TWO DEAD BILLIONAIRES

TWO DEAD BILLIONAIRES

LUKE PATRICK SHELDON

LOS ANGELES, CALIFORNIA

ISBNs: 979-8-9899816-1-8 (paperback),
979-8-9899816-0-1 (digital online)

1. Fiction—Mystery and Detective—General 2. Fiction—Thrillers—Suspense

Northern Lights Publishing
Los Angeles, California

For Dad

PART ONE

CHAPTER ONE

His throat was slit. A fistful of cash had been shoved into the wound. Blood soaked the money—100,000 Icelandic krónur, 700 U.S. dollars, and 600 euros.

Detective Hekla Rafney Fritzdóttir, of the National Bureau of Investigation, looked up from the body and into the hotel suite. The room already was teeming with cops and technicians. None of them had ever seen anything like this. Not in Iceland, where six years could pass between murders. And certainly not in the fanciest suite at the Azure Spa and Hotel—which shares space with Iceland's most famous tourist attraction.

"Shit," someone mumbled from inside.

Hekla forced herself to look back at the body. She knew it wasn't just the manner of death or the location—not even the three different types of currency in the dead man's throat—that had everyone on edge. It was identity of the victim. Jack Drumman. A billionaire. An American. His death would be a big deal even if he had died peacefully in his sleep at one of his half-dozen compounds in the States.

But that's not what happened. He was killed here. In the private hot spring surrounding his suite. Then his body was posed on the wooden deck that led to the water. Brutally murdered with a symbolic flourish in one of the most peaceful nations on earth.

And it was Hekla's case to investigate. She closed her eyes and let out a barely audible sigh. Then she stepped over the body and got to work.

CHAPTER TWO

Five Hours Earlier

A LONE FIGURE STOOD OUTSIDE, STARING AT A seemingly endless stretch of snow and ice. Their silhouette was the only human form for kilometers. "Am I really going to do this?" they wondered. They shook off the thought. They wished someone else was there with them—to encourage them if nothing else. But they decided long ago that they had to do this part alone. They had help, but not here. Not now. They were on their own.

They moved before the doubt convinced them not to. They broke into a jog, deftly maneuvering around jagged rocks, and gingerly stepping across slippery layers of ice that threatened to crack at any moment.

They glanced skyward, caught a glimpse of the moon, and cursed their carelessness. Months spent preparing, countless hours making practice runs on similar grounds, yet they never thought about the moon. But there it was: three-quarters full, low in the sky. And bright. Bright enough to illuminate the rugged terrain, thankfully, but also luminescent enough to expose them. It was their second oversight—a small one, sure, but more than they could afford with such a slim margin for error.

They already were kicking themself over their first oversight— the car. The vehicle itself was fine, but they had never driven it before, and they were on edge the whole time. Because they didn't know the car's quirks, and were unfamiliar with the way it handled, they had to drive slower than they wished. The painfully slow pace made their anxiety worse. A delay could derail the entire operation.

As it turned out, they arrived early. This quelled one anxiety, but triggered another. While they sat in the car, staring at the clock, all they could do was try—and fail—to think of something other than the enormity of what lay ahead.

So although jogging on ice was difficult, it was a welcome change after all that time sitting idly. It forced them to concentrate on the immediate. All they had to do was move fast and not fall.

They held their breath once they got close to the hotel. They were afraid that lights from the resort would illuminate them, likely accompanied by hostile shouts that would mark the end of their mission, their career, their life, and anything else they could think of. But there was nothing. No light, no screams.

Their associates—people whose names and faces they did not know—had come through: The group had knocked out one of the outdoor lights that otherwise would flood the area. This was part of the plan, but they were never really convinced it could be accomplished. It wasn't that they doubted their associates' ability to take out a light or two. It was just that a random blown bulb seemed precisely like the kind of thing that the entitled asshole staying in the suite would notice and complain about.

They stood perfectly still for about a minute just in case. Then they got undressed. They pulled off their gloves and laid them on top of the black, waterproof bag they had been carrying. They removed their parka and stretched it out on the ground. They untied their boots and stepped out of them onto their parka. They slid off their insulated snow pants, folded them and placed them by their side. All that protected them from the brutal cold now was a polypropylene jumpsuit, and they were about to take that off. They unzipped the jumpsuit, freeing both arms before tugging it off one leg.

That's when the cold hit them. Hard. It sucked the air out of their lungs and seized control of their body. They shivered uncontrollably and clenched their jaw in a futile attempt to stop their teeth from chattering. Their brain screamed at them to put their clothing back on, to jump off the ridge, to move, to run—to do *something*. Then their brain went silent for just a moment, conserving its energy before repeating its demands with even greater urgency.

It was wasting its time though.

They weren't retreating. Neither did they have any intention of taking a shortcut or deviating from the plan. They weren't going anywhere until they finished what they had started years ago. Their nervous system eventually got the hint and relented, releasing just enough adrenaline to allow them to move again. They finished undressing and unzipped their bag.

⸻

A geothermally heated pool surrounded the suite, protected by a steep rock wall. They peered over the edge. It was a long way down to the water. This, at least, was a risk they were more prepared for. There were obvious difficulties and moments of chance in their undertaking, but most were products of circumstance. If not for their end goal, the risk would be minimal. Climbing down the rock wall to the water, however, posed very real danger: One slip and they could break their arm or smash their head. And now, they had to navigate the treacherous surface in near-total darkness, knowing that a mere scratch could be as damning as a siren. They hoped their neoprene shoes and water-proof knitted gloves would keep them stable.

But no such luck.

The moment they started climbing down, they realized that some high-tech shoes and gloves were no match for the steep and slippery rock wall. As they inched their way toward the water below, they were certain they'd fall. They held their breath, afraid that the slightest shift in their weight would send them crashing. Their stomach sank when they made the mistake of looking down. Every portion of rock they managed to grab onto, every groove their foot could find was a miracle.

And then they reached the bottom.

Any relief they felt for successfully navigating the rock wall disappeared once they lowered their body into the water. The sudden change from the frigid cold to the hot water was excruciating. It took all they had not to scream. An extra minute of exposure to the elements meant everything—it was like putting a cold finger under hot water, except now, their entire body was submerged. And there was nothing they could do. They had no choice but to endure the pain as their eyes welled with tears, adding another layer of distortion to their already compromised field of vision.

They were under water, in the dark, breathing through a snorkel. As they waited, the idea hit them that despite all the careful planning, this whole thing was ridiculous—they were doomed to failure. They brought their smartwatch close to their face. They were well past the time they had promised their associates they would retreat, and were now a few minutes past the time they had promised themself they would leave if the target didn't appear. There was a limited window to successfully complete their mission, but there was also a limited period to have any chance of getting out undetected, regardless of whether they had met their objective. Terrible thoughts swirled in their mind. They tried to calm themself, but their efforts only increased their anxiety. Deep breathing doesn't work through a tube, and relaxation seemed like an awful idea. They felt tension in their neck and suddenly realized they felt weak. The hot water was sapping their energy.

That's when their mind drifted. The details and technicalities of their schedule and plan slipped away, and they were forced to think about what they were *really* doing. They searched desperately for something else to focus on, but they could find only truth, and the truth of what they had set out to do was horrifying.

Panic flooded their brain. Waves of nausea roiled in their stomach. "No," they thought to themself, "I can't do this. I need to leave." Anything would be better than what they had planned. They relaxed their grip on the wall. Their body floated up as they reached for their mouth. But almost as soon as they decided to abort, they heard the sound.

Pshhhh.

Or did they? They carefully pulled themself from the water so they could hear better. See better. They didn't dare get too close—not yet. If they were spotted, the plan that so many had worked on would come crashing down. They only had one chance at this. Once they committed there was no going back. Their mind raced.

What if I fail? What if it's someone else? No. They would have warned me. What if someone can see me already? What if—

They felt his movement in the pool. It was time.

Move.

Now!

They sucked at the air once more before pulling their body down and pushing off the side of the pool.

They swam underwater until they were behind the man. In one decisive movement they wrapped both legs and one arm around him. They lifted their head out of the water and threw their free arm forward, pressing their knife against his neck.

"Jack?" they asked in a hoarse whisper. But they knew it was him.

Press hard and pull.

They had prepared for a struggle, but Jack barely moved. He made a sound, but it wasn't the scream they expected, just a startled "hey." By then, it was too late. They repositioned the knife and sliced his throat.

The cut didn't go deep enough. Jack's body jerked with ten times the energy he had shown just before. They swam back, holding the knife in front of them, certain he was about to attack. But no. Jack's flailing was just reflexive. They had to watch though, as he convulsed, blood gushing wildly from his neck, his eyes locked in a terrified gaze. He let out a ghastly gurgle trying to breathe. His head fell beneath the water, and then somehow reemerged in a final, desperate attempt to get some air and stay alive. He gasped for air and choked on hot water and blood instead.

They had prepared for Jack's death to be gruesome, but it was worse than they could possibly imagine—loud, unnatural, and excruciatingly long. No one should imagine such a thing, let alone witness it. They certainly shouldn't *cause* it. It was wrong. And they knew it.

CHAPTER THREE

HEKLA STOOD IN THE MIDDLE OF THE SUITE, EYES locked on her tablet. This was her first murder investigation and the first known murder in Iceland in three years. Her tablet played cellphone footage that the first officer to arrive, Gunnar Ottóson, shot after clearing the area. Gunnar's video didn't differ much from what Hekla could see in the room. There was an urgency and dread in the footage, however, that could not be replicated. A slight shake or wobble, the sound of Gunnar's heavy breath. He must have been terrified, she thought.

The thought of anything terrifying Gunnar was surprising. He was enormous, with giant shoulders that filled the hallway outside the suite. A thick beard hid his genial face, making him seem all the more imposing. At the moment, Gunnar was towering over his boss's boss's boss, National Police Commissioner Kjartan Bjarnasson. Although Kjartan was probably the only one in the room who had ever seen a murder victim up close before, he looked sicker to his stomach than the rest of the officers combined. Probably because of who Jack was.

Hekla turned off the video. She ran her fingers through her thick blonde hair, which she had cut short a few days earlier. Her hand closed around air where up until recently, there were longer strands of pale-yellow hair. She was still getting used to the length. She signaled for Gunnar to join her.

"Where's the wife?"

"She, um, she—she spent the night at another hotel," Gunnar answered. "The uh, Envoy in Reykjavík, I think."

Hekla furrowed her brow. "She didn't stay in the same hotel as her husband?"

"Yes. I'm sorry—was that a question? No. she had a morning meeting scheduled in Reykjavík and thought it would be more . . . convenient to stay there."

Hekla tried to comfort the big man by patting him on the shoulder, but she only reached his mid-back. It would have to do. Her attention turned to an untouched Azure-branded tote bag overflowing with a fluffy turquoise towel and matching slippers. She scanned the room before bending over to check underneath the furniture.

"The body was found by an employee?" she asked.

"Um, yes," Gunnar checked his notepad. "Elísa Pálsdóttir. Nineteen. Employed for about a year and a half."

"Still here?"

Gunnar nodded.

"Good. Can you go get her?"

The Azure Spa and Hotel was a tourist trap that had recently focused its attention on catering to rich foreigners. To be fair, most of Iceland's tourism industry had been actively pursuing, or grudgingly resigning itself to, this business model by the time the first luxury suites opened. And to be even more fair, after the pandemic, many other countries also had decided that if the Americans were going to let the world go to hell for the benefit of their wealthiest, they might as well grab what they could before the ship sank. But still, it struck Hekla—and a whole lot of Icelanders—as grotesque that their beautiful, welcoming country had suddenly put up signs that said, essentially, "rich visitors only."

That certainly seemed to be the case at the Azure. Suites inside the sleek, two-story monument to excess were designed for tourists who wanted an "authentic" Icelandic experience without having to venture too deep into Iceland. Or interact with any Icelandic people who weren't being paid to cater to them.

The Spa and Hotel felt more like a spa and two separate hotels—one for "regular" rooms, and one for suites. The suites occupied a private wing, removed from the mere rooms and *far* removed from the spa, which was open to day visitors. Nearly a million people—close to three times the population of Iceland— visited the spa every year to soak in hot water piped in from a nearby power plant. Day visitors generally spent about three hours in the water. Some stuck around for lunch or dinner at the wildly expensive restaurant.

As posh as the restaurant was, the suites were a different world. And as sumptuous as the suites were, Jack's made the others seem shabby. The "Virtu Suite" had three walls that provided unobstructed views outside. Like the six other ground-floor suites, Jack's had a balcony with steps leading to a private area of the water. It was the only non-communal bathing option available to visitors of the hot spring. Technically, they still shared water with the masses, but privacy walls kept *most* of the refined guests from complaining too much. 700,000 krónur a night to stay at the edge of a hotel at the edge of a resort at the edge of the world. That seemed to Hekla like a lot of money to drop just to be alone in a place that was undoubtedly colder, darker, and smaller than the sprawling estates that the suite's guests were used to.

Hekla shook her head as she looked around the suite's living room. It really was enormous. She figured she could fit her entire flat inside at least three times over. It was sleek, spotless, cold— a streamlined mix of polished concrete, slate, stainless steel, and walnut. It looked like what an American would imagine Scandinavian design to be if their only reference points were Restoration Hardware and the Fortress of Solitude from the 1980s Superman movies. Towering windows looked out onto the private spa and rocky terrain surrounding the hotel. Two sets of sliding doors led to the balcony, one in the bedroom and the other in the living room.

She briefly examined the bathroom and bedroom before making her way to the balcony. This terrace was smaller than the one off the living room. Three people could stand on it, but no more. She gazed out onto the surrounding area. It *was* nice, she thought. It looked almost nothing like the place she had visited as a child, but the sight of steam rising off the water in the winter still kindled a wondrous feeling. It was a feeling that couldn't be fully eradicated, no matter how much money tried.

When Hekla was a little girl, she and her parents once made the long trip from Akureyri, in Northern Iceland, all the way south to what was now known as the Azure Spa and Hotel. Back then, there were just a few showers and a fake beach next to the geothermal plant that heated the hot springs. Nonetheless, it was a thrilling experience for 10-year-old Hekla. She remembered being entranced by the seemingly endless number of coves and hideaways, made even more magical by the steam and mist. She and her brother imagined they were explorers on a distant planet, and that the handful of adventurous tourists, all speaking strange languages, were alien creatures that they were on a mission to study.

Hekla swallowed hard at the thought of her brother. So much of what she had done was because of him, but the motivation and influence had become distorted over time. She forgot how much it hurt to remember him as an actual person.

Back when her family would visit, they would spend the night at a nearby hotel. It still operated as a more affordable option for those traveling to the hot springs, but aside from that, almost everything other than the rocks and source of energy was new. First, they built the visitor center and a restaurant. Then came the first iteration of the on-site hotel along with a standalone structure for spa treatments. And just five years after Iceland's economy collapsed, work began on a massive overhaul of the hotel, replete with the addition of two new restaurants and more trappings of luxury. The suites were the final flourish, and Jack's was the highlight of the pitch deck created for investors.

Hekla once read that the spa "put Iceland on the map." It was in an article that masqueraded as news but really was a puff piece that a public relations agency had convinced an editor to publish. The line seemed ignorant and insulting at the time. Hekla wondered if the hotel owners wished their hotel weren't so "famous" right about now.

∏∏∏∏∏∏∏∏∏∏∏

Hekla walked the narrow portion of the balcony that wrapped around the corner of the suite until she was at the sliding glass door to the living room. Jack's body, now covered by a white tarp, lay next to two stylized chairs and a small table. A folded towel lay neatly on the table, and another was placed carefully next to the steps that led into the water. An Azure-branded bathrobe hung over the back of one of the chairs.

Surrounding the pool outside Jack's suite were rocky bluffs that rose at least four or five meters high above the surface of the water. They were steep, almost perpendicular to the water in most places, jagged and covered in moss wherever conditions would allow. The terrain above the bluffs was similarly unforgiving—kilometers of snow and ice, peppered throughout with sharp rocks.

Hekla spotted Ólafur Jakobsson, the NBI's head of forensics, through the open sliding doors. "Can I go in?" she asked, nodding toward the water.

Ólafur arched his brow in response.

"Well?"

"If you want," Ólafur slowly replied.

"No evidence issue?"

"No," he said. "Four thousand people are in that water each day. It doesn't recycle for forty-eight hours. We can't get a clean sample of anything."

Hekla had removed her boots and jacket before Ólafur finished speaking. She continued stripping until she was down to her her bra and panties. She looked fit, with slender curves and lean muscles that showed themselves as she moved toward the water.

"You're not really going to—" Gunnar started, but Hekla already was up to her shoulders. She quickly made her way across the water and began grabbing at the rock wall.

"You think they came in that way?" Ólafur called out.

"Maybe," Hekla shouted to the head of forensics, who now stood on the balcony with Gunnar. "Or maybe this is where they left."

Hekla continued her inspection of the wall as Gunnar and Ólafur stared, half-confused, half-awestruck.

"There's nowhere to go," Gunnar responded, sounding much more composed than he had been upon Hekla's arrival. "Even if they did make it out, they'd be soaking wet. They'd freeze to death. Or they would come up on one of the cameras."

Kjartan poked his head outside. "What's she doing?"

Gunnar and Ólafur both shrugged. Kjartan shook his head. "Hekla," he shouted, "the girl is here."

Elísa Pálsdóttir was 19 years old but she barely looked old enough to drive. Her dirty blonde hair was pulled back in a tight, tidy ponytail. Hekla stood with her in the hallway outside the suite. The girl seemed confident for her age, self-assured, holding eye contact when answering the detective's questions.

Elísa told Hekla that when she arrived, she found the door to Jack's room open. Jack's assistant had ordered several bottles of water the night before, and Elísa was bringing them to the room. Elísa noticed the door was ajar, knocked and announced herself. When there was no reply, she pushed the door open and entered. She was only a step or two inside when she felt the cold wind and saw the balcony door was open. Another step and she saw blood. That's when she screamed and ran out.

The web of communication among Jack, Jack's wife, their assistant, and the staff at the hotel was confusing. It seemed to Hekla as though everyone was speaking on behalf of someone else—to the satisfaction of no one.

And Jack, being Jack, only added to this confusion with his *unique* communication style. As the founder and majority shareholder of a company that specialized in quasilegal surveillance, Jack was obsessed with privacy and refused to speak by telephone. Instead, he insisted on communicating via a secure app. So, the on-site manager assigned the hotel's youngest staff member, who grew up using apps, to be Jack's contact person. That staff member was Elísa.

"Is it normal for you to communicate on a private app with a guest?" Hekla asked.

"No," Elísa responded without hesitation.

Hekla looked into the girl's eyes. Elísa met her stare.

Hekla gave a curt nod. "Did you know Mr. Drumman's wife was away?"

"Yes."

Hekla narrowed her eyes, but Elísa continued before she could follow up, "They told us she'd be away. They made a big deal out of their visit."

"Who did?"

"Everyone—my boss, the manager. Someone else came to talk to us too. I think it was one of the owners."

"What did they say?"

"Nothing." Elísa shrugged. "Same thing they always tell us— do our jobs, treat every guest like they are special, all that stuff. But they had something for us to sign too."

"What was it?"

"Contract or something. Saying we promised not to tell any- one anything about their visit."

"A nondisclosure agreement?"

"I guess."

Hekla's eyes searched the hallway. "Are you concerned you might be violating it now?"

"No. Should I be?"

"I can't imagine it being an issue."

"Right, well if that's what his wife's worried about, she can go ahead and sue me."

"You don't like her?"

Elísa tilted her head defiantly. "I don't *know* her."

"But you knew Mr. Drumman. You were the only one who texted with him, right?"

"Not by choice. My manager asked if I could download an app on my phone. I said 'okay,' and he just started texting me."

"Mr. Drumman started texting you?"

"Yes."

Hekla noticed Kjartan make his way into the hallway. He looked anxious, but Hekla kept questioning Elísa.

"How many tote bags were here?"

"How many *what*?"

The question seemed to catch the teen by surprise. "Tote bags," Hekla repeated. "The ones the hotel leaves for the guests."

Elísa instinctively looked toward the room, even though all she could see from her vantage point was the doorframe. "There—should be two. Usually."

Hekla felt like the girl knew there was only one bag in the suite, but she kept an impassive face.

"One for each adult guest," Elísa continued with more certainty.

"I only saw one."

Elísa started to answer, but Kjartan interrupted.

"I'm sorry." Kjartan had maneuvered around the police personnel crowding the hallway. He leaned toward Hekla. "Do you mind—can I speak with you a moment?"

CHAPTER FOUR

It was cold.

His stomach hurt all the time.

His chest felt like someone had wrapped their hands tight around his lungs and heart, arrhythmically squeezing whenever they got the urge. His jaw was clenched, with his tongue pressing firmly against the roof of his mouth.

He had stopped going out almost completely.

He felt paralyzed. There was a heaviness, a dread in his mind that spread throughout his entire body, making any actual movement seem impossible. It felt like his brain was slogging through thick mud or knee-high snow, each step only bringing him close to where he began in the first place. He would have a thought to do something, to change his immediate surroundings, if not his circumstances or long-term prospects. But there always were too many options. The seemingly endless number of possibilities accompanying each decision made the process so difficult that it was always easier to just stay where he was. The simple act of going to the store seemed impossible. A maddening buzz filled his mind, like an incessant, stifling weight pressing against his head and shoulders.

There were many ways to characterize the various mental and physical ailments that plagued his daily existence. In fact, there were many ways that they *had* been quantified, treated dutifully by patient and practitioner alike. However, none of the exceptionally qualified individuals who plied their trade on his brain had ever been willing to accept or prescribe for the one diagnosis he insisted on. For as open as he was to help, as willing as he was to accept the premise that his mind was more sensitive than others to stimuli—more susceptible to patterns of thought that might, occasionally, devolve into cycles of madness—there was one suggestion that he would never entertain. August Sorenson refused to believe that his misery was anything but deserved.

There wasn't really any reason for August to be in Copenhagen anymore. He hadn't been an FBI legal attaché—a legat—for years. Not since everything went to hell. He was a Danish citizen, but Copenhagen wasn't home. His only friends were Petar and Jenson, but the latter's job might be in jeopardy if they spent too much time together—at least that's what August told himself to assuage the guilt he felt for not making more of an effort. And Petar's affections almost certainly depended on the maintenance of their sexual relationship.

Also, August hated the cold and dark.

Established weather patterns likely played more than a small part in his general misery. Even when he was regularly employed, August spent as much of the winter as far south as his job permitted. And right now, the sporadic heating in his second-story Vesterbro flat, directly above what was either a busy restaurant or disruptive sound factory, was doing all it could to rattle the last of his nerves. The source was an old wall unit with a mind of its own. It went on automatically, without any discernible pattern or rhythm, sounding like a jet engine as it blasted out steam. Almost immediately, the flat felt like a sauna. Then, just as abruptly, the unit would turn itself off. And within an hour, it was freezing again.

There was one upside to the wretchedly ineffective heating

system: It gave August an excuse to go back to bed. He spent many of his waking hours putting on, or pulling off, various layers of sweat-stained shirts, dirty sweatpants, and oversized cardigans. It was much easier for him to retreat to the covers whenever temperature regulation became difficult and allow sleep to block out the noise, relieve the weight, and give him some respite from his thoughts.

⁕⁕⁕⁕⁕⁕⁕⁕⁕⁕⁕⁕⁕

It had recently come to August's attention that not everyone has a narrator inside their head. This was a fascinating revelation. He had taken for granted the presence of a real-time commentator in his brain, figuring that was just how brains worked—they say things to you. They process *and* explain. What good would it be if the mind caused you to take actions without informing you of the thinking behind them? Show your work, right?

No, the narrator was fine, he thought. In *theory*. The problem was, his had morphed into a traitor and a masochist. Specifically, his personal voice-over seemed to be actively conspiring with the world to enhance his suffering. It was like a broken alarm system that had turned against itself, no longer scanning for danger but instead focused on finding and exploiting August's own weaknesses and vulnerabilities. If he was upset about something, the voice would explain all the reasons why he should be even more upset. If he was burdened with an unpleasant thought, the voice would reintroduce the topic whenever August had a moment of peace.

He had experienced something like this before, back when he was still drinking. *That* narrator seemed most interested in terrifying him until he found refuge in malt liquor or watery beer. Abstention, treatment, and medication had done a world of good.

The voice became quieter, less hostile. He did the type of things that the audible voices and culture at large told him he should. He graduated law school, got a job, used his savvy and lucked-into advantages to engineer a move abroad. Within a few years, he had risen to a position in life where he had the privilege of working alongside some of the worst people in the world as an agent of the United States government.

But now he was free of all that. And because of how he got free of it, the voice had come back louder than ever. And August had no defense. In fact, he felt as though the foul-weather companion in his head made a good argument. He *had* fucked up. It *was* his fault. He *should* be miserable and cold and alone forever. The only thing he had control over now was how long forever would be. It was hard to tell, but he was pretty certain that it was his own true voice that was assuring him, with increased regularity, that he could make the pain stop anytime he wanted.

CHAPTER FIVE

JACK AND HIS WIFE, SUSAN TEELE, ARRIVED AT THE Azure on Saturday evening. They flew directly to Keflavík on a privately chartered plane that left from Virginia's Dulles International Airport, about a half-hour drive from Washington, D.C. Along with them on the flight was Jack's personal assistant, Emma Weinstein, whom they put up at the Crystal Hotel—the cheaper hotel near the hot springs.

Jack and Susan stayed in their suite and ordered room service their first night at the hotel. On Sunday, the couple spent the day together at the onsite Fire and Ice Spa, where they received massages and other "detoxification treatments." That night, they had dinner at The Assuana, the most upscale of the Azure's three restaurants. They were joined for dinner by Steingrímur Eggertsson, Iceland's wealthiest citizen. The trio sat by themselves, somewhat apart from other diners, at a table on the far side of the restaurant. Their server provided a detailed account of the dinner to Hekla.

Everyone appeared to get along well at first. Susan and Steingrímur seemed to be on more familiar terms with each other than Jack and Steingrímur. Jack didn't make eye contact with the server, but Susan was pleasant. Steingrímur was patronizing, making unnecessary asides and complaining in Icelandic to the staff whenever anyone stopped by.

Susan didn't drink, but Jack and Steingrímur drank heavily. As the evening went on, things grew a bit contentious between the two men. The server couldn't discern exactly what the problem was, but it was clear they were arguing about something. Susan, obviously embarrassed, tried to keep the peace.

After dessert, Jack had another drink while Susan walked Steingrímur to the door. She appeared to offer a few words of apology before kissing him on the cheek and saying goodbye. Then she returned to the table and exchanged a few sharp words with her husband before they both headed to their suite.

Susan stuck around for about 15 minutes and then went to the lobby, where a chauffeur was waiting to drive her to the Envoy Hotel in Reykjavík. Susan had scheduled a business meeting in the city the next day, and staying at the Envoy, rather than 40 minutes away, would make for a more pleasant morning.

That pleasant morning, Jack was found dead on the balcony of his suite.

*

After speaking with the staff at the restaurant, Hekla left the complex alone and clambered into the slate-blue Toyota SUV she had abandoned more than parked on the pathway directly in front of the hotel. It was a 45-minute drive back to the NBI's headquarters in Reykjavík, but she pulled off the main highway after about 15 minutes. She made another turn down a dead-end street before yanking the steering wheel to the right and parking the car.

As soon as the car stopped, she flung open her door and threw up the coffee and remnants of a protein bar she had consumed earlier onto the side of the vehicle and pavement below. She sat for a good 30 seconds before stepping out of the car. She did her best to avoid the vomit as she found her footing, and then spent another minute or so hunched over, trying desperately to quell the nausea that had set in. She managed only to cough up some mucus-laden saliva and coffee-tinged stomach acid.

Hekla shuddered, walked around to the passenger side of her car, and retrieved a lighter and nearly full pack of American Spirit cigarettes from the glove compartment. She lit a cigarette and took a deep drag. It hit hard, the nicotine providing a brief high and temporary cover for the poor state of her stomach as a pleasant dizzy sensation distracted her. She took another drag and noticed that her fingers were trembling. She sucked hard on the cigarette and then moved it to her left hand so she could warm her right hand inside her pocket.

Her conversation with Kjartan hadn't done much to settle her nerves. Most of what he told her she could already have gleaned from a quick search online or from the fact that her phone hadn't stopped ringing since Jack's body was discovered. This was a *big deal*. Any homicide at the Azure would be a national headline for years. It was like being killed at Disneyland in a country where people weren't killed. And any American meeting their end abroad naturally raised the stakes considerably.

But Jack Drumman was no ordinary American. Kjartan had made this point very clear in their conversation.

Hekla put her cigarette out in the snow and placed the butt in one of the dozen or so empty coffee cups in her car.

⁓⁓⁓⁓⁓⁓⁓⁓

Hekla was familiar with the recently deceased. To her, Jack Drumman was a 43-year-old sociopath. He made his fortune as an early investor in some cursed social media platform and then quickly went all in on the data mining business. His chief concern for the past few years was Palezar, a company he founded after cashing out of his glorified advertisement hustle. Jack met Susan when the private equity firm she was a member of purchased a sizable share of Palezar stock.

Palezar was, ostensibly, an information and technology company, though it would be hard to tell what exactly they did based on their public-facing materials. The firm's website was packed with inane marketing jargon like, "outcome optimizing," "efficacy enhanced," and "solution-oriented." Palezar's true "utility" was best discerned by looking at its contracts and investors. Anyone taking a close look at these materials, as Hekla had, would see that all Palezar did was turn the human experience—in the form of personal information given, bought, bartered, or stolen—into a commodifiable product.

It seemed to her like the future that Jack and his ilk were ushering in was just the past repeated. He was not an innovator, and his business, as fancy as the tools had become, was not any different than the businesses that had come before. Achievements in science and technology were being utilized by these "titans" in much the same way previous generations had used their advancements: To exploit and profit.

Hekla knew that even in Iceland, most of the population had come to accept companies like Palezar as inevitable. But she also knew that Palezar was special. Even in a landscape of deified grifters and legally sanctioned cons, Palezar stood out. Its biggest customers, the U.S. military and various law enforcement agencies around the globe, weren't simply trying to exploit humans, they were intent on confining and killing them as well. With offerings like facial recognition, location analysis, statistical models, and artificial intelligence, Palezar provided the powerful with an array of high-tech tools that made them even more powerful.

So the question of who would want to kill Jack was rhetorical—anyone with a conscience would. What concerned Hekla right now, and what Kjartan had ominously alluded to in their conversation, was what the response to his murder would be.

People like Jack didn't die like this, so it was hard to predict how the many individuals, entities, and countries he and his business had entangled themselves with would react to the news. It was unlikely to be pleasant.

⁓⁓⁓⁓⁓⁓⁓

As soon as Hekla arrived at the hotel that morning, she could tell that something other than the murder—as awful as that was— had gotten to Kjartan. At 59, after a lifetime spent in law enforcement, Kjartan had seen some things. Hekla worked with him as an officer in the capital before they both were promoted to national positions, so she knew him well. In general, he was the picture of Scandinavian stoicism—decisive and calm. He rarely raised his voice unless his beloved Fram Football Club was playing KR Reykjavík or Valur. If something was upsetting, viscerally or emotionally, his only giveaway was a momentary pause as his light blue eyes became distant. He was a good boss, a good man in her opinion.

But today he was fidgety. He kept removing his hat and adjusting his silvery gray hair before putting it back on and adjusting its angle. And when he spoke, he sounded uncertain, maybe even worried, as though he were asking permission or seeking her assurance.

"We need to look at everyone who was here," Kjartan had told her after he cut short her interview with Elísa. "There's the hotel guest registry. Employees. And then a list of visitors to the spa. Surveillance video is being sent over now but there aren't any cameras in the bathing area or in the rooms. Obviously."

"Obviously," Hekla replied.

"The U.S. embassy. They were notified—I notified them. They're going to want to speak with you."

"Okay."

"There's a . . . " Kjartan flipped through his notepad, "Lisa Harris. A director there. I forget her title exactly. But she's the one. Look out for her call."

"I will. We've handled dead tourists before." Hekla immediately regretted the choice of words, but Kjartan didn't seem to notice.

"This needs to be done right. I'll oversee. Help coordinate. Whatever you need. But you'll take the lead. You'll be in charge."

Under most circumstances, Hekla would have been more than happy to lead a significant investigation. Since she moved to the NBI, she'd spent most of her time chasing down hackers, which meant sitting behind her desk, sorting through documents, and occasionally speaking with computer scientists. It was that or immigration and drug trafficking—dubiously immoral crimes at best, in her not always humble opinion. But these were not normal circumstances.

"Aldís Eva was here," Kjartan said.

"What?" Hekla figured that name was at least half the source of Kjartan's angst.

"She visited the spa this morning."

"How do you know? Did someone look at tape already?"

Kjartan replied with a shake of his head. Hekla did her best to hide her annoyance at being stonewalled by her boss less than a minute into their first real discussion regarding the murder.

"It's just—do everything as you normally would," he eventually replied. "Just, you should know. We can't waste time if she was involved."

CHAPTER SIX

Aᴜɢᴜsᴛ ɢʀᴜɴᴛᴇᴅ ᴡɪᴛʜ ᴘʟᴇᴀsᴜʀᴇ. Hᴇ ʀᴏᴄᴋᴇᴅ ʜɪs hips slightly, allowing Petar to thrust deeper inside him as he lay on the edge of his bed with his legs splayed and knees pulled back near his chest. A bead of sweat fell from Petar's forehead onto August's stomach. August rubbed the moisture into his skin, wrapped his fingers around the base of his penis and scrotum, and gave a light tug.

He locked eyes with Petar. He was doing his best to stay in the moment and ensure that this was a memorable experience for his partner. Petar deserved that much, at least.

Petar was wonderful, a much better companion than August felt he deserved. He was strong, but not in the superficial, closeted-terrified ways often displayed by confused men who believed indifference was akin to power. He was able to meet August where he was, offer empathy while retaining his own sense of self. He was kind and charitable, not out of need or with expectation, but because that was who he was and how he felt like acting. August suspected that Petar didn't quite understand August's angst or self-imposed exile from the rest of the world, but he was still respectful, despite the strictures it put on their encounters.

He was hot, too. August enjoyed that. Thin, with lean muscles, about August's height—average for an American, slightly short for a Dane. He had wavy, jet-black hair that always looked perfect no matter how it fell. His features were well-defined, like August's but less delicate. Petar used to wear a short beard but had taken to arriving with a clean-shaven face—a sacrifice made without fanfare after August had let slip his preference one night. And his legs were long, much more muscular than August's, with a firm ass that was highlighted by his choice of jeans and habit of tucking in his fitted T-shirts.

Petar worked his way to a climax as August increased the pace and intensity of his own genital manipulation. August let out a prolonged, strained grunt, and ejaculated onto his stomach and chest. Petar let August's contractions guide his final few pelvic movements before he pulled out and came into a tissue from a box on August's nightstand.

Petar sat on the edge of the bed as both men took heavy breaths. After several seconds, Petar turned to August. The unconscious relaxation of August's muscles must have exposed a facial expression that alarmed Petar in a way that his usual forlorn look did not.

"What's wrong?" Petar asked.

"Huh?"

"Something's wrong. What is it?"

"No. . . . Nuh—nothing," August meekly replied. Petar raised his brow. August realized he would have to do better. He quickly searched his memory for past experiences where he felt depleted and disoriented after good sex, hoping to summon a tone and countenance that seemed more natural. He cleared his throat. "That was just . . . that was really . . . good."

Petar didn't appear entirely convinced, but August knew it was hard to argue with a lover in a moment like this. He fortified his words by lifting his shoulders off the bed, placing his hand behind Petar's neck, and pulling him in for a deep kiss. That seemed to do the trick. Petar nodded, announced his intention to go to the bathroom, and handed August the box of tissues.

August cleaned himself off and fell back on the bed. He could feel the preemptive soreness of muscles that were no longer able to hold hard angles for extended periods of time without consequence. He groaned—this utterance full of much less pleasure than his previous vocalizations. Age-related aches were annoying, but he was much more frustrated by the fact that a subjectively satisfying experience had only managed to provide a single second of post-coitus bliss before the darkness showed itself on his face again. Fucking, like everything else, had become a distraction. It was nice, but he still wanted to kill himself.

August switched places with Petar in the bathroom. When August stepped out, Petar was in the kitchen unpacking the groceries that August hadn't given him an opportunity to put away earlier. August smiled ruefully and felt a faint tug near his heart as he watched the beautiful naked man refill his depleted pantry and refrigerator with meat-and-dairy-free provisions.

August felt a pressure behind his eyes. He hurried over to help Petar with the groceries before *that* bodily function had an opportunity to evolve into anything more revelatory.

⁓⁓⁓⁓⁓⁓⁓⁓⁓

August awoke the next morning with more energy than usual.

"Excited for me to leave?" Petar asked when he finally managed to lift his head off the pillow.

August scowled. It wasn't fair that he couldn't express excitement without coming under scrutiny, and it wasn't fun having his otherwise innocuous behavior so accurately interpreted. "Stop," he instructed. "You're . . . welcome to stay . . . as long as you'd like."

"You know I have work."

August held up his palms as a proclamation of innocence.

"I guess I could call in sick though," Petar continued.

A fleeting look of panic crossed August's face. He wondered if he might have caught it in time. Petar rolled his eyes and shook his head. Apparently not.

"I just . . . I like to plan," August said defensively, but with a smile. "You know that." He playfully nudged Petar in the side before pulling him in for a hug. Petar gave a wry smile and wrapped his hand around August's arm so that it stayed tight against his body.

It was true. August very much enjoyed the time he spent with Petar. He loved being fucked and even found comfort in the company before and after, but this was only because there was a previously established, mutually agreed-upon endpoint to their encounters. The knowledge that he was guaranteed indefinite alone-time again took the pressure off the present. And he *did* like to plan. Usually, the plan was just to spend time alone, but in his world, this was as prioritized an activity as anything else. He had bigger plans for today, but Petar didn't know that.

A half-hour later, Petar was dressed and ready to leave. The tinge of excitement August usually felt walking him to the door was all but extinguished by Petar's accurate analysis of his facial expressions. Something else was bothering him though—he was unsure of its origin, but he could feel it in his stomach.

When they got to the door, he gave Petar a long kiss, saying goodbye but also trying to subdue whatever new emotion was bubbling inside him.

Petar pulled back and searched August's eyes.

"What?" August asked.

Petar held his gaze a few more uncomfortable seconds before shaking his head slightly. "Call me if you want to do something today," he said, as he often did before departing. But this time the offer had a trace of urgency. "I can leave early. Or if you just want to talk. I'm around. You know that, right?"

"Yeah . . . of course." Petar's tone only added to August's discomfort. He needed this to be over.

But Petar was not so easily assuaged. "Promise me," he added with unmistakable gravity.

"Okay . . . yes." August forced a smile. "I will." He tilted his head to the door. "C'mon . . . you're gonna be late."

Petar nodded. He opened the door and walked into the hallway.

"Have a good day," August said as Petar turned his head back. "You too."

August watched Petar until he disappeared down the stairwell. As soon as Petar was gone, August shut the door and allowed the tears he had been holding back for the past 12 or so hours to flow.

"Fuck," he muttered to himself.

CHAPTER SEVEN

THE NBI HEADQUARTERS WAS ALREADY BUZZING when Hekla arrived. It looked like every member of the force on active duty, and some who weren't, had shown up. Too many toys for them to play with, she thought.

The facility had recently been upgraded thanks to a grant from the government of Norway, which had ratcheted up its fight against terrorism and trafficking. After two decades, "suspicion of terrorist activity" no longer had the power to convince the public to shut up and let the people with money do what they wanted, so the new evil lurking in the dark was human trafficking. It was a real issue to be sure, but it was often overblown and cynically deployed, in Hekla's opinion. In any event, Norway's law enforcement had a budget surplus, so now the NBI offices looked more like mission control for a space launch than a police unit in charge of the welfare of fewer than 400,000 humans.

"Why haven't we arrested her yet?" Bjarni Pálsson was in Hekla's face before she was halfway to her desk.

Bjarni was in his mid 40s, about ten years Hekla's senior. He had hair that was too short for any accidental style and a face that was as weathered by resentment as it was by the twice-daily shavings he inflicted on his skin. Hekla viewed Bjarni as the type of guy who watched way too many American police dramas and felt like he was missing out.

"Who?" she responded with a manufactured naivety that always managed to evade Bjarni's suspicion.

"You know. Aldís."

Bjarni followed her as she walked the rest of the way to her desk and sat down.

"Why would we arrest her?"

"You know that bitch had something to do with it."

Hekla raised her eyes at Bjarni. She did her best to keep her lips relaxed as she gritted the teeth behind them. Inhale through your nose, she thought, exhale through your mouth. "We don't know anything yet. We'll talk to her. Like everyone else. When's the wife coming in?"

Bjarni gave a dismissive shrug and abruptly turned his back on her as he mumbled something to himself.

***

It didn't take long for Hekla to locate Aldís on the security camera footage. Just a few clicks and there she was. It looked like Aldís had managed to appear front and center on every camera they had. Except, of course, any of the ones focused on the luxury suite wing. Those cameras, the ones that mattered, showed nothing unusual at all. No one other than Jack was recorded entering or leaving the suite from the time his wife left until Elísa arrived the next morning. The only people in the wing during those hours were a few guests coming from, or going to, their own suites, and a small cleaning crew sweeping the hallway. And none of these people were covered in blood or holding a knife.

Neither could Aldís be seen doing anything that would normally draw suspicion. She arrived at the spa early, just as it was opening, entered the visitor center, and rented a locker. She exited into the changing area that led to the showers and hot springs. A little more than an hour later, she was inside again, fully dressed, purchasing a drink. She wasn't captured on any of the cameras that led to the greater hotel or luxury suite wing. She looked like any other visitor enjoying a morning at the spa.

Of course, Aldís's mere presence at the Azure Spa and Hotel was, in and of itself, highly unusual—even suspicious.

There weren't a lot of plausible reasons for a lifelong resident of Patreksfjörður to spend a Monday morning in December at a tourist hotspot in Grindavik. This was particularly true when the resident was an outspoken critic of both the hotel group that controlled the spa and the commercialization of nature in general. And, when that person was an *even more* outspoken critic of a prominent American businessman murdered at the adjacent hotel when she was visiting said spa—well, that might lead even the most objective observer to conclude that the critic was somehow involved. Hekla didn't dispute this logic, so she understood Kjartan's direction to focus on Aldís. Still, the person she was most interested in speaking with wasn't Aldís. It was Susan Teele, the dead American's wife.

⁓⁓⁓⁓⁓⁓⁓⁓⁓⁓⁓⁓

Hekla was in the middle of leaving her second voicemail for Susan Teele when Lisa Harris called.

"Hekla speaking."

"Hello, is this Hekla Fritzdóttir?" Lisa spoke in English but with excellent pronunciation of Hekla's traditional last name.

"Rafney."

"Excuse me?"

"It's Hekla Rafney." She switched to English. "How can I help you?"

"Oh. I'm sorry. Ms. Rafney. Of course. My name is Lisa Harris. I'm with United States Embassy."

"Right." Hekla wished she hadn't answered. "You spoke with Kjartan earlier. Our national commissioner."

"Yes. I did."

"Okay. Well, I'm afraid we don't have much else to add at this time. But please let the family know we have everyone working hard to figure out who's responsible for Mr. Drumman's death."

"Have you spoken to any suspects?"

Hekla closed her eyes as her shoulders sunk. "At this point, we're still trying to get in touch with anyone who interacted with Mr. Drumman. As a matter of fact, I should get back—"

"Actually, that's something I wanted to talk to you about." There was a short pause before Lisa continued. "Susan Teele, Mr. Drumman's wife, informed me that you had left a message for her. I wanted to let you know that she will be available to talk tomorrow."

Hekla felt her cheeks fill with blood. She tried, with only moderate success, to keep her voice steady. "We need to speak with her now. Her husband was just murdered."

"Well as you can imagine this has been very hard day for her. She'll be available tomorrow."

"That's not good enough. I understand it must be very difficult for her, but time is of the essence here. We can come to her if that's easier."

"She's not available today. I'm sorry."

"What do you mean 'she's not available'?" Hekla's ire was obvious.

There was another pause, as though Lisa was deciding how to respond. "She's not available. We'll see you tomorrow."

Lisa hung up and Hekla stared at her phone as though it owed her an apology. "*We'll* see you," she repeated in her head. What the hell did she mean by "we'll"?

Hekla tasked Bjarni with figuring out what Susan and Steingrímur Eggertsson were up to after leaving Jack. Independent of her personal distaste for the man, Hekla knew Bjarni to be effective at gathering information. More important to her though, was her desire to keep him as far away from Aldís as possible.

Bjarni's earlier pejorative was not the first time Hekla had to endure his unsolicited opinion on the prominent journalist. Bjarni was part of a growing contingent of delusional Icelanders who blamed Aldís and her activist-minded contemporaries—but mostly Aldís—for any parliamentary decision, real or imagined, they disagreed with. "Parliamentary decision" was probably being too kind, as most of the complaints from self-identified *real* men like Bjarni had to do with the light criticism they faced for acting like assholes. It was grievance theatre, with every other sentence prefaced with a "we're not allowed to" or "it used to be," as though they were trapped in a bubble, helplessly watching society collapse because they got flak for being sexist. It was exhausting. Hekla shuddered to think what he would say or do if Aldís actually did something wrong.

Fortunately, most of the other officers and investigators were more evolved. Hekla wasn't convinced they had the resolve to stand up to the outside influences that were almost certain to show up, but she'd worry about that later. She dispatched most of the detectives and senior officers to interview everyone who had been at the Azure during the 48 hours leading up to Jack's murder. She instructed the more junior staff to review surveillance footage from the hotel. Her focus was on proximity and knowledge. She wanted to know the identity and whereabouts of everyone who either knew where Jack and his wife were, or who were close enough to have committed the murder.

Hekla asked Gunnar to join the team in Reykjavík. Though the capital police and NBI officers hailed from all over, Hekla wanted to have at least one uniformed officer who lived and regularly worked in the district where the murder took place. This type of crime was a few degrees removed from the petty theft and drunken tourists that usually defined his beat, but his perspective would still be useful. Gunnar seemed a bit apprehensive about leaving his post in Grindavik, but Hekla assured him that most of his work wouldn't require any physical presence in the Capital.

Hekla met with Kjartan in his office after giving out orders. Kjartan informed her that he had spoken with the Ministry of Justice and been assured of their active assistance in the investigation. Hekla wasn't quite sure what "active assistance" meant. Normally, when she asked the Ministry for something like a search of financial transactions that she suspected would show fraud, it could take weeks to hear back. But now, in the time it took her to drive from the hotel to headquarters, it seemed the NBI had been given carte blanche to examine any electronic record Hekla wanted. She did not find this reassuring. She just hoped that visiting Americans weren't exempt from these orders.

Given the evidence left in Jack's throat, records of all currency exchanges seemed like the most natural place to start. The major banks had this data uploaded and available for review almost immediately after a transaction, but some small, standalone banks and kiosks might take a day or more to provide it. Hekla enlisted Val, an administrator whom she knew had previously studied to be an accountant, for the job of pouring through several weeks of money exchanges. Val was a little nervous, having just graduated from answering phones to sorting files, but they were sharp.

"How do you know the killer didn't convert that money elsewhere? Or couldn't they have taken the money from the victim?" Val asked.

Hekla gave a tight-lipped smile and nodded. "I don't think Jack was the type to worry about local currency. At least not in those denominations. And the numbers suggest a conversion that started with krónur."

"Why?"

"Well, the foreign currency found on him is what you get if you exchanged a hundred thousand krónur and just used the hundreds. If you went the other way—exchanging dollars or euros for krónur—you would have at least a thousand in dollars or euros. And I think if the killer had a thousand dollars or euros, they'd put them down next to the hundred thousand krónur. Don't you think? Unless there is some significance to leaving exactly seven hundred dollars and six hundred euros on him. But I doubt it. Double check the exchange rates, but I don't think they've changed enough in the past month or so to affect that."

Val was left with their mouth slightly parted, impressed, but unable to do more than grunt in agreement.

"Thanks." Hekla smiled. "Call me if you find anything."

᠁᠁᠁᠁᠁᠁

It was early morning when Hekla returned to her apartment complex in the Rimar neighborhood of northeast Reykjavík. By the time she reached the building, her body was trembling. She made it to her door, somehow, but had to hold onto the doorknob and brace herself against the doorframe to keep from falling. Her head was spinning—she needed water, she needed food that didn't come in a foil wrapper. Both of those would have to wait, however. When she managed to open the door and stagger inside, the couch was as far as she could go. She collapsed, face first into the cushions, and let sleep mercifully take her away from the events of the past 24 hours.

CHAPTER EIGHT

It was ten o'clock sharp when Susan Teele, Lisa Harris, and a bland-looking man in a suit entered the offices of the NBI. Susan wore a coat that looked like it cost more than twice Hekla's monthly rent. She was in her late 40s but appeared at least a decade younger. Her skin had a glow and was taut around the top of her brow and neck in a way that wouldn't seem odd unless you were sitting across from her in a small room with unforgiving lighting. She didn't appear to be in mourning, Hekla thought, but she did look upset. Maybe disturbed would be a better word. She held herself like a confident person used to being treated with deference, but there was something in her eyes that belied the rest of her body's certainty. Hekla wondered if this was what sadness looked like for a person like Susan. Or perhaps it was fear.

Lisa also was in her 40s, a few years younger than Susan, with a diplomatic charm that terrified Hekla—extremely polite and engaging until challenged. When Lisa's eyes locked in on you, it felt as though they were telepathically conveying a strong argument for why you and everything you held dear were insignificant. She was dressed more conservatively than Susan, like someone who had spent some actual time in Iceland. But she still stood out. Unlike her attire and demeanor, this wasn't her fault. It was just that her presence on the island increased the percentage of Black people in the population by at least five percent.

The other man, Mark something or other, identified himself

as a lawyer. He looked the part—50s, with a shock of gray hair, and a pale, portly, chinless face that disappeared into the light blue shirt and deep red tie that he wore underneath a navy suit. Hekla thought he would fit right in as a background actor in an American political drama. Only the fabric of his suit and style of his shoes gave any indication that he had perhaps stumbled upon an even more lucrative hustle.

Mark spent a good minute or two whispering in Susan's ear near the door before they joined Hekla and Lisa at the table in an interrogation room. Hekla informed the group that Kjartan was observing behind the glass, prompting another 30 seconds of whispering before Hekla could begin. She didn't waste any time. "What did you and Steingrímur Eggertsson talk about after you left the Azure hotel that night?"

Susan's head reflexively moved back a few centimeters as her features struggled against her skin to express dismay. Lisa and Mark both started to speak before they had settled on actual words with which to object.

"What are you talking about?" Lisa finally sputtered out.

Hekla kept her focus on Susan. "On the phone. I imagine it was around the time you were driving to the Envoy."

Lisa gave Mark a sharp look. They clearly did not expect her to have a copy of Susan's phone records. That was likely because someone representing Susan had taken the highly unusual step of trying to seal those records in Icelandic court before this interview.

"I'm not sure—" Susan started.

"What does this have to do with Mr. Drumman's death?" Lisa interjected. "You know, the violent murder of an American citizen that just took place in your country?"

This was going to be fun, Hekla grimly mused.

*

Throughout the brief interview, Lisa did her best to steer them away from specifics regarding Susan's life or her activities in Iceland. Mark did his part, ensuring Susan would have ample time to consider her responses by employing the garbage lawyerly tactic of seeking clarification on every word in every sentence until they were devoid of all meaning, and no one remembered what the hell they were talking about. None of this impeded Hekla, however, as there was only one topic she wanted to talk about. She didn't even need any further information, really, as she already knew almost everything about the subject. She just wanted Susan to admit it. What Hekla wanted was a public acknowledgment of the *real* reason Susan was in Iceland.

*

After the initial objections, Susan provided some details on the argument between Jack and Steingrímur the night before Jack's murder, as well as the general nature of her conversation with Steingrímur later that evening. According to Susan, Jack was interested in a business expansion that Steingrímur thought might pose a threat to his telecommunications empire. Steingrímur was offended, so Susan called him later to apologize on behalf of her uncouth husband.

Hekla could tell by the way Susan revealed the information that this was the area the trio wanted her to focus on—Jack's business and his grand ambitions. It was like chum thrown in the water. A juicy tidbit "reluctantly" given up, and that she should be eager to feast upon. To her though, it was more like the small confession you give to an inquisitor to conceal the bigger truth, like tearfully telling your spouse about a night of indiscretion, when you have an entire family and two dogs in another town.

"So, Jack had his eyes on conquering the Icelandic market?" Hekla asked as seriously as she was capable.

"Yes," Susan responded quickly, before adding, "I think he believed it would allow him easier access to some of the European countries that are reluctant to do business with Palezar."

"I see. And you think this has something to do with why he was killed? His business interests?"

"That's your job, isn't it?" Lisa asked. "His business affairs certainly seemed to rile up some of your more deranged compatriots."

Hekla clenched her teeth, attempting to mask the slight smile she felt coming on. Lisa couldn't help herself, she thought, but did they really expect her to believe that Jack and Susan traveled to Iceland in the middle of winter so Jack could get a piece of the prized Icelandic market? Hekla wondered if they really thought so little of law enforcement in her country. Or maybe this was just an extension of the shit they pulled at home. Maybe, she thought, getting away with everything had warped their brains to the point where they took it as a given that whatever they said, no matter how nonsensical, would be accepted and repeated as fact without question or debate.

"Where were you when you found out your husband was killed?" Hekla asked.

"I told you, I was in a meeting," Susan answered. "At the Harpa."

Mark spoke without glancing up from his legal pad. "We agreed, she's not answering questions about her meeting or her business dealings."

"I'm not interested in her business dealings," Hekla replied, lying. "After you found out your husband was dead, you went back to your room at the Envoy, right?"

Susan nodded.

"Why didn't you go to back to the suite at the Azure? Didn't you want to see your husband one last time?"

"Why would I want that?" Susan's eyes narrowed and her voice wavered. "I didn't want to see him—his *body*—not after what was done to him."

Hekla nodded. "Okay. You got my messages though?"

"Yes." Susan forced a sniffle.

"Why didn't you return my call? Didn't you want to help the people investigating your husband's murder?"

"I talked to the embassy. That was all I could do. They said I could come today. I don't know that I would have been able to talk yesterday. I was scared, I didn't know what to do—how this would work, what I should do."

Hekla believed part of that. "Then what *did* you do?"

"What do you mean?"

"Yesterday. You didn't come to speak with us. What did you do instead?"

Susan shook her head. "I cried."

"Of course. But then?"

"I don't understand what you're getting at."

Mark rapped the edge of his legal pad against the table.

"Is this really what we came here for?" Lisa asked sharply.

"What were you expecting?" Hekla shot back.

Lisa glared at Hekla. Mark started in with some objection, but Hekla spoke over him. "Where were you yesterday afternoon? Were you alone?"

Susan just stared back with wide, tearless eyes.

"You met with Steingrímur again, didn't you?"

No one spoke, so Hekla continued, "After Jack was killed. You left the meeting and returned to your hotel. You spoke with Ms. Harris and then you met up with Steingrímur. Again. Because he was at the meeting with you earlier, wasn't he—the one at the Harpa?"

"This is a waste of our time," Lisa said as she placed her note-pad and pen in her black leather briefcase.

Hekla ignored her. "You met him again at the restaurant, right? Downstairs, in the corner of the hotel. Who else was there? There were other people from your meeting that morning, weren't there?"

Mark grumbled something about "business confidentiality."

Hekla's eyes moved quickly between Mark and Susan. "It *was* a business meeting. That's what you were doing after you found out your husband had his throat slit and stuffed with money— wasn't it? Having a business meeting."

Lisa forcefully pushed her chair back and stood. "That's it. We're done."

Susan gave an uncertain look at Lisa before tentatively reaching for her bag.

"Do you think your husband's death might have had some-thing to do with what *you* were here for?" Hekla asked. "Do you think it could have been related to *your* business?"

Susan bit her lower lip.

"That's why you all met again, isn't it?" Hekla continued. "You *were* scared."

"I—" Lisa grabbed Susan by the shoulder before the widow could continue.

"You don't have to answer her," Lisa instructed.

Hekla noticed a look in Susan's eyes again. Just like earlier, there was something vulnerable and authentic about it, like a glimpse behind the mask. Hekla remained seated as the three Americans pulled on their coats. "You'll be staying in Iceland for the time being?" she called out as the three made their way to the door.

Susan didn't respond.

"Well, please make sure to keep us informed if your plans change."

Lisa held the door open as Mark led Susan out of the room. Then she turned back to Hekla and spoke loud enough so Kjartan and anyone else in the office could hear.

"Maybe you should focus on the woman who actually threatened Mr. Drumman's life. And her radical little friends." Lisa's lips contorted into a crooked smile. "The Fólk? That's their name, isn't it?"

Lisa shut the door hard behind her, leaving Hekla alone in the room.

There it is, Hekla thought. It took her long enough.

⁓⁓⁓⁓⁓⁓⁓

"What are you doing? You can't do that."

Kjartan was either angry or stressed. Possibly both. It was hard to tell, since the only real indication of his ire or angst was a slight twitch on the side of his otherwise impassive face. Right now, his cheek flared more than twitched.

"They were relevant questions."

Kjartan gave her a look. "It won't get us anywhere good."

"There has to be some connection. Jack wasn't doing anything of significance here, but what Susan was up to—the secrecy and lengths they're going to in order to hide everything . . . "

Kjartan shook his head. "They won't stop."

Hekla furrowed her brow. "Who? Who's they?" She hesitated a moment. "Do you know about the deal?"

Kjartan made eye contact with Hekla again but said nothing. He looked tired, she thought. Already, hundreds of journalists were pestering their office. That wouldn't shake her boss though. Neither would even the most overbearing diplomat. This was something else. Hekla pushed on. "Did you know?"

"Did I know what?"

"Why Susan was here—what she was working on with Steingrímur and the others. Did you know?"

Kjartan didn't blink. His cheek moved again though. And then his Adam's apple expanded, moved up, and then quickly back down. "Just focus on Aldís," he finally said. "And The Fólk."

Hekla scoffed. She stared back at him in disbelief. It was the first time she heard Kjartan use that name in this context.

At its most basic, The Fólk was just the title of a newsletter that Aldís published from her small home in the Westfjords. But to its detractors, and maybe its supporters as well, it had come to symbolize much more. Aldís was an acclaimed journalist and author who gained international fame for exposing financial fraud at the top levels of government in several European countries. She was beloved in progressive circles and a frequent guest or panel member on news shows and at conferences around the world. But her eyes never strayed too far from Iceland, and she was most loyal to The Fólk. The Fólk was her vehicle for pushing back on the corroding influence that countries like the United States had on Iceland. Depending on who you asked, The Fólk could also be a subversive group of Icelandic revolutionaries intent on destroying Iceland by protecting its natural resources and preserving social safety nets.

Hekla never imagined Kjartan would be influenced by this kind of nonsense.

"She made threats, Hekla," Kjartan added, as if he could read her mind. "They won't be satisfied unless we've exhausted that angle."

"They?" Hekla turned away before Kjartan could respond. She didn't see the utility in letting Kjartan see the expression she had on her face right now. There was The Fólk and there was the threat. In her mind, *They* were the threat—whoever *They* were—and The Fólk, whatever its shortcomings might be, was against the threat. What Hekla didn't know was where Kjartan stood in all of this, and how much say he really had. Especially since his chief concern in the investigation was appeasing *Them*.

CHAPTER NINE

Aᴜɢᴜsᴛ sᴛʀᴏᴅᴇ ᴀᴄʀᴏss ʜɪs sᴍᴀʟʟ ʟɪᴠɪɴɢ ʀᴏᴏᴍ and entered his equally compact kitchen. He opened the cupboard next to the stove and retrieved a sleeve of nicotine gum. He pressed a piece out of its foil wrapper, popped it in his mouth, and chewed on it for several seconds before parking the partially chewed piece between his gums and cheek on the left side of his mouth. He took two more pieces out of the wrapper and put them in his pocket before putting the rest of the package away.

He moved to his bedroom, stepping over small piles of neatly folded, dirty clothing until he reached his closet, with sliding doors that hopped off their track every time he pulled them open. He yanked hard, halfway hoping the doors would fall off and the ceiling would cave in, rendering this exercise moot, and mercifully removing the end result from his hands. The doors slid smoother than ever before. Of course, he thought to himself.

He scoured the shelf above the rack of hanging shirts, lightweight jackets, and cardigan sweaters. He couldn't see farther than a few centimeters deep on the shelf, so he fumbled around with his hand above his head, navigating via touch around and underneath the underutilized or unloved clothing and accessories that he once imagined he'd eventually donate. His hand brushed against a sturdy object that made a light scraping sound as it moved on the wooden shelf. There it was.

He wrapped his hand around a belt and pulled it down from the shelf. It was dark brown, well-worn—it used to be his favorite. It felt tough, particularly around the edges. He remembered buying the overpriced leather and grumbled softly at the indifference that marked his past life's purchases.

He scanned the rest of his bedroom.

In truth, he didn't really know what he was doing. There probably were much better ways of doing this, but *belt* leapt to the front of his mind when he thought of asphyxiation techniques, and asphyxiation always was in the top three of August's rotating list of hypothetical suicide methods. Suicide, naturally, was a constant consideration.

So, belt it was.

But August wasn't trying to kill himself now. Not consciously at least. Really. His *non*-plan was much more realistic and practical. Maybe just a little more asinine.

However it would be categorized, comfort was still of paramount importance, so he would need to do something about the belt's surface. He pulled open the top drawer of his dresser. There wasn't much there—a pair of too-small cotton briefs that he had worn once, two mismatched dress socks, a largely unused notebook, buttons and thread enclosed in a small plastic bag, and two screws that rolled down across the open drawer until they hit the edge.

August glanced around the room. The socks he was looking for were in a large pile on the floor. Surprisingly, they were clean, just waiting for their neglectful owner to pair them. He fished through the pile until he found one to his liking.

⁓⁓⁓⁓⁓⁓⁓⁓⁓

August rested one knee on the chair next to his desk as he hovered over his laptop in the living room. He mechanically entered a few terms in the search bar of a pornographic website, as though trying to find a restaurant he knew existed but had forgotten the name of. An unusual sensation of self-consciousness emerged as he absentmindedly scrolled through the results. Normally he had no issue with his kinks, but his lack of arousal highlighted the bizarre nature of this endeavor and brought particular attention to the combination of genitals, orifices and individuals that might be left interacting on his screen long after he was gone. He grimaced slightly and typed "two people in love." He hit enter and stood up. He took the pieces of gum out of their foil and placed them on the table. Then he took off all his clothing.

⁓⁓⁓⁓⁓⁓⁓⁓⁓

August couldn't kill himself. He knew this. He could, and did, think about suicide daily but he wasn't ever able to get any further than the *idea* of a plan. It was like his mind threw a dark sheet over itself as soon as it recognized the contours of a contraption that it knew could end its existence. He was certain he could bypass these security measures with drugs or alcohol, but he had no interest in going out like that—plus he figured there was a good chance they would only prolong the process or cause him to botch the execution.

The brilliant lawyer—multilingual, former personal representative of the director of the Federal Bureau of Investigation in Copenhagen—was able to come up with one idea though. A workaround of sorts to the problem of wanting out but being stuck within. He would create an artificial circumstance where a not *un*pleasant death might *accidentally* occur. It was a rationalization, he knew. He was going to kill himself. But he would overcome his brain's annoying instinct for self-preservation by creating an alluring combination of sexual gratification and physical jeopardy that he knew he couldn't consciously object to. Brilliant.

But as soon as he was naked in his living room—his dick

flaccid, his belt, a single sock and two pieces of unwrapped gum lying next to a laptop computer whose screen was overloaded by gifs and thumbnail videos wedged between advertisements for masturbation video games—he felt more than a little foolish. It would have been better if this setup aligned with one of his sexual preferences, he thought. It would have been better if everything didn't remind him of *her*. The cigarettes he used to smoke, the animals he used to consume—even the cartoonishly large penis with its missing foreskin on one of the jerk-off game ads made him think of her. She never did miss an opportunity to opine on male genital mutilation. After the fourth or fifth diatribe, he found it necessary to gently remind her that, while he agreed with her absolutely, his inability to resurrect the protective layer of skin on his own dick made it kind of a bummer to hear about the sensations that were lost for him forever due to the actions of a medical practitioner when he was an infant.

And now he was crying.

He snatched the gum from his desk and tossed it into his mouth.

""""""""""""""""

An unadorned nail protruded from the wall above the desk, where a framed reprint of a Piet Mondrian painting used to hang, *Composition with Oval in Color Planes II*. August picked up the belt, slipped its end through the buckle, and then worked the first notch of the belt over the nail. It was tricky, and for a moment he thought he might have to widen the notch, but eventually he got it over the head of the nail.

He pulled the desk away from the wall and inspected his work. The loop in the belt hung much lower than he had envisioned. He briefly considered taking it off and trying a different notch, but wasn't confident he would be successful. This would be awk-ward—*more* awkward—but at least the belt wouldn't slip off. It likely was almost as secure as if he had driven a nail straight through the notch itself. *Why hadn't he done that,* he immediately asked himself. He could very easily have affixed the belt via ham-mer and nail, so he wouldn't have to add 'squatting position' to the list of indignities on the future police report. He sighed and rolled his eyes before closing his lids. Maybe he could at least give himself a break on this one, he pleaded as much as thought.

He turned the laptop to face the wall and leaned onto the desk to pick a video. A disparity between what he envisioned when he entered the phrase and the videos being offered quickly became apparent. He imagined high-resolution clips of beautiful people, shot with artistry, passionately making love to each other with just a dash of intimate filth for realism. What he got was fake spy videos and staged sex parties, along with the ever-present thumb-nail images of frightened nude women above captions for videos that could double as cocaine-addled descriptors of empire-build-ing—*destroy, devastate, conquer, impale.* He waded through the results until he found an 11-minute clip where all the participants were attractive, in focus, and gave the appearance of enjoying them-selves. He pressed play and enlarged the video.

He placed his back against the wall and slid down until the loop of the belt was near his head. He worked his head through the loop. He took the sock that he had been holding with his fin-gers and slipped it between his neck and the belt. Then he crouched lower to eliminate the slack.

But the small adjustment caused him to lose control of his weight distribution. He lost his balance and the loop quickly cinched his neck, much tighter than he anticipated or desired. He felt a flash of heat behind his face, and a rapid swell of pressure.

The discomfort was as alarming as it was unpleasant, a dense, dizzying cloud that moved swiftly, threatening to overwhelm all his senses.

He threw his arms back against the wall to stay upright and stop any further movement. The muscles in his shoulders and triceps flared.

His hands slid a millimeter and the belt squeezed even tighter around his neck, cutting into the skin just below his ear. The pressure in his head was unbearable. His arms shook, devoid of strength. He was certain this was it—an accident within a purposeful act designed to replicate an accident. How dumb. How fitting.

But the back of his arms remained in place against the wall.

He still had a chance.

With all his remaining strength, he pressed even harder into the wall with his triceps and elbows. He wormed his body up, slowly but surely, a centimeter or two at a time. And that was enough. He yanked at the belt.

"Aaguhahhh," he choked out before taking a greedy gulp of air.

His deep relieved breaths were interrupted by light coughing fits, but he was okay.

After a moment, he adjusted his feet and carefully lifted his body, keeping one arm firmly on the wall until he was standing.

Fucking hell, he thought, why the fuck did everything have to be so fucking hard?

A woman shrieked. August looked around with alarm. His eyes stopped on his laptop. An oiled-up woman in stilettos and intentionally smeared makeup straddled a disembodied cock on a pleather couch; a similarly shiny man stood next to her with a fistful of her hair, alternating between hurling insults at her and jamming his swollen member in and around her mouth.

August closed his eyes in frustration. This wasn't helping. He stretched his right leg out and used his foot to close the screen of his laptop.

What *was* he doing, he thought to himself. This wasn't going to change anything. He couldn't Rube Goldberg his mind into permitting self-annihilation, just like he couldn't distract himself from the truth in his waking life. He could either accept reality or not. And why shouldn't the end be painful? Everything else was.

He failed her.

He failed them.

It wasn't an ordinary failure, that was true. It was extraordinary, a *feat* of failure, an accomplishment. But however perceived, no matter how he categorized events, and no matter how he chose to view the personal and professional *devastation* that *he* had inflicted, it was over. Past tense. It was what it was, and it would be what it would be. He was here, they were not, and that was that. These were the facts and there was nothing he could do about them now.

Except this.

August used one hand to brace himself against the wall, placed his other hand around the buckle of the belt, and gently lowered himself until the length above his head was taut.

CHAPTER TEN

JACK'S ASSISTANT WAS GONE. EMMA WEINSTEIN WAS on a flight back to the States within hours of Jack's death. Of course, Susan's attorney withheld this crucial piece of information until *after* Susan's interview.

The Ministry of Tourism offered complimentary stays at nearby hotels to potential witnesses who lived abroad, but there was no guarantee they would accept, and if they did, they could leave at any time. The police couldn't really keep tourists in the country unless the tourists had a direct connection to the murder, so it was essential that the investigators got as much information as possible now, while most everyone was still here.

Few witnesses were more critical than Emma. Still, an unfiltered assessment from Jack's assistant seemed like a tall order. Hekla didn't know if Emma's ambitions were to have assistants of her own one day or just to eat and sleep in comfort, but she did know that Emma's success—however she defined it—was dependent on staying in the good graces of people like Susan.

Later that evening, Ólafur met Hekla at her desk to review the medical and forensics reports. He looked exhausted. His small team had been working around the clock.

The Norwegian government offered to send assistance, but Kjartan didn't deem it necessary. Hekla agreed. As rare as murder was in Iceland, the national police were more than capable of investigating, no matter how shocking the circumstance. Still, Hekla couldn't help but wonder if someone—maybe Kjartan, maybe someone else—was eager to keep outside eyes away from this.

Ólafur didn't have much to share that wasn't already apparent from viewing the corpse. There were no foreign substances on Jack's body, no sign of sexual assault, no stray hair or fibers that could be tested. Neither did they find any unaccounted-for fingerprints or DNA in or around the suite. There were no defensive wounds. Jack was likely approached from behind, his throat slit from left to right with a medium-sized blade. There was a tiny cut on the left side of his neck, something like a hesitation mark, but the deep and smooth nature of the wound suggested that the killer was just adjusting the knife. The cut was deep enough that Jack would have bled out, but it was lack of oxygen that killed him. He suffocated, drowned really, as water and blood filled his lungs.

"So, they knew what they were doing?" Hekla asked.

Ólafur nodded.

"How strong would they have to be?" Hekla held up her hand, "what size guy are we talking about?"

"It depends. The water works both ways. You have to be fit to move around quickly. But when you are up to your shoulders, height and other advantages could be neutralized."

Hekla nodded. "He was killed in the water, though—we're sure about that?"

Ólafur nodded again, "Absolutely. Lungs were filled with blood and water. Skin was soft, hair soaked, no blood anywhere but the balcony—and not much there considering the manner of death."

"Right."

"It would have been gruesome to witness," Ólafur added with an expressive tone that took Hekla by surprise. "He would have been conscious— at least five to ten seconds, probably more. Even when he did slip out of consciousness, his body would still be trying to survive."

Hekla furrowed her brow. This was a bit more opinion than Hekla was used to receiving from Ólafur. "What about the money?"

"Yes. I think they had trouble there. The incisions were much less refined. It looks like they tried different methods of securing the currency. We found vertical perforations on some of the bills. I suspect the killer ended up using the knife to force the ends of the currency inside as they pried the skin apart. Like I said, real gruesome stuff."

Hekla glared at Ólafur. "Thanks. We'll make sure to focus exclusively on gore aficionados now."

Ólafur gave a weak shrug. "Sorry, I was just—sorry."

"It's okay." Hekla rubbed her eyes. "I'm just tired."

"Understandable. Let me know if you need anything else."

Hekla nodded. She turned her attention to the report on her desk for a moment before looking back up. She watched Ólafur disappear into the corridor lined with offices that divided the detectives and support staff from the high-tech toys and the whiz kids who monitored them. As soon as Ólafur was out of sight, Hekla made a beeline for the door.

She rushed down two flights of stairs and exited into the hallway on a quiet floor that was used mostly for record keeping. She made a sharp left around a corner and continued until she was in front of the door to a rarely used single-stall bathroom. She gave a quick knock before opening the door and slipping inside. She locked the door, pulled her shirt over her head, and tossed it on the sink as she grabbed a stack of disposable towels.

The vomit flew from her mouth before she hit her knees.

After she was done, she spent several more minutes hunched over the toilet, watching the remnants of her tears and spittle swirl within a sickly-yellow base. Finally, she lifted her head. A loud rattling sound jolted her. She looked at her hands, grasped tight around the sides of the toilet seat. She realized she was shaking uncontrollably.

nnnnnnnnnnn

Kjartan was gone by the time Hekla returned to the office. She called him from her desk to let him know that she would be traveling to the Westfjords in the morning to speak with Aldís. Kjartan sounded relieved that he did not have to order Hekla to go there.

Before she left for the night, Hekla spoke with Val, who was still reviewing currency exchanges.

"Nothing fits what we're looking for," Val explained after showing Hekla their progress. "But we're going to get the rest of the small banks and kiosks in a few hours."

"Okay. Call me. First thing if you find anything—anything at all."

Val nodded as Hekla walked away.

Hekla had a cigarette in her mouth and her thumb on her lighter the second she stepped outside.

nnnnnnnnnnn

Hekla parked her car in the lot near the harbor, just south of the peninsula that marked the northernmost boundary of Reykjavík— not counting the uninhabited Geldinganes island or barely inhabited northeast corner close to her flat. She wore a hooded, brick-red parka over her work clothes and a faded, denim-blue baseball cap low over her eyes. She stepped out of her car just as a strong gust of wind rose from the water. She pulled the hood over her hat and tugged on the drawstrings.

To her left, she could see the glass walls of the Harpa Concert

Hall, its sharp angles cutting into the night sky. The designers behind the project said the reflection on the glass was meant to highlight the natural elements and unique light conditions that gave Reykjavík life. At times, it was truly phenomenal. Tonight though, it just looked like a cold, dark rock whose sides had been sanded flat and polished. Hekla knew that Susan, Steingrímur, and whoever else was part of their godforsaken business deal met there the morning Jack's body was found. Maybe tonight's reflection was more accurate than at first blush. Not far from the Hall, construction had begun on what was to be Reykjavík's fourth five-star hotel. A large area next to the harbor had been cordoned off. Monstrous earth-moving machines lurked ominously where an offbeat shipping museum once stood. Progress.

Hekla continued walking along access roads until she reached the more postcard-worthy streets that led to the center area of the city, and finally, the Envoy hotel. The Envoy was a stately, six-story building tucked between two narrow streets in the northeast part of downtown Reykjavík. Compared to the Azure suites, the Envoy was a testament to restraint. Diplomats and businesspeople often stayed at the modern but understated hotel.

Hekla entered the hotel and walked briskly past the lobby to the elevators. She pressed the "up" button and tapped her foot nervously as she waited for the doors to open. She rode to the third floor, watched the doors open again, and discreetly scanned the hallway before stepping out. She kept her head low as she marched down the hall, stopping at the second door on the left. She raised her hand to knock without looking at the number. Before her arm moved a centimeter, the door swung open.

Hekla looked up at Logi Stefánsson. Logi was at least a head taller than Hekla, and thin, with piercing brown eyes and textured, dark brown hair that wound its way near the base of his neck in soft curls and waves. Hekla's eyes widened as though eager to communicate, but the rest of her body remained perfectly still.

Logi didn't hesitate. He took a full stride out into the hallway, placed his hand behind Hekla's neck and gently pulled her in for a deep kiss. Hekla closed her eyes and let herself be taken away for a moment. Then she grabbed Logi by the shirt and pulled him with her into the hotel room. As he stepped inside, Logi hooked the door with his foot and extended his leg to push it shut.

Not a second after the door clicked shut, Hekla broke off their kiss. She took another step inside and fell to her knees.

Logi looked alarmed. Hekla continued onto her forearms and let out a guttural cry. Her shoulders heaved forward and her back arched, expanding and contracting along with her uneven breath and heavy sobs.

"What's wrong?" Logi asked as he knelt and placed his hand on her back.

Hekla just shook her head.

"Hekla. Please! What's going on?"

She kept shaking her head, but managed to collect enough oxygen between unintelligible cries to croak out a few discernible words. "No . . . It's too much . . . we can't—I can't."

"What? What are you talking about? I don't understand."

Suddenly Hekla tilted her head sharply toward Logi. Logi flinched. Hekla's eyes were watery and red, but her stare was intense and focused.

"Don't do it," she shook her head forcefully. "You don't need to. Please. Don't."

Logi furrowed his brow. "What?" he asked again with genuine confusion, but Hekla had already resumed crying.

Hekla stepped out of the shower feeling more refreshed than she had in several days. The light, clean feeling remained even after she pulled her dingy work clothes over the pair of fresh panties she had smuggled into the hotel. She still hadn't gotten enough sleep or consumed enough real food, but perhaps the hot water had induced an optimal level of delirium. It was a ludicrous but amusing thought that caused a slight smile to emerge on her face as she exited the bathroom.

Logi was sitting up in bed. His eyes were locked on Hekla and his expression was one of deep concern.

"What?" Hekla asked defensively.

Logi didn't reply.

The ping of Hekla's phone interrupted the silence.

Hekla kept an eye on Logi as she made her way to the nightstand next to the unoccupied portion of the bed. She grabbed her phone. There were several missed calls and a slew of text messages from Val. "Fuck."

"What is it?" Logi asked.

Hekla placed her fingertips against her temple as she read Val's texts to herself. They found something. An individual had made two separate transactions over the course of four days. Both transactions were money exchanges. Ten days before Jack's murder, the individual exchanged 100,000 krónur for U.S. dollars. Three days later, the individual swapped 100,000 krónur for euros. Both exchanges took place at the same small bank in the Westfjords. And Aldís Eva made both transactions.

CHAPTER ELEVEN

The United States military keeps a video and electronic record of every drone strike conducted by its personnel. Not just the strike itself, but evidence used to ascertain targets, communication between staff, and footage showing the aftermath of the deployment of the missile or missiles.

Strike. Deployment. August still couldn't help but fall back onto the jargon of his former employer. You strike something with your hand. They bombed with a robot. And they weren't deploying anything—they were murdering from the fucking sky. *Fucking hell.*

Anyway, everything that anyone saw on a screen during a robot-bomb assassination was simultaneously recorded and stored on a local server. Then, supposedly, it was uploaded onto a secondary server that was accessible to other branches of the government or military. August was never able to get much information on the secondary server, but the local server, that, he knew a good deal about. It was never *actually* a secret, at least not to those involved in the quasi-clandestine operation of remote killings based on cell phone data.

The local recording made sense though. By reviewing the footage and related evidence, the military could find patterns, look for missed clues, instruct—theoretically, they could even discipline. As such, access was not all that hard to obtain. If you had the right codes and ID, you could enter the room, sit in front of a computer, and pull up—and print—all the information you wanted via a user-friendly database. All told, it was fairly easy to walk into the room and, 15 minutes later, have a record of war crimes that might even cause a U.S. Department of Defense ghoul to blush.

The videos were bad. Horrible. No one who took more than a cursory glance could deny the humanity that was being devastated by the bright light and smoke that covered the screen after a "strike" was "initiated." August shuddered at the details. Even from a distance, it was clear that the figures were human beings living their lives. The functionaries pushing buttons and dropping bombs chose not to see that humanity. But August recognized it. The small figure moving toward a slightly larger figure was obviously a child running toward a parent. At night, the red dots moving inside houses painted a more realistic portrait of a loving family than any high-definition closeup possibly could.

As appalling as the videos were, they were nothing compared to the accompanying materials. When August reviewed the chat logs, directives, and flow charts, he had two revelations:

First, the people who decide life and death were no more qualified to make those decisions than Randoms on the street. August felt they were less qualified. It wasn't just the teenagers pulling the trigger or their sociopath bosses who were out of their depth, but everyone involved in the process. As someone who was fully aware that he had no business deciding life and death, August was quite sure on this point. He didn't have the fancy upbringing that the executives and politicians in charge of these operations had, but he had enough in common to know what was and what wasn't taught at their pay-to-play universities and law schools. A lifetime spent avoiding consequences and embracing the worst of humanity in pursuit of self-interest doesn't bestow the wisdom, insight, and compassion necessary to assess the value of life.

Second, *no one* actually had any idea what the fuck they were doing. The haphazard, arbitrary, unaccountable—just fucking random—way that these death squads operated was probably the most horrifying aspect of it all. A country that could obliterate any individual or group, in any region, at a moment's notice managed this awesome responsibility with *a goddamn flow chart.* And boy, August thought, did it fucking flow. The chart had arrows pointing to and from "POTUS," "SECDEF," "JSOC," and "PDC/PC." Even if you understood the acronyms, none of it really meant anything. The mountains of documents seemed to exist only to ensure that no one with power would ever lose the ability to kill someone if they really, really wanted to.

August had not sought out any of this information. In fact, he spent much of his life and career actively avoiding full knowledge of his employer's business dealings. He was no naïf, but he joined America's domestic spy agency because it offered him a realistic path out of the country. He justified the decision by telling himself—and anyone who would listen—that as an "insider" he could work to rein in the worst of their actions. He was clever, an attorney after all. Selfish. He used his intelligence and Danish passport to escape and create a better life for himself. In Copenhagen, there was a buffer between his work and the effect it had on people and society. He was proud of what he'd been able to accomplish for himself. In his mind, he had used America for what he needed and discarded the rest. Things were good and he believed himself to be happy.

That all changed when he met Aldís Eva.

***

Aldís was a radical.

"Radical" was one of the descriptors used in the file that the legat shared with Danish intelligence.

To August though, she was the real thing. Her actions aligned with her values, and the values she touted centered around the betterment of humanity, protection of the most vulnerable, and the sanctity of all living things on the planet. This was extreme.

Aldís was Icelandic, but she became known internationally when her reporting on financial crimes led to the resignation of the Swedish prime minister and several high-ranking cabinet members. Since then, she had become a sort of right-wing bogeyman. Any time a corporate interest felt the slightest pushback, Aldís's name found its way into the mouths of their army of defenders. Consequently, various Nordic law enforcement agencies often asked August's office to assist in investigations into specious conspiracies in which Aldís was a person of interest. It was nonsense. August ignored them when possible. When it wasn't, he sometimes manufactured fake reports to satiate those seeking his aid.

When it appeared that Aldís herself was being targeted though, August took immediate action. He called her and, much to his surprise, she answered. Hundreds of pages of her writing, read with a delight that quickly morphed into awe, hadn't prepared him for the voice on the other end of the phone. He felt the earth move during their one hour and seven-minute conversation. As soon as he hung up, he booked a flight to Iceland. And the next week he found himself outside a red-roofed home in Patreksfjörður.

⁓⁓⁓⁓⁓⁓⁓⁓⁓⁓

Aldís's house was at the westernmost end of Patreksfjörður—a little fishing village that occupied a narrow strip of land along the coast. Past Aldís's house, near a small café that her parents once owned, was an abandoned farmhouse, but otherwise, there was nothing but grass until the steep hills assumed their rightful place against the water.

Aldís's parents had both died when she was 17—her father from a brain aneurism, her mother in a car accident less than a month later. Her parents didn't leave her in great financial condition, but a large contingent of townsfolk chipped in to cover costs and expenses so she could study in Reykjavík. They even kept paying the mortgage on her house so that Aldís always had a place to come home to. Aldís's successful career had provided her plenty of opportunities to upgrade her dwelling or choose a more glamorous city to call home, but she was committed to her hometown and to the house that her neighbors had kept for her.

August's excitement carried him from his office in Copenhagen to this odd but beautiful little town. He made decisions quickly, the answers coming to him easily. He chose not to expense his trip, opting instead to use vacation time. It didn't really matter. At that time he had the run of the legat, but he had a romantic notion that paperwork and pretext might sully his time with the fascinating person he had set out to meet.

As August stood outside Aldís's home, however, it dawned on him how ridiculous his thinking had been. *Sully* his time? What the fuck did he think he was doing? Aldís had indeed invited him to visit, but it was in response to a joke he had made regarding her supposedly clandestine activities. Did she even know he was joking? What exactly was funny about that kind of joke anyhow? She probably was just being polite, he thought then, or daring him to travel—offering to prove her innocence with a bluff of hospitality. Yet here he was, standing outside her door without even the guise of official duty, thinking she really wanted to spend time with him. He felt like an idiot. A fool, undone by his own arrogance and sense of exceptionalism. The very same type of person Aldís consistently railed against.

He almost turned around. But after close to a minute lost in thought, standing suspiciously outside her door, he felt it would be worse if he didn't at least knock.

So, he knocked. Ten seconds later, a tall woman with unwieldy auburn hair answered. She had sharp features, eyes that danced, and lips that always appeared on the verge of a smile. The photographs and video August had seen had clearly failed to capture the joy that exuded from the human standing before him in a thick, oversized sweater, form-fitting jeans that faded naturally at the knees, and scuffed, dirt-stained boots.

"Mr. Sorenson." Aldís's face managed to light up even more as she spoke, "I'm so glad you decided to come."

Before August could respond, he caught a glimpse of a roguish young man sticking his head out of a back room. "Oh. Sorry, am I . . ."

Aldís followed August's look. She smiled. "That's just Logi. He works with me on the newsletter."

She waved him over.

Logi sauntered to the front door. He looked August up and down contemptuously. August marveled at Logi's long hair, intense eyes, and the ease at which his slender frame occupied his substantial height. How was everyone so fucking tall over here, he thought to himself for the thousandth time.

"He promised he wouldn't be wearing a wire," Aldís teased as she looked between Logi and August. "Isn't that right Mr. Sorenson?"

"August. Please."

"August?" Logi scoffed, "you're allowed at the Bureau with a name like that?"

August was speechless. There was something about being mocked by Danes, or now Icelanders, that left him at a loss for words. Maybe it was the accent. Or maybe he just expected them to be nicer.

"August is a lovely name," Aldís kindly volunteered, "it's Danish, right?"

"What—yes," August stammered. "It is. My father—he's from there. He was born there, and he lived there. For a time. Me too. Well—I wasn't born there. But I live there. Now."

Logi rolled his eyes. "Right," he said in English before adding, "maybe you should go back then, fascist pig," in Icelandic as he walked away.

Aldís narrowed her eyes as she studied August's face to see if he understood. August gave an innocent smile. He recognized enough. Fascist wasn't really a difficult word to pick up, and he caught the root of the word "leave," so it wasn't hard to discern the general contours of Logi's remark. But he decided it was better to just to play dumb for now. Besides, he thought Logi's response was more than justified, all things considered.

"Nice to meet you," August cheerily called out as Logi returned to the back room.

Aldís motioned for August to come inside, smiling to herself as she closed the door behind him.

CHAPTER TWELVE

As soon as she finished reading Val's texts, Hekla left the Envoy hotel and sped to the NBI offices. She wanted to be angry with Val, but she knew she had no right. Val had done everything they were asked to do—they called Hekla several times, left almost as many messages, and when she didn't respond, they took the information to Kjartan.

Of course, Val's diligence meant that by the time Hekla got to the office, orders already had been issued to arrest Aldís. The arrest order was objectively premature. The currency evidence was circumstantial. A reasonable interpretation of the surveillance footage at the Azure would find it to be *exculpatory* for Aldís. There wasn't a timeline that could be proffered that gave Aldís time to kill Jack, stage his body, *and* appear on camera as she did. But even Hekla had to admit that this new evidence made Aldís more than a "person of interest." Hekla could almost forgive the civil liberty protections the Ministry of Justice was willing to chance in authorizing the arrest.

Almost.

"I would have been there in a few hours," Hekla practically shouted at Kjartan as soon as she stepped inside his office.

Kjartan responded by lowering his eyes.

"She wasn't going anywhere," Hekla continued. "You really think this is the best way to get information?"

"There are bigger things here." Kjartan shook his head as he spoke. "It looks like an attack on us. People are scared."

"I'm sure they are. But we don't put people in jail because

other people are scared. We both know she didn't do it. And we're not going to find out who did by storming her home at five in the morning."

Hekla followed Kjartan's glance as he looked at a digital clock on the wall: 6:52. He returned his attention to Hekla. "No one is storming in."

"Really? So, officers from Patreksfjörður are going to arrest her? Not a team from Akureyri?"

Kjartan's cheek flared. He looked down at his computer.

Hekla scowled. "This isn't how we should do things. If we really want—"

The abrasive ring of Kjartan's desk phone cut Hekla off.

Kjartan picked up and listened for a few seconds.

"Okay," Kjartan spoke into the receiver. "Stay there for now. I'll get back to you."

Kjartan hung up and looked at Hekla. "She's gone."

⁂

The investigation that Hekla was only nominally in charge of to begin with slipped almost completely from her grasp. Kjartan stepped out of the confines of his office and administrative duties to coordinate a countrywide search for Aldís. Police in every jurisdiction went to the homes of anyone who had exchanged more than a "hello" with the woman. Several powerful people in government advocated for the police to be permitted to search the properties of the contributors to her newsletter as well, but the Ministry of Justice was finally willing to draw a line at that. Such an intrusion into the privacy rights of journalists based upon a nebulous connection to an attack on an American was still a step too far.

Only a few years had passed since the prime minister

dramatically demonstrated Iceland's commitment to free press by expelling all FBI agents from the country. The expulsion came after the Bureau aggressively "investigated" journalists and justified its probe as a "terrorism investigation." Perhaps, Hekla thought, the Ministry had that episode in mind when it denied the request for full searches. Or maybe the Ministry was afraid of what such a search might uncover.

An initial search of Aldís's home provided nothing of immediate value. The team returned with knee-high stacks of her printed work and several terabytes worth of electronically stored information—much of it encrypted—which would take time to process. Nothing they found gave any clue to her present location. Of course, the NBI already had a file on Aldís and The Fólk, which gave them some direction.

According to the file, Aldís was unmarried and lived alone. Several times a month, for two or three nights in a row, Logi Stefánsson, a man in his early 30s, would stay with her. When he wasn't helping with the newsletter, Logi worked in Akureyri, in sales for one of Iceland's largest beer producers.

The police in Akureyri located Logi and questioned him for over an hour. He claimed to have no idea where Aldís was. And while he did not deny a romantic relationship, he said he hadn't talked with her in several days. He had an alibi for the morning of Jack's murder—he was staying at the Envoy hotel for a work-related trip. Staff at the hotel confirmed seeing him there.

Hekla was glad to be excluded from this part of the investigation.

""""""""""""""""

Hekla could tell that the Americans were growing impatient. *More* impatient. In the ensuing days, she watched Lisa Harris, often accompanied by Mark and/or similarly joyless suits, meet with Kjartan for long stretches of time. On one occasion, she spotted someone who she believed to be the Minister of Foreign Affairs. Hekla wasn't sure what the various groups discussed, but each time they left, Kjartan looked more beleaguered.

Thus far, the Americans had managed to respect the jurisdictional restraints on their authority. It was well established that the murder of a foreign national was to be investigated by local authorities. The corresponding embassy was to be kept apprised of developments, but the embassy was to have no active role in the investigation. Local authorities could ask for assistance, but even then, any outside officers or agents were to serve solely as advisers.

Lisa was smart. She knew which lines she could and could not cross. This allowed her carefully calibrated threats to be plausible enough to cause concern.

"Do you need assistance locating her?" Lisa asked Hekla on the fourth day of the search for Aldís.

They were meeting in Kjartan's office. Hekla had expected the question, but still had to resist the urge to snap back. "No," she answered calmly. "We have officers in every district searching. It's only a matter of time before we find her."

Lisa nodded. "You have what—three hundred ninety thousand people here? On an island the size of Kentucky. That's one of our smaller states. How hard can this be?"

"We're not all gathered in one place."

Lisa let out a dissatisfied grunt. "I think we should issue a travel advisory. How can I trust Americans are safe on an island where the authorities can't even find one of their most famous citizens?"

Hekla turned away so Lisa wouldn't see her eyes dart up.

"There's no reason to suspect this is anything but an isolated incident," Kjartan offered.

"Really?" Lisa countered. "Is it normal for you to find money sticking out of a dead man's throat? Because it's not normal to me. And the longer that woman is gone, the more likely it is she's receiving assistance. Coordination."

Hekla knew where this was heading.

Lisa continued, "I've been urging our office not to jump to any conclusions—trying to give your team time. But really, at this point, I'm not sure anymore why we shouldn't consider this an act of terrorism."

Hekla met Kjartan's eyes.

"A single individual was killed," Kjartan reiterated. "It's tragic. But that's all there is—it's all the evidence is telling us."

"And what if this *was* an act of terrorism?" Hekla challenged. Kjartan glared at her, but she couldn't help herself. "Are you going to invade Iceland over the death of a billionaire?"

Lisa gave a smug guffaw. "Please. Detective. My concern is only the safety of our citizens abroad." She turned her attention to Kjartan. "I'll leave it to others to reevaluate our countries' relationship if necessary."

"Reevaluate our relationship?" Hekla asked incredulously.

"You can't do that," Kjartan added.

Hekla noted a trace of worry in Kjartan's voice. She considered the possibility that it was the Minister of Finance or Industry instead of the Minister of Foreign Affairs who met with Kjartan earlier.

"I think any action like that would only make it more difficult to apprehend the perpetrator," Hekla said, helping her boss before expounding on her own views. "Especially considering how likely it is that at least one of your citizens was involved in Mr. Drumman's death."

Lisa narrowed her eyes.

"Unless it was a *business* associate." Hekla purposely let her words hang in the air a moment. "The only people who knew where Mr. Drumman was were American. They were the people closest to him." She decided there was little point in stopping now. "I understand you already helped coordinate the departure of one such individual? His assistant?"

Lisa stewed a moment. She looked like she wanted to indefinitely detain Hekla on the spot. Instead, she gave a sharp look to Kjartan before glaring at Hekla.

"We won't interfere. But it's not just our government that should concern you. Mr. Drumman was involved in a number of highly classified business deals. We're concerned about the response if other groups or associations believe their information is at risk."

"What the hell is that supposed to mean?"

"Hekla," Kjartan practically shouted as he shot up his hand. "Can you give us a moment? Please?"

<center>~~~~~~~~~~~~~~~</center>

Hekla was only at her desk a minute or two before Kjartan summoned her back to his office. Lisa held the door open. "It was good speaking with you again," Lisa said before twisting her lips into the same menacing smile she displayed the other day. "Keep me updated."

Lisa shut the door, and Hekla stood alone in front of Kjartan. Her look dared him to try and justify whatever he was about to tell her without referencing the Americans.

"There's a former associate we haven't checked," Kjartan said as nonchalantly as possible.

Hekla looked over her shoulder, to where Lisa had just been standing. "Is that so?"

"Yes. There's reason to believe the former associate might be helping her out—or at least know where she is. I want you to pay a visit."

Hekla let out a tiny sigh and looked off to the side. "Okay."

Kjartan looked surprised by her response. He nodded a few times before adding, "You'll have to travel a bit."

Her eyes hardened.

CHAPTER THIRTEEN

Hᴇᴋʟᴀ sᴘᴇɴᴛ ʜᴇʀ ᴛʜʀᴇᴇ ʜᴏᴜʀ ᴀɴᴅ 15-ᴍɪɴᴜᴛᴇ flight watching video of Aldís giving speeches and interviews. In another case, she would already have scoured the web for this kind of information. Here though, she was familiar with most of what she would find. Just one detail escaped her memory.

The first video she watched was from a speech Aldís gave at the University of Iceland.

"As many of you know, I'm often accused of hating America, but this could not be further from the truth," a slightly younger Aldís said from her position behind a lectern in a packed hall. "I hate neither America nor Americans. They are our brothers and sisters. The siloing off that has occurred . . . their siloing off . . . this is something that has been done *to* them. It is a purposeful act. Destructive—"

Hekla skipped forward. She'd heard this speech before. It was not the clip she was looking for, but she still couldn't help but be drawn in by the fugitive journalist's passion. She resumed the video.

"Exceptionalism creates blindness. That belief that you are better than—that 'at least we don't have those problems in *our* country' type of attitude—causes us to miss what's happening right under our noses. It's already happened to many of our friends to the east. Hard-fought gains are given up for small indulgences or the privilege of indifference. The compromises don't seem like much at first, until one day you wake to find you no longer have a choice."

Hekla skipped to the end.

" . . . cannot claim to be a beacon of freedom if they neglect and abuse their own population. The time for pragmatism is over. It ended a long ago. It's not too late here, but we must be imprudent, rash even."

Hekla stopped the clip as the already building applause overtook the speaker. She pursed her lips. She returned to the search results on her laptop, scrolling until she found a video from an interview Aldís did with a popular news program. She skimmed along until she found the exchange she was looking for.

"So, would it be okay to kill then—if it's in furtherance of your goals?" the host asked Aldís with a sense of astonishment. The host was an older-looking woman wearing horn-rimmed glasses, a dark brown suit, and perfectly applied makeup. The two sat on an unadorned stage with no audience.

"My goals?" Aldís calmly asked in reply. She had exchanged her boots for flats, but otherwise wore her usual outfit of jeans and a sweater.

"The causes you believe in—the betterment of society, increased equity, all of that."

"Those aren't *my* causes."

"Well naturally you claim to be speaking for *the people* . . . " the disdain in the host's voice was much more noticeable than Hekla recalled from her first time watching. Aldís's tone, on the other hand, was much more even.

"Right. I understand. I'm not trying to be pedantic or avoid an answer, it's just . . . well, it's the *betterment of life*. I can't let it be reduced to an issue or a stance. Are we honestly opposed to that now?"

The host cleared her throat. "That's not what I was saying."

"No, but . . . " Aldís shook her head, "I think this is as

important as anything I might say. We're letting people in power convince us to adopt perspectives that are diametrically opposed to our wellbeing. There's no better example of this than *a better life* for *all human beings* being viewed as a *cause,* and not the ultimate goal of everything we do in our limited time here."

The host tilted her shoulders toward Aldís. Her exasperated tone was devoid of any nuance now. "I appreciate your thorough explanation, but as you've acknowledged, that was not my implication. And if we could please go back to my original question—"

"Yes."

The host's eyebrows shot up. "I'm sorry. Did you—"

"That's my answer to your question. Yes. I think it's okay to take a life under certain conditions."

"You do?" The host appeared genuinely shocked.

"There are circumstances." Aldís looked down for a moment. "It's not something I would advocate for—I do believe it's immoral—but, yes, there *are* circumstances . . . ones where I couldn't cast judgment.

"How can you justify that?" the host shot back. "With all that you've said about humanity—the sanctity of life."

"We're protecting the innocent. Aren't we?"

"That's not the scenario that was presented."

"I know, but no one doubts that right—self-defense, preventing an innocent's death. Well, right now, these deaths are rampant. The great capitalists kill every day—"

"Yes, you've made your position on *that* subject very clear. But please, back to my question—what are the circumstances that you believe would justify taking a life?"

Aldís gave a soft shrug and rolled her lips between her teeth. "It's all related. I think it's about consequences. There must be consequences for actions. For some, there have been none. And what's happened? They torture and kill with impunity. The only ones who suffer are those trying to survive or improve the welfare of others."

"You're not answering my question."

"I don't *have* an answer. But when the status quo is the literal end of the world, an action to change that circumstance might be justified. Maybe I'm wrong. But for a chance at survival—for any hope whatsoever—it's something we have to consider. If an innocent is killed, someone must be held to account."

The host started to speak but Aldís silenced her with the wave of a hand.

"That's what I think. If there are consequences—remorse—then maybe. Consequences give hope. I can't tell you the exact scenario and I have no interest in speculating on something so awful. To save humans . . . humanity . . . the planet—that's when it would be okay. I don't want anyone to die, but some people have shown that they have no regard for human life. So, the only honest answer I can give to your question is 'yes.'"

Hekla stopped the video. Her face had settled into an uncomfortable grimace. She had forgotten the part where Aldís had theoretically identified potential targets with the words "some people."

CHAPTER FOURTEEN

THE PAIN WAS EXCRUCIATING. THE SNEAK PREVIEW August endured moments earlier did nothing to prepare him for what he felt now. It was a horrifying—a previously unimaginable level of agony that he would do anything to stop.

That was his first, and clearest thought.

After that, everything got fuzzy.

The belt was tight around August's neck as he hung in a seated position—his legs stretched out, feet on the hardwood floor, but bottom hovering about ten centimeters above. After the distinct sensation of pain came a heedless panic. He wanted to live, but his rising tide of disorientation was smothering even that desire. It was as though his thoughts were being drowned out by blood.

He tried to move his arm.

When the belt tightened, both his hands immediately drew to his neck, instinctively trying to pry the belt loose. But now his left arm dangled lifelessly by his side. He could see it. He knew his brain was instructing the limb to reach up and grab the belt to create some slack, but he could not. As the disconnect between his will and his abilities became apparent, a flash of terror tore through his clouded mind like a bolt of lightning. He was helpless. There was nothing he could do. He had been hanging like this only a few seconds, but he knew he was quickly running out of time.

Suddenly, August's left foot moved—he could feel it again. He pushed the bare foot against the hardwood floor, trying desperately to gain traction and lift his body. His first attempts did nothing, but his third push squeaked along the floor, gaining just enough of a hold on the floor to elevate his body a centimeter or two more.

A tiny bit of oxygen ran through his nostrils and his left arm shot up. He grabbed the belt above the loop and pulled. He tugged as hard as he could. He couldn't tell if he was making any progress. It was as if he was pulling at an anchor rope tied to concrete. With his right hand, he clawed at the belt again, but it wouldn't budge either. It felt like it had been welded onto his neck.

Almost as quickly as it had come in, the oxygen was depleted. The effect was immediate—the strength in his arms disappeared, and the darkness descended over his mind. An incessant buzzing sound filled the tiny pockets of space where he had previously been able to hide away an idea or instruction.

It hadn't worked. His effort to pull himself upward to relieve tension had failed. He had one last, semi-coherent thought: Instead of pulling *up*, maybe he could pull *out* and free the belt from the nail.

It felt like his head was about to explode. He would have only one chance at this. It might already be too late.

August mustered every resource in his body. He directed all that was left of his focus and energy to his left arm and visualized his body pulling forward. He clenched his fist around the belt and yanked.

The belt moved.

The nail bent slightly, and the notch of the belt pulled at the head of the nail.

But it didn't break free. The belt stayed on the wall.

That was it—the valve between August's brain and body closed tight. The light went out completely. His arms dropped and his body went limp.

As the full weight of his unconscious body pulled on the belt though, the nail began to give way. And then, with a light *pop*, it came loose.

August tumbled onto the floor. His lifeless body rolled onto its side and remained motionless. Then his shoulders jerked and his lungs filled with air. He tore at the belt until he was able to get it loose from his neck.

"Gawwwhhhh," he wheezed and gasped as he rolled onto his stomach.

He slid his knees up but kept his forehead planted firmly on the floor. He rubbed his neck and continued trying to inhale as much oxygen as possible in between coughs. Everything hurt. A new type of fog covered his mind. He was disoriented, and it felt like a candle burned within his skull. And he could still hear that indistinct buzzing.

But he was alive.

He wiped at his watery eyes. After about a minute, his breath returned to a steadier rhythm. The buzz continued though, sharper than before. And it was changing—from a consistent drone to something more distorted, like a guitar played with a pedal effect. Very quickly, August realized that the noise wasn't the product of his near-death experience. It was the door. And a person. A person was knocking at the door. And screaming.

Who the fuck was bothering him now, he thought.

"Police!" a young man shouted.

CHAPTER FIFTEEN

Not even 12 hours after accepting the assignment from Kjartan, Hekla found herself standing outside a flat above a bustling cafe, next to an overgrown teenager dressed in a police uniform. Her eyes kept returning to the handgun in the supposed officer's holster. His height and build suggested adulthood, but his cherubic face—marked near his chin and next to his nose by benignly infected, clogged pores—and his nervously styled hair painted a picture of a boy who should not be playing with firearms.

The officer must have been knocking on the door for a good minute. Hekla didn't realize anyone had answered until the officer started talking.

"Good afternoon, sir," the officer spoke in clear English. "I'm Officer Pederson with the Copenhagen police. Is it okay if we speak with you for a moment?"

She finally pried her eyes off Pederson's weapon and turned her attention to the man on the other side of the doorway. The man she was supposed to care about.

He looked terrible. He was dressed in sweatpants and a long sleeve T-shirt, both of which were impressively stained. His eyes were puffy, watery, and red. He was barefoot, his face was flush, and his hair was matted on one side. She would have thought they interrupted sexual congress, but there didn't appear to be anyone else in the flat. Maybe he was masturbating. That would account for the delay and the shuffling noises they heard when they first arrived. It likely wouldn't explain the distinct red mark below his ear though, she thought to herself.

The man turned to face her. There was a curiosity in his look. Even in their unamused state, weathered and tired, she could see that his eyes were instinctively searching. She found her own interest peaked by them. The rest of his features were not unpleasant either. They were subtle, entrancing, and only partially muted by what must have been several weeks worth of unkempt hair on his face and neck. He was about her height, maybe a little taller. She could imagine a world where this man could be quite attractive, maybe after a thorough cleansing with a hard sponge and a bonfire for his clothes.

The man's eyes moved between Hekla and Pederson. Hekla tried to sneak a glance into the flat, but the man deftly maneuvered his body to block her view.

"No," the man croaked.

Then he shut the door.

Pederson gave Hekla a look before knocking again.

The man answered right away this time. "What . . ." he closed his eyes and sighed, "do you . . . want?" His speech was slow and uneven, as if each syllable he uttered required great effort and caused great pain.

"I'm speaking with August, correct? August Sorenson?" Pederson asked.

August didn't respond. He rubbed the side of his neck.

"We'd just like to speak with you for a moment."

"Mmmh," August grunted, still rubbing his neck. "I don't . . . want to speak . . . with you." He looked studiously at Hekla.

"It's about a murder investigation."

August shook his head. "I don't . . . care." He continued to stare at her.

"Please sir. If we could just have a moment of your time . . ."

August let out an exasperated groan as he tilted his head back.

He brought his head forward and looked Pederson square in the eye. "Go . . . fuck . . . yourself."

Pederson's face pinched tight with confusion. August gave him a look of pitiful disdain in return.

Hekla opened her mouth to speak, but found she had nothing to add. Even with his stilted delivery, that was the most clear and confident "go fuck yourself" that she'd ever heard delivered to a uniformed officer.

"Fucking cops," August grumbled as he started to shut the door again.

Hekla shot out her hand.

August looked with surprise at Hekla's palm pressed firmly against the door. She looked somewhat surprised herself, but she quickly locked eyes with August. "It's about Aldís Eva."

The change in August's demeanor was instantaneous. The bravado evaporated. Genuine concern appeared on his brow and on the corners of his uncertain lips. "Is she . . . is she okay?"

So, they *were* close, Hekla thought to herself. "We're not sure. We're trying to find her. I'm with the police in Iceland and—"

"She's not . . . dead?"

"No. At least, we have no reason to believe so. She's not the victim. She's a person of interest in a homicide."

August guffawed, which apparently tickled something in his chest. He coughed for a few seconds while Hekla and the too-young cop waited.

"Do you know where she is?" Hekla asked.

"Who—" August cleared his throat, "who *is* dead?"

"Do you mind if we have a look around?" Pederson interrupted as he indicated inside August's flat. August scowled.

Idiot, Hekla thought to herself, he was *talking.*

"Please . . . just . . . leave me alone." August took a step back inside his flat.

"We're worried about her safety," she called out.

August stopped and gave her a piercing look. "Why?"

A few neutral responses cycled through her brain. She didn't really have the time or energy to get further involved here. But something about this man made her want to know more. "The embassy told us about you," she said. "Your old American colleagues."

August's eyes continued trying to penetrate Hekla's while the rest of his face remained neutral. Then, without a word, he turned his back on them and slammed the door.

After her brief interaction with August, Hekla stopped at a nearby cafe. Officer Pederson had offered her space to work at the local station, but she didn't really feel like being surrounded by an entirely new police force right now.

The other reason she had eschewed the station for the cafe was her hope that August might contact her. Before leaving his flat, she slipped a card with her personal number underneath his door. The way his face changed when she mentioned Aldís—she couldn't be sure, but it felt like he wanted to know more. And at this point, Hekla could no longer deny that *she* wanted to know more.

Lisa's suggestion that August was the key to finding Aldís always seemed far-fetched. Aldís had devoted her life to countering the misinformation and misdeeds of the powerful. She was too smart to run to someone who already was on their radar. Lisa had to know this. So why did she send Hekla to wake up this washed-up lawyer in the middle of the afternoon?

Hekla had been informed that August used to work as an FBI legal attaché at the American Embassy in Copenhagen. She obviously knew that there were American cops everywhere, but the extent to which they had established an official presence around the world still took her by surprise. Apparently, the Americans had around 47 legats, which were essentially satellite offices of their domestic spy and policing agency. With the legats, the Americans could share with the world their organized system for suppressing dissent.

Denmark was the only Scandinavian country with a legat office, and August had been in charge of that office. From what Hekla could gather, August left this cushy post several years ago. It didn't appear as though he'd done much of anything since. He let his license to practice law expire, and she couldn't find anything suggesting a new job or career. Clearly something had happened to him. Putting aside his appearance, he seemed much more hostile to law enforcement than most of the bureaucrats whom Hekla interacted with. And while most American agents weren't exactly respectful of the work of their foreign counterparts, they also weren't likely to tell uniformed officers to go fuck themselves.

On the other hand, the man was easy to find. If something significant had happened, why was he still here—not just in Europe or Denmark or even Copenhagen, but at the very same address that was on file from his legat days?

CHAPTER SIXTEEN

AUGUST LOOKED AT THE CARD THAT THE TALL Icelandic woman had left: Hekla Rafney Fritzdóttir, detective with Iceland's National Bureau of Investigation. There was a handwritten number scrawled in blue ink on the back. He moved a neglected pile of mail and papers from his couch and sat down.

He hadn't spoken with Aldís in years. They had to know that. He wondered what they were trying to pin on her now. Maybe Jack's murder? Petar had told him about Jack's violent end the other night. Gnarly stuff. Petar took issue with what he described as August's "gleeful" look when the news was relayed. August disputed the characterization, suggesting it was, at most, an expression of bemused reverence—he couldn't believe anyone had managed to pull something like that off. Petar was only somewhat reassured after August told him all he knew about Jack.

August shook off the thought. There was no way the police could truly believe Aldís was responsible for the billionaire's death. He wouldn't be surprised if she had called for it, placed his name within proximity to a call for retributive justice, but that was just her way with words—her passion. And it was reserved for the worst of the worst, the kind of people she believed held humanity captive while forcing them to watch a live production of their very own snuff film. Jack fit the bill, but any serious investigator would know that prominent threats by perpetrators were the province of fiction. Serious assassins didn't broadcast their intentions.

Aldís was special, she was extraordinary, but she'd only be able to effect change if she were alive and innocent. And she knew that.

The woman he had known knew this, at least.

How much could have changed?

August stared at a mystery spot on his shirt—a stain within a greater stain. He rephrased the question in his mind. How much could have changed *for her*?

So, if not reasonable suspicion, what would motivate the cops to visit him? Sending a top investigator here simply to bother him seemed like a waste of time and resources. It might please a few American officials who held old grudges, but he had trouble believing they were *that* involved at this stage. He knew as well as anyone not to underestimate the Americans' ability to interfere. Even, or especially, now that they were really just a hollowed-out war machine propped up by a carnival game economy, he thought. But Iceland had always been uniquely immune to their overtures and "strong recommendations."

August wondered if the cop had been telling the truth—maybe Aldís *was* in danger. He always held Icelandic cops in higher regard than most of the other protection rackets he had dealt with. That didn't mean he thought they would be especially concerned for her welfare, but it also didn't mean her safety was assured. There were more than a few who posed a threat to Aldís in *good* times. A high-profile murder like this could easily create perilous conditions for her—an opportunity for the powerful to accomplish goals they only dreamed about back when he was at the legat.

He thought back to the Icelandic detective and how she had looked at him. It was a look he rarely saw in cops who carried agendas or preconceived notions—two things police tended to treasure. It was only a brief interaction, but she didn't appear to be like the others. Even when she tried to look inside his apartment, it didn't appear to be with any expectation or hope of guilt. She looked curious, as though she were truly trying to learn as much about him as possible.

"Fuck," he murmured to himself as he ran his hand over his face.

He was probably just imagining things now, trying to convince himself that what he had already decided to do was rooted in reason. But it wasn't. He could list all the good reasons in the world, and they still couldn't overcome the truth that what he was about to do was driven by emotion. The last time his heart led him to the front lines people got hurt. He failed. After that, he gave up. He shut out almost everyone and settled into a life of adequacy. *Near* adequacy. But at least no one got hurt—well, at least he wasn't putting *others* at risk, he thought as he rubbed his neck again. Near adequacy was enough. He wasn't sure he deserved better anyway.

But there was another truth that he could no longer deny—this life *wasn't* enough anymore. He was less than a half-hour removed from trying to end it with a belt for fuck's sake. He was sad—*miserable*—and was clearly getting worse. In an instant, that cop reminded him of the last time he felt alive. It was a glimpse of real life that made retreat into his cocoon of despair an unpalatable prospect.

He picked up the landline telephone next to his sofa and dialed the number on the card.

CHAPTER SEVENTEEN

HEKLA LOOKED AROUND THE BUSY CAFÉ: TIGHT groups of young people laughing over drinks and snacks, angelic faces made rosy by the cold. Copenhagen was lovely, but not exactly welcoming to foreigners looking for a new home. Maybe it was different for August. With a name like August Sorenson, no one would question his roots, but Hekla knew plenty with similar bona fides who still weren't able to overcome the Danish "way of life" social barrier.

She thought about what it must be like for anyone crazy or desperate enough to want to start anew in *her* homeland. It'd been quite some time since she'd been out of the country. In her relative isolation, it was easy for her to focus squarely on the Americans, as though they were unique actors in the mad world. Being back with her Scandinavian neighbors, she was reminded of the xenophobic creep that threatened even some of the most "progressive" nations in the world.

Just as her mind was ready to dig deep into the issues plaguing the region, her phone rang and vibrated on the table in front of her.

"Hekla," she answered.

Strained breathing and static.

"Hello?" she asked in English.

"Hi . . . this is . . . this is August. Are you still . . . around?"

"Yes. I'm at a cafe—"

"Ok. I'll speak with you. . . . Just you. Not that Dane."

August gave her an address and told her to meet him in 15 minutes.

Exactly 15 minutes after he called, August arrived at a cafe a short distance away. He had changed into a pair of dark jeans and a light brown cable knit sweater that he wore underneath a navy blue parka. His hands were covered by thin, knit gloves. As he entered, he pulled a beanie off his head, exposing hair that—even with the effect of the hat—wasn't quite as asymmetrical as before. His skin also had significantly more life to it. To Hekla, it still looked like he had just woken up, but now his appearance could be mistaken for an aesthetic choice as opposed to his life's reality.

August's eyes wandered around the room as he made his way to the corner stools Hekla had chosen. His eyes locked on her phone after he sat down.

She followed his stare. "Do you want—I'll turn it off?" No response. She turned off her phone anyway, holding up the screen for him to see before putting it away.

He continued staring at the empty space where her phone was for a few moments before his eyes roamed around the room some more. "Why . . . why do you think . . . she's in danger? Who was killed?"

Normally, Hekla would prefer to be the one asking questions, but August wasn't *her* suspect. And in this case, she was as interested in what August might be interested in as anything else. "This is regarding the investigation into the murder of Jack Drumman. He was—"

"You think . . . *she* killed him?" A wide smile emerged on his face.

Hekla looked curiously at him. It was the first glimpse of anything resembling joy she'd seen on him. "Do you have any reason to believe she would?"

"Well . . . she had a conscience."

"I'm sorry—what?"

"A conscience. Anyone . . . anyone with a conscience . . . would have a good reason to kill him."

Hekla's lips parted involuntarily.

August grimaced and looked away. He ran his fingers back and forth along the collar of his sweater. "No. . . . I don't . . . I don't think she would."

"Okay. Has she been in contact with you?"

He shook his head.

"Do you have any idea where she might be staying?"

August returned his focus to Hekla but said nothing.

"Would you tell me if you did?" she asked.

"Stop," he said, as if her efforts were an embarrassing affront. "Stop . . . please." He stood up and took a step away. He manipulated the zipper on his parka without making much of an effort to align slider and pin. "You said . . . " he looked back at her. "The embassy sent you. . . . Who exactly?"

"It was my boss, really. Our police commissioner."

He narrowed his eyes.

"But I think the direction came from your embassy," she added.

"*Who* . . . who at the embassy?"

"Lisa Harris. She's a director there. Do you know her?"

August's expression answered the question. His jaw clenched, his face hardened, his eyes sparked with more than a hint of rage behind heavy lids.

"Yeah," he finally answered. He zippered his parka with one violent tug. "I know her." There was silence a moment before he added, "And it's not . . . *my* embassy. Please . . . stop saying that."

Hekla flew back to Iceland that evening.

She had suspected August would contact her. And now she was convinced he would make his way to Iceland, as well. This was probably what Lisa wanted—a way to tie August to Jack's murder or bring him back into her orbit. August certainly knew this. He seemed to have an informed type of paranoia—the type that errs on the side of distrust. But Hekla also recognized the look in his eyes when she mentioned Lisa. That was a fury that couldn't be mitigated by reason. It was the type that drove people straight into the fire.

She believed him when he told her he hadn't been in contact with Aldís, but she also suspected he would have no problem finding her if he wanted. This would be useful. She probably could figure out where Aldís was on her own, but she didn't want to risk her source being revealed. Following August solved this problem.

She didn't like how it would look to August. Whatever his background, she felt that he—like her—was keenly aware of who the real enemy was in the greater saga. She didn't want to alienate him, and she didn't want to inflict more pain on a man who obviously had been through some real unpleasant shit—likely precipitated by his relationship with some of the same people bothering her. But she didn't have many better options. His name had come up, and if he decided to get involved, she'd be foolish not to take advantage of the opportunity. She was certain August would understand if he knew the whole story, and maybe one day he would. She just hoped his zeal didn't make things more difficult in the interim.

CHAPTER EIGHTEEN

After meeting with Hekla, August stopped at two electronics stores and one supermarket before finding what he was looking for at a tiny convenience shop a block from his flat. He purchased three prepaid mobile phones and a box containing 100 pieces of cinnamon-flavored nicotine gum. He paid in Danish kroner and left the change with the clerk.

August hadn't owned a mobile phone in years. His luddite leanings were more sentimental than practical. He knew his former colleagues could still find him if they felt like it—he hadn't made much of an effort to stay off grid otherwise. The cellular phone was just a constant reminder of things he did not want to be reminded of. And after adjusting to life without, he realized the phone's primary function in his life was to remind him of things he *did not need* to be reminded of.

He spent the rest of the night trying to learn about what happened in Iceland and who might be trying to benefit. He started with Jack Drumman, but he quickly became much more interested in Susan Teele.

Jack's once-robust media presence all but vanished when he no longer needed investors, but he still had to bother with a nominally adversarial media. Susan operated on a different level. She didn't say things that she'd have to retract when they became an impediment to profit. In fact, she didn't really say things at all. August marveled at her ability to use so many words to say nothing. He was equally impressed with her resume, which was sparkling at first glance but incomprehensible upon closer inspection.

August had dealt with people like Susan before. They went to great lengths to hide reality behind the façade of human experience. They were the people he feared most. He had to wonder what the hell she was doing in Iceland while her husband was being murdered.

As expected, he had no luck finding out what Lisa had been up to since their paths last crossed. He'd need some help with her. Most of the people he counted as friends during his time at the embassy had quickly disassociated themselves from him after things went south, and he wasn't sure how much he could trust the few who did reach out. There was one person, however, whom he never doubted: Jenson.

CHAPTER NINETEEN

Hekla's flight from Copenhagen to Keflavík landed just after midnight. She took off her clothes and stepped into the shower as soon as she got home. She turned the knob to make the water hot—as hot as possible—and directed the scorching water onto the parts of her body that itched ferociously. It was not a medically sound remedy for her irritated skin, but it felt wonderful, and was surely better than using the seams of her clothing to sandpaper her body, as she had been the past few days.

After showering, she half-heartedly dried herself as she crossed into her bedroom. She dropped the towel, sprawled out on top of the covers, and let herself sink deep into the bed. To her pleasant surprise, visiting the American gave her a sense of ease that had been absent since Jack's murder. She felt she wasn't entirely alone in her fight. Colleagues like Val and Gunnar seemed up to the task, but there was a limit to what she could share with them—to what they might be willing to do if the real enemy was not so clearly defined. With August, she felt there was someone who could see things through even if she came up short. It probably was wishful thinking—it did after all require her to consciously disregard the state in which she found the man—but for now it allowed her to drift off peacefully for the first time in many nights.

⁂

Hekla felt a chill. Her body reflexively shivered. Her mind conjured dark thoughts, grotesquely morbid musings of her naked flesh exposed to a carnivorous landscape, unable to find safety or comfort as an icy wind lashed at her skin and jagged rocks rose from the dark water that encircled her.

She opened her eyes. It took her a few seconds to recognize her surroundings and accept that she was not about to be swallowed whole by her blankets or the hungry world around her. The last image of her writhing, helpless and alone, however, remained locked in her mind as she reached for the phone on her nightstand.

It wasn't there.

Hekla growled to herself as she recalled the carefree mindset that allowed her to end up phoneless and freezing on her bed. The large window that ran the length of her bedroom offered no insight as to time of day—it was just dark. With another grunt, she grabbed the comforter and wrapped it around her body as she pulled herself off the bed.

She found her phone in the pocket of the coat she had tossed on the floor outside her bathroom. 4:36. Impossible, she thought. There was no way her body wouldn't take greater advantage of the rare opportunity for rest. She shuffled into the living room, where, to her dismay, the digital clock confirmed the time.

uuuuuuuuuuuu

Less than an hour later, Hekla pulled into the parking lot across the street from the NBI. It was way too early, but she knew she wouldn't be able to fall back asleep. At least she'd be able to slip into the building before the reporters had set up for the day.

Kjartan and the public relations team had done as good a job as possible at minimizing the sensationalist aspects of the crime. They kept the focus local, pushing back against any suggestion that Jack's killing was a coordinated attack or part of a larger conspiracy. But the tone of coverage had shifted dramatically in the past few days. Words that had been relegated to the final paragraphs of articles—included only in sentences that disclaimed their necessity—were increasingly common: *terrorism, plot, assassination.* These words ushered in a whole new contingent of media and twice as many independent reporters with handheld production studios.

It was obvious to Hekla that the press was being manipulated, and she had no doubt about who would benefit most from the hysteria. There was no chance that Kjartan or anyone else with sufficient knowledge would point the finger where it belonged, so she was stuck holding a truth that she could not divulge. But neither was she willing to lie, so rather than risk being hit by a stray question, she carried her tray of store-bought coffee across the street, walked the long way around the garden that occupied much of the block next to the offices, and entered the building through the rarely used utility door.

uuuuuuuuuuuu

At eight sharp, Gunnar entered the office. He was similarly punctual every day Hekla called him in. She told him he needn't be so rigid, but Gunnar said he was like this in Grindavik as well. He wanted to do his job, but spending time with his family and enjoying his life were equally important. He showed up on time so he could leave on time. Hekla heard other officers grumble about the lazy officer from the South, notably Bjarni, a man whose favorite pastime was shirking responsibility, but she couldn't find any fault with Gunnar's life prioritization.

Hekla waved Gunnar into a conference room, where he gave her details about his interviews with the last few hotel guests he had tracked down. Most had no useful information. There was one encounter, however, that excited him.

"She was staying in these—cabins, near the harbor," Gunnar said as he gestured with his hands. "Real square, modern. Like cubes. There's a dozen or so there."

"Is there a registry?"

"No. At least nothing at the site. I think they rent them on a secondary market. Probably to avoid taxes or regulations. She was a tough find."

Hekla gave an appreciative smile.

"A Swedish woman on holiday," Gunnar continued. "She recognized Aldís,"

"Really?"

Gunnar nodded and took out his notepad.

"Not just that, here's what she said—'she,' Aldís, the woman is referring to, 'was flaunting her money. It was so obvious. I think she was American.'"

Hekla furrowed her brow.

"I asked her what she meant, where she saw Aldís. The woman said that Aldís was in front of her in line. The money thing was apparently from when she opened her bag to buy something."

"The woman saw the currency?"

Gunnar tilted his head in a slow, swooping nod, before responding, "Both euros and American dollars."

"Huh. Well that's something." She looked off in thought a moment before returning her gaze to Gunnar. "So, what do you think?"

"What do I think?" He seemed surprised by the question. "Well, I believe her—the woman. I think she saw Aldís and the currency."

"But?"

He gave a half-shrug. "It still doesn't make sense."

"What doesn't?"

"Aldís. If she killed Jack or if she had something to do with his murder—it wouldn't make sense. Why risk being seen with the money? I can't imagine anyone going through all that planning and then being that reckless."

"Yeah. I agree." Her phone vibrated in her pocket. She checked the screen. It was a number from Denmark. She held her forefinger up to Gunnar and answered.

"Hekla speaking."

"I'm coming to Iceland," August told her. He sounded like a different person, speaking with much greater clarity and conviction. "I understand that Aldís is wanted on suspicion of murder. I'm traveling to offer support to her as a friend. I will not interfere with any attempts by law enforcement to arrest her. I will not offer her any assistance in evading arrest. If I happen to see her, I will encourage her to turn herself in to the proper authorities immediately."

Hekla started to stammer out a reply, but August kept going. "I'll be staying at a hotel near the airport. I can give you my flight number and the name and address of the hotel. Are you ready?"

PART TWO

CHAPTER TWENTY

THE AIRPORT WAS TERRIFYING. AUGUST ENTERED confidently but made it only as far as the first digital screen before freezing up. He stood, practically motionless as hundreds—possibly thousands—of bodies swarmed around him. He stared vacantly at dozens of high-definition images advertising the wonders of the Copenhagen airport by showing the shit you could buy. The ads were interspersed between a single image showing where any of that shit—or the bathroom—was located.

It was all too much. Too much noise, too much light, too many people—everything and everyone competing for an attention that had already been divvied up a thousand times over. His occasional visit to a cafe or convenience store had not prepared him for the sensory overload that was the airport. It was overwhelming—the people and the activity. It made him feel incredibly alone.

All those screens in people's hands. It wasn't new for August. It had been well over a decade—maybe two, maybe three—since they had become the preferred dopamine provider for most people. The hold seemed even stronger now though, like they were the real center of gravity for society. He supposed that made sense. They combined vice with necessity—offering the small benefits and large drawbacks of things like cigarettes and slot machines, all on the same device used for work and to keep in touch with family. August would have liked to blame his discomfort on the misery merchants behind these technological "advancements," but it's not like he'd done much better on his own. It was probably even easier to manipulate him, he supposed. All it took was a cop mentioning a name and here he was, doing exactly what they wanted.

The muscles in his face moved suddenly, like an exaggerated wince—his eyes clamping shut, his cheeks bunching up high.

He lowered his head and pushed through the crowd, his suitcase bouncing as much as rolling behind him as he maneuvered around the bodies. The airport was undergoing another renovation. An enormous plywood wall served as a temporary barrier, blocking access to one of the terminals and funneling people toward the main shopping area. A partially shielded floor above looked like it was still accessible. August made a sharp turn and scurried up the stairs.

He crossed a narrow strip, where a few savvy travelers had set up camp to eat and browse their phones, until he reached a desolate annex. It was like he remembered—a walkway made of long wooden planks that bisected the carpeted floor. Years of neglect were showing themselves on the chipped wood and faded carpet. Still, the attribute he found most attractive, its relative quiet, was in pristine condition.

He removed his backpack and sat down on a padded bench against the wall. His jaw was still tight, he noticed with dismay, the tip of his tongue in its familiar place, firmly planted against the roof of his mouth. He massaged his jaw before stretching his mouth and neck in unison.

He tried to remember a breathing exercise Petar suggested to him not too long ago. It was something simple, noting the breath. But before he could start, he thought of an article criticizing the wellness and mindfulness movements as coping mechanisms for the brutality of capitalism—a commodity sold by neoliberals to mitigate the effects of their policies instead of providing a decent standard of living.

"Christ," he whispered to himself.

He tried again. This time, he managed to inhale fully through his nostrils before his mind intervened—was he supposed to say "in" or "one," he wondered as the breath escaped his lips. And was each act independent, or did he have to double up either number or direction? Another two rotations passed before he recalled the explicit instruction that there was no *proper* way of doing it.

"In," he said to himself as he aggressively pulled air through his nose.

"Out, one," he thought as he forced the air back out.

His brain wasn't satisfied. If there was no right way of doing this, then what was wrong with thinking about why he was doing it wrong? Was it because that would be believing he was doing it the wrong way? Which was wrong, even if there *was* no wrong?

"Fuck!" he exclaimed loud enough to draw the attention of a couple sitting at the other end of the hall.

He opened his backpack and took out two pieces of nicotine gum. He bit down hard on the gum and leaned back against the wall. He shook his head. What the fuck *was* he doing? Everything about this was wrong but he still couldn't convince himself to retreat.

"Fuck," he said again, in resignation as much as anything else.

⁕⁕⁕⁕⁕⁕⁕⁕⁕⁕⁕⁕⁕⁕⁕⁕

August felt better once he was safely—if that was the word—in his seat. Window. Middle of the plane. Even the semi-confined space of the security queue had allowed his mind to rest a bit. The lack of options and consistent physical presence provided a sense of ease. It reminded him of when he would wedge himself between the seat and back cushions of a couch as a child. The plane was chaotic, but controlled, with only minimal intrusions into his 48-by-78-centimeter haven.

The flight gave him an opportunity to think through the information he had uncovered the previous night. Although Lisa Harris's activity remained a mystery, there was plenty to discover about her boss, the U.S. ambassador to Iceland. Before becoming an ambassador, Lewis Kessel had been a partner at a white shoe law firm. His specialty was the defense of giant energy conglomerates. Kessel was the guy you called when your company spilled enough oil to destroy an eighth of the habitable land in a Central American country, or, more precisely, he was the guy you called when anyone *took issue* with that spill.

Kessel's law firm, like every other similarly sized entity in America, made annual bribes—they called them "contributions"—to both political parties. Kessel appeared to enjoy this activity more than ruining the lives of environmentalists. He personally led massive fundraising efforts that helped clear a path for his preferred candidate to reach the highest office. And for that, he was given an ambassadorship. August figured Kessel must have been disappointed to learn he'd be ambassador to Iceland. Guys like him usually prefer countries that are only a train ride from the glamorous cities in Western Europe, or at least ones with a favorable climate. It didn't occur to him that Kessel might *want* to be in Iceland.

Nothing he found on Kessel was all that surprising. It was standard fare for diplomatic posts in countries where hostilities were limited to disapproving frowns. What he could not figure out though, was why Lisa would want to work for this guy? No matter what title they gave her, this had to be considered a significant demotion. That didn't seem like something she would willingly accept. And of course, there was the more pressing question of what she wanted with him now that she was in Iceland.

She had won. Winning was never enough for the U.S., but an example had already been made. Was this really about Aldís, or did Lisa still think he was a threat?

There had to be another relationship. Or something he was missing. It felt like the information was pinging off his brain and falling to the floor. He used to make these kinds of connections naturally. Maybe he'd been inert for too long.

August managed to remain calm until the plane was about to land. But then, as the landing gear was deployed and the other passengers murmured with excitement, he began to realize the extent to which he was out of his depth, and his panic returned.

He had no plan. He had no power, no authority—no true allies or friends he could trust. All he had was a few numbers in a phone. And one of those numbers belonged to a fucking cop. What exactly did he think he had to offer?

The plane rose and fell in quick succession.

August tugged at his hair. It was arrogance, he concluded. It managed to find a tiny window between his walls of self-loathing to jump inside and convince him that he could help—no, that he was somehow *uniquely qualified* to help in a situation he knew nothing about. And now, just like before, other people would pay the price. He *knew* they wanted him to look for Aldís, that the police and Lisa were baiting him, hoping he would be so foolish as to board this plane. How could he dismiss all of that so quickly? He thought he was smarter than them, but he wasn't even sure who "they" were.

The wheels of the plane bounced hard against the ground, jostling the passengers in their seats, before finding a gentler glide onto the tarmac.

August pulled at his collar. He tapped his fingers against his thigh in a rapid and evolving pattern—three taps with his ring finger, once with his middle, and once with his index; three times through this rotation before starting a new one with three taps of the middle finger, one with the ring, and one with the index; and so forth until he lost track of taps.

Even if she was in danger and he could assist, he knew there was no reason for him to believe Aldís would *want* his help. The two hadn't spoken since everything fell apart. There wasn't anything in the intervening years he could point to that would alter these facts. If anything, all he had proven was how uniquely unqualified he was for the job of keeping people safe. He couldn't even guarantee his own welfare if left alone for too long.

He groaned loudly. Then he bent over and yanked his backpack from under the seat in front of him. He unzipped the bag, pulled out an old stenographer's notebook, and flipped through the faded pages. There was one more number he had to add to his phone, someone he needed to talk to before he did anything. He'd avoided making the call since he decided he would come over, but there was no getting around it any longer. They weren't exactly friends. August figured they were allies. At least, that's what he hoped. The truth was, he didn't really have a clue anymore.

CHAPTER TWENTY-ONE

Steingrímur Eggertsson's home in Reykjavík's posh municipality of Garðabær was a three-story assault on aesthetic decency. At a distance it was unfortunate, another blight on the landscape initiated by excess wealth. The close-up view Hekla got as she parked her car near a concrete square that she guessed to be a garage, however, truly set the home apart from others in the neighborhood. The random juxtaposition of hard angles, dead spaces and cramped windows, the miniature towers and oversized annexes, the slate gray and polished steel—every element of the place was as ludicrous as it was hideous. It was no wonder that Steingrímur spent most of his time in London, she thought.

She pressed a button inside a small metal enclosure next to an oversized front door that was approximately her body length in width and nearly twice that in height.

To her surprise, Steingrímur answered himself.

"Detective Fritzdóttir?" he asked with a sly smile.

"Rafney," she clarified with a placid face. "Do you mind if I come in?"

⚬⚬⚬⚬⚬⚬⚬⚬⚬⚬⚬⚬⚬

It was Steingrímur's idea to have Hekla visit him at his home. One of his lawyers had communicated this message to her after declining an invite to the station on Steingrímur's behalf. She half-expected to be greeted by a phalanx of attorneys and assistants that couldn't reasonably fit into an interrogation room, but perhaps the solo presence was its own type of power play.

The inside of Steingrímur's home was almost as offensive as the outside. A cavernous hallway led to a spiral staircase that interfered with the openness of an open kitchen, but did provide a lovely staircase view for those seated in the living room. Abruptly vaulted ceilings gave each room its own uniquely unsettling vibe. Sparsely furnished, generic, it looked like it was staged for a sale.

Steingrímur led Hekla to the living room where she marveled at a poorly paved piece of cement situated in a four-by-six-meter frame above a black leather couch.

"It's brilliant, isn't it?" Steingrímur told as much as asked. "Löfgren. An artist I met in Sweden. He lives in the countryside. Only makes two pieces a year."

"It's something."

"Can I get you anything to drink?"

"Coffee?"

"Of course. Just give me a moment."

She sat down on the leather couch as Steingrímur navigated his way into the kitchen. Across from her, a fireplace ran about a third the way up the wall. In between the couch and fireplace was a cloudy glass coffee table that must have been about twenty centimeters thick, with a surface area as large as Hekla's bed. The only other piece of real furniture in the room was a stunning wood and leather armchair and ottoman set. Hekla wondered how such beauty found its way into the home.

Steingrímur offered her a stone mug.

"It's black. Is that alright?"

"That's fine. Thank you." She accepted the mug from Steingrímur. "How long are you in town for?" she asked as he sat down diagonally from her on the magnificent chair.

He studied her a moment before responding. "As long as I'm needed."

Hekla knew Steingrímur took great pains to act the part of a character he had created. Physically, this was easy enough. He was in his late 40s, tall with broad shoulders. He had a decent jawline that took on comic proportions with his thick, reddish-brown beard meticulously carved to add five or six centimeters to his chin. His hair was slicked back to the nape of his neck, dark brown and glistening, with a hairline that had only just begun to recede. He was dressed in what could be considered his uniform—a crisp, bright white button-down shirt, stretched to capacity by an owner hellbent on showcasing his pectoral muscles, tucked into dark denim jeans, with a tailored navy blue blazer and matching blue suede shoes.

The real work wasn't in appearance though. It was in his performance of the role of *Steingrímur the Icelander.* The myth Steingrímur had created for himself was easy to debunk and full of glaring holes, yet it persisted up to, and perhaps a little past, the point where he was able to do lasting damage to the country. It drove Hekla crazy.

In truth, Iceland was only Steingrímur's home when he was doing interviews or dodging taxes. He spent time here as a child, but by the time he was a teenager, he was out of the country most of the year. In his teen years, he attended a private school abroad, which prepared him for enrollment in one of America's most prestigious finishing schools for future war and financial criminals. Afterward, he went to Eastern Europe with his father—and his father's money—to see what the economic ruin brought upon by the collapse of the Soviet Union could offer them. It was here that Steingrímur cultivated his reputation, encouraging rumors of risky enterprises and hard-nosed, dangerous negotiations with assorted toughs. Really, he had some money, and he borrowed some money. He used the combination to buy things, then he used the equity in those things to borrow more money to buy other, bigger things. Soon enough, he didn't have to risk any of *his* things to make money.

But Steingrímur desperately wanted to be seen as deserving his windfall. The "Swashbuckling Scandinavian" persona gave him an identity that obscured the pedestrian origins of his wealth. It also gave him the delusional self-confidence to sit at the same table with those who had been using capital to destroy lives for generations and think he would still be received as a hero at home. To Hekla, he was just another prick who conflated power and bravery, taking all the wrong lessons from the Viking stories he read as a child. The schtick worked for a while, but when things got tough, his true cowardice showed, and the receptions for his occasional visits home became as frosty as the winters he would absolutely, without a doubt in her mind, never be here for. Unless there was *a lot* of money at stake.

"But you'll return to London soon, or perhaps Sweden?" she asked.

Steingrímur tilted his head slightly and narrowed his eyes.

She wondered if this look was supposed to intimidate her. "Don't you have a home in Sweden?"

"Iceland is my home," he finally replied.

"Of course. You were scheduled to fly out last week though, correct?"

"That's right. But things change when your friend's husband is murdered."

"And business partner."

"Excuse me?"

"Susan. She's not just your friend, right? She's your business partner."

Steingrímur tried to mask his surprise with a straight face and silence.

"You had dinner with them," Hekla continued. "Susan. And her husband, the night before he was murdered."

"Yes. I did." He pursed his lips and looked down a moment.

"What were you arguing with Mr. Drumman about?" Hekla asked as she took her tablet out of her bag. She opened a file with interview transcripts and flipped through with a flick of her middle finger.

"Arguing?" He shook his head. "I don't think there was an argument. We were drinking—probably got a little loud. That's all. You know how it is."

"I don't." Hekla looked at her tablet as she continued. "After your argument with Mr. Drumman, you spoke with Susan. Once at the end of dinner and then at least once more on the phone. Probably not long before Mr. Drumman was killed."

Steingrímur leaned forward. "I'm sorry, do you think I had something to do with his murder?"

She looked up from the tablet. "Did you?"

"Of course not."

Hekla nodded. "Okay. No. Not directly at least." She held his eyes a few seconds. "Where were you staying that night?"

Steingrímur looked like he was ready to snap back with an answer before he thought better about it. He settled on a sharp tone and a poor imitation of his "menacing" glare from earlier. "What's this about?"

"It's a murder investigation."

"Right. And I think I've been more than accommodating. I've invited you into my home—"

"Because you refused to come to the station—"

Steingrímur raised his voice. "I've *invited you* into my home, and I'm more than happy to answer any questions that relate to the murder of Mr. Drumman. But I'm not going to let you interrogate me about my personal life or business affairs."

"You don't think your business affairs had anything to do with his death?"

Steingrímur's forehead crinkled. "No. How could they?"

Hekla nodded again. She looked back down at her tablet and flicked her finger on the transcript without any real destination in mind.

Steingrímur continued with indignation, "Some lunatic kills a man, and instead of arresting her, you decide to come here and waste my time with this nonsense?"

Hekla raised her eyes from the tablet. "So, it wasn't about the mining deal?"

Steingrímur expelled a short burst of air through his nose and lips. "That's what you're here for?" he asked, a cocky smile emerging on his face.

"That's why Susan was calling you, wasn't it? She wanted to make sure her drunken husband hadn't bothered you too much—with all that was at stake."

"Well, you certainly seem to know a lot." He shook his head as he lifted his large frame out of the chair. He straightened the lapels of his jacket and pulled on the cuffs of his shirt. "Like I said, I'm not talking to the police about my business affairs. If you have any further questions, you can direct them to my attorney. I think you have his information."

Hekla looked up. Steingrímur was now towering above her.

"Okay." She put her tablet away and stood up, but remained facing him, just a few centimeters from his puffed-out chest, as she addressed him. "I do think it's important that we explore all the possible motives of . . . this *lunatic*. It would probably be a good idea if you stay local for a while. At least let us know if you intend on traveling—wherever that might be. The safety of all our citizens is paramount."

Steingrímur glowered as Hekla turned away.

She could feel his presence behind her as she walked to the front door. He remained silent until her hand wrapped around the handle.

"I take it you have a problem with what we're doing?" he asked.

She turned her head. "I'm still trying to figure out what exactly that is."

"What do you think our future is here—in Iceland?"

She let go of the handle and turned to face him.

"Do you think fishing and tourism are really going to be enough in the next few decades?" he continued. "Is that what people like you want for us? A place for rich tourists to gawk for a few days, piss in our waters before going home?"

She narrowed her eyes. "And you'll save us? Like last time?"

Steingrímur growled but didn't let the jab deter him. "We have an opportunity to bring Iceland into the future. Jobs. Security. A real improvement in the standard of living for our people. You might not like me, but I consider myself a patriot. Everything I do is for my homeland."

"If you're helping Iceland, why are all your negotiations in secret?"

He remained silent a second before dismissing her with his eyes and a nod. "Have a nice day, detective."

CHAPTER TWENTY-TWO

AUGUST COULDN'T REMEMBER THE LAST TIME HE was actually *in* Patreksfjörður. It bothered him. He tried counting the summers spent in Copenhagen since his departure, but the winters all merged together, forming an indefinite block of cold, dark sadness in his mind. He had vivid recollections of the events leading up to his departure—they were seared into his memory. But the details of his last moments in the village escaped him entirely. Did he really just *leave?* He knew the answer but still flagellated himself with variations of the question throughout his drive.

He had left his hotel near the airport early that morning. He could have flown to Patreksfjörður, but he didn't want to be restricted by a limited schedule or responsible for any more coordination or interaction than necessary. Besides, driving to Patreksfjörður was all he had ever known, so he rented a car without a definitive return date. He made sure to get an SUV with navigation, but the dashboard panel was so complex, he briefly considered speeding into the nearest embankment and hiring a driver. Once he was on the road and past the Capital, though, everything became familiar.

The last three or so hours of the drive north from Keflavík were as majestic as he remembered. Steep bluffs and mountains sprung up from nothing on one side, and sparkling water, topped off with a horizon of snowcapped peaks, dazzled on the other. It might be even more beautiful now, he thought, as he had never made the drive in the winter months before. It was wondrous, but what once inspired awe and gratitude, now served as a painful reminder of who he used to be, how he used to feel, and what he used to have.

The small fishing village looked foreign at first, its brightly colored roofs made white by layers of snow. But as he rolled the car slowly down the streets, the shape of the town triggered his recollection. By the time he approached Aldís's home, it was as though he had traveled back in time. He remembered *this*. He remembered what it felt like the first time, and how it was so many times after that, when he arrived on foot and his time away was limited to a few hours at most.

Now he remembered the last time, when what he had done was so awful that all he could do was grab a few things and rush out the door before anyone saw him. The memory clawed at him as he pulled his car around the side of the house and parked behind an all-too-familiar, rust orange Jeep 4x4.

He turned off the engine but remained in the car. Just like he did the first time he came here, he considered turning around and going back where he came from. It would be a more justified decision now compared with his decision *not* to run years ago. This move would be rooted in solid rationale, a conclusion drawn from an objective analysis of the available evidence. The drive was long though, and he'd hardly slept. A cup of coffee might be too much to hope for, but even if he was refused entry, he could at least take a piss behind the house before getting back on the road. He steeled himself, unbuckled his seatbelt, threw the door open, and hurried to the house.

It was far too cold to rap his knuckles against the door, so he tried pressing a doorbell that he never used before. A few frigid moments later, the door opened, and the owner of the familiar car looked him over.

"You look like shit," Logi remarked without emotion.

mmmmmmmm

August's heart sank as soon as he stepped inside. It was clear that the police had aggressively searched the place, undoing decades of care in a few hours of malicious indifference. Logi, or someone, had tried to clean up. Salvaged belongings were arranged against one wall, destroyed objects and furnishings piled in the corner along with an assortment of fragments and debris. But these efforts only highlighted the magnitude of the destruction.

Aldís's home had always given him a sense of ease. It was clean, modern, and filled with life. The objects and arrangements all seemed intentional, with thought and meaning in every detail, and nothing just for show: Everything in the home appeared to be actively read, used, worn, or admired. Now the opposite seemed true. He looked around the room, searching for familiarity but feeling only dread and discomfort.

He spotted Aldís's reprint of Piet Mondrian's *Composition with Color Planes* on the ground. Its metal frame was broken, and the glass shattered, the neatly arranged squares of muted pink, purple and yellow left clinging precariously to the pressed cardboard backing. After some more searching, he was able to locate the large tome on the history of jazz in the United States that Aldís was always trying to get him to read. It was next to a dark red, velvet throw pillow that somehow survived the search.

Logi let August soak in the emptiness a while. Then he gestured for him to sit in one of the two chairs from the kitchen that had been moved into the living room and placed around a surviving end table.

"What do you want?" Logi asked as soon as he sat.

"Is . . . she okay?"

"What do you care?"

August answered with an intense look that needed no explanation.

Logi stared back, unblinking, for several seconds, before responding to the original question. "I don't know."

"Do you—do you know where she is?"

Logi looked incredulous. "Do you think I'd tell you if I did?"

"I'd never let anything happen to her. You *know* that."

"You wouldn't, but your friends would."

"I don't—I don't work for them. Any of them. I haven't even spoken to anyone since I—since I left . . . here."

 Logi studied August's face.

"I'm just worried," he added.

"Okay. Well, I don't know where she is."

August looked over at a pile of coats and heavy sweaters near the front door. "You're sleeping . . . spending nights here?"

"Yeah. So what?"

"So . . . she didn't tell you where she was going? When she'd be back . . . anything?"

"She's her own person. You know that."

She was, August knew, but she also told people she cared about where she was going. Unless doing so might get someone killed. He decided to try a different tact. "Why'd you want to meet here?"

"In case she comes back. I don't want to miss her."

"You still have your place—Akureyri, right?"

Logi scoffed. "Fuck off."

August winced. This wasn't getting anywhere, he thought. He looked away for a second. "Look . . . I'm—I'm sorry."

"For what?" Logi snapped back.

"Everything." August shook his head. "What happened. I know you hate me. I don't—I'm not trying to change your opinion. I fucked up. You were right . . . the whole time, you were. I never should have talked her into it. It was my fault and I'll . . . I'll never forgive myself. I just want you to know that—that I'm sorry."

Logi stared back at August for what felt like an eternity. "Is that it?"

August nodded. "Yeah," he said as he stood up. "Thanks for seeing me." He walked back through the living room. There were more questions he wanted to ask—about the murder, about Aldís and what she was up to—but they all seemed trivial in the face of Logi's righteous anger.

He had one foot out the door when he heard Logi's voice.

"So that's why you came?"

August turned around. "What?"

"To tell her that. Or me. Is that why you came back?"

He narrowed his eyes. "I'm—I'm worried about her. The fucking cops came to my door."

Logi's brow furrowed. "Who? Who was it exactly?"

"I dunno. Some fucking . . . Danish prick. And a cop from Iceland. Rafney. . . . Hekla Rafney."

Logi's lips parted.

August turned back around and left the house. He was tired of Logi's inscrutable looks. His conciliatory energy was depleted and he was growing annoyed. He had driven five-and-a-half hours to get here, and he hadn't even been offered coffee. His head hurt, he was hungry, he was exhausted. Now he'd have to stop somewhere before another interminable drive when all he wanted to do was lie down and rest.

August was halfway to his SUV when Logi shouted again.

"Hey!"

August closed his eyes in annoyance before turning back. "What?" he asked with exasperation.

"I do hate you. But it's not for what happened with him. That wasn't your fault. She didn't blame you—neither of us did. So, if that's why you're really here, you should just go home. You didn't convince Aldís of shit. She thought you were doing the right thing."

August looked perplexed. "Then what? What's your problem . . . with me . . . still?"

Logi looked back with contempt. "You left her. You just left. No call. Nothing. When she needed you most. You ran away. She really loved you. And you just abandoned her. She was devastated. That's why I hate you."

⁓⁓⁓⁓⁓⁓⁓⁓

August stood motionless outside Aldís's house long after Logi stepped back inside and shut the door. It felt as though the insides of his body had dropped, the weight moving to his feet, which now felt glued to the ground. After all that time wishing for a different truth, he finally had one, and it was even worse than the original: Aldís upset at him, not for what he did, but for how he responded afterward. Not merely upset, as Logi made clear, but *devastated*. August could have stayed back then, he could have salvaged something. The past however-many years of self-exile and self-indulgent misery never needed to have occurred. And the pain he caused this human whom he loved so dearly was entirely preventable.

He felt faint with a sudden warmth behind his face. The heaviness left his feet and for a moment he thought he might topple over. It was as if the outside world, with its weather and gravitational pull, no longer affected him—his mind and body had their own orbit.

He inhaled sharply through his nose. The cold air stung but the oxygen brought life back into his body. He placed his hands on his knees and drew another deep breath. How was it that he kept ending up in this position, he asked himself. He didn't even need the help of a belt; all it took was a bad thought and he'd find himself unable to breathe.

After a minute, he was able to drag himself to the car. He started the engine, put the car into reverse, and accelerated. Almost immediately he slammed his foot down on the brake—he slid forward until his chest pressed against the steering wheel. The car jerked to a stop just centimeters from the side of Aldís's house.

He looked down at his hands. They were trembling on the edge of the dashboard. He gripped the steering wheel tight to stop the shaking and took another deep breath. He straightened the car, turned around, and drove for a bit before merging onto the road that ran along the water to the center of town. When he reached the main shopping area, he pulled into the small parking lot next to a market and stopped the car.

By now, tears had completely obscured his vision. As soon as he shifted the car into park, he unleashed a loud, painful sob. He continued crying for several minutes that felt like many more.

Finally, he pulled himself together. He wiped his face with the inside of his hands and looked through the windshield. Staring right back was an old man holding a grocery bag, and a middle-aged woman with a young child in tow. August's mind had begun to formulate insults for the intrusive crowd until he looked out the side window and realized his car was more *on* the sidewalk than off. It *had* been some time since he had driven. And that was in much better conditions than today.

August arrived back at his hotel in Keflavík—a block-shaped outpost of a megachain, directly adjacent to the red-roofed airport—in the early evening. He stopped at the front desk and spoke with one of the clerks. Then he went up to his cookie-cutter room. He spent about 40 minutes composing letters on cheap stationery hidden amongst the stack of tourism brochures on the small table next to his dresser. He could feel himself beginning to crack, but he forced himself to push through until he had completed his task.

Whether Logi knew where Aldís was or not, her presence at the scene coupled with her disappearance was not a good sign. What had seemed like the most remote possibility to August before—Aldís having anything to do with Jack's death—now had to be considered. Logi had always loved Aldís, he would do anything for her, and she could trust him absolutely. If she told him where she was and he was keeping it a secret, that was bad. If she felt as though she couldn't even tell him, it was worse. It had appeared to August as though Logi was lying when they spoke, but he wasn't convinced it was with respect to his knowledge of her location.

There were plenty of places in Patreksfjörður or Akureyri where Aldís would be able to stay, but most all of these would already be on the cops' radar. There was one place August could think of where Aldís might go if she really thought herself to be in danger. There were only two people besides him and Aldís who knew about the spot. He was pretty sure he could still get in touch with one of them.

He had already taken it as a given that he was going to try to meet Aldís. He was being reckless again, he knew, but after what

Logi had told him, he felt like he had to see her. He needed to know she was okay, he needed to hear from her—he needed to know if Logi was telling the truth.

August's mental and physical exhaustion made it easy for him to fall asleep. Late the next morning, when he was finally able to pry himself out of bed, he went to the Pósturinn near the airport. He mailed his letters and went straight back to his room.

CHAPTER TWENTY-THREE

Hᴇᴋʟᴀ ʜᴀᴅɴ'ᴛ ᴇxᴘᴇᴄᴛᴇᴅ ᴛᴏ ᴏʙᴛᴀɪɴ ᴍᴜᴄʜ ɪɴ ᴛʜᴇ way of useful information from Steingrímur. Her primary objective in visiting was to let him know that *she* knew—bump into him without apology and see how he responds. In that regard, she was successful. Still, she couldn't help but be somewhat agitated by their interaction, or, really, by the bullshit that people like him still shamelessly promoted. He reminded her of a man she used to date in university. In the early days of their courtship, the man's voice would fill with excitement and his eyes would grow wide when he talked of the future. He had the same vision as Hekla, but unlike her, he had what sounded like a realistic plan for bringing it to fruition—small compromises for the greater good, a pragmatic hope, that sort of thing. Just like Steingrímur, he wanted to build with the tools available—without, of course, acknowledging that those tools had only worked before for a tiny segment of the population.

It didn't hurt that the man was beautiful or that she wanted to believe—desperately. The romance gave her license to pursue what seemed like an easier path than the ones her friends were taking. It certainly made her family proud. Looking back, she wasn't sure the man ever really believed what he was saying. Exuberance fades fast, and the eyes grow dim when you use your spiel only to convince an idealistic young woman to disrobe. Steingrímur, to his credit—the only credit she was willing to concede—seemed more like a true believer. Perhaps the degree to which people believe their own bullshit is relative to the success they've had in applying that bullshit.

••••••••••••••••

Hekla held the corner of the document between her thumb and forefinger. It was a memo, a few pages long, with the word "confidential" stamped in bold, capital letters across the top of the first page. Only partially marred by the black ink of the secrecy designation was the distinct letterhead of the National Energy Authority.

It was dark again outside, but you couldn't tell that from the windowless room that Hekla, Val, and Gunnar were using. Separated from Kjartan's office by only a few meters, the meeting room served as a sort of sanctuary, not just from the brief appearance of natural light, but from the rest of the force and whatever their latest focus was. Right now, that attention was still devoted primarily to the search for Aldís, with Kjartan continuing in his unusually involved role managing day-to-day operations.

This was all more than fine as far as Hekla was concerned. She took the opportunity to move her own informal team into the room devoted to storing paper copies of the electronic files obtained from the search of Aldís's residence. Almost all of the sleek, oversized table that occupied the center of the room was now covered by stacks of paper. After running every conceivable search term through the devices' data, the tech team had transformed a laptop, two portable hard drives, and a phone into mountains of paper. They even managed to have some success decrypting files. A corner of the table was devoted exclusively to this recovered data, which was where Hekla now stood, confidential memo in hand.

"Did you get the list I sent?" Gunnar asked.

Hekla nodded as she flipped through the memo. "Everyone from the mining deal group is included?"

"Yup."

While everyone else was looking for someone who could *not* have possibly killed Jack, Hekla tasked Gunnar with revisiting the murder from the ground up. As part of that effort, he had sent Hekla a list of every person believed to be aware of Jack's visit to Iceland.

"Anything further with the itinerary?" Hekla asked. A paralegal at a law firm that employed one of Susan's attorneys had been kind enough to forward a metadata-free copy of an email with Jack's schedule that his assistant sent to the hotel. The hotel already had given police paper copies of an itinerary the assistant sent before the trip. This new email contained an updated version of Jack's schedule with the notable inclusion of an entry for "spa time" in the early morning hours.

"Only sent to the hotel staff," Gunnar answered. "As far as we know. But obviously, we can't confirm that with records or the assistant."

"Right."

"Aldís didn't have a copy of it," Val chimed in. "She didn't have any of Jack's personal information. Nothing in all of this."

"So, the assistant wasn't her source?" Hekla asked.

"No." A look of concern appeared on Val's face. "What if we do find her source? You know, for all of the—other stuff. We're not going to . . . "

Both Val's and Gunnar's eyes were on Hekla now. Hekla responded silently but decisively with a shake of her head. Val appeared relieved. Gunnar looked more nervous.

Hekla felt fortunate to have Val with her. Even without their accounting background, Val was more qualified for this type of investigative work than 90 percent of Iceland's police force. Hell, they were probably more qualified for *any* type of work than *most of the population*, Hekla thought, but there seemed to be an artificial cap on their career prospects regardless of profession. Something about those who defied easy categorization still terrified most in power, even in an "enlightened" country like Iceland. Val was motivated to seek underemployment with law enforcement rather than continue their underemployment with corporations after one of their friends was viciously assaulted. They were angry. Hekla understood that. Personally, she felt that Val's move to the police was closer to a show of solidarity for the assaulters than a stand in support of the assaulted, but she kept that opinion to herself. For now, she was just happy to have a skilled person she could trust.

There was a noise out in the hallway, the thud of heavy boots against the floor. Hekla barely had time to register what the sound was before a group of four men barged into the room.

The men were dressed in the steel-gray assault uniform of the Sérsveit Ríkislögreglustjórans—a Special Unit of the National Police, referred to almost exclusively as the *Viking Squad*—replete with black body armor, gloves, and leather combat boots. Hekla quickly noticed that there was no identifying information on any of their gear, no name stitched into their shirts or emblazoned on their Kevlar vests, and no winged badge that the 60 or so special operations officers rarely, if ever, missed an opportunity to adorn on their uniforms. They also didn't have any guns, she realized, a tradeoff that made the conspicuous attempts at anonymization slightly less unpalatable.

Three in the group fanned out in front of the door as the fourth stepped forward. Those in front of the door were remarkably indistinct men in their late-20s and 30s, each with well-manicured facial hair of varying length and style, and self-serious scowls locked onto their faces. The man in front was the oldest, barely in his 40s, if that, and the only one who was clean-shaven. He was slightly shorter than the others too, with a compact build, a long face that appeared to naturally draw down the corners of his lips, and multicolored brown eyes—one with a swath of sea-green occupying a corner of the iris.

Gunnar stood up and took a step toward the men, positioning himself as best as he could between the group and Hekla and Val. Even a few meters away, and backed by a trio of goons, Gunnar seemed an intimidating presence to the man with multicolored eyes. He shot Gunnar a wary look, the sliver of green in one eye sparkling as it caught the light.

"It's our understanding that your office is in possession of stolen property," Multicolored Eyes said as though he were reading from a cue card. "We're here to collect it and return it to its proper owner."

"Who the hell are you?" Hekla shot back.

Multicolored Eyes simply stared.

"This is evidence," she continued, "do you know where you are?"

Still no movement from his etched-on frown. Instead, Multicolored Eyes motioned with his left hand. The men behind him took their cue and stepped forward.

"Hey!" Hekla shouted to no avail.

One of the men went shoulder-first into Gunnar.

Perhaps the man thought Gunnar would move, or at least concede the space after this show of force, because he seemed woefully underprepared for the effect of trying to bowl over a stationary Gunnar. The man bounced off Gunnar like a kid off a trampoline, stumbling backward and only just managing to secure his footing to keep from falling.

This act of passive resistance sent the other two scurrying to back up their humbled colleague. Hekla took the opportunity to move closer to the men, just a pace behind Gunnar and to his right.

"Tell us who you are," she demanded.

Multicolored Eyes ignored Hekla, speaking instead to Gunnar. "Sir, I'm going to need you to move. Now."

Gunnar *didn't* move. At least not his legs or torso. Instead, he tilted his head to look down at the man who charged into him. His expression was as neutral as one could convey, devoid of malice, not even a trace of the gloating bemusement one might expect from a person who almost floored an armored idiot without moving. But his glance was sufficient to cause the man and his colleagues to take defensive postures.

Before things could progress, Kjartan made himself visible in the doorway. "It's okay," he said.

Hekla's eyes burrowed into Kjartan's. He looked sick again, she thought. His voice was soft, as if he were embarrassed to be delivering this message.

Kjartan practically sighed as he continued. "Hekla. Please. Let them in. It's okay."

"Not until someone tells me who they are." Her glare moved from Kjartan to the mute men. "And who sent them."

Kjartan shook his head. "Not now. I'll explain later." Kjartan's eyes had look of urgency Hekla had never seen before. "Please."

Gunnar's eyes moved from Kjartan to Hekla and then back again. His face registered a peculiar uncertainty.

Hekla clenched her teeth and closed her eyes. She let a stream of air pass forcefully through her nostrils, but then tilted her head and opened her eyes, signaling to Gunnar to let the men pass.

It was snowing when Hekla stepped outside. She attempted to light a cigarette but neither her lighter nor thumb appeared up to the task. Each ridge of the serrated spark wheel felt like it was carving into her flesh as a weak flame sporadically appeared and quickly vanished. The soft numb from her skin's exposure to the elements did little to mitigate her discomfort.

One upside to the rapidly plunging temperature and generally miserable weather was its effectiveness at chasing away even the most intrepid reporter—there wasn't another soul in sight. But the solitude offered no practical benefit, Hekla mused, if she remained unable to light this *god damned* cigarette.

Suddenly, there was a break in the wind.

A moment later, a pair of large hands cupped themselves around the lighter. The flame held, Hekla lit the cigarette and clasped it awkwardly between the fingers of her gloved left hand as she shoved her freezing right hand into her pocket.

"Thanks." She smiled at Gunnar. "Why are you still here? You should go home."

Gunnar raised his brow and gave her a side-eyed look. "I thought I should stay to make sure everything was okay. What did Kjartan say?"

She shook her head. "Nothing. Nothing useful at least. He said the group had authority from the Ministry of Justice. He wouldn't say who they were. I'm not even sure he knew."

"They were Viking Squad, weren't they?"

Now it was Hekla's turn to shoot Gunnar a look of incredulity. "They weren't working for *us* tonight."

"Then what, mercenaries? Private contractors? Do you think it was Steingrímur?"

"Or Susan." She shrugged. "Someone who didn't want us to know what Aldís knew." She stared at the ember on her rapidly diminishing cigarette. It was nearly three-quarters burned. "I'm surprised we had that much time with them to be honest."

"But how are they going to prosecute her if we give all the evidence back?"

"I'm sure they'll get what they need when the time comes."

She took one last drag before extinguishing her cigarette in the snow and depositing the butt in a metal trash can next to the building.

Gunnar looked confused. "Aren't you angry?" he asked.

"Did I seem angry?"

"Yes. Back there at least."

"Good."

"But now you're fine? I don't get it. What exactly *did* Kjartan say to you?"

Hekla chuckled. She reached up to pat Gunnar near his shoulders. "We have copies. Val made them as soon as we got everything. I had a feeling they'd do something like this."

Gunnar looked slightly awestruck.

"It's good. Now we know Aldís was really onto something. Might even have a better idea how far it goes." She gave Gunnar a warm smile. "You should go home now. We're okay. But thanks for your help today. Really. I mean it."

And she did. She was now pretty sure the big guy was someone she could trust fully as well.

CHAPTER TWENTY-FOUR

August stood facing the shower head as the water beat down on the back of his head and upper back. He slowly twisted the handle, increasing the temperature of the water. Steam began to surround his body. The muscles on his shoulders and arms rose as they filled with blood. His face contorted into a defiant grimace and his body began to tremble as thousands of droplets stung his flesh. It felt like he was being pelted with fire.

He squeezed the handle. Then, with one quick movement, he turned it as far as it would go.

"Ahhhh!"

August leapt forward. He pressed his body tight against the light-gray tiled wall, lifting himself on his toes with his legs spread to avoid the scalding water. He yanked blindly at the handle—pushing and pulling until the shower finally turned off. When it was safe, he took a step back and lowered himself onto his knees before leaning forward and resting his forearm and forehead against the wall of the shower stall.

After a few minutes, he lifted himself up and pulled himself out of the shower. He made a halfhearted effort to dry himself before dropping the towel on the floor. As he stepped out of the bathroom, he caught sight of his reflection in the full-length mirror next to the front door. He stood still and examined his naked body for the first time in a long time. He didn't look *that* bad, he thought to himself. Maybe it was the lighting, but it was better than he expected. He was a little thin. And pale. But all in all, not so terrifying.

His hair was a mess, its length and thickness disparate and disjointed, making any attempt at styling *void ab initio*. There was a similar lack of cohesion with his facial hair. It covered his face well enough, but it was so uneven that it looked more like a showcase of styles accidentally merged than a purposeful beard. His chest hair was much more robust than usual. As was his pubic hair, which had all but swallowed the top half of his penis in a forest of tight, curly hair.

He returned his attention to his face. The skin appeared thin, like it had been stretched as far as it could go, the only reserve of flesh showing itself around his eyes. It was jarring—the unmistakable signs of age changing his reflection without warning. His lower lip flared out and down into a forlorn frown. Not halfway through an average life cycle and his body had already decided that it couldn't be bothered to keep his facial fat pockets in place. He had always looked young for his age, and he wondered what had accelerated the decline. Had his age simply caught up with him or was his face unable to overcome the reality of his existence? In either case, he looked how he felt. Thin. Pale. Weary.

He turned away from the mirror and lumbered across the small room, leaving damp footprints on the brick-red carpet as he moved from the bathroom to the bed. He pulled hard at the top sheet to loosen it from its secure position underneath the queen-size mattress. Then, with skin and hair still thoroughly wet, he crawled into bed and pulled the comforter over his head.

""""""""""""""

August had believed, quite reasonably in his opinion, that things couldn't possibly be worse for him in Iceland. He had negative history with this country, but his last full day in Denmark included a suicide attempt—surely things could only improve elsewhere. What he didn't realize until now, however, was how much of a controlled environment his flat in Copenhagen offered. One glaring exception aside, he knew how to handle his sadness there and was strict in regulating any potential disturbances. Here, alone in a new space, without his routines and the threads that connected him to society and provided a bare minimum of nourishment, the sadness had gotten out from under his control.

Somewhere in his mind he knew there were different thoughts, positive memories, a different perspective. He tried to remind himself that he was just unable to access these thoughts right now, that this was only a temporary condition. But as each avenue for optimism or hope in his mind was blocked, he became more desperate and less rational. More and more, he felt cornered, trapped once again by the thought that he needed to end the bad thoughts for good.

As before, sleep was a temporary salve. Even the worst and darkest thought was no match for a body drifting out of consciousness. He did his best to prolong the brief period of sentient bliss that occurred right before he fell asleep, when his fears about sadness, and sadness about fears, were almost entirely neutralized by exhaustion. But inevitably, he would wake, and his mind immediately would dredge up the worries that sleep had put aside. It was just like in Copenhagen, maybe even worse. He could almost feel his brain's excitement at being unleashed, giddily searching for compromised areas it could burrow into, reviving useless distortions and reanimating lifeless fears.

And then he would be stuck, forced to occupy his body again and coexist with a mind that was actively conspiring against him. He'd putter about in the hotel room, watch shows he didn't understand, drink shitty coffee without wanting to stay awake—whatever he had to do to distract himself while his body used up what little energy it had. Then, when he felt weak enough, he would return to bed and lie still. His thoughts would grow fuzzy, and he might be able to float away again. This was the best he could hope for and how he occupied his first days and nights in Iceland.

One night, August woke with a terror that dwarfed all those that had come before. It wasn't an intrusive thought or unwelcome memory this time, but a feeling—a terrible feeling that seized control of his entire being. It felt like his brain had truly snapped, broken in two, as though there were a very real crack in his mind.

He fell out of bed and staggered around the room. His face sporadically twitched and tightened, as if someone was jabbing sharp objects into the small of his back. He put on, and then quickly discarded, clothing and blankets. He was too cold and then immediately too hot. There was no comfortable temperature or position. He wrapped his arms tight around his body, enveloping himself in a hug to try and find comfort—or hold himself together.

"Uhgghhhh," he groaned as he fell to one knee by the corner of his bed.

An arrhythmic pounding in his skull forced out any clear thought. There was just noise. His stomach twisted with nausea, but he couldn't vomit. He leaned forward and watched, mouth agape, as a drop of saliva stretched downward from his lip before breaking apart and falling on the carpet.

He thought having a plan might help, something to look forward to. He wrote the letter; sent it in the mail. But even if someone, somehow, had the ability to guarantee him a future full of peace and joy, it wouldn't make the slightest difference to him now. His eyelids drew heavy with tears. He sucked desperately at the air before yanking the comforter off the bed. He wrapped it around his body and curled up on the floor. Iceland or Denmark, here or there, it didn't matter. He couldn't go on like this.

⁓⁓⁓⁓⁓⁓⁓

Do not disturb. Privacy as a privilege. A modern-day luxury, but historically part of the shelter-for-money transaction at the center of the hotel business. They even provide a fucking sign. And, lest there be any doubt, both sides of the sign that August slid around the metal handle of his door displayed the phrase in multiple languages. The system was foolproof. And yet the knocking continued.

"One second," he croaked.

His eyes were practically sealed shut as he gripped the comforter and lifted himself off the floor. He pulled the blanket around his body and shuffled to the door, but the blanket caught beneath his foot and yanked his body forward. He stumbled, heading straight for the wooden dresser. He managed to free his arm and catch hold of the top edge of the dresser just before his head smashed into it.

"Jesus Christ," he grumbled. He pulled himself upright and readjusted his comforter cloak before continuing to the door. He opened it halfway.

Hekla was staring back at him.

"What . . . the fuck?"

"Hello."

"Noo . . ."

"Are you—I heard a noise. . . . " It looked like Hekla was doing her best to keep her eyes from wandering. "Everything okay?"

August stared as defiantly as his eyes were capable. He let the door open slightly, allowing her a glimpse of his partially exposed chest and bare legs. "What . . . what do you want?"

Hekla pursed her lips. It looked like she was reformulating what she wanted to say—another expression August wasn't used to seeing in cops.

"Can you help me?" she finally asked.

CHAPTER TWENTY-FIVE

Hekla had a large coffee waiting for August when he crawled into her car. He did not love the presumptuousness of the gesture, but he did enjoy the improvement over the coffee-flavored water he had been swigging at the hotel. The car smelled odd—stale, like old ashtrays but not recent smoke.

They drove to the Holmsberg lighthouse, a yellowish-orange cylinder not far from the hotel. August occasionally looked over at Hekla as they traveled, expecting her to say something. But she remained quiet, focused on the road. Or something beyond that he couldn't see.

The lighthouse was near the northern tip of a small piece of land that jutted into the water on the northwest side of the Southern Peninsula. There wasn't much of a border between the land and water, and at the edge it just dropped—about 20 meters of nearly vertical rock plunging into the Atlantic Ocean. In the late spring and summer, the visual experience was enhanced by large flower beds and lush grass. Now, there was just snow.

Hekla parked on the side of the road. August shivered as he stepped outside. He pulled the hood of his parka over his head and shot a look at Hekla, who seemed to be handling the frigid conditions with aplomb. Hekla and August made their way along a narrow path that was marked by the treads of brave, foolish, or lost travelers who had come before. They passed a middle-aged couple on the path, but otherwise, they were alone.

When they got to the lighthouse, August kept walking. It was tricky ground to traverse. His feet sunk into the unpacked snow with each step, but he continued until he was close to the eastern edge of the land. He shuffled carefully toward the edge of the cliff, peered over, and studied the long drop to the water.

He could feel his heart beating faster. Heights had never really bothered him, but accessible ledges at high altitudes, particularly ones with low or nonexistent barrier walls always stirred something within him. It was as if he was feared he might decide to fling himself off—and that he would somehow be powerless to stop. He wondered if anyone else felt like this. If the urge was not unique, man-made barriers served their purpose by making it just difficult enough to keep everyone from satisfying their natural desire to just fucking end all of the madness.

"You wouldn't die."

He turned to see Hekla standing to his right.

"Not right away," she added. "Maybe if you hit a rock, but . . . " she shook her head, "even then, likely a very unpleasant time down there. There are better ways."

He took a step back. "I don't—I don't know where she is."

She nodded as she took a cigarette out of her pack. He eyed the cigarette like he wanted to fuck it.

"Do you mind?" she asked.

"Can I have one?" The words bypassed his brain.

She smiled.

He took a cigarette from her outstretched hand. She lit it, her free hand cupped around the flame. He took an overeager drag and immediately coughed like it was his first smoke. Undeterred, he put it right back to his lips and took a more mature puff. "God that helps," he thought.

Hekla allowed August a few more drags before speaking. "I don't think she killed him."

"Mmh," he grunted. "You've shared this . . . opinion . . . with your colleagues?"

"She still needs to come in. I was serious before. I'm worried about her."

"Of course."

Hekla looked expectantly at him.

"What?" He shrugged. "I don't—there's nothing for me to tell you. I don't know where she is. You're wasting your time . . . with me."

Her expression didn't change. "That's not why I'm here. Do you know who Steingrímur Eggertsson is?"

He gave her a curious look. "Didn't he . . . that's the guy who fucked you guys, right? During the financial crisis . . . his company almost bankrupted the whole country."

"Iceland's most successful businessman," she deadpanned.

He smirked, though he wasn't sure if that was intended as a joke or not. "Why . . . what's he got . . . to do with anything?"

She gave him a long, studious look. He responded by lifting his hands in confusion.

"Jack had dinner with Steingrímur the night before he was killed," she revealed. "Him and his wife. Susan Teele."

"Okay . . . so . . . ?"

She took out a neatly folded document from her coat and held it out for him. He took it in his hand, but she didn't let go. "I don't trust the people from your embassy," she said.

"You shouldn't."

"We found documents—research from something Aldís was working on. This is one of them. There are businesses—companies, contracts, deals. It looks like there's a lot of American involvement. I could use some help figuring it out. Can I trust you?"

nnnnnnnnnn

August returned to his room with the document and a small stack of papers Hekla had given him before dropping him back off at the hotel. After less than an hour reviewing the documents, he called her.

"These are Kessel's," he said while inserting a pod into a tiny machine to make himself half a cup of bad coffee. "Lewis Kessel . . . the ambassador. They're his companies—the ones you highlighted at least."

"How do you know?" Hekla asked. "They're not associated with him on any of the Secretary of State filings in your country—"

"It's not . . . " He exhaled quietly, choosing to let the offensive association go this time. "That's a good place to look . . . normally. Kessel made it even easier though. The companies—they were mentioned at his confirmation hearing."

"I don't understand."

"For his appointment . . . I read the transcripts. A senator kept asking about these—it's the same companies. Kessel wouldn't give up control of them . . . to remove conflicts of interest. I thought they were just oil companies. But this . . . this looks like a whole other thing."

"Is that allowed? Keeping his business while he's an ambassador?"

August chuckled. "Fuck. . . . Do you know what he did before? *That* shouldn't be allowed."

Hekla was quiet.

"Yeah," he continued. "They make a show, but . . . his confirmation was unanimous."

"Oh."

August ran his finger along the document until he came to a section he had underlined. "This memo . . . or whatever. . . . It refers to another document. And some . . . 'consortium' that's defined there. Do you have that—do you know what that is?"

"I think so."

"Well?"

"There's a lot of language," she said. "One document refers to another which refers to another. But it looks like the consortium is just a group of private companies and individuals."

"That . . . are doing . . . business with your National Energy Authority?" he asked, his brow furrowing with surprise.

"It's worse than that. These documents just approve the structure. I think what might be going on is that this group is being given the authority to negotiate an energy deal with those companies you recognized. Authority on behalf of Iceland—"

"While also . . . receiving ownership shares in the companies?"

"I believe so."

"No fucking way."

There was silence on the line again. August thought back to when he would get particularly excited about a subject with Aldís and start liberally cursing. It took her some time to figure out when he was genuinely angry and at whom. "What kind of . . . deal is this—what's it even for?"

"Mining."

He laughed heartily. "This secrecy . . . for what? Aluminum?"

"No. It's something else. Something new they found. Offshore. There's an old volcano underwater. Some hybrid mineral. Must be pretty valuable."

"Hmm." he pondered this a moment. "How do you know all of this?"

This time the silence on the other line seemed more intentional.

He accepted the non-response. "Okay. Well . . . what does it have to do with Jack's murder?"

"I don't think it has anything to do with him. I think it has to do with his wife."

"His wife?"

"Yes."

"So you . . . you think his wife's involvement with this sketchy deal . . . that's why you think he was murdered?"

A long pause. Then, "Yes."

〰〰〰〰〰〰〰

August opened his laptop as soon as he got off the phone. He knew a bit about Iceland's energy policy—not a lot, but it was enough to know that if any of this were true, it was bonkers. By law, natural resources in Iceland belong to the people. Allowing a shadow group to negotiate in secret with a foreign company for the extraction and refinery of a mineral—even if it *was* just aluminum—would be unheard of. It would certainly be the kind of story that Aldís would sink her teeth into. He wondered though if there might be other aspects of the deal that interested her.

After a quick search, he downloaded Iceland's *1998 Act on the Survey and Utilization of Ground Resources.* He scrolled through the document. Several sections on the permits and licensing needed to survey and prospect caught his attention. The process was very strict, with multiple levels of approval and review required if anyone wanted to put more than a shovel in the ground. When he got to *Chapter VI: Extraction of Materials From the Earth,* he slowed down. He focused on a passage in Article 47, *Authorization for extraction*:

> All extraction on land and from or under the seabed within
> the netlaying area, shall be subject to the operating

permission of the local authority concerned, cf. Article 27 of the Planning and Building Act, No. 73/1997.

It was written in the obtuse, backward-ass style of lawyers, but "operating permission" and "local authority" gave him direction. It told him that a representative from the area closest to any offshore mining—a member of parliament, for instance, or a local board—could veto the operation. He opened another browser and entered a pair of longitude and latitude coordinates listed on one of the papers Hekla had given him. It took him several attempts to enter the information properly, but when a location just off the shore of the Northwest District popped up, he knew he got it right. This was practically Aldís's backyard.

August tilted his chair back and stared at the eerily flawless, muted white ceiling. If what Hekla was telling him was true, Aldís had uncovered a massive scandal: The consortium was making a secret deal with itself to sell minerals that rightfully belonged to the Icelandic people. And it involved an American company. In Iceland.

"Fuck," he thought to himself. It seemed unbelievable. Maybe it was.

The next part was undoubtedly true though. Susan Teele's husband was murdered. Brutally. With a symbolic flourish. According to Hekla, Susan was part of this consortium, and Aldís was going to bring her clandestine dealings to the public's attention. Now Aldís was accused of killing Susan's husband. And she was missing.

CHAPTER TWENTY-SIX

Six-and-a-half months after meeting Aldís, August resigned from his position at the embassy. Because he had ten years of service and had managed to be on good terms with a human resources representative, he was able to salvage a decent portion of his pension. Coupled with the additional savings he had accrued by spending most of his career abroad, he would be set financially even if he spent a significant period unemployed. None of that mattered though. He was ready to quit before she even asked.

After their first meeting, August had spent every weekend, holiday, or 18-unencumbered-hours-in-a-row with Aldís in Iceland. During the winter holidays, she spent the better half of a month with him in Copenhagen. They were close, but he wanted to be closer. He could tell she was holding back from him. One day, toward the end of her stay, after she had deftly avoided engaging in a discussion of the future, she told him what was bothering her.

"You need to quit your job," she told him as he poured non-dairy creamer into her coffee.

"Okay," he replied without hesitation.

"I'm serious."

"I know."

She shook her head. "It's not—I don't want you to—it can't be because—"

He gently placed his hand on her forearm. "I know," he repeated. "It's something I should have done a long time ago. You're right. There's no excuse for me to be working for them. There never really was."

"It's that easy now?" she asked, leaning away from him. "What about making a difference from inside? Being one of the good guys. Isn't that what you always said? Was that just bullshit?"

"No." He gave a pained expression as he looked away. "I meant it—I did. It's just . . . I dunno. I think I was always trying to convince myself of it too."

"What do you mean?"

He held up his palms. "I wanted a nice life. I wanted out . . . and I didn't want to feel bad." He let out a tiny nervous laugh. "Being out here, removed from most of what they do— what *we* do—I had that. I thought I was using them. I did . . . and I did try. I always tried. But . . . "

Aldís placed her hand on his back. He looked her in the eyes.

"It was a half-truth," he continued. "At best. It let me do what I wanted. Some . . . rhetorical bullshit." He sighed. "You know the truth. It's what you said . . . I uphold the system. 'Any good that I might accidentally do is negated by'—what was it—'our lending credibility to an institution and nation that turn perceived moral authority into blood.'"

A small smile emerged on Aldís' face. "I did say that. Or some-thing like that."

"It was good."

"So why?" her tone was serious again. "Why would you keep this up for so long?"

"Why wouldn't I? It *is* a nice life. *Was*—I thought. I thought I was happy. It's what you did . . . " August gave a half-shrug and looked down, "People like me. It was selfish but . . . we didn't call it that. I didn't know any other way to live. I certainly didn't think there was anything better."

"So, what, it's your country's fault?"

"No," he shook his vehemently. "People over there do much better . . . with much less. I'm just trying to explain . . . what I was thinking—how it was for me."

As a youth, August was taught that he was free. That Americans were *the most* free. And he believed it—for a time. It wasn't until much later that he came to view his country with suspicion, and then contempt. Now, it all seemed like propaganda and indoctrination to him. Everything and everyone reinforcing the same story, the same dream, where August was the hero, narrator, and author. *He'd* be happy if *he* did well for himself and everyone would be better off if they had the same opportunities as him. It all sounded deranged to him now, but it wasn't even worthy of articulation for most of his life. It was just the way the world worked.

Aldís left for Iceland soon after their conversation. August quit his position unsure if he would ever hear from her again. He didn't blame her. She might not ever be able to trust his motivations, and that was fair. He would be disappointed but grateful for the time he had with her. He also was immensely relieved that he would never have to justify his continued employment with the FBI again.

But Aldís did contact him. She called just one week later. In the spring, he moved in with her at her home in Patreksfjörður. A few months later she told him about Client.

,,,,,,,,,,,,,,,,

Client was nothing like August. He grew up poor, in a rural community in the Southern United States. After high school, he struggled to get by with a series of dead-end jobs. There wasn't a well-tread path of university, internships, graduate school, and professional job for him; no family business or familial support. If he wanted to eat, sleep, or shit with a roof over his head, the military was his best option, so he enlisted in the Air Force. But he never had any illusions about what he was doing.

Since he was seven, the one thing Client *did* have was access to a wide variety of news sources. He'd spend extra time after school, and weekends at the library two towns over, reading or listening to podcasts for hours on end. The outlets and voices that Client naturally gravitated to, the ones that made the most sense to him, were on the left of the political spectrum. Unlike August, Client did not rely on a tortured, self-serving analysis to defend his employment with immoral actors. To him, it was just a job. He needed a job so he could live. And the military was hiring.

After enrollment, Client took an exam and then another exam. Soon he was spending more time with a computer than a gun. And before long, he found himself as an analyst, sitting in a converted hangar, watching a high-definition video feed as three bombs obliterated a camp for displaced women and children in quasi-occupied land in the Middle East. After the first bomb dropped, Client could see the survivors try to get away—tiny figures rushing toward the aqueduct bordering the camp, some of them dragging even smaller figures. Then the second bomb fell. By the time the dust from the third bomb settled, there were no more moving figures. More than 70 women and children were killed that day. The carnage was so vicious that body parts once belonging to the same human could be found in separate piles, some rising several meters high.

By this point in his career, Client had become familiar with the many ways the United States justified what he considered murder. There are rules of engagement and then there are rules for the rulers. The thing about *this* incident, however, was it managed to violate even the loosest interpretations of the most liberal of the military's own secret rules. There wasn't a classified memo or back alley legal opinion that would ever permit such an obvious and reckless use of force against civilians. And if there *were*, as Client quickly recognized, it wouldn't have been necessary for the strike log entries to be changed or the camp to be bulldozed the next day. This was a war crime by any definition—a crime against humanity.

So Client did what he was trained to do. He spoke with the legal officer on site. He brought his complaint up the chain of command, to the Office of Special Investigations. When that produced nothing, he wrote a memo to the chief legal officer for the region. A letter to the Senate Armed Services Committee soon followed. And finally, Client made a hotline complaint to the Inspector General's Office.

Client did everything by the book, working within the system to ensure that those who committed this mass murder would be held responsible. Every free moment he had, from the time of the bombing to his honorable discharge two years later, he spent pushing for accountability. There were meetings, investigations, reports—promise after promise after promise—but it all went nowhere. The closest he got to an explanation, or answer to the question of, "Why were all of these people killed?" was a line in one report that stated, "Women and children in the area have been known to take up arms against allied interests." That was it. They didn't do a goddamn thing.

So after doing everything he could within the system, Client left. He returned home and applied for a few jobs in Washington, D.C., where his high security clearance would all but guarantee him a generously compensated position. He got hired at a fancy consulting firm with a start date two weeks out. Then he went on vacation.

On his first civilian flight out of the country, Client took with him the contact information for a journalist he had first heard of as a teenager, a woman whose tenacious reporting about financial fraud forced the prime minister of Sweden to resign. Having come of age in a country where money matters were only criminal if you didn't have enough, he was awed by her ability to hold people to account. Over the years, he continued to follow her, and he came to believe that if there were anyone he could trust, it would be her. So, Client's holiday would be spent in the offbeat destination of Iceland. Accompanying him on the flight was every piece of tangible information—video, file, data—relating to the massacre of civilians by the U.S. government that he was able to get his hands on during his time as an analyst.

⸺⸺⸺⸺

Aldís was militant when it came to protecting the identity of those who risked their lives for others. She had never given up a source and was confident in her ability to protect Client after he told her his story. Her plan was for Client to act the part of a tourist and then return to his job in the States. She knew people who could scrub the data he had given her so that no one would be able to tell where it came from. She would write a story, and then make the information public in a time and manner that would protect him.

August was living with Aldís when Client contacted her. At first, Aldís told August only that she was working on a new story but wasn't ready to share any details. After meeting Client in the South, and deciding that Client was credible, she told August her plan. August felt a chill go up his spine as he heard the story. His response was instantaneous.

"No."

"What do you mean, no?" she asked, offended.

"It's not going to work. They'll find him—"

"No. They won't. I'll make sure of it."

"They always do," he snapped with a ferocity that surprised him. He softened his voice, taking on a solemn, almost pleading, tone. "Aldís. It won't work . . . you can't. Please. He's not going to be safe. He'll never *know* if he's safe because he never *will* be. Please . . . you can't—don't do this."

"So what? What are we supposed to do?"

August held her stare. There was an urgency in his look that he felt her respond to, as though she would trust whatever he said next. That his response was so reflexive, that he didn't have a plan at first, these things gave him some comfort in the years that followed. They made him think that perhaps his intentions were pure, that he was trying to do what was best for Client. But inevitably, the thought that he was once again motivated by selfishness, trying to pursue his own glory or make up for his own failures, would creep in. And in these times, he would think back to Aldís's eyes, staring back at him, willing to follow, and trusting him with that which was most sacred to her.

⁂

August knew what life was like for whistleblowers in the United States. The only ones who did okay for themselves were those who remained committed to the bad conduct right up until the moment it became more lucrative, or beneficial to their career prospects, to switch sides—mostly people already starting from a position of power. They were nothing like Client.

The story usually unfolded in similar fashion. Those who called attention to the crimes of big business and government when it wasn't fashionable had their lives ruined. Examples were made of them. They were imprisoned and tortured or they lived in fear or in exile. At best, they were forced to live without a real future in or out of the States.

Rarely were there consequences for people higher up on the totem pole, those most responsible for the heinous acts that a whistleblower exposed. When confronted with evidence of their misdeeds, they would offer mealy-mouthed excuses and maybe sit in the "time out" corner for a year or two. Then they'd be back. Some would even tout their insider knowledge of the *bad* as a reason why they were specially qualified to lead the country back to the *good*. When asked what should be done about the whistleblower, they would defer to whatever laws they knew would punish the whistleblower most. They took issue not with a whistleblower's intentions, of course, but with the *way* the whistleblower went about divulging the information.

So, the whistleblower would have to hear from a mocking guard transferring her back to isolation or learn from a nightly news program in the frigid land he'd been banished to, about the book written by their former boss, bravely denouncing the system that they fucking built. It was all so depressingly predictable.

August thought he could do better for Client. He came up with a plan where he would represent Client. His goal would be to protect Client legally, leverage his insider knowledge to get a non-prosecution agreement signed by government officials who could make it binding. This would be coupled with a real investigation into Client's allegations of war crimes, secured by the public release of some of the information that Client possessed. It might not be as sweeping an exposition as Client or Aldís envisioned, but the key information would come out and, most importantly, Client wouldn't have to look over his shoulder for the rest of his life.

"It's the best of both worlds," August told Aldís the next morning, after explaining his plan.

She bit the corner of her lower lip.

"I can do this," he went on. "If there is some . . . benefit to my career—something good it can do . . . this is it. I know who to talk to. He can be protected—actually safe."

"I've never had problems before."

"I know. I believe you. . . . I just don't trust them. They don't lose. I'm telling you—they don't fucking lose."

There was a moment of silence.

"Will you ask him?" August continued. "Tell him my plan. Just see what he thinks."

Aldís stared at him a long moment before nodding her head. He gave a tight-lipped smile, pulled her close, and kissed her on the forehead as he rubbed the back of her neck.

"We can do this," he said.

Later that morning, Aldís drove south to meet with Client again. August waited nervously at the house, his smartphone next to him with the volume up. He watched the time, imagining where Aldís might be on her journey as each minute passed. When he estimated that she was with Client, he grew even more tense. Just seconds later, his phone rang.

"Okay," Aldís said as soon as he answered.

August's insides unwound as he exhaled. Apparently, Client didn't need much convincing. It took a few more moments for the nerves to return as August realized that it was now up to him to make this work.

CHAPTER TWENTY-SEVEN

At 1 p.m., the phone rang in August's hotel room. He reached to the nightstand and poked around until he was able to dislodge the receiver from its base. The plastic phone clacked on the edge of the wood before tumbling off the side of the table.

"Mmmhggg," August groaned.

He pulled himself close to the edge of the bed but remained under the covers. He wondered what kind of record was kept for automated wakeup calls—if people even used them anymore. A log of the time guests wanted a ring would probably be some decent data to sell if smartphones hadn't all but monopolized the alarm business. He was sure that there would still be an account of his wakeup call somewhere. In this rare instance, he welcomed the sharing of his activities with unknown individuals and entities. Ever since Hekla had visited him, August had made a point of keeping to a relatively strict and purposefully obvious routine.

First, he showered and dressed, layering himself in every variety of cold-weather apparel he owned. Next, he left the hotel and walked east, away from the airport, along a barren stretch on Aðalgata. The cold didn't bother him quite as much since his walk now doubled as an opportunity for a smoke. After passing a few multi-family houses and apartments, he made a right on Hringbraut, continued a few minutes, and then made a left on Vatnsnesvegur, which took him to the southern edge of downtown Keflavík.

August's destination was a 1950s-themed diner. Today, just

like every other day, it was nearly full by the time he arrived. The place suited him fine, but he couldn't really figure out its appeal to others. He considered the diner's proximity to a large hotel as a causal factor, but there did just seem to be something about nostalgic diners in tourist centers that drew consistent crowds. Maybe it comforted visitors, reminding them of a not particularly impressive place where they used to eat back in their home-towns—or, if you were American, of a time when the country didn't bother with artifice.

He entered the diner and walked straight to the wobbly half-table in the back that was always unoccupied. As usual, he tried a few words in Icelandic on the waiter, and, as usual, the waiter answered with a polite smile and confident English. August returned the smile and ordered his usual midafternoon breakfast of whole grain toast with jam, coffee, and fruit. After finishing his meal, he gave an overenthusiastic goodbye to the staff in Icelandic and stepped outside.

August scanned the area. The space in front of the restaurant was relatively open. There were wide streets, a traffic circle, and low buildings. Each day he had spotted plainclothes officers, but never the same one twice. There were usually at least two of them, one who would follow from behind, another in front, in whatever direction they suspected he was going. They must be going through half their force watching him, he thought with amuse-ment. He gave an exaggerated wave to one of the suddenly flus-tered cops and started his walk back to the hotel.

Although nearby Keflavík was nice, it wasn't what motivated August to stay in the area. His hotel happened to be quite close to the place he believed Aldís would go if she needed to disappear. The Westfjords, or an isolated spot in the North or East, might work, but oddly, their remoteness made them poor hiding spots.

It was far too easy to become trapped. If you needed to get supplies or see someone, having to drive an hour or more on a road that may well be covered with a meter of snow wasn't ideal. And no one could go to you without being noticed. More populated areas offered more options—and the opportunity to disappear in a crowd.

August was employing a similar strategy with his public appearances and his routine. The idea was to establish a pattern that could serve as a cover. If he always did the same thing, the people watching him were more likely to stop paying close attention. Staying stagnant would have shone a spotlight on every detail of his day. It was harder to notice small discrepancies when there was more going on, and therefore much easier to hide something in plain sight.

This day, however, he was struck with a thought that threatened to disrupt his carefully constructed schedule. About halfway back to the hotel, seemingly out of nowhere, he wondered, *what if she's dead?* It felt like someone had shoved a dagger into his spine. He hadn't truly considered the possibility before, but now it seemed just as plausible—if not more so—that the reason Aldís hadn't been in contact with him wasn't because she didn't want to see him, or because she thought it was too risky, but because she *couldn't.* It took everything in him not to sprint back to the hotel. In his head, all the evidence rearranged itself to support his new theory—Hekla's warning about Aldís's safety, the oddly disconcerting look on Logi's face, his knowledge of how his government deals with threats. Why would he think she was in hiding? She probably was just dead. He considered bypassing the hotel and going straight to the safe house.

No, he reprimanded himself. He had to stop these thoughts. There was no reason to believe the Americans cared more about Aldís than they did about the rest of Iceland's citizens, a level of concern which hovered between not at all and something a bit less than that. What he needed to do was slow down, maintain a consistent pace, and not do anything to draw the attention of the officer 30 meters to his left who was pretending to browse his phone as he monitored August in the side and rearview mirrors of his awkwardly parked car. The worries kept coming though. New information combined with old, and fresh paths merged with well-trod avenues of fear and doubt in his brain.

After what seemed like an hour of walking in slow motion, he arrived at the hotel. He kicked the snow from his boots as he covertly watched his tail pull into a "random" spot in one of the three areas of the parking lot the police had deemed sufficient for monitoring. His legs felt weak as he walked inside and ambled to the front desk.

"Any mail for August Sorenson?" he asked the clerk. It was the same question he asked every day after returning from the diner. He did his best to keep his voice neutral, only letting his eyes betray his concern as they burrowed into the back of the clerk's computer screen—doing everything in their power to will an affirmative message.

The clerk started to shake his head before answering, "No."

August's heart sank. He had to push himself off the desk to get his legs moving again. In the elevator, his thoughts of visiting the safe house returned. He was confident in his ability to lose the officers, but less certain of his ability to travel to the house undetected. He knew he couldn't drive. Maybe he could get a ride— pay in cash, get dropped off somewhere a few kilometers away. He would need a way to get back as well. *If she were alive.* His chest tightened. There were way too many pitfalls, but by the time the elevator doors opened he had decided he would go to her. This resolution alone was enough to ease some of the tension in his torso, though he still couldn't help but increase his pace as he strode down the brightly lit hallway to his room.

He stopped abruptly a few meters from his door when he caught sight of the Do Not Disturb placard hanging from the handle. He crept closer, making sure to avoid the peephole on the door as he moved. As gently as possible, he ran his hand up along the crevice where the front of the door met the frame.

The sign shouldn't be there. He kept it inside after he canceled daily cleaning services in accord with the hotel's conservation efforts. But affixing the sign after breaking in would be a strange thing for the cops to do. Maybe it was just a reminder for the hotel staff, he allowed himself to consider. His fingers probed the area near the top corner of the door until he found what he was looking for. He brought his hand down and inspected a piece of clear plastic tape stuck on his middle finger. Someone had been inside.

Without thinking it through, he inserted his keycard into the slot above the handle. The fluctuations in adrenaline had left him feeling almost numb as the lock clicked. Only when he pushed open the door did it dawn on him that he could be in actual danger. It was too late now though, so he stepped inside. His worries washed away when he saw Aldís standing next to his bed.

CHAPTER TWENTY-EIGHT

Aᴜɢᴜsᴛ sᴛᴀʀᴇᴅ ᴀᴛ Aʟᴅís ɪɴ ᴅɪsʙᴇʟɪᴇғ. Iᴛ ғᴇʟᴛ like his body was in a suspended state. He was conscious of what was happening, but unable to do anything. When he finally was able to move, he shut the door and walked toward her. He stopped several paces away. Aldís didn't look like someone who had been on the run, he thought. She looked good. Like she did the last time he last saw her.

Aldís's lips curled into a smile as she tilted her head. "August," she said, her voice both sweet and sad, "What on earth are you doing here?"

He opened his mouth, but no words came out. There was so much to say, he didn't know where or how to start. His eyes began to fill with tears. "I'm sorry," he finally uttered. "I'm . . . I'm so sorry."

"No," her voice cracked. "Stop that. You didn't do anything wrong."

"Yes. I did—I'm—" a sudden sob interrupted his words.

Aldís closed the gap between them and pulled him in for a tight hug. He choked out another cry and let himself be held. After a few seconds, he whispered into her shoulder. "I didn't . . . even call. I didn't know. I thought . . . I thought you'd never want to see me again. I'm so sorry."

"It's okay." She rubbed his head with one hand and leaned back to look him in the eyes. "You should have at least called, but it's okay."

He chortled and she flashed a mischievous grin. They

embraced again. Then he pulled back, his face growing serious. "What's going on here?"

"What do you mean?"

He gave her a knowing look.

Her eyes darted away momentarily. "It's probably best if you don't know."

"Are you in trouble?"

"I'll be okay." A wry smile emerged on her face, "You know how it is."

"Yeah . . . I do. . . . It's not fucking great."

They shared a round of dark laughter.

He sighed and wiped his eyes. He was at a loss. He had spent so much time trying *not* to think about her that all the thoughts and feelings he now wanted to express were logjammed. His mind was overwhelmed. So it was only in retrospect that he recognized the significance of the tiny beep he heard after their laughter died down. The second beep was just as easy to overlook. But the more pronounced click that followed was impossible to ignore.

And then, all hell broke loose.

Six police officers burst into the room, equipped with weapons and body armor that August didn't even know they possessed. They shouted, first in Icelandic, then in English. Their words barely registered. All August could focus on were the guns pointed at their chests.

Two of the officers quickly moved toward them. August turned to see Aldís fearfully lift her hands up.

"Hey!" August yelled as one of the officers forcefully grabbed Aldís's arm. "Get the fuck off her!"

Almost instinctively, he shoved the officer. The officer's legs caught the foot of the bed, causing him to tumble onto the floor.

It looked much worse than it was, but that distinction was clearly lost on the other officer, who swiped August's legs and threw him to the ground in one quick movement. On his way down, August's head slammed into the bottom corner of the dresser, making contact just above his right eye. His head hit hard, affecting his memory of the ensuing events as everything turned hazy.

What he did recall, however, was the oddly comforting sensation of warm liquid trickling down his forehead. Less pleasant was the feel of the carpet as his face was ground into its fibers, and the impression of a large Nordic man's knee just beneath his shoulder blade. Nothing bothered him as much as what he saw next though. Although blood now interfered with his vision, and everything was compromised by a spaced-out dizziness that would soon turn into an agonizing throb, he could still clearly see Hekla's form as she took Aldís by the elbow.

August shouted. He meant to direct an expletive at Hekla, but it was unclear to him if anything more than incomprehensible gibberish came out of his mouth. Hekla did turn to him though. He recognized that familiar look of pity in her eyes, maybe also accompanied by a hint of guilt. Then his head was shoved further into a carpet that had suddenly become spongey.

The last thing he remembered was Aldís's voice. Her reassuring tone was more comprehensible than her words. It sounded like she was saying something to the effect of "it's okay," or "it will be okay." He even thought he might have heard, "fault," like, "it's not her fault."

⁓⁓⁓⁓⁓⁓⁓

The jail cell was notably uncomfortable. August allowed for the possibility that his perception was affected by the abrupt transition from the luxurious confines of the hospital. There clearly had been concern for his welfare at first, the flashes of memory he retained all involved grim faces whenever someone looked at his injury.

Perhaps his expectations were also unreasonably high. During his time at the legat, he had the opportunity to visit several Nordic prisons. Many of them were like resorts compared to how most people in his home country lived. Maybe the comforts in Iceland were reserved for the actual prisons, or for guests who weren't associated with the most sensational murder in the country's history. Still, August would have appreciated something more than ice in a paper towel and what looked like children's aspirin. This place reminded him more of a jail in America, like the one he had the misfortune of visiting when he was younger— too drunk and too loud in the wrong state. At least he was alone here. The steel bench, toilet, and thin mattress on another flat, steel surface were reserved exclusively for him.

He was lying on the sad little mattress, trying to figure out what time it was, when someone pounded on the door. The sound of metal sliding against metal preceded a loud clank as the deadbolt moved. The door creaked open, and a guard stuck his head inside.

"You have a visitor."

August sat up too quickly. "Ahh," he groaned as he put his hand to his forehead. This only elicited another pained gasp when his fingers touched swollen flesh that had no business extending out so far. The excruciating throbbing sensation returned as blood rushed to the injured region. The sudden reallocation of critical fluid left him dizzy, forcing him to grab the edge of his bed.

When he could finally focus, he saw a man in a dark suit standing a few meters away, watching him impassively as he writhed in pain.

"Errgh," August croaked, "the fuck . . . are you?"

"Mr. Sorenson. Hello. My name is Mark Carney. I'm an attorney at the embassy—"

"Ehnno." He lowered his head. This helped with the pain somewhat.

"This is just a consular visit. But I think that, maybe with some cooperation—"

"No."

"It really would be in your best interest—"

"Ahhrgh," August seethed, lifting his head back up. He sized the man up with his one good eye and the slit of vision remaining in his other. Carney looked like an American attorney—miserable, with an arrogance that swallowed any self-awareness. This version clearly had that extra layer of unearned confidence that came from working in the upper echelons of the U.S. government, knowing that he was preemptively above any law that could be written. "I said . . . no. I don't want you. . . . I don't want the embassy. Please . . . fuck off."

Carney studied August's face for a moment and then replaced the haughty but accommodating tone he had been using with a cold, bullying one that he seemed much more comfortable with. He had satisfied the obligatory duties of his profession and now could move on to the real business. "Fair enough. Lisa Harris would like to speak with you. She'll be expecting you at the embassy at 2 p.m. tomorrow. I assume they'll be letting you out by the morning. Unless you managed to commit a few more crimes in between arrest and detention?"

Carney shot an inquisitive look at August, seeming to consider it entirely possible that he had, in fact, squeezed in a few extra offenses.

August only managed to meekly whisper, "I'm not going."

Carney grunted softly and gave a short nod. He knocked on the door before looking back at August. He took an awkwardly exaggerated breath, like a poor parody of a parody of a sympathetic sigh. "It would be a good idea if you met with her." He gestured at August's wound. "Hope you feel better."

CHAPTER TWENTY-NINE

Hekla sat across from Aldís in the interrogation room. On her tablet was a photograph of Aldís's home. The picture was of the exterior of the house, with a focus on the rust-orange, Jeep 4x4 parked alongside.

Sitting next to Hekla was Bjarni. Hekla didn't want him there, but Kjartan had insisted. Kjartan was in his customary position on the other side of the glass, but Hekla could sense the many others who would be watching, either via live feed or video later. Kjartan had gone so far as to float the idea of questioning Aldís in English, though he quickly retreated from the idea when Hekla said that doing so could compromise the integrity of the interview. He didn't press the issue. In fact, his demeanor suggested he was ashamed to have even asked.

Aldís looked calm, practically serene compared to everyone else in and around the room. She was exceedingly polite to the guard who brought her in and removed her handcuffs, and she sat patiently with her hands folded on the table in front of her as she waited for Hekla to begin.

Hekla closed the picture of Logi's car on her tablet and brought up a document with an outline she had prepared. "When did you find out Susan Teele and her husband would be in Iceland?" she asked.

There was a nervous quiet, as if everyone were holding their breath.

Hekla looked up.

The corner of Aldís's lips lifted, ever so slightly. "Susan?" she asked, as if she were offering Hekla a chance to edit her question.

"Yes. And her husband. Jack Drumman."

Aldís nodded once. "I didn't know Jack would be here." She paused. "But I knew Susan was coming for the meeting."

"What meeting?"

"I'm sure you've looked at my research by now." The sly smile Aldís had hinted seconds earlier was now unmistakable. "I would hope there would be some point to all that destruction at my home."

"We apologize for any inadvertent damage," Hekla curtly countered. "The research though—are you referring to the classified documents from the National Energy Authority we found on your computer?"

"Classified? I didn't think that was possible. It's our energy, isn't it?"

"When did you receive the documents?"

Aldís moved her head slowly, first in one direction and then the other, signaling "no" as she kept her eyes on Hekla.

"Who provided them to you?"

Aldís gave a quicker shake of the head this time.

"You mentioned a 'meeting,'" Hekla continued. "You're referring to a group that was meeting to discuss a proposal for a mining operation—is that correct?"

"I think they'd moved past discussions."

"But that *is* what you are referring to?"

"Meetings. Yes. And I imagine they're still going on. These aren't the type of people to let death get in the way of a business opportunity."

"Uh-huh. So, you knew when Susan would be traveling here.

And you also knew who she was married to. Did you know where they would be staying?"

"All I knew is what's in the documents."

"Is that a 'yes' or a 'no'?"

"It's a no. I didn't know where they would be staying. My guess would have been somewhere overpriced and charmless. But I also would have assumed they'd be staying together."

Bjarni shuffled impatiently in his seat. Hekla ignored him. "Did you share the information about Susan's expected arrival in Iceland with anyone?"

"Well, she *is* here, right?"

"Excuse me?"

"It's not 'expected.' She came. They've been meeting. Haven't they? She's *still* here. Isn't she?" Aldís's eyes moved to the one-way mirror behind Hekla. "I don't know why you all keep acting like this is a hypothetical."

"Mr. Drumman's death isn't hypothetical," snapped Hekla.

Aldís locked eyes with Hekla. "And that's why Susan is still here?"

"Did you have anything to do with Mr. Drumman's death?"

"No."

"Do you know who did?"

"No. Do you?"

Hekla held Aldís's stare for several seconds before looking down at her tablet. "You certainly didn't have much nice to say about him when he was alive."

"There *isn't* much nice to say about him."

"Then you're happy he's dead?" Bjarni's eyes darted over to Hekla in surprise.

Aldís looked pensive, taking a moment to respond. "I'm not

sad. He made the world a worse place. But that's done. I don't know that his death will make it any better."

"But you're okay with murder. The murder of people like him." Hekla placed a finger on a portion of her outline. "You once said that it's 'okay to take a life under certain conditions,' that you 'wouldn't cast judgment.' Those are your words, aren't they?"

"They were."

"And do you still believe that?"

There was a long pause. "I do," Aldís finally said.

Hekla nodded. She minimized the outline on her tablet and brought up a document showing financial transactions. "You made a currency exchange recently. What was that for?"

"Travel."

"What did you do with the money?"

"I left it with a friend. My traveling companion."

"Really?"

"Yes."

"Why would you do that?"

Aldís shrugged. "Safekeeping. You never know who's going to raid your home."

"You think this is a joke?" Bjarni spat out as he leaned forward, his backside raising off his chair.

Aldís didn't flinch. Instead, she looked at him calmly, almost serenely.

Hekla gave him a withering glare. "Please," she muttered. Bjarni reluctantly returned to his seat. Hekla took a deep breath.

"So, you're planning a trip to both Europe and the United States. You exchanged currency, but you haven't booked a single flight or hotel. We didn't find any travel guides, there were no relevant searches on your laptop—that's kind of odd, no?"

"We're planning for spontaneity, I suppose."

"That's cute. Who's this traveling companion?"

Aldís's eyes flickered mischievously. "His name is Logi."

Hekla froze. She looked uncertain for a long moment and then flicked her fingers aimlessly on her tablet. "We'll need his information," she murmured.

"I'm sure you have it already."

Hekla looked back up.

"But I'd be happy to share it again," Aldís continued. "I'm sure he'd love to talk."

Hekla grunted softly. "What were you doing at the spa the morning Mr. Drumman was killed?"

"What anyone does at a spa. I was enjoying a day off."

"Five hours from your home to visit an *overpriced and charmless* tourist trap? The same day Mr. Drumman is murdered there? A man who you've relentlessly attacked in writing, who you have secret documents about—documents that relate to an energy deal that you *also* oppose. We're supposed to believe it's all a coincidence?"

"Yes." Aldís looked directly at the small camera in the corner of the ceiling. "But for the record, the documents you found aren't about *Jack Drumman*. They're about a deal. A deal that a group of private citizens, businesses and public officials are negotiating with an American company. It's for the extraction and refinement of minerals located in Iceland. It's being done in secret and in violation of the law. If allowed to proceed, it will destroy the relationship between the Icelandic people and the land that we live and work on." Aldís paused for effect. "And, if I'm being charged with any crime, I'll obviously need these documents for my defense."

Hekla and Bjarni entered the small room that occupied the space between the station's two main interrogation rooms. The floor was elevated and monitors were set against the wall. Beneath the monitors was a long table with computers and a phone that Kjartan hung up when the detectives entered.

"She knows something," Hekla said, visibly frustrated. "I'm not sure if it's about the murder or something else, but it's like she's playing with us."

Kjartan looked from Hekla to Aldís, who had resumed her relaxed position in the adjacent room, hands folded neatly on the table in front of her.

"There's no real evidence besides the currency transaction though," she continued. "It's strong, but still just circumstantial, even if her story can't be verified."

"What about obstruction?" Bjarni volunteered.

"Yeah?" Hekla asked with more than a trace of disdain. "What about it?"

"She won't say where she got the classified documents."

"What documents? *We* don't even have them anymore. Besides, we can't make her give up a source—"

"There's no source. She's not a journalist, she's a traitor."

Hekla exhaled loudly through her nose and shut her eyes. "I'll look into her claim regarding the currency," she informed Kjartan.

"The traveling companion?" Kjartan asked in a tone that she couldn't quite decipher.

"Yes," she replied. "I'll follow up, see if the individual she identified has the money."

"That won't be necessary."

"Why not?"

"Searches are being conducted now."

Hekla narrowed her eyes. "*Searches?*"

Kjartan gave a curt nod. "The Ministry of Justice has authorized searches on all individuals associated with The Fólk publication."

Hekla was aghast; Bjarni looked gleeful. "When were they authorized?" she asked.

"Recently."

"*When?*" she demanded. "There wasn't any new information obtained tonight. When was the request made? Were you going to tell me?"

Kjartan's cheek flared, it looked like he was deciding between answering her question and dismissing her outright. He decided to address the other occupant of the room first. "Bjarni, leave us alone for a minute."

Bjarni groaned before skulking out of the room.

"These are raids," Hekla declared as soon as the door shut behind Bjarni.

"They are lawful searches," Kjartan responded. "Of individuals believed to be in possession of evidence related to a murder."

She shook her head. "There's nothing to suggest they have any information. I doubt the Ministry would approve a search of the homes of journalists—even these journalists—on such flimsy grounds. What else is there?"

Kjartan met Hekla's glare. "Suspicion of terrorist activity," he muttered before turning his head away.

"Fucking hell! So that's what this is turning into now? Why didn't you tell me?"

"It was just approved."

"That doesn't answer my question."

"I am the only one who knew. We needed to make sure everything was properly considered before making any decisions."

Hekla stared at Kjartan until he turned back to face her. "I don't believe you," she said. She walked toward the door. "I can't do my job if I don't know what you're planning behind my back," she added before storming out.

Hekla grabbed her coat and left the office. By the time she reached the ground floor, she had sent two texts. As she walked down the hallway, she popped a cigarette in her mouth and pulled on her coat. She fished around her pocket for a lighter as she approached the front doors, but stopped short when she looked outside. Reporters. Some on their phones in their cars, a few huddled in makeshift heating stations that extended from the sides of two vans.

She growled to herself as she turned around. She located the lighter, but now was trying to ascertain whether she had the separate key card that would allow her reentry through the back doors. All the while she stared at the screen of her phone, trying to will a response from the recipient of her texts.

⁂

"**B**ack on the death sticks, huh?" Bjarni cheerfully asked Hekla when she returned to the office. Hekla knew for a fact that Bjarni's hobbies included getting blackout drunk and watching adult humans pummel each other until one was unable to move. But she smiled. "Ready to talk with Mr. Sorenson?"

Hekla followed Bjarni into the mirror-image interrogation room where August sat. He looked terrible, she thought. The right side of his face was badly swollen, the only visible part of his right eye was marred by the bright red streaks of popped blood vessels. There were several prominent stitches under and above his brow, and the area still contained a fair amount of dried blood. She tried to suppress the urge to stare at his injuries, a task made more difficult by August, whose gaze remained fixed on her as she sat down next to Bjarni.

Bjarni made some introductory remarks, but August kept his eyes locked on Hekla.

After August ignored another of Bjarni's attempts to begin the interview, Bjarni changed his tactics. "Look at me!" he yelled.

Finally, August took his eyes off Hekla and gave Bjarni his attention. "How . . . can I help you?" August smiled.

Bjarni cleared his throat. "Thank you." He looked at a report laid out in front of him. "As I was saying—assaulting an officer, aiding a fugitive. These are very serious offenses."

Bjarni looked at August, who kept a stoic face.

"Personally, I don't think this is all your fault," Bjarni continued. "It's a bad situation that an old girlfriend got you involved in. I understand."

Hekla had trouble believing Bjarni could relate to that circumstance, unless it was a deep Oedipus metaphor, where the girlfriend was his mother, and the "bad situation" was his miserable existence.

"I want to help you," Bjarni implored. "But I'm going to need your help too. You understand? All you need to do is tell me the truth. That's it. If you do that, I can help. But if you're not going to tell me the truth, I can't do anything for you."

August put his hands together as if in prayer, then he cupped them around his nose and mouth. He closed his eyes and took a deep breath. "You . . . you want to help me?" he asked as he opened his eyes and slid his hands off his face.

"I do," Bjarni replied. "But you have to tell us everything you know."

"Mmh." August nodded. He leaned forward and tilted his head to the side, a faraway gaze showing itself in his good eye. "If I—if I tell you the crimes . . . I've committed. Or implicate others . . . in crimes. Ones that—that right now, you don't have sufficient evidence of to warrant detention. But if I provide that information to you . . . " August turned back to face Bjarni. "You . . . someone whose job it is to gather admissible evidence justifying detention, will . . . help me? Provide . . . unspecified assistance for me, in my—I dunno, life?"

Bjarni's throat contracted and expanded as he swallowed. "You think you're real clever?" he barked. "What are you? Some disgraced lawyer? No one cares about you here."

"I thought you wanted to help me."

"I don't need to waste my time with you—"

"Don't."

"If you don't want to talk—"

"I don't."

"With us, then we are going to charge you with—"

"With what?" August raised his voice. "Getting thrown into a dresser? By one of your . . . Stasi officers? Fuck!" There was a deep, powerful anger evident in the last expletive, as though something much more significant than an overly ambitious detective was bothering August. The outburst caused Hekla to pull back and even Bjarni to be momentarily subdued—a look of fear briefly registering on his face.

Bjarni tried to compensate for the display of vulnerability with volume. "Don't you dare talk to me like that!"

"Sorry," August's voice was low and contrite. He offered his hands up in apology. "I'm . . . I'm sorry. I shouldn't . . . have raised my voice."

Bjarni shuffled the report in front of him. He started to speak but August cut him off with a pained groan.

"Ehhmmh. It's just . . . " The left side of August's face spasmed, and he started tapping the fingers of his right hand against the back of his left in some sort of poorly executed pattern. "I can't always . . . find the right words. It's . . . in situations like this. I want to make sure . . . I'm clear."

"We can understand," Bjarni interjected. "You just need to answer my questions."

"Please," August's voice hinted at its earlier amplification. "Please . . . let me finish. I have *trouble* . . . properly expressing myself. These situations . . . with a cop, or law enforcement— someone in your position. When you suggest . . . to someone in jail, or prison, a witness—really anyone. When you tell them to *trust* you . . . that you're going to *help* them."

August's lip twitched. Bjarni opted to let this second of silence pass without opening his mouth.

"It's rare . . . this opportunity," August continued. "All I can really say . . . or do . . . with such a kind offer . . . is to tell you to *fuck of* and *go to hell.*"

Bjarni yowled something incomprehensible as he leapt to his feet and slammed his hands on the table, his chair falling to the floor behind him.

August was undeterred. "Just . . . fuck off," he continued as Bjarni cursed in Icelandic. "Fuck the fuck off. . . . Do you hear me? Go to hell. And fuck off."

Bjarni pointed aggressively at August. "You're going to be sorry!" He shoved the report toward August before storming out of the room and slamming the door behind him.

August sat back in his chair. Hekla shot him a look as if to ask if that were truly necessary. But there was also more than a hint of concern in her eyes. She took a deep breath and got to her feet. She gave August a nod and then quickly walked away. He managed to throw her one last unpleasant look before she left.

CHAPTER THIRTY

AUGUST WAS LED OUT OF THE STATION BY A GIANT.
He wondered if the giant was playing the role of bouncer, ensuring the disgruntled suspect didn't break anything on his way out. They had forced him to stay the night in the cell, but, as August and the bloated attorney from the embassy had anticipated, they didn't have any basis to keep him longer. They could have charged him with assaulting an officer, he supposed, but that would also likely require them to justify the condition of his face.

Once they were outside, the giant looked at him for a moment. Then he reached into his pocket. "Hekla thought you might want these," Gunnar said as he held out a pack of cigarettes and a lighter.

August looked skeptically at Gunnar. He reached into his coat pocket and retrieved his own pack of cigarettes. The package was crushed. August pulled back the top to see that nearly every cigarette was broken. His lips curled into a frown. He gave a resigned nod, put the smashed pack back in his pocket, and accepted the gift from Gunnar.

"Thanks," August said. He slid off a glove to light a cigarette before quickly pulling it back on. He then waited for Gunnar to follow the nicety with some sort of request. Instead, Gunnar just looked around.

"Do you need a ride?"

August furrowed his brow. "Ah," he winced, reflexively lifting his hand to his face. This time he stopped himself before his fingers made contact. "Okay," he mumbled, unsure of how he could communicate with a cop without employing a look of disbelief.

It was quiet for most of the 40-minute drive to August's hotel. American pop-punk music briefly burst from the speakers of Gunnar's well-worn hybrid SUV when he started the engine, but Gunnar quickly turned the volume off. August quite liked the music, though silence was preferable to the risk of conversation, so he spent most of the ride staring out the window at the incredible early morning sky.

When they got close to the hotel, Gunnar started to grin. "Fuck the fuck off," he said, letting out a small chuckle that was soon followed by a deep belly laugh. "I like that."

August smiled sheepishly.

"Bjarni," Gunnar added. "He does suck."

Now August laughed as well.

Gunnar stopped the car at the hotel's main entrance.

"Thanks for the ride," August said as he opened the door and stepped out.

"One more thing," Gunnar said.

August looked back inside the car.

"Hekla wanted me to tell you she's sorry. She didn't mean for it to happen like that."

August contemplated this for a moment. Then he nodded. "Right. Well . . . thanks again." He shut the door.

The lighting inside the hotel made August flinch. The disorienting effect of moving from darkness to bright, artificial light, coupled with his head injury, also made him skip his usual check-in at the front desk.

"Sir," one of the clerks called out. It was a young kid who often worked the desk—exceedingly polite, with dark blond hair that he was always pushing away from his eyes. "Excuse me. Sir."

August stopped in his tracks. Oh right, he thought, the arrest. The hotel probably had some clause that lets them cancel a reservation when Seal Team Viking grabs you from your room. He turned around with nervous anticipation. The clerk's head pulled back as he gasped, with an inhale so sharp that August could hear.

August was confused a moment before he remembered how he looked. "Oh," he said as he pointed to his face. "This . . . yeah. Cops."

The clerk laughed nervously.

"Is my, um . . . room . . . still available?" he asked.

"Of course," the clerk cheerily responded. "There's still a small area that's drying. They needed to do a second treatment on the carpet from where—" the clerk gestured on his head, approximating the location of August's injury.

"Yeah. I'm sorry . . . about that."

"No, don't apologize," the clerk sounded genuinely upset. "We're sorry for what happened to you. We thought the room would be ready by now. We can move you to a new room if you'd like." He looked down at his computer. "Let me see what's available."

"No. No . . . it's okay. I'm—I'm good."

"Are you sure?"

"Yeah. Thank you though." God they were lovely here, he thought, apologizing for the bloodstain that *he* left when the cops arrested a fugitive in *his* room. Unauthorized bleeding was probably a misdemeanor, at a minimum, in the States these days. He smiled and gave a wave. "Have a good day."

"Wait." The clerk rifled beneath the desk. He pulled out a thick envelope and placed it on the counter. "You have a package."

August's face lit up—the left side, at least.

The clerk held out a pen. "Here. You just have to sign for it."

CHAPTER THIRTY-ONE

*D*EEEE-DEE-DEE-DEE-DEE-DEE DEEEE-DEE-DEE-DEE-
dee-dee deeee-dee——

Hekla silenced the alarm on her phone. In addition to her usual alerts, she had now taken to setting periodic alarms whenever she was engaged in a task that left open the possibility that she might inadvertently doze off. She hadn't fallen asleep this time, but considering the way her lifeless eyes were staring through the papers in her hands, she might as well have snuck in a nap.

She was sitting in the driver's seat of her police wagon, parked on the street in front of the Envoy hotel, reviewing a flow chart Val had created. It was close to 1:40 p.m., and she was exhausted. Beyond exhausted, actually. It had been a day since she arrested Aldís and August, and she was spent.

She had come to the Envoy to inform Susan of the arrest and to give her a general update on the case. She was certain that Susan already knew as much about the case as she did, but she wanted to speak with her anyway. Kjartan could articulate no procedural objections when Hekla informed him of her planned visit, but he certainly didn't sound pleased with the idea.

In general, though, the mood was much more relaxed at the station. The extra staff that had been brought in for the manhunt had been sent back home, and most of the NBI and Reykjavík police who had been working nonstop since the murder were given the day off.

Aldís was being held indefinitely on a Ministry of

Justice-approved "charge first, find evidence sufficient to convict later" basis, and Kjartan either didn't know or wasn't telling Hekla what the raids had turned up—if anything. It seemed like someone should keep the actual investigation moving along, Hekla thought. Providing information to the spouse of the victim didn't quite fit that description, but it was something. If she also used the opportunity to stop by the room that she knew Steingrímur was occupying, well, that just showed efficient police work, she reasoned.

She looked at her watch again. Almost time. She downed the last few sips of her room-temperature coffee in one gulp, got out of the car, and made her way to the hotel.

After Jack's death, Susan had hired a security team that accompanied her whenever she went out in public. Not coincidentally, so had a very specific set of government representatives and business executives. The hotel already was a safe space for people like Susan and Steingrímur though. Access to the top floor was restricted to occupants of the two suites and their guests. People needed a keycard or assistance from a member of the hotel's staff to reach the floor by elevator. There were two stairwells, but they were exit-only. Hekla didn't have a card or permission from the suite occupants, but her badge was enough to convince the staff to let her up.

She rode to the top floor and tried to spot all the security cameras between the elevator and Susan's room. At about 1:50 p.m., she knocked on the door.

Susan answered the door wearing leggings and what Hekla was quite certain was one of the fleece pullovers she saw in Jack's wardrobe. Hekla's chest briefly grew tight upon recognizing the fleece.

"What do you want?" Susan asked with a weariness that seemed new to her.

"Can I come in?"

Susan gave a resigned nod and Hekla followed her inside.

"Are you alone?" Hekla asked as she looked around. This suite was unnecessarily large. There was a formal sitting area, separate entertainment and dining spaces, a full bathroom, and a bedroom with an en suite bigger than most ordinary hotel rooms.

"I think you know the answer to that," Susan responded dryly.

Hekla grimaced. "No business meeting, I meant." She gestured to the large coffee table that had been turned into a makeshift office—a wireless printer, two laptops, pens, binder clips, a stapler, and all manner of documents spread across its face.

Susan gave a nod and soft grunt in response. Hekla took a seat on one of the two sofas facing the table. Susan sat in a plush armchair across from her.

"I'm also aware that you've hired private security," Hekla asked as much as stated.

"Can you blame me?"

"No—I just—" she decided to abandon this line of inquiry. "We made an arrest in your husband's case."

"I heard."

"There were a number of documents found on the suspect's laptop."

Susan's expression hardened.

"Most of them didn't have anything to do with your husband," Hekla continued. "If his death has something to do with your business here, there could still be a threat."

Less than ten minutes after Hekla arrived, Susan asked her to leave. It was strange, Hekla thought, watching money conflict with the personal welfare of the grotesquely rich. Money was what gave these people their sense of invulnerability. It was safety, it was power. She supposed that in Susan's mind, there might not *be* any room for the idea that a business interest—the acquisition of more money—could be an *impediment* to life.

Still, Susan's firm response was surprising. Hekla thought she had seen something in her back at the station—a break in the façade, a glimmer of recognition, some sort of understanding that death is equal even if life isn't. It wasn't like she was asking Susan to take a vow of poverty in exchange for justice. She was telling Susan that her *life was in jeopardy* for Christ's sake. She was asking her to risk one business deal for exponentially higher odds of not being fucking murdered. And Susan would have none of it.

Hekla stood in the hallway outside Susan's room for a good minute. She sent a text and then walked to Steingrímur's room. Before Steingrímur even answered the door, Hekla realized that she wouldn't be able to interact with him for long. Her body and mind were simply not up to the task. Steingrímur invited her in and seemed willing to repeat at least some of the song and dance that he had performed when Hekla visited him at his house. But she had no interest in reprising her role. She could barely even look him in the eye. After a few minutes, she excused herself.

She found herself gripping tight to the metal rail on the side of the elevator car as it carried her back down. She felt lightheaded, and the urge to vomit had returned. The doors opened and she walked slowly toward the front doors. She stopped near the center of the lobby and turned back. To the right of the elevators was a bar. To the left was the hotel's restaurant, a highly rated seafood establishment.

She wasn't sure what to do next. She didn't want to leave, but she knew there was no good reason for her to hang around the hotel after making her official visits. Standing around foolishly didn't look much better though. Her body decided for her. She half-sat, half-collapsed on a firm chaise lounge, light blue with velvet throws—part of a set of similarly styled furniture in the center of the spacious lobby. Her stomach and head continued to swirl and now her jaw was clenched tight.

After a minute, Hekla took a strained breath and pushed herself off the couch. With wobbly, uncooperative legs, she forced herself toward the entrance. Her arm tingled as her palm, and then her fingers, wrapped around the cold brass handle of the large glass doors. She leaned back and pulled. The door started to move when an unearthly sound forced her hand open and brought her shoulders to her ears.

⁂

The sound was so loud and jarring that Hekla's instinct was to recoil as though she were being physically attacked. She scanned the room. Five or six guests were in the lobby. Two employees stood behind the front desk. The guests looked around, part perplexed, part annoyed, as they gravitated toward the front doors. The two employees looked helplessly at one another before one of them disappeared into a back room. There was no visible smoke or other indication of an active fire.

After the initial shock, the noise gave Hekla a jolt of energy. She ran to the front desk. Before she could even open her mouth, a terrified scream broke through the sound of the fire alarm.

"Hellllp!"

Hekla looked over and saw a horrified Susan rush out of the elevator. As Susan ran for the front doors, she let out a sound that was part plea for help, part anguished wail. By now the lobby was filling up with confused guests evacuating the other floors. Hekla dodged them as she sprinted to intercept Susan. She threw out her arm and Susan ran into it. Hekla gently cradled her for a moment before turning her body so that they were facing one another. She held Susan tight by the shoulders. Tears streamed from Susan's eyes.

"What is it?" she asked.

Susan's eyes, full of terror and dread, answered before she did. "He's dead!"

"Who? Who's dead?"

"Steingrímur!"

"""""""""""""""""

Hekla was caught between securing the scene and investigating a crime that demanded immediate attention. Fortunately, it didn't take long for two patrol officers to arrive. The officers helped with the increasingly panicked crowd as Hekla went to check on Steingrímur.

Officially, she should have waited for backup. A situation like this might even warrant a call to the special unit that she was becoming all too familiar with. But she had no intention of standing around. She declined the officers' offer of non-lethal weapons, as well as their suggestion that she retrieve her firearm from the trunk of her wagon. She wasn't afraid anyone was waiting to ambush her. She just needed to see what was up there.

The on-site manager gave Hekla a master access card and the detective hurried to the elevators. The doors shut behind her as though she were being enclosed in a crypt. The restless crowd and sirens from approaching emergency vehicles went silent, leaving her alone with a more somber, elevator-muffled version of the earsplitting fire alarm. She could feel her heartbeat speed up as the elevator rose. She wasn't sure if she wanted the ride to go on indefinitely or be done with at once. It didn't matter. Within seconds, it eased to a smooth stop and the doors slid open.

She hesitated. Not a half-hour earlier, she stood in this exact same space. But now everything seemed different. The sense of emptiness was palpable. Even with the alarm blaring, the floor seemed like a ghost town. She stuck her foot out to prevent the elevator doors from automatically closing, and quickly peered out in the direction of Susan's room. Nothing. Hekla turned to look the other way. A blue suede shoe was sticking out of the door to Steingrímur's room.

Hekla stepped out of the elevator and walked cautiously toward Steingrímur's room. When she got closer, she could see that the shoe was Steingrímur's. His foot was in the shoe, and all parts of his body were appropriately attached. But the normalcy ended there. Steingrímur was splayed out on his back, with a thick pool of blood encircling his head and the top half of his body. It looked almost as if he were floating. A deep wound punctured the center of his neck. Streaks of crimson marked his neck and colored the top of the white T-shirt he wore underneath his blazer. A large hunting knife was positioned conspicuously inside the room. Haphazardly scattered about his body, soaking up blood, were hundreds of U.S. dollars and euros, and thousands of krónur.

Hekla wasn't sure how long she spent staring at Steingrímur's body. She blinked and the floor was filled with every cop, investigator, technician, and forensics personnel that could fit in the hallway. They carefully made their way along paths of plastic steppingstones that had been arranged to prevent evidence contamination. Both rooms on the floor, as well as the elevator and one of the stairwells were being carefully pored over.

Kjartan placed his hand on Hekla's shoulder. He seemed to be trying to offer words of assurance, saying something like, "it's not your fault," or "you did everything you could." When she was able to recognize what was going on, Hekla shook him off and made her way to the other end of the hallway. She took a pair of latex gloves and paper booties from a technician, put them on, and made her way into Susan's room.

The hotel was a zoo, but within a few hours, some semblance of order was bound to return. And when it did, Susan and the Americans would undoubtedly do all they could to keep curious eyes from looking into Susan's role in the mayhem that had besieged this peaceful island. But right now, at least, this entire floor, up to and including any potential entrances and exits, was a crime scene. Hekla took out her phone and started to record video.

CHAPTER THIRTY-TWO

It was strange how a fight to survive could quell any doubts about the merits of survival. A sense of purpose did the same thing. In the days leading up to the cop's first visit to his hotel, August had concluded for the second time in a very short period that he no longer had any interest in continuing life as an active participant. Passive participation not really working for him either, his options were limited. The only thing he knew for sure was that he was done. Having weighed the pros and cons, he would prefer to not really bother anymore. His unsuccessful attempt at the ultimate exit back in Copenhagen hadn't really changed his calculus. It had just eliminated one path from consideration.

But then the cop showed up. She engaged his mind, and he remembered what it felt like to believe, to care, to potentially even matter. Immediately following that, other humans took away his autonomy. When they restrained him and held him captive, they made his fate their decision instead of his own. So in short order, he had both a purpose and a fight to survive, or, at least, a fight to be put back in charge of his own survival. Doubts were quelled. Life was worth pursuing.

Or maybe it wasn't either of those things, he considered. Maybe it was just about distractions. Most people had so much to deal with that they never had an opportunity to question their purpose with any real urgency. They may think it's all for family or love, or any of the other, undeniably beautiful but exceedingly rare, unevenly distributed, and fleeting experiences that life offers. But that's just shit that keeps us busy. The search and struggle kept everyone from wondering *why*—every single waking moment of every single fucking day—they should keep bothering with the searching and the struggling. It prevented the exploration of alternatives to a game that no one ever volunteered to play, where the only prize is the ability to temporarily abate suffering, and where participants are forced to continue until all their beloved teammates die, their body stops working, or some other tragedy befalls them and those they love.

Fucking Christ, August chided himself. It took him just a minute to turn the notion of not feeling suicidal for a decent amount of time into something almost as bleak as the act itself.

"It's okay," he said to himself as he took a deep breath.

All in all, he was doing well, particularly considering it hadn't been much more than a day since those goons broke into his hotel room, arrested Aldís, and smashed his face. He was concerned about Aldís, and not particularly pleased with the cop who had used him, but Aldís was tough, and cops were cops. It was a relief just to see Aldís, to know she was okay, to hear her voice and apologize to her, finally, after all these years. His head hurt like hell, but there were a few moderately strong painkillers in his coat pocket that the hospital must have provided. That helped. He was also excited to have received a package from Jenson. He had given it only a cursory glance before passing out for what turned out to be just a few hours. But it was sure to make for good reading later. The cops had confiscated his laptop and phone. Fortunately, the documents Hekla had given him were safely secured, although he wasn't quite sure whom he was protecting most by keeping them hidden.

And now, he was heading back to the diner. A little later than usual, but there was still some light left in the sky. He was so lost in his thoughts that it wasn't until he was a few meters away that he noticed something was off. Almost everyone inside was looking at their phone or looking at someone else's. Most of them were on their feet, too, exchanging words and worried glances with one another when their eyes moved from the screens.

August traveled the remaining distance in several long strides. He threw open the door. His entrance garnered significant attention, as though he were there to provide answers. But he just looked back at them with confusion.

"What's up?" he asked in an Icelandic that would frighten most native speakers, even if his face did not.

⁘⁘⁘⁘⁘⁘⁘⁘

Having just been released from the custody of the Icelandic police and with the military-adjacent arm of his former employer paying close attention to him, August was certain it wasn't the *best* idea to show up at the scene of Iceland's second shocking murder in less than a month. Given both parties' apparent indifference to the guilt of those they detained, however, it didn't necessarily seem like the *worst* idea.

To the best of his knowledge, Aldís was still in prison for a crime that she almost certainly couldn't have committed. The bloated billionaire who was just killed had a strong link to the dead American asshole, a link August was only aware of because one of Iceland's finest spent a recent afternoon going over it with him—another aspect of this whole mess that confused the hell out of him. The dead men weren't just hoarding all the money while people suffered, they were part of, or closely associated with, a mining deal that could permanently alter the relationship between the land and people in Iceland. August didn't expect this piece of information to be shouted out, but he thought there would be some mention or strategic leak—something to assure a populace as unaccustomed to wanton killing (as the *modern* Icelanders were, at least) that they were unlikely to be targeted next.

August needed to know what the fuck was going on. The fact that the connection between the mining deal and the murders remained secret made him even more interested.

The city was packed by the time August arrived. Barricades prevented vehicles from traveling on any street in a two-block radius around the hotel, resulting in another five blocks that were largely unnavigable. Fortunately, he recognized the signs of traffic and turned back on the 41 before he got too deep into the city. He drove along the water and parked near the Harpa. He got out of his car and walked along the water until the 41 turned into Lækjargata street. He crossed over the various, hectic intersections, and headed west across a parking lot toward the hotel. He wasn't more than a few steps into the lot when he spotted that familiar looking, rust-orange Jeep.

CHAPTER THIRTY-THREE

It was pitch dark when Hekla left the hotel. By that time, Kjartan had already given an impromptu press conference to the throng of reporters that had congregated on the street outside the cordoned-off area. A large crowd still waited to shout questions at Hekla as she finally made her way through the front doors. She checked the time. Soon an international set would swell these numbers, she thought. She still had nothing to say but would be grateful for their presence. A critical mass would make it harder for the media to be manipulated. At least she hoped that would be the case.

On the adjacent street, she saw a reporter for RUV getting ready for a shot. One member of the team was setting up a light box while the cameraman adjusted his equipment. Hekla recognized the reporter, Margrét Harðardóttir. Margrét had a round, youthful face and long auburn hair. She usually only ventured outside the studio for festive occasions, like the Icelandic National Day parade. The cameraman gave a thumbs up sign. Hekla stepped behind another spectator in the small crowd that had gathered to watch the report.

"Today, in a terrifying act of violence, prominent businessman and philanthropist Steingrímur Eggertsson was found dead in his room at the Envoy hotel after an apparent knife attack," Margrét announced.

Hekla cringed at the utterance of the word *philanthropist*. She immediately began to question her belief that such startling incidents could leave room for an objective analysis of the deceased and their business operations.

"This comes less than one month after the killing of American billionaire Jack Drumman at the Azure Spa and Hotel," Margrét continued. "These acts of violence have frightened the country and raised serious questions about law enforcement's ability to solve and prevent brutal crimes. Most troubling is the lack of information being provided by authorities."

Hekla slinked her way back out of the crowd. *Lack of information.* Margrét was right about that. She was just wrong to think that most of the police investigating the crime *had* the information. There was nothing Hekla would have liked more than to share with the public *all* the details surrounding the murders, including the links between the victims and possible motives for the crimes. It was the kind of knowledge that would assuage any fears that average citizens might have regarding their own safety. The problem was, much of the information was still being kept secret from *her.* Even if she knew, she couldn't reveal it. That should change soon though. At least, she hoped it would.

She got in her car and waited while a uniformed officer cleared a path for her to leave. She was on her way back to the station when Gunnar called. Still at least a kilometer away, she could already see that a crowd had formed outside of the station—it seemed as though everyone who was not still at the hotel had moved the short distance to the police headquarters. Hekla pulled over and answered her phone. "Yeah?"

"The bag," Gunnar's excited voice came through her car's speakers.

"What bag?" Hekla asked in response, even though she had a good idea what Gunnar was referring to. She had sent Gunnar and Val the video from her walk-through of Susan's room the second she stopped filming—the video she shot just in case something should happen to the room or items in it after she left. The video she sent just in case something should happen to her phone or her.

"The tote bag. From the Azure. Susan had it in her room at the Envoy."

"So?"

"It's too many. It means the girl was lying."

Hekla furrowed her brow. "What do you mean? There were two per room. Now we know where the other one was. Susan took it when she left."

"No. The girl brought another one to the room. Her supervisor saw her take it after Jack checked in. The girl said the couple asked for an extra."

"Wait, what? *What girl?* And why didn't you tell me?"

"It was the girl who works at the Azure. The one you spoke with. Elísa Pálsdóttir. She told you there were two bags in the room, right? But her supervisor told me that Elísa brought them another bag—that the couple requested an extra. He inspected the suite before they checked in and was certain it had two tote bags. I thought it might just be a mix-up. That's why I didn't say anything. I wanted to confirm with the girl before making a big deal."

"Well, maybe the supervisor was mistaken—Jack or Susan could have just been asking for a second bag. Right?"

"Then why wouldn't the girl tell you about that? It seems like something she would remember. And then the supervisor would have to be wrong too. If one bag is in Susan's suite at the Envoy, the girl's story doesn't make sense. Either what she told you or what she told her supervisor."

Hekla pursed her lips. "Maybe. She could have been confused.

It was probably quite a shock finding that body. You couldn't speak with her?"

"No. She wasn't at work when I spoke with the supervisor. The hotel manager said she needed to take some time off. He said he'd tell me when she was back. I left a message, but she hasn't called. I was going to follow up this week but haven't had a chance with everything else going on."

"Mmh," Hekla grunted as her face turned sour. She certainly would have liked to have been informed of all this, but understood and, in some ways, appreciated Gunnar's tact. Of course, she also had noticed the tote bag in Susan's room and knew there was almost certainly an inconsistency in the girl's story. But she did not like the focus that it put on a surely frightened-out-of-her-wits teenager and didn't know it would turn out to be such a pertinent clue. "Okay," she finally added after a long pause, "follow up with the girl and keep me updated. But Gunnar, keep it quiet. I don't want to see this get out of our hands before we even know if it's something."

"Of course."

She ended the call and looked out her windshield at the mass of reporters waiting outside the station.

It all hurt Hekla's head to think about, but she knew that Gunnar was onto something, even if he couldn't articulate it clearly. In fact, Hekla sensed a weakness in the girl's story well before seeing the tote bag in Susan's room.

Gunnar realized that the girl's story didn't add up. Literally. She told Hekla that there were two bags in Jack's suite. But she told her supervisor that she had brought over a third. So, that's why Gunnar was suspicious. Why would she lie about the number of bags—and what else was she lying about?

CHAPTER THIRTY-FOUR

THE STATION WAS JUST AS CHAOTIC AS IT APPEARED from a distance. Hekla spent a fair amount of time working her way through the crowd just to get into the building. When she arrived at her floor, she was confronted by a line of officers and witnesses stretching the entire length of the hallway. She shuffled past them into the office, only to find another, smaller line of witnesses being funneled in and out of interrogation rooms.

Hekla's gaze immediately fell on a haggard-looking gentleman swaying back and forth near the front of the queue. It was Logi, and he looked high, drunk, or both. As he staggered forward, his head turned just enough to face Hekla. They locked eyes—hers wide, his glassy and unfocused. She tried not to react, but the moment was gone in a second anyway as Logi turned his attention back to some undefined spot on the floor.

Hekla put her head down and marched straight to Kjartan's office. He was on the phone but beckoned her inside.

"Yes, that's fine," Kjartan said into the handset. "Listen, I have to go now, but I'll see you shortly. Call if anything changes. Okay." Kjartan hung up and turned his attention to Hekla. "Officers from Akureyri are coming down to help. Their chief is on his way, too."

She nodded.

"Here," Kjartan said, handing her a report.

"What's this?" She looked over the document. It appeared to be a list of items seized during the raids on the staff at The Fólk. She stared inquisitively at Kjartan. "When did you get this?"

"Just a few hours ago."

She shook her head.

"Third page," he said.

She turned to the third page and ran her finger down the list. "Oh hell," she moaned. There it was. Among the items seized from Logi's home were U.S. dollars and euros matching the amount Aldís had converted several weeks ago. "Damn it. She was telling the truth."

"Appears so."

"We wasted our time on her." Hekla angrily held up the report. "How can this just be coming to us now? They must have known about this last night."

"I told you—I just got it myself. It was above me."

"There isn't supposed to *be* anyone above you."

Kjartan's cheek twitched as he gave an almost imperceptible shrug.

Hekla half-sighed, half-growled. "We should have been focusing on finding the real killer."

"Nothing is certain yet."

"What do you mean? Don't tell me we're still going to hold her."

"They're running DNA samples from the knife and double-checking with the bank to see that the money is the same. If the knife is clean and the notes match, they'll release her."

"Unbelievable," she muttered.

There was a moment of silence before Kjartan spoke again, "He was at the Envoy you know."

"Who was?"

"Logi Stefánsson. The traveling companion."

She nodded. "I saw."

"It's curious, don't you think?"

"I'm not sure what to think anymore," she snapped back.

Her phone vibrated. It was Gunnar. She answered, pressing the phone tight against her ear.

"She's not at her home." Gunnar sounded out of breath. Hekla looked over at Kjartan who stared back with curious eyes. "I spoke with her roommate. She says she hasn't seen her in days."

Hekla winced. "Shit."

There are more than a few reasons why a 19-year-old may suddenly decide to leave town for a few nights. The world of possibilities narrows dramatically when the teenager is as mature and responsible as Elísa Pálsdóttir seemed to be. So, when her disappearance corresponds with an increased focus on her by law enforcement who believe she has critical information regarding two murders, it's hard not to jump to conclusions.

These assumptions were Hekla's biggest fear now, and they informed the decision she made immediately following Gunnar's call. She knew that information about Elísa—her job and sudden disappearance—would get out one way or another. Whoever it was exactly—the Americans, Kjartan and the people above him—it was clear that someone was conducting an investigation in the shadows. And it was clear to Hekla that whoever was conducting that investigation had motives and a sense of justice that differed considerably from hers. She wanted to make sure that she got to Elísa first, and she concluded that making the search for Elísa public would afford the girl the greatest protection in the meantime.

So, Hekla told Kjartan about Elísa and what Gunnar had learned regarding the Azure tote bags: That there were inconsistencies in Elísa's story—the one she told Hekla, her supervisor, or both. She asked Kjartan to send her to Grindavik to search for Elísa, but he said no. He said he needed her to focus on the investigation into Steingrímur's murder. She didn't argue. There wasn't much that could trump the investigation of a murder of an American billionaire at the Azure, but this would qualify.

⁕⁕⁕⁕⁕⁕⁕⁕⁕⁕⁕⁕⁕

Hekla met with Bjarni and another senior detective, Einar Ingólfsson, so they could compare notes before moving forward. Einar was mostly bald, with his remaining straw-colored hair meticulously groomed into what looked like a perfectly even, upside-down crown that went around the back of his head from ear to ear. He was an affable man in his mid-40s, with an almost inhuman level of patience when dealing with members of the public and with suspects. Hekla invited Val along as well, ostensibly to take notes, but really to listen in so she didn't have to spend time going over the same information with them later.

"What's *she* doing here?" Bjarni said derisively upon spotting Val. Val looked away.

"*They're* helping," Hekla stated in a manner that precluded debate. "What have you both got?"

"Have you seen the video?" Einar asked.

Hekla nodded. There was surveillance footage from the hallway that showed most of Steingrímur's attack. His assailant, wearing a mask and a hooded parka, entered from one of the stairwells, walked to Steingrímur's suite, and stabbed Steingrímur in the throat after the victim answered the door. "No luck with an ID, I imagine?"

"No," Einar responded. "His face isn't visible. Based on height and general proportions, it seems safe to say it's a male, but we can't confirm yet. And no one at the hotel saw anyone dressed like him. If it is indeed a him—which, as I've mentioned, we believe it to be."

"Right. How about a timeline?"

"Yes." Einar looked at his notes. "According to the surveillance video, you left Steingrímur's suite at 14:07. At 14:10, we have the assailant entering the hallway from the stairwell—"

"Is that when the fire alarm sounded?"

"No. Interestingly enough, it's not." Hekla raised an eyebrow. Einar continued, now without consulting his notes, "The assailant proceeds to Steingrímur's door. He waits there a moment—he's very close to the door so it's hard to see if he's knocking or what—and when Steingrímur answers, he immediately thrusts the knife into his throat. Steingrímur falls backward into the room and the assailant follows. The whole thing takes just a few minutes, and then the assailant goes back to the stairwell."

"So, the alarm goes off then?" Bjarni asked.

"No, there's still another delay." Einar looked back at his notes. "He exits the room at 14:14 but the alarm doesn't sound until 14:26."

Both Hekla and Bjarni looked perplexed.

"It's an automatic alarm?" Hekla asked.

"Yes. If the door opens, the alarm sounds—unless it's been disabled. According to the manager I spoke with, all the alarms had been inspected recently and were working properly."

"Double check that."

Einar nodded.

"How do you disable it?" Bjarni asked.

"There's a key," Einar answered. "It allows the door to be opened without setting off the alarm."

"Okay, well find out who had access to the key," Hekla directed. "If it wasn't triggered when the assailant entered or exited, what do you think set it off?"

"If I had to guess, I'd say the back door. Unless he went back into the hotel, but then he would have been easy to spot. On the ground floor, another door opens to an alleyway behind the hotel. That would have set it off."

"But if he had a key, why would he set the alarm off then, after being so careful?" Hekla asked.

Einar shook his head. "I'm not sure. Maybe he was flustered after the murder and forgot to use it. Or he just wanted to get out quicker."

"Maybe he wanted to set it off," Bjarni offered. "Create chaos."

"Could be," Hekla said. "See if there is any footage from around the hotel, maybe a witness who saw him leave. I wasn't there long, but I didn't see anyone inside the hotel with a hood up and face covered. I'm sure he was also bloodier when he ran off. That might attract attention."

"Okay," Einar said.

"He must have been waiting for you to leave," Bjarni said as he looked at Hekla. "Are you sure you didn't see anything?"

Hekla held Bjarni's stare. "How would he know I'm there?"

Bjarni gave a low grunt.

She returned her attention to Einar. "Do we have a full record of who was on the floor?"

"Yes," Einar said as he looked back at his notes. "That day Steingrímur came up at 8:50—"

"He didn't spend the night?"

"No. He was basically using the suite as an office while Susan was there. He used his card to enter his room at 8:54 and then again at 12:35. Ms. Teele had a guest who was let up by the front desk at 9:28—no name was provided. Room service delivered coffee to Ms. Teele at approximately 10:06. At 10:35, housekeeping cleaned Steingrímur's suite. Room service for him at 13:10. You at 13:47 and that's it."

After going over the basics, Bjarni and Einar caught Hekla up on the interviews that had been conducted so far. Unsurprisingly, Susan had opted to give a statement through the embassy attorney. Hekla wondered if it struck anyone else as odd that Susan had co-opted an active American State Department attorney to serve as her personal counsel. Things had gotten pretty lax in America as far as ethics were concerned, but this seemed over the top even for them. The brief statement described Susan as returning to work after Hekla left the room, hearing Hekla—outside Steingrímur's room she presumed—followed by the sound of a door being shut. A few minutes later, Susan heard another voice, a woman who sounded like Hekla, though Susan was less certain this time. She didn't hear anything else until the fire alarm. When the alarm went off, she left her room and saw Steingrímur's foot sticking out of his door. That's when she saw he had been attacked.

Detectives had already spoken with every staffer who had been on the floor that day. They noted the unidentified guest in Susan's room, but had only been able to provide a vague description that could apply to a quarter of Iceland's population—middle-aged white guy with dark blond or light brown hair. Hekla instructed Einar and Bjarni to try and ID the man from security footage. She also told them to find out who had visited either Susan or Steingrímur the previous few days.

"Who else did we talk to?" Hekla asked.

"Logi," Bjarni practically yelped out.

Hekla nodded as casually as she could. "Right. The currency holder. What did he have to say?"

"Not much. Said he was at the bar. Drinking."

"Was he?"

"Bartender said so. I don't trust him though."

"The bartender or Logi?"

"Either."

Hekla narrowed her eyes at Bjarni. "Okay, well what am I supposed to do with that?"

"He's still here," Einar volunteered. "Given his connection, we thought it would be good if you had a chance to question him too."

Hekla put her hand to her mouth. She had hoped they would have finished interviewing Logi by now.

"You do, right?" Bjarni asked. "Want to ask more questions?"

Hekla gave Bjarni a brief stare. "Yes. Let's go."

As they left the room, they split, with Bjarni following Hekla to the interrogation room, and Einar and Val going the other way.

Hekla stopped abruptly. "What are you doing?" she asked Bjarni.

Bjarni held up his hands.

"You conducted the first interview with him, right? I'm not having you in the room again."

Bjarni sighed and rolled his eyes.

A slight grin briefly showed itself on Val's face.

Hekla gestured with her head to Einar. "You come with me. Bjarni, find out who could have gotten the key and go over that footage."

⁕⁕⁕⁕⁕⁕⁕⁕⁕⁕⁕⁕⁕

Right before entering the interrogation room, Hekla informed Einar that she wanted him to conduct the interview. He was surprised but seemed excited for the opportunity. She wasn't convinced she had the stamina to deal with Einar's exacting style, but it was a small price to pay to get out of having to ask the questions.

Logi appeared to be either passed out or asleep, with his cheek pressed flat against the table and arms encircling his head like a halo. Einar gently tapped the table near Logi's head as he sat down across from him. Logi roused. He looked tired and still reeked of alcohol, but he seemed to be more alert and cognizant of his surroundings than he had been when Hekla first saw him at the station.

Einar opened a folder. Hekla glanced over his shoulder. To her surprise, it appeared as though Einar had an entire list of questions ready to go.

"Mr. Stefánsson," Einar began. "What was your purpose for staying at the Envoy hotel?"

Logi grumbled incoherently.

"The reason you were staying at the hotel?" Einar rephrased.

"Work," Logi managed to articulate. "I told your jackass colleague already."

"You checked in two nights ago—are you saying that you were here for work the entire time?"

Logi shrugged. "I stay an extra night—two—sometimes."

"What for?"

"Why not?"

"Where were you last night?"

Hekla subtly shifted her eyes between Logi and Einar.

"Where was I?"

"It appears that you left the hotel in the middle of the night and didn't return until almost five in the morning."

There was a slight pause before Logi responded. "I don't know—I don't remember."

"You don't know what? If you left your room or where you went?"

Logi shook his head. "Either. I was drinking. I don't remember."

"What about today?"

"Definitely drinking."

Einar stared back, unamused.

"Is that against the law now?" Logi asked.

"It depends on what you do after."

Logi gave a sarcastic-sounding grunt in response.

Einar was much more precise than Hekla figured he'd be. Maybe it would have been better letting the aggressive but dim-witted Bjarni conduct the interview, she thought.

"Were you here for work anytime in December?" Einar asked.

"December?"

"That's right. Last month."

Logi shrugged. "Maybe. I think a few nights."

"Any idea which nights those were?"

"No."

"The hotel would have a record, you know."

"That's great. Go ask them then."

Hekla watched Einar scribble a note and then run his pen down the paper, toward the end of his prepared questions.

"When is the last time you traveled outside of the country?"

Logi stared defiantly at Einar. Whatever damage a day's worth of alcohol had inflicted upon his body and mind, it seemed to clear up, at least for a moment, rather quickly. "I think I'm done now," Logi stated with clarity. "If you're not charging me with something, I'm going home."

⁕⁕⁕⁕⁕⁕⁕⁕

Hekla settled into a trance as she watched the security camera footage of Logi at the bar. She had memorized the exact number of clicks it took to return to various timestamps in the video, and how many real-time seconds it took to cycle through 20 minutes of footage played at all the various speeds on the media player of her desktop computer. She watched, again and again, as Logi came in and out of the frame, sat down and got up, stayed still, and moved about. No matter how many times she viewed the video, all she could see was that Logi left the bar area at 14:02 and didn't return until 14:20. Eighteen minutes unaccounted for. Right when a guest several floors above was being murdered.

"His boss confirmed he was here for work."

Hekla startled in her chair. She looked up to see Einar standing next to her. "Whose boss?"

Einar nodded at the monitor. "Logi's."

She squinted at the time display on the screen. "It's 3:15. Tell me you didn't call someone at this hour."

"I don't think a lot of people are sleeping tonight. Everyone is on edge. I called—just to leave a message—but I received a call back right away."

"Christ. Do people really think they're the next logical victim after two billionaires are killed?"

Einar shrugged. Hekla let out a slight groan. The lack of sleep was affecting her differently now. She had stopped feeling tired and was now just angry. She stretched her neck, trying to wake herself up. "What did he or she say exactly?

"The boss said that Logi regularly traveled to Reykjavík for work. He used to just make day trips—returning late at night— but in the past year or so he started staying for a few nights sometimes. The people at the Envoy like him so they give him a courtesy discount."

"Why'd he suddenly go from day trips to overnights?"

"Not sure. He told his boss he liked the city. Something about wanting to enjoy himself more while he was still young enough to do so. He's been with them for over a decade, so the boss didn't have a problem with it. Company covers the first night but otherwise Logi pays himself."

"Hmm."

It was quiet for a moment. Then Einar spoke again. "Curious, isn't it?"

"What is?"

Einar gestured toward the screen.

"He's clearly piss drunk, but the bartender lets him stay there."

Hekla nodded. "Right. What did the bartender say about the time when Logi is off camera?"

"The bartender said he was in the bathroom. He even checked on him after a few minutes." Einar pointed to the screen. "I think it comes up at around 14:09."

Hekla scrolled the video to the 14:09 mark. Sure enough, the bartender left the frame for about 30 seconds before returning.

"I see. I guess that's a decent enough alibi then."

Einar nodded. "He also returned about seven or eight minutes before the alarm went off, so we know he wasn't the one who triggered it. Still curious."

She nodded. Einar took a step to leave.

"Oh. That thing you asked about being here in December—you don't think Logi had anything to do with *Jack's* murder, do you?"

Einar shook his head. "No. The only connection would have been Aldís, right? And we both know that's nonsense now. I just wanted to see how he'd respond."

"Right." She rubbed her eyes. "Well, good job."

CHAPTER THIRTY-FIVE

THE NEXT MORNING, HEKLA STOOD IN THE HALLWAY outside Steingrímur's suite at the Envoy hotel, her back and head resting against the wall. She watched Einar reenact the assailant's suspected movements—occasionally nodding and saying "yeah" or "okay" when he would look at her—without really paying attention. She was much more focused on her phone, taking it out repeatedly to make sure it was set to both ring and vibrate for incoming calls.

It wasn't like Einar was providing any new insight. The killer hadn't hidden from the camera, at least not here in the hallway, and forensics had already scoured every centimeter of the floor.

Now Einar was indicating for her to join him in the stairwell. She tried not to growl as she lumbered over.

"Sure," she uttered absentmindedly after Einar said some words with a slight raise in pitch on the last syllable. Unfortunately, this didn't seem to do the trick, as Einar kept staring expectantly at her. "But how?" he asked.

She followed his eyes to the fire exit door which had been kept open for the investigative team. There was no handle, just a reinforced metal bar that could be pushed to open the door. A narrow rectangular box with a keyhole at the bottom protruded eight or nine centimeters from the top of the door. Her eyes moved to the base of the door.

"Propped it open," she said, guessing that Einar's question related to the assailant's exit.

He nodded slowly. "Ah, yes. That would do it."

She guessed right. Fortunately, none of this was too hard. The assailant moved quick and packed light. It wasn't particularly noteworthy if she deduced that the killer didn't have time to fumble with a key while also keeping any trace of DNA off the door.

She followed Einar into the stairwell, and they made their way down.

"The manager said only one key disables the alarm on these doors," Einar said as they arrived at the landing at the bottom of the stairs. "He keeps it in his office. I saw it earlier. It's on the wall with a few other keys. It's hard to miss. He swears he never saw it missing and he's certain he locks his office when he's gone for more than a few minutes."

"How long would it take to make a copy?"

Hekla's question was more rhetorical, or at least not a line of inquiry she was seriously interested in right now, but Einar answered anyway. "I'll find out."

Two doors, both of which also were kept open for the detectives, were at the bottom of the stairwell. One door led inside to the bar area. The other led to the alley behind the hotel. The detectives spent a few minutes outside, walking the alley, before returning inside and heading to the bar area. The security camera that caught Logi was focused only on the bar itself, so Hekla and Einar spent some time testing various pathways that would allow someone to walk to the fire exit without being caught on video. It was possible, but it would require a route that would seem odd to anyone watching in the vicinity.

Hekla sat on a contoured stool with her back pressed against the glossy wooden bar. She watched as Einar made his fifth, and the pair's combined eighth, walk on a hypothetical path from the edge of the bar area to the fire exit door. Afterward, he came back to her with a slightly discouraged look on his face.

"Hard to imagine someone about to commit a murder walking around like that and not drawing attention, huh?" she asked.

"I find it hard to imagine anyone walking around like that at all. I suppose he could have entered from any floor though— perhaps even from outside?"

"Yeah. We'll have to look at the footage from each floor, see if there is anyone walking toward the stairwell that doesn't have a good reason for doing so."

Hekla's phone rang. She yanked it out of her pocket so quickly that she almost sent it flying. It was Kjartan.

"Yes," she answered.

"Have you heard from Gunnar?"

"No. Not yet."

Kjartan grunted.

"Did we get the results back from the knife?" she asked.

"Hm? Oh. No. We didn't."

There was a long pause that made Hekla nervous.

"I think we should ask for help," Kjartan finally said. "At least with finding the girl."

"We don't need help," Hekla responded sharply. "She's a 19-year-old girl, gone for a few days. We can find her."

"With help we can find her quicker. This does pertain to the murder of an American citizen. We have an obligation to keep them updated anyway. If they can provide us with some assistance as well, I don't see any reason why we shouldn't accept."

Hekla felt her face heat up. Her phone dug into the skin of her palm as she squeezed it tight. "It's not necessary," she said as calmly as possible.

Kjartan started to respond but Hekla cut him off. "Just give me one more day. Please. There's no reason to involve anyone else. It won't help us get information. It will only make things worse."

There was another long silence. Hekla considered saying more but wasn't quite sure how to further make her point without raising her voice and risk losing Kjartan completely.

"Okay," Kjartan said. Hekla could feel the muscles in her upper back and chest unwind. "One more day. But if we can't find her by then, we're going to ask for help."

CHAPTER THIRTY-SIX

Aldís didn't kill Steingrímur. The police didn't need a forensics report to know that. She was in their custody when he was attacked. What the forensics report did show, however, was that the knife used to kill Steingrímur had traces of Jack Drumman's blood around the base of its blade. Aside from Steingrímur's blood, there were no other substances or DNA on the knife. Additionally, while the wounds on each of victim's necks differed somewhat, they were consistent with what one could expect from an attack with the knife that was recovered. It was safe to assume that the same knife was used to kill both men.

And, *obviously*, there was the money. Both victims had thousands of U.S. dollars, euros, and krónur in, on, or around their bodies. It was a statement. To Hekla, the best way to determine the identity of the killer would be to figure out what that statement was, exactly. Similarly, the best way to figure out what that statement was, would be to figure out the connection between the victims. Kjartan disagreed. Hekla suspected that the pushback had something to do with what the two victims had in common. Actually, she suspected the pushback had something to do with *who* the two victims had in common: Susan. And Susan's business dealings.

"I'm not saying you're wrong," Kjartan said when Hekla suggested investigating what Jack and Steingrímur had in common. "We just need to focus on what's in front of us now."

Hekla had left Einar at the Envoy and was now back in Kjartan's office. "This is what's in front of us," she retorted. "It's *literally* in front of us. We have the knife. It's the same one that was used to kill Jack. We have to look at the connection between the victims."

"And you will, but we need to investigate all avenues before we start digging into the affairs of the spouse of a victim—particularly when they were both foreign guests."

"What does that even mean—all avenues? And foreign guests? They were here to make money. Christ. Why are you protecting her?"

Kjartan narrowed his eyes. "It's a delicate situation."

"So what? Should we pretend that a murder that was nearly identical to her husband's—that took place, what, less than ten meters away from her—still has nothing to do with her?"

"That's not what I'm saying."

"Then what *are* you saying? Exactly?"

Kjartan's cheek flared as he turned his head ever so slightly. It appeared to Hekla that she was close to crossing a line that was very hard for anyone to reach. "I *want you* to get all the information you can first," he said. "Find out what's going on with the girl, talk to her—"

Hekla started to protest, but Kjartan beat her to it, "*and* we can look at the relationships between the victims. Internally. Quietly. But I'm not going to let you put the wife of one of these victims on trial until we know everything we can about the murders."

⁕⁕⁕⁕⁕⁕⁕⁕⁕⁕⁕⁕

An hour later, Hekla sat with her head resting on her forefingers in the room where she had stored the records from the search of Aldís's house. Neither Gunnar nor Val had made any progress locating Elísa, and Hekla didn't know what she should do next, but she'd fallen asleep with her eyes half-open when Val called out a question.

"Why would he leave the knife?"

"Huh?" Hekla tried to wake herself by blinking her eyes.

"Why would the killer leave the knife?" Val repeated.

"I don't know," Hekla said as she felt around the table for a coffee or energy drink. "He might have just wanted to get rid of it."

"It looked purposeful. The way it was left. Not like he dropped it or threw it in the room. Like he placed it."

"Yeah," Hekla nodded in agreement as her hand wrapped around a quarter-full can of room-temperature caffeine and chemicals. She took a swig like it was a shot of cheap liquor. "I think so too."

"Do you think he wanted us to know it was him who killed Jack too?"

"I think the money would do the trick."

"Anyone can throw money. No one else would have had that knife."

"True. So why do you think he wanted us to know—for certain—that it was him both times?

"Maybe he was doing it for Aldís."

Hekla gave Val an inquisitive look.

"I don't mean at her direction," Val explained, "but sometimes people who do these types of things aren't well—not in a good mental state—so their motivations don't always make sense. Aldís gets a lot of attention, maybe this person took the wrong message from her work, but still didn't want her in trouble."

"Mmh. That's a lot of reasoning for someone who's not well. I'm not sure the rest fits—a crazed fan. There's a lot of planning here. A high level of execution you wouldn't normally have with someone like that."

Val nodded. There was silence for about a minute before Val spoke up again. "You hate them, don't you?"

"What?" Hekla looked back at Val with surprise. "What are you talking about?"

Val gave a knowing look toward the rest of the office. "Them."

Hekla chuckled lightly.

"I'm sorry," Val quickly added. "That was inappropriate."

"No. Don't be. It's perfectly appropriate." She finished off the last of her wretched drink. "I don't hate them. Not all of them at least. I hate what they are having us do—making us complicit in. You've seen the same documents I have. Are *you* okay with all this?"

Val shook their head adamantly. "No. Not at all. All of this should be public. We should be investigating what that mining group—the consortium—is doing, not helping to cover it up. I hate that too."

Hekla nodded. "But . . . ?"

"It's just—well, it just seems like it goes deeper for you."

"Mmh."

"We don't have to talk about this. Again, I'm sorry."

"Val," Hekla raised her voice slightly. "Stop apologizing."

"I'm s—" Val stopped herself and they both shared a smile.

"It's fine. I can tell you if you want."

Val looked eager to hear more.

"What do you want to know exactly?" Hekla asked.

"Um . . . I guess, why'd you join? In the first place?"

Hekla looked thoughtfully at the table. "Hmm. My brother. Probably."

"Is he a cop?"

"A cop?" Hekla looked back at Val with surprise. "Oh. No. Doctor. Just—the whole public service thing. He and my parents were big on that. I was trying to follow in his footsteps in that way. And I did care about what was fair." She shrugged. "So, I joined.

I knew what it was like elsewhere, but I thought we were different. Part of the community."

"You don't think that's true?"

Hekla shook her head. "No. After I joined the NBI, before any of this with the consortium putting together the mining deal, I came across a file. There was a unit, some offshoot of intelligence I guess, and they had been investigating the people at The Fólk."

Val furrowed their brow, "For what?"

"There *wasn't* any reason. No complaint, no accusation. Nothing I could find in the entire file. And it wasn't just background. They had detailed accounts of their private lives—intimate details. No criminal activity but they were still monitoring. *Spying.*"

Val looked horrified. "So that's why . . . "

Hekla's lip pulled into a frown. "It just made it obvious—more obvious. I think before finding that, it was easier to lie to myself. Pretend that, because we didn't carry guns or whatever, we were different. Better."

"Aren't we?"

Hekla held out her hands. "What do you think we're doing here?"

"We're looking for the truth."

"*We* might be. But as a whole. This system. We protect it don't we? We make sure the structure stays in place. It looks better here—in our country I know. But I think that's just because we're smaller."

Val tilted their head skeptically.

"If Iceland was ten, fifty—let's just say a hundred times the size," Hekla continued, "what do you think things would look like then? What would our jobs be like? I think it'd be just as bad as elsewhere." She glanced toward the rest of the office. "Just look at how differently we treat those with money already."

"Mmh," Val uttered thoughtfully.

"It's a variation of the same theme. I think if we aren't careful, we're going to go the same way as the rest of them. That's what I care about now. Making sure that doesn't happen. That's all I care about."

CHAPTER THIRTY-SEVEN

AUGUST WAS HARD TO MISS. HEKLA SPOTTED HIM AS soon as she stepped into the diner. He was an odd man who looked like he was constantly on the losing end of an argument he was having with himself. She suspected his quirks and eccentricities might be temporarily magnified by circumstance. His borderline deranged state wasn't compatible with his former occupation. Hekla doubted it was compatible with *any* occupation—any *existence*, really—for any extended period. Right now, though, August was just a loner in the corner of a tourist trap restaurant, sporting a ghastly injury on side of his face.

She sighed as she made her way to his table. In another life, she might have wanted to participate in his imaginary conversations—rare was such a combination of crazed and cute.

August looked up from his coffee as Hekla sat down. She tried not to react to his face, which somehow looked even more frightening now than it had during the interrogation. Half the white in his right eye was now a bright, almost iridescent shade of red. The area around, above and below his eye was gnarly, with shades of sea green, pale rose, and far too much purple—as if an infected bruise had melted.

"Sorry about that," Hekla said, gesturing with her head toward his face.

He grunted as he eyed her with the same contempt as he had at the station.

"And I'm sorry about the rest of—well—I know how it must look . . . "

August let out another low grumble that told her he wasn't interested in her explanation.

"Well, thank you for meeting with me." She *was* grateful he had agreed to see her. She hadn't expected him to call back. She was prepared to show up unannounced at his hotel room again, even though she was certain that would only hurt her chances of getting the information she sought. It was a long shot already, but she was desperate.

"He's fucking dead?" August exclaimed suddenly. Hekla quickly shot a look around the restaurant.

"What?" she asked quietly, hoping to inspire August to modulate his volume as well.

"You . . . you tell me Aldís was investigating a mining deal involving some Icelandic guy . . . and then he's killed?" He was still loud. "What . . . what the fuck is going on? And what if they found the papers you gave me when we were both arrested? Is that—is that why you gave them to me? Was it some . . . setup?"

Hekla grabbed him by the wrist. He looked down in surprise.

"Listen to me," she whispered forcefully. "You need to calm down. I'm not your enemy. I know how it seems, but I also know you're not a fool. *Think.* I was the one at risk by giving you those papers. Me. Not you or anyone else. And believe it or not, you're still not the one in danger."

August pulled his hand out of hers. He looked at his forearm as though she may have wounded him with her light grasp. "What about Aldís?"

"What about her?"

"Is she . . . is she still in jail?"

Hekla remained silent.

"She is . . . isn't she? Fucking Christ. I'm supposed to trust you?"

"It's not my choice. It never was. And she'll be out soon. It should be tonight."

"Right."

A waiter came by to refill August's coffee. The waiter asked about August's injury, and he ended up spending about a minute conversing with the middle-aged server. Hekla watched, bemused, as August's entire demeanor appeared to shift. He went from anxious and surly to relaxed, friendly, and—dare she say it—charming in a snap of the finger. She wondered what it was that caused the change. Then she realized that she had only seen August interact with police. Maybe the key to unlocking the more amiable August was to not be associated with her line of work.

After the two were done chatting, Hekla ordered a coffee, and the waiter left them alone. Fortunately for her, the effect of engagement with an outsider seemed to linger, and August returned to the conversation noticeably less angry.

"I saw your boss . . . last night," he said. "First time I've heard someone in law enforcement acknowledge the murders might be . . . connected. Still nothing about how though—how long with that secret?"

She gave him a knowing look. "It never should have been a secret. You know how I feel. Why do you think I risked my job giving a disgraced American lawyer with ties to a suspect key evidence?"

August's lip twitched, clearly trying to suppress, before finally allowing a small smile. "I wasn't . . . expecting your colleague to have my resume."

They both laughed. After a moment Hekla asked if there was anything else that he would like to know from her.

August looked contemplative before asking, "How long have you known Logi?"

The question caught her off guard. "What do you mean?" she replied, buying time as she searched his face for clues.

"You do know him . . . right?"

She tried to determine how much information she felt comfortable sharing with August. Her ask was big enough that she wanted him to feel comfortable—vent as necessary, ask questions as he saw fit—but this wasn't a topic she cared to explore with him. She needed to be honest, but the less she said the better. "Logi Stefánsson? He's a publisher of The Fólk with Aldís. He was also a guest at the hotel when Steingrímur was murdered. I'm not sure—"

"Stop . . . stop that. You grew up together."

"Oh" Hekla thought to herself before saying it aloud. This opened a different world of possibilities. "Akureyri. That's right. We were both born there. It's a big city though."

August let out a bitter laugh. "C'mon . . . it's not even a big *town.*"

Hekla gave a defensive smile.

August continued, "Especially when you're the same age . . . just a few blocks away. Same school too. . . . Right?"

"Mmh. You've done some research?"

"Only fair."

Hekla nodded. "I knew him. Like you said, we grew up together. We were friendly, I guess, as classmates—same birthday parties, that type of thing." She shrugged. "No one is that far removed from anyone else here."

"Nothing . . . that would interfere? With an investigation?"

"That's right. You know him too, I presume?"

"Yeah," August answered. "Not well. He was close . . . with Aldís. I think they're dating now."

"We're aware of their relationship," Hekla quickly responded.

"Uh-huh."

"Anything else?" she asked, with as pleasant a tight-lipped smile as she was able to muster.

August shook his head. "No. . . . Not right now."

"Okay."

"So what do you want?"

Hekla stared at the coffee in front of her. She hadn't noticed the waiter place it on the table. "I need your help."

August stayed quiet.

Hekla looked up from her coffee. "There's this girl—a teenager. She's gone missing. We think she might know something about Jack's murder."

August shook his head and turned his palm up, appearing to signal confusion. It was better than ire, thought Hekla. She was still afraid of how he would respond when she told him her theory, but she didn't have any more time to waste.

"I need your help finding her," she blurted out.

"Ha!" August exclaimed with a wide smile, loud enough for diners nearby to notice. "You've got—you've got to be kidding. . . . Right?"

Hekla gave another quick glance to her side before leaning forward. "No," she said, using all her body and voice to convey a sense of urgency. "She's in danger."

August looked genuinely perplexed. "You know . . . you've used this line before." He pointed at his battered face. "How'd that turn out? I'm not helping you . . . round up people. And honestly . . . if I did find the person—the person who killed that sociopath—I'd do everything I could . . . to help keep them *away* from you."

"The girl didn't do it."

"Of course not. You're just worried . . . about her safety. Again."

"I am."

"Fuck you."

Hekla closed her eyes tight and lowered her head. She rubbed her brow and clenched her teeth. Finally, she opened her mouth just enough to mumble, "How is she?"

"Wh-What?"

Hekla opened her eyes and looked back at August. "How *is* she?"

"Who?"

"Aldís."

"She's . . . she's in jail."

"Yeah, but how is she?"

August shook his head.

"She's safe, isn't she?" Hekla continued. "No one hurt her."

"I don't . . . I don't know that she ever *was* in danger."

"Really? Is that why she was hiding? Do you think she's afraid of the *Icelandic* police?" Hekla was out over her skis now, speculating—hoping, was more like it—that some aspect of August's history with Aldís and the Americans evoked the same sense of fear that she felt.

August's face contorted for a split second, almost like an involuntary half-wince, as her words landed. It seemed she hit on something.

"I'm not—I'm not helping," he said. "You're the only threat . . . to anyone's wellbeing that I've seen." There was another pause. "But why—what makes you think . . . I could help?"

Hekla wondered if it was even worth telling him now. There wasn't much to gain. It seemed like his mind was set, and, theoretically at least, there was a lot to lose.

"What is it?" he asked with greater force.

If there was even the smallest chance she could change his mind though, she needed to take it. She also still trusted the man, as admittedly irrational as that might be. More important, she knew *his* trust could be instrumental later, and if she didn't tell him the connection now, there was no hope she would ever regain it.

"I'm not entirely sure," she started, "I haven't told anyone this, but—I have a feeling she knew Aldís. The girl. I think she might be hiding out in the same spot Aldís was."

August gave Hekla another confused look. "Well, if she's there . . . then she's safe. No one found Aldís . . . not until she came to see me. Remember?"

Hekla shook her head. "It's not the same. I don't think Aldís was ever really a threat to them. They knew she didn't do it. They just wanted an excuse to raid The Fólk and their homes—find out what information they had. It's different with the girl. I'm not sure what they'll do."

August pursed his lips.

Hekla's heart fluttered in hopeful anticipation.

"Right," August began. "Well . . . that's not what you told me—not at my apartment and not at the hotel."

Hekla deflated.

"And so what?" August went on. "You think I'm going to help you . . . arrest someone *and* implicate Aldís? Are you—are you out of your fucking mind? Have you listened to anything I've said? It's just . . . fucking . . . unbelievable—"

"August!" Hekla shouted, surprising herself with her decibel and timbre. "She's in danger. Please. I know how this might look, but—I'm telling you the truth, I'm worried. Please, I'm begging you."

August shook his head and stood up. "I never knew . . . where Aldís was staying—still don't. So . . . sorry. I can't help. It was good . . . *seeing* you again." He reached into his pockets for his hat and gloves. "Oh . . . and thanks for the cigarettes. That was very thoughtful."

CHAPTER THIRTY-EIGHT

Approximately 36 hours after the police had conclusive evidence that Aldís was innocent of Jack's murder, they released her from jail. The decision to let her out seemed at once delayed and rushed, as though it suddenly occurred to someone that it might not be a great idea to hold a high-profile journalist on a nonsensical obstruction charge. Especially when the details surrounding the mining deal scared someone so much that they couldn't even trust the police to hold evidence of the obstruction. This likely also contributed to the decision to release Aldís early in the morning, perhaps hoping authorities could dispense with her when no one was paying attention.

Hekla learned about Aldís's release via a phone call from Val. Kjartan had approved Hekla's request to promote them to a flexible position as special assistant, with a more defined role and retroactive pay increase. The seizure of the mining deal documents from the NBI drove home Hekla's fear that, despite assurances from Kjartan, she never could tell for sure what was going on with the investigations. Her goal was to have either Val or Gunnar at the station when she wasn't.

After her disappointing meeting with August, Hekla had spent the rest of the day and early evening with Gunnar, trying to find Elísa. They chased down every lead, partial lead, or part of a part of a lead, in and around Grindavik and the Azure Spa and Hotel. Nothing bore any fruit, and when Hekla started to display a startling inability to perform basic motor functions, Gunnar forced her to go home. She protested the whole drive back but was sound asleep seconds after her head hit the pillow.

The selection of horror that played in Hekla's mind every time she slept had a decidedly more frightening quality to it this evening. There were still the vivid depictions of death, and the painful, bizarrely abstract allegories of suffering and consequence conjured by her subconscious. But underlying everything tonight was dread, a sense that something else bad was about to happen—like time was running out. When her phone rang, she practically leapt out of bed, certain she was too late.

"Hi," Val said. "I'm, um, sorry to be calling you now."

Hekla had no idea what time it was. "It's fine. What's going on?"

"They're releasing Aldís."

A wave of relief washed over Hekla. This was probably the best news that Val could have delivered. "Okay. Is that it?"

"Yes. Well—yes and no. There's a lot of people outside. Cameras and everything."

Hekla pulled her phone back to check the time. "Really?"

"Yes. That's why I called. I thought you'd want to know. You can probably see it on the news."

Hekla made her way to the living room and turned on RUV. The camera had just panned away from Margrét to show the large contingent of reporters outside the station. It was clear that someone had given them a heads-up. Hekla wondered if she should call August, who didn't appear to be adhering to a very strict sleep schedule. She settled on a text. This way he would at least know that *she let him know* of Aldís's release as soon as she did. Maybe that would help at some point.

Margrét was in the middle of recapping Aldís's illustrious

career as a journalist when there was a commotion behind her. "Hold on," Margrét said, "I think she's coming out now."

Margrét stepped to the side and the camera focused on Aldís as she exited the station. Aldís exchanged what looked like a few friendly words with an officer who held the door open for her. She had no hat or gloves, but the cold didn't seem to bother her. She had a melancholy smile as she walked toward the reporters, appearing surprised but undaunted by their presence. The reporters were anything but calm as they shouted out questions and quickly encircled her. Aldís nodded politely and waited for them to settle down.

The picture of Aldís was striking. Lit up against the black sky, hair swirling in concert with thick flurries of snow, reddened cheeks a sign of defiant life in the darkness, she looked radiant. And when she politely held up her hand and began to speak, it was as if all the other sounds in the world collectively ceded their time.

"Thank you," Aldís began. "Several days ago, I was arrested for a crime I did not commit. The police who arrested me, the prosecutors who approved my detention, and their bosses with the Ministry of Justice knew I was innocent. They knew I did not murder Jack Drumman or anyone else, but they arrested me anyway. The reason I was arrested—the reason my home was ransacked along with the homes of my friends and colleagues at The Fólk—is because I was trying to expose the truth about my government—the truth about *our* government and its involvement with the United States."

Hekla's heart skipped a beat. Her mouth parted but the rest of her body remained still as she stared at the television, transfixed by Aldís's speech.

"With approval and encouragement from the highest levels of

our government, private citizens and corporations have been negotiating a secret mining deal with a U.S. company—a deal to
drill in our waters, to give away our land, and to exploit our resources for their own personal benefit. I tried to tell the truth
about this illegal deal. For that I was arrested. The police violated
our constitution. They threatened and intimidated us. They allowed their co-conspirators to label me a terrorist, all because I
tried to tell the truth. And here is the truth: Our elected leaders
are betraying our way of life. *They* are the traitors—not just to our
country, but to humanity, and the land that all of us—regardless
of the happenstance of birth—are responsible for.

"I have harmed no human being, but I was imprisoned for one
simple offense, more serious to those in power than murder ever
could be. I threatened their profits, their gains, their capital. But
I will not remain silent, and we are not powerless. The people of
Iceland still have a voice.

"The local representative where drilling is planned can veto
the mining deal. Right now, that representative is *Ragna María
Sigurðardóttir*—an individual who has been part of the secret negotiations with the U.S. corporation. I intend to run against Ms.
María Sigurðardóttir, to unseat her, and to prevent the destruction of our land and the betrayal of our principles. There is still
hope for us. All of us. Thank you."

CHAPTER THIRTY-NINE

The U.S. Embassy in Iceland was a strange little building in the Laugardalur district of Reykjavík. It looked as though the architects were unsure if they were supposed to be designing a library or a prison, so they split the difference. August had several opportunities to visit when he was working out of Copenhagen. The diplomats here were some of the more pleasant ones he encountered, but that was an exceptionally low bar. American diplomats were, in his opinion, awful. They had no qualms running game theory scenarios on dead civilians or divvying up clean water based on a system that always favored the powerful over the thirsty.

Still, August decided he'd visit the embassy. It was that cop. He didn't trust her—after all, she had burned him once already—but there was something earnest in her demeanor. It made him curious as to the extent the Americans were really interested in some runaway teenager. His other motivation stemmed from several documents that Jenson had managed to secure regarding America's sudden interest in Arctic-adjacent mineral exploration. There was a link between Lisa's past and Iceland's (apparent) future that he wanted to better understand.

He sat in the embassy's tastefully decorated waiting room, eyes fixed on an expensively framed reprint of a Louisa Matthíasdóttir painting. He liked the painting and the painter, but he doubted there would be such a prominent place for artwork created by someone who moved from the States to Iceland, instead of vice versa.

Being back in such familiar environs, he couldn't help but reflect on all the times he had failed to help people when he worked at the legat. His office wasn't really in the people helping business, but there were still countless occasions when he knew he could have done more, or *less*, to produce a just outcome. He would rationalize his indifference by telling himself that the loss of power that would result from extending himself wasn't worth it—that he would ultimately be able to help more people by following protocol. It still made sense on a superficial level. But deep down, he knew that this way of thinking underestimated both the power of doing the right thing, and the unseen consequences of ignoring a wrong. And that made him no better than the cretinous diplomats he loathed so much.

The Matthíasdóttir painting was one of the those with two horses. It was lovely, but August preferred those that also featured a solitary, despondent human lurking in the background. It always seemed to him that the one human was searching for a good cliff to jump off, or a deep enough spot in the water to drown in. A secretary called his name before he could dwell too long on the people not in the painting.

Lisa met August outside her office door. She was dressed in a light gray pencil skirt cut a fashionable length above the knee, a matching jacket, white blouse, and black pumps with block heels. She looked good, he thought, unnervingly relaxed with a plastered-on smile, but good. For a second, he felt self-conscious about his own appearance before he remembered why he was here and who, exactly, he was dealing with.

"I'm so glad you were able to find the time to come by," Lisa said, extending her hand for August to ignore as he walked into the office.

Lisa smoothly transitioned to the large leather chair behind her desk. August looked around as he sat in a chair apparently designed to make visitors feel uncomfortable. He studied another Matthíasdóttir painting on the wall. Unlike the reprint downstairs, this one looked like an original. He imagined they had a fucking pallet of them somewhere in the basement. On top of a small bookshelf was a framed photograph of Lisa and the ambassador, Lewis Kessel.

"It's been a while," Lisa said, leaning back in her chair. "I know things didn't go exactly as you hoped after our last meeting. I understand you were upset, so, don't worry. No hard feelings for how you behaved."

August narrowed his eyes and pressed his tongue hard against the back of his teeth. "How I . . . behaved?" he eventually replied with unmasked contempt.

Lisa gave a smug smile that only increased the feeling of heat radiating behind August's face. "The phone call. Your language. I think we'd both agree it was unprofessional—to say the least."

He shook his head in disbelief.

Lisa ran her eyes over him. "To be honest, you still don't look that great." Her smile was replaced by a look apparently meant to resemble sympathy. "That's unfortunate. I would have hoped you'd move on by now. Then again, it didn't take much—"

"What—what are you doing here?"

"What are you talking about?"

"Why are you here . . . in Iceland?"

"I was offered a position. I accepted. There's not much more to it than that."

August blinked hard. "Your last post . . . was in the Middle East. You were with the Secretary of Energy before. This . . . this is a demotion."

"I don't see it that way." She adopted a casual tone that

somehow infuriated him more than her patronizing one. "Quality of life matters to me too, believe it or not. I'll admit, I was a little hesitant at first, but it really is a beautiful country. Majestic. Truly."

"Uh-huh. And Lewis . . . that's why he's here. . . . Big nature guy."

"Ambassador Kessel brings a great deal of geopolitical experience to the job. It's a pleasure working for him."

"Jesus." August looked around. "Who . . . who the fuck are you talking to? Can you stop . . . this bullshit?"

"Is this why you came? To curse and complain about presidential appointments?"

"I want to know what you are doing here."

"Serving my country—"

"*Money?* A rock? Some . . . mineral? Something you can use for . . . faster chips, or better death tech—some shit like that? That's what you found. Right? That's why . . . that's what dragged you out here. Tell me I'm wrong."

"You're wrong."

August exhaled loudly and rolled his eyes.

"I'm sorry things don't always fit into the narrative espoused by people like your girlfriend—quite a speech by her this morning, by the way—but our government isn't involved with any mining operation." Lisa paused for a moment. "We will, however, do absolutely everything in our power to protect our citizens from terrorist attacks."

He grunted. "Heard that before."

"And it was true then just as it's true today. You know, Americans including yourself have benefited immensely from the work you now deride. Before you suddenly decided we were the enemy, you had a pretty nice life because of our country's strength. It's easy to dismiss something after you've enjoyed it. Most people go their whole lives without knowing the ease you took for granted."

"It wasn't—it wasn't sudden."

"Excuse me?"

"I didn't . . . *suddenly* decide. I just . . . it just took me some time . . . to do the right thing."

"Of course." Lisa's lips twisted into sarcastic smile. "My point remains."

August shook his head again. This was pointless, he thought to himself as he got up to leave.

"I would caution you against getting too involved with criminals again," she continued. "A lot of people thought you should be charged last time. I had to lobby hard to keep them from going after you. I'm not sure I'll be able to help you if you wind up on the wrong side of things again."

"You're . . . you're threatening me?"

"It's not a threat, it's a fact. They murdered two people. We have to protect ourselves."

"Who's *they?* . . . And who's *we?*"

Lisa gave another contemptuous smile. "You should go back to Denmark, August. Or wherever else you'd rather be than home. I know you've been through a lot. I really would hate to see you get hurt more."

⁂

August came close to lighting his cigarette in the yard between the embassy and the gate. A petty act of defiance by the powerless. *God*, he thought, Lisa really did make him feel like a child. All the arguments and carefully laid-out reasoning in his head were wiped out in an instant by her condescending smile and above-it-all tone.

He made his way past the gate and onto the sidewalk, where he lit his cigarette under the disapproving eye of a Marine. After a slower than necessary drag and exhale, August walked toward his car.

Maybe Lisa was right, he considered. Maybe it was all just a power thing. August never felt this weakness before because whether he was conscious of it or not, he had a confidence derived from his citizenship. He had always felt safe and secure, even as an attorney for a domestic policing agency operating within *another* country's border. He could swear off violence, badmouth his employer, disclaim their actions, but in the back of his mind, didn't his comfort come from knowing that his team could annihilate its opponents with impunity? If it wasn't in the back of *his* mind, he knew it was always in the back of everyone else's mind.

He rolled the cigarette butt tightly between his thumb and middle finger until the ember fell to the snow. He put the extinguished butt in his pocket, got in his car and slammed the door behind him.

Something else was bothering him. He had watched Aldís's speech several times—they were running it almost non-stop on RUV—and he couldn't figure out what she was doing. The idea of Aldís representing her district made sense, but that press conference was bizarre. It was too perfect—like she had the whole thing planned. And this didn't seem like an area where she should be so cavalier. Aldís was fearless, but to him, this was reckless. And that was coming from a man who knew a thing or two about recklessness.

He had only driven a few blocks when the ring and vibration of his phone nearly caused him to steer into a parked truck. He stopped the car and flipped open his phone. "Hello?"

"Hello," Aldís replied.

August was speechless. He'd forgotten that he shared his new number with her.

"This is August, right?" she asked with a trace of uncertainty.

"Yes. Hey. Sorry. . . . I just . . . I wasn't expecting you to call."

"You gave me your number."

"Right . . . right. It's um . . . been a while since I had one of these."

"I gathered as much. Fancier models now, but they still make and accept calls."

He chuckled. "Of course. Well . . . pleasant surprise then."

"Good. It's nice to be able to reach you again."

"Good to be reached. Hopefully . . . it goes better this time?"

Aldís laughed. "I'm sorry about that. Are you okay? It looked like you took the worst of it."

"Yeah. . . . Yeah, I'm fine."

"Good. Then you can come visit me tomorrow."

CHAPTER FORTY

The last time both Lisa and Aldís were in August's life, things did not go well. One day he was driving from the safe house to Aldís's home, and the next thing he knew, it was all over. He had taken Client from the safety that Aldís had provided and led him straight to his demise. August's plan had failed spectacularly.

He should have known better. From the moment he first contacted U.S. officials, they were waiting for their opportunity to arrest Client and undermine his revelations. They bided their time as August foolishly gave them everything they needed to prosecute Client. And when it came time to arrest Client, they barely had to move. August had assured Client that he was protected. August beckoned him out of the safe house and let him fly to the States.

The first forewarning August had missed was the presence of Lisa Harris at the meetings. At the time, she was in a position directly beneath the ambassador in the Middle Eastern country where the most horrendous of the crimes Client witnessed had taken place. The other officials insisted that Lisa was necessary to tie together various pieces. But she never should have been there. She wasn't a prosecutor, she had no power to provide Client immunity, and she had no business being made privy to the details of a war crime prosecution that could very likely implicate her boss in some very serious crimes. She shouldn't have been there, and when her presence was insisted upon, he should have walked the fuck away.

It was equally foolish to believe he could ever protect Client in the first place. The ease in which the U.S. got around its agreements was shocking. All it took was a military tribunal ruling that those with whom August negotiated didn't have the jurisdiction to bind the government in matters relating to national security, and Client was at the mercy of military prosecutors.

August didn't see the actual ruling until two weeks later. When he didn't hear from Client in the days following Client's arrival in the U.S., he worried. When he answered the phone only to hear an automated message announce a call from a federal prison, his heart dropped.

Client had no interest in being a martyr, but he was better prepared for his government's betrayal than August was. After all, Client spent much of his career watching real-time video of his government abandoning any pretense of principle. What hurt Client more—the twist of the knife in his back—was what they managed to do with the truth.

As soon as Aldís learned of the arrest, she and her group at The Fólk, went about transforming the scaled-down story they had into a full-blown exposé. But it was too late. The U.S. government, with the help of enablers and sycophants, had already gotten its version out. The story the government spun was about a troubled former contractor who had been arrested for treason after stealing documents and endangering American lives. There were also whispers about behavioral issues and some allegations of misconduct. It didn't matter that it was all bullshit. Corrections took time. In the end, the water was muddied and time was bought. And that's all that needed to be done.

Maybe the story never would have gotten anywhere. By the time it was published, most Americans had already been desensitized to horrific violence abroad, and many of the other powerful nations had either given up on reeling America in or were secretly pleased someone else was doing what they couldn't. But August knew it was heartbreaking for Client to have his voice muted before he ever got to speak. All Client had wanted was for the truth to come out, for the unvarnished reality of American warfare to be presented to the people. August's involvement not only caused Client harm, it also robbed Client of his truth.

About a month after Aldís's story broke, the U.S. Department of Defense released a statement on the bombing that had prompted Client to act in the first place—the one that killed more than 70 women and children. A team had investigated and determined that "mistakes were made." "Were made." A passive-voice phrase meant to acknowledge that someone had done something wrong without assigning any blame. The word "profound" was used a lot, as in "profound mistake" and "profound condolences." The statement did not offer details of disciplinary action that would be taken against those involved because there would be no disciplinary action.

Many media outlets commended the acknowledgement of "tragic mistakes" and a "breakdown of systems" as extraordinary admissions from the U.S. government. A few mentioned the money that surviving relatives would receive.

Lisa was the first person August spoke with after learning of Client's arrest. He didn't remember every word he said to her, but was sure there was at least some profanity. August never made the other call—the one to Aldís. He came close. The night after he learned of the arrest, he had his phone in hand and her contact information pulled up. He didn't call then, but he promised himself he would the next day. That day came and went. So did the next one. August kept promising himself he would call—on certain days, or within specific windows of time. But soon weeks went by, and, in the end, he never could make that call. He put it off until he could convince himself it was too late. And in that, he finally found success.

CHAPTER FORTY-ONE

THE U.S. WAS NOW INVOLVED IN THE MURDER investigations. Officially, it was on a very limited basis, and the Americans were only to provide technical assistance locating Elísa, but Hekla was still worried. She stayed glued to her phone in the ensuing days and nights, unsure if she would be getting an address or an announcement of a military junta. The more time passed, the more nervous she became. Kjartan had promised that she would be the first to know, but even if he were being truthful, she wasn't convinced that *he* would be the first to know.

She was at the station when the information finally came in. She had an extra monitor at her desk and was watching synced-up footage from various security cameras in and around the Envoy hotel. It was past 8 p.m. when Kjartan beckoned her.

"We got two addresses," he told her as soon as she walked into his office. She raised an eyebrow. "They're not sure which one she is at. But they're reasonably certain it's one or the other."

"How'd they get them?" she asked without expecting an answer.

Kjartan gave her the hopeless head shake she *did* expect.

"Right," she muttered. "Well, let's see." She walked behind his desk, and he turned his computer monitor toward her. The screen was filled with an email. There was no subject, and the only text in its body were two addresses separated by a double space. She glanced quickly at the email's sender before studying the addresses. "Really?"

"It's the best we've got."

She took a step back.

"What do you think?" he asked.

She pursed her lips. Her eyes fixed absently on the reflection in the deep-gray tinted windows of the office. After a few seconds, she turned back to him, speaking with conviction, "We go to both places. Early tomorrow morning. Same time."

Kjartan nodded. Hekla looked at the clock.

"Send Bjarni and Einar to Vik," she continued. "I'll go with Gunnar to the place in Keflavík."

"You don't want someone else with you?"

"I want Gunnar. He's right around there and I trust him. Is that okay?" There was a gentleness in her voice, like she was asking her boss for permission for once.

Kjartan nodded. He seemed to appreciate the consideration.

⁓⁓⁓⁓⁓⁓

The first address in the suspiciously sparse email that Lisa sent to Kjartan was for a cottage in Vik. Vik was a small village about three hours from Reykjavík, just below the Mýrdalsjökull glacier. Vik was isolated and beautiful, particularly in the spring and summer when the surrounding cliffs were green. The views from the old church or on the black pebble beach were magnificent. The plan was for Bjarni and Einar to leave now and spend the night in one of Vik's hotels or guesthouses.

Hekla was almost certain that Elísa was not in Vik.

The second address was for a place in Keflavík. Hekla was to go home and rest for a few hours before meeting up with Gunnar. At eight the next morning, both teams would search the respective locations. This was the plan that Hekla told Kjartan and Gunnar. But she never intended to follow it. She hoped Gunnar wouldn't be *too* upset when she showed up, unannounced at his home so soon after her after-hours phone call.

Hekla left the station at around 10 p.m. About 40 minutes later, she stood shivering outside Gunnar's one-story house on Staðarhraun street in Grindavik. Gunnar's place was part of a group of similarly sized houses east of the harbor. It was white with red trim, neatly bordered by hedges and a red, two-rail fence. Hekla hadn't shown up *completely* unannounced—she was pretty sure the gruff voice that had answered her call from the car a minute earlier had responded affirmatively.

The door opened. A tall young woman with a beaming smile that did not match the time or occasion greeted her. Hekla started to apologize but the young woman held up her finger. "We have a little one asleep," she whispered.

The inside of Gunnar's home pleasantly complimented its exterior. There was lots of blonde wood and round edges, cute accents, and colorful appliances in the kitchen. It was all very tidy except for the clear territorial markings of a toddler. The young woman sat across from Hekla at a circular table a few meters from the kitchen.

"You must be Hekla. I'm Ingibjörg. It's so good to finally meet you."

"It's nice to meet you too." Hekla lamented not having the opportunity to ask Gunnar more questions about his personal life. She heard footsteps and turned in her chair to see Gunnar emerge from the other wing of the home. He gave her the slightest look before moving his attention to Ingibjörg. "Did she wake her?" Gunnar's voice must have been several decibels louder than he intended. Noise came from another room. Ingibjörg raised her eyebrows at Gunnar, who grimaced.

A few seconds later, a sleepy-eyed young girl emerged. She looked confused at first, but quickly decided the presence of adults meant more time to play. In an instant, her sleepiness disappeared, and she bounded into Gunnar's dutifully outstretched arms.

It took some time, but eventually the adults negotiated a deal where the young girl would get ten minutes of playtime in return for a solemn pledge to go back to bed without debate or delay when time was up.

"Anna," Gunnar said as the group watched the girl play. "She just turned four."

"I didn't know you had a girl," Hekla said to Gunnar. "Or . . . " she looked to Ingibjörg.

Gunnar smirked. He got up from the table to get the coffee that was brewing in the kitchen.

"She's mine," Ingibjörg said. Then she gestured with her head toward Gunnar, "*his* niece."

"Ah." Siblings, thought Hekla. That explains the height.

After exactly ten minutes, Ingibjörg got up and escorted Anna to her room before retiring to her own bed.

When the last door was shut, Gunnar gave Hekla a stern look. "What are we doing?"

"Elísa's not in Vik. It wouldn't make sense."

"You really think she's at the Keflavík address?"

Hekla gave a half-shrug. "If she's in either of these places, that'd be the one."

"And we can't wait till tomorrow?"

"No," Hekla said firmly. "We need get there first. Whether she had anything to do with this or not."

Gunnar looked conflicted.

"You saw them," Hekla continued. "They took evidence from

us. They were ready to fight you. Imagine what they'd do to people without badges."

He made a low grunting sound.

"If you're not comfortable with this . . . " she glanced at the door to Anna's room. "It's okay. I understand. I probably shouldn't be trying to drag you into—"

"No." Gunnar shook his head. "I think you're right."

Hekla's lips tightened into a small smile.

"If we get in trouble, I can just blame it on you anyway, right?" Gunnar asked.

"Absolutely. It was—it is an order."

"Good. So, when do we go?"

CHAPTER FORTY-TWO

THE KEFLAVÍK ADDRESS THAT THE AMERICANS provided was for an old house that once belonged to a lighthouse keeper. It was near the coast on the southwestern edge of the peninsula. The lighthouse was now fully automated and operated by the government, but the house had been passed down through generations of the keeper's family. The place was relatively isolated, the last of a handful of country homes and farmhouses on a long road, perpendicular to the highway. Unless you lived in one of the houses, or wished to visit the fourth-most interesting lighthouse on the Southern Peninsula, you wouldn't have any reason to be there.

"Who lives there now?" Gunnar asked as they drove.

"Ownership is listed under a Sívar Bergsson," Hekla replied. "Great-great grandson of the original lighthouse keeper, I think."

"In the business of hiding fugitives now?"

"Persons of interest," Hekla corrected. Gunnar nodded. Hekla glanced at him from the driver seat. "And maybe. What else does he have to do? Lighthouse takes care of itself these days."

Gunnar smiled.

Hekla turned off the highway and slowed to a near crawl as they traveled the narrow road to the house. She parked behind a farmhouse about 400 meters away, grabbed two Lögreglan vests from the back seat, and handed the larger one to Gunnar. After putting on the vests, they both got out.

It was almost three in the morning and it was bitter cold.

Hekla and Gunnar walked briskly along the road, and then on a dirt path that had recently been cleared of snow.

"Should we be worried?" Gunnar asked.

Hekla gave him a look.

"Showing up in the middle of the night like this?" he continued.

"We're just seeing if anyone is there. It's an inconvenience, but it's an urgent matter related to a murder."

Gunnar nodded. But now Hekla wondered if she *should* be worried. Her concerns so far had been confined to Elísa—making sure she got to her first and ensuring Bjarni would be as far away from her as possible. She realized now that she hadn't thought about what exactly would happen when she and Gunnar showed up at a stranger's isolated home in the middle of the night. It was unlikely to be the gracious reception they deserved.

They rounded a large snowbank and found themselves about 20 meters from the house. There were no lights on, but the moon and its reflection off the snow gave everything an ethereal glow. It was a two-story home, pale white with what looked like a red roof. Even in the darkness, it was clear that it was a gorgeous structure. Its partially illuminated silhouette against a backdrop of rolling hills, a jagged cliff, and the ocean was like an illustration in a children's book of dark fairy tales.

Hekla signaled for Gunnar to check around back while she approached the front of the house. In a well-trodden area to the side, an old Jeep was covered in a thin layer of snow. There were only a few windows on the front and side of the house, all high off the ground with shades or curtains drawn. After walking around the circumference, Gunnar met back with Hekla at the front corner of the house.

"No door," he whispered. "Nowhere to go."

"Okay. Stay here. I'll knock."

He nodded.

Hekla approached the front door. She hesitated a moment before knocking. Here, at last, she felt real worry. It surprised her. She didn't think her body could find new levels of displeasure. She went ahead anyway, pounding her clenched fist against the door. "Police! Open up!"

She waited a few seconds before repeating the call and knock. Nothing. She looked back at Gunnar, but he just shook his head. "Police!" she shouted.

A faint noise soon was followed by the sound of a door unlocking. Hekla stepped back just as the door swung open. A sturdy-looking man in his 70s pointed a shotgun at her face.

"What do you want?" the man demanded.

"We're with the police," she responded while doing her best to keep the rest of her body still.

"I don't care." The man aimed the gun away from Hekla to a point over her shoulder and then back to her. She snuck a quick glance to see that Gunnar had moved closer to her.

"Put down the weapon, sir," she stated firmly.

"Why are you here?"

"We need to check the home. We have reason to believe a person connected with a murder may be here."

"You're not coming in."

Only a few hours ago, Hekla was quite pleased with her plan. Now, the gaping holes were obvious. She heard snow crunching behind her and saw the gun move away from her again.

"I'll shoot," the man said in a manner that made clear he would. Gunnar was just a few steps behind her now and seemed intent on getting next to her. She could feel her heart beating.

"It's okay," a quiet voice said from the darkness. The man kept his gun on Hekla, but his expression softened. The voice seemed to get through to him in a way that their vests and badges could not.

Hekla peered into the darkness as the shadow of a young woman made its way from the back of the home to the front door. In the partially illuminated doorway, Hekla recognized Elísa Pálsdóttir. "It's okay," Elísa repeated, gently placing her hand on the man's shoulder. "Let them in."

<div align="center">~~~~~~~~~~~~~~~</div>

The inside of the home was stately. A staircase with a thick wooden handrail, wrought iron banisters and a hand-carved volute ran along the back wall. The living room featured an ornate, tufted sofa, love seat, wingback chair, and ottoman that also had hand-carved wooden accents. A large, antique bookshelf was filled with both new and old volumes. A floor lamp with a puzzle-piece glass lampshade that looked as though it belonged in a museum was between the wingback chair and the sofa. To the right of the front door, a small mudroom led to a hallway.

In the surprisingly sufficient light provided by the floor lamp, Hekla got a better look at Elísa. Hair down, out of her uniform, and dressed in loose sweatpants and a wool, cable-knit sweater jacket, she looked every bit the teenager she really was. The girl shouldn't have to deal with this, Hekla thought.

While Hekla followed Elísa into the living room, Gunnar remained behind in the mudroom, trying as best he could to negotiate rather than force Keeper to put the gun down. Before Hekla had a chance to speak, there was a sound. At first, Hekla could only *see* the sound in Elísa's eyes—the rapid movement in her pupils, and then a questioning look, which quickly transformed into fear.

"Shh," Hekla said as she jutted out her hand. Everyone froze as they listened to the night. Nothing was out of place. Just a slight wind that had returned after resting for a bit. Then Hekla heard it. It was outside, just a subtle shift really, but she recognized the sound of snow being displaced.

She quickly moved to the front wall and signaled for Elísa to take cover. Keeper tightened his grip on the shotgun and exchanged a look with Elísa. He looked pained, she thought, like he wanted—no, *needed*—to be next to her, but Gunnar's big frame blocked his path.

There was a window about two meters to Hekla's right. She covered the distance in two long strides, pulled the shade back and ducked her head so she could see outside. A black SUV sat idle at the entryway to the path. Three of its four doors were open. There was no sign of the vehicle's occupants.

Hekla didn't waste time trying to trace footprints in the dark. She hopped back to the door, opened it halfway and shouted. Before she could finish the word "police," a rock ricocheted off the door and landed inside. She stared curiously at the symmetrical rock before recognizing what it really was. She started to scream.

"Cover your—"

There was a light popping sound, and suddenly everything was illuminated by an intense light. The pop was followed almost immediately by a thunderous bang that rendered any further instructions Hekla could give moot. The light seared Hekla's skin, but the bang was worse: It shook her body *and* brain, deafening her and disrupting her ability to process information coherently.

And then Hekla found herself alone on the wood-planked floor. It was as if the needle on the record of time had skipped, and when the music resumed it was at a different tempo. Nothing

Hekla heard, saw, or felt, seemed natural. There were some echoes and feedback—elements and signifiers of noise—but mostly just pain in her ears while chaos unfurled in front of her.

An unnatural fog had descended upon the room, and the floor tilted back and forth. Through the fog, she could vaguely make out a group of people moving about the center of the room, pushing and pulling one another in some sort of violent ring dance.

She shifted her focus. Above her, a wooden ladder disappeared into the fog. She kept staring at the ladder until she was able to recognize it as the bookshelf. She returned her attention to the group in front of her. None of the dancing figures had the build of a teenage girl. With great concentration, she was able to keep all of them still long enough to recognize Gunnar fighting off what appeared to be three sizable men. Hekla pushed herself off the floor and stood, only to find that the ground beneath her feet was still slanted. She hit the floor hard. She watched Gunnar before dragging herself back to where she imagined the bookshelf to be.

The images of the intruders remained unsteady, but it was obvious that they had some sort of training. They approached Gunnar in unison and tried to take away his leverage while protecting their vitals. Their tactics, however, were matched almost equally by Gunnar's strength and will.

Gunnar absorbed and blocked body blows from two of the men, using his left arm as both a shield and a weapon. The third man attacked from behind, wrapping his arm around Gunnar's neck. Gunnar bent forward to lift him up and negate his leverage, but the maneuver left his face unprotected, and the other two men used the opportunity to attack. Gunnar took a staggered step as the third man adjusted his hold. One of the other men landed a fist square on Gunnar's jaw. The big man swayed. There was a brief pause as the attackers prepared for Gunnar to collapse.

But the punch only enlivened him. Instead of bending forward more, Gunnar stood straight up. The two men in front of Gunnar pummeled him, but it seemed to have no effect. Gunnar dug his fingers into the protective gear and clothing near the nape of the third man's neck. Gunnar continued forward, lifting the man over his head and flinging him forward. The man rolled off one of the others before crashing to the floor, landing with almost all his weight on his right shoulder and the side of his head. The man's mask and headgear were jostled by the fall, and Hekla saw one of his eyes briefly glimmer through the smoke.

The two other men looked at each other. One signaled toward the door and the other bent down to help his fallen accomplice. Suddenly, they both froze.

Hekla, now standing and holding onto the bookshelf, looked for a visual clue but found nothing. Then she saw the barrel of the shotgun clearing a path for Keeper. The intruders raised their hands and Keeper slowly moved into the living room. Keeper was a little wobbly, but he held the gun with conviction. The intruders did not budge. As Keeper came close though, a fourth man emerged from near the front door and tackled Keeper from behind. Gunnar moved toward them, but one of the other attackers hurled himself at Gunnar's legs.

Hekla felt the ground shake as mighty Gunnar tumbled down. She managed to lurch forward a bit, but by the time she was near, the fourth man had wrested the shotgun from Keeper. And he was pointing it at Hekla. Keeper lay helpless on the floor, the attacker's boot on his back.

The other attackers scrambled to their feet and moved behind Number Four. The man pointed the gun at Hekla, then at Gunnar, then at Keeper, then back at Gunnar. Four's uncertain moves worried Hekla. The attacker was improvising while holding a firearm—always dangerous. The attackers made their way to the front door, with Four walking backward, keeping the gun trained on Gunnar. The intruders rushed out as Four stood guard in the doorway.

Four took another step backward, so one foot was inside, the other was outside. He scanned the room once more. Then his upper body moved. It wasn't much, and it might have just been his shoulders, but it was movement.

And then, a single, sickening sound.

Bang!

It wasn't deafening, like the first one. But it was familiar and foul. The movement and images that followed the noise made it worse than any sound—or loss of sound—could be. A spark of light, a tiny puff of smoke, the recoil of the shotgun in the man's hands. He shot Gunnar.

CHAPTER FORTY-THREE

THE FLASH GRENADE THAT INTRODUCED CHAOS TO
the quiet cottage a few minutes earlier had been effective. Hekla
was dazed and deaf. And she was furious.

"Gunnar!" she tried calling out, forcing air from her lungs. She
hoped he could hear her, even if she could barely hear anything.

Something else, besides her hearing and balance, was off. It
was too dark for a lit room, but the swirl of odd shadows and
spectral lights told Hekla the room was not in total darkness. She
alternated blinks and wide-eyed stares as she slowly turned her
head. A few meters to her right was the glass lampshade. It lay
perfectly intact and right-side up on the floor, bulb still shining.
So that was the light source. She looked back to the left. Gunnar
should be there. Why wasn't Gunnar there?

Keeper flew across her line of vision. Hekla started to call out
but decided to save her energy and not risk the delicate balance
she almost lost looking around the room seconds earlier. Instead,
she took careful, bow-legged steps toward the back of the room.

The images still didn't seem right. Keeper was gone already.
Had he made it up the stairs or down the hallway? She navigated
around the toppled wingback chair. And where was Gunnar?
The large sofa was upright, but appeared to be moving. She scru-
tinized its form as she carefully made her way around. She had to
walk for longer than made sense, as if the mayhem had doubled
the sofa's size. When Hekla finally reached the edge, she stared
with curiosity at the moving mass near her feet.

There was Gunnar—his face, his hands. And there was

Keeper, too. Even in this fractured light, with her sensory perception so compromised, Hekla immediately recognized the look on Keeper's face. She kept moving though, until she could see the reason for his expression herself.

Elísa lay motionless on the floor. Her sweater jacket was ripped open. Gunnar's large hands pressed firmly against a blood-soaked T-shirt. Hekla grabbed her phone. She rang emergency services and shoved her phone toward Keeper. The look in her eyes was enough to convince him to finish the call. Then Hekla collapsed to her knees and applied pressure to one of the wounds on the teenager's body.

Elísa died before emergency responders could reach the house.

Paramedics rushed to help Hekla, whose physical injuries were severe enough to warrant a trip to the hospital. Her mental clarity was even more battered. All she knew was pain: guilt, grief, anger, regret, and their brethren. They flooded all the systems in her body at once, and it hurt. It hurt to the point that even when the doctor directed her attention to the burns on her calf, she felt only the ache in her head and torso.

Hekla felt everything, but she couldn't move. It was as if a force was pulling her from the inside in an endless series of agonizing implosions.

The doctor who had attended to Hekla's calf returned with a nurse. Hekla could still only make out fragments of sound. Voices would fade in, seemingly at random, before disappearing again. It seemed like the people at the hospital found her state to be equally unmanageable. The nurse handed a syringe to the doctor, who emptied its contents into a port on Hekla's IV line. And then she didn't feel anything.

CHAPTER FORTY-FOUR

HEKLA AWOKE TO THE SOUND OF THE TV. FOR A moment she was unsure of where she was. One of her legs was freezing and the other hurt immensely. She had a headache and her mouth was dry. Next to her, on her large, wooden coffee table, sat a bottle of Finnish vodka and a nearly full tumbler. She let out a deep sigh. Now she remembered. She had decided to drink.

It was an odd choice. She had never been much of a drinker, and in the past year had all but given up even the occasional libation. She had too many things to do that practically and morally required a clear mind. The brand made more sense. To her knowledge, the Finns had never shipped concussion grenades to her country, so she was okay with buying their booze. Why she had opted for alcohol instead of the strong painkillers that had been prescribed was more complicated.

She tried lifting herself to a seated position.

"Ahhck," she groaned.

It wasn't just her head and leg. Everything in her body hurt tremendously. It felt like all her bones were bruised and all her muscles, known and unknown, had been torn. She looked at the clock. 2:36.

If she felt like this, she wondered how Gunnar must feel. Or . . .

She let out a softer groan. She reached out and grabbed the tumbler. She lifted her body and head in unison as she poured the liquid down her throat. She finished her drink before she was upright. She refilled the glass and attempted to take stock of the past few days—what she could remember of them at least.

She figured it had been around 48 hours since they were at Keeper's house. Not seconds after Hekla placed her hand on Elísa's stomach, her hands were almost as bloody as Gunnar's. The girl had no chance. The shot had torn deep wounds all over her torso. Hekla kept pressing though. She and Gunnar both did. At some point, emergency responders came and pulled Hekla and Gunnar away from Elísa. After they left with the girl, the medics seemed most concerned with Hekla.

She could remember seeing the faces of Gunnar and Keeper, illuminated by flashing lights outside of the house, as the responders forced her into an ambulance. It was like an incomplete nightmare, as frustrating as it was horrifying, with audio and key scenes missing throughout. She remembered feeling isolated and impotent watching Gunnar and Keeper from the back of the ambulance. She couldn't hear much, but she could see their pain and profound sadness as the chaotic lights amplified and exaggerated their every movement.

How did this happen—how did *she* let this happen, she asked herself.

She took a large gulp of vodka.

The hospital was mostly a blur after they knocked her out. She remembered being moved to a different floor at some point, and a cluster of doctors paying close attention to her leg. All she could see from her vantage point was a smooth swatch of bright red where her skin used to be. She recalled calling out and not getting a response to a question she knew was important. Maybe she had forgotten what happened to Elísa.

More memories began taking form. It was dark out when they released her. At first, she thought it was night, but it must have been the next morning because the sun was out when Einar drove her home. Had Einar been at the hospital? She didn't remember speaking much. She hoped she hadn't. She needed more information and a sharper mind before confronting either Einar or Bjarni.

Einar! He hadn't been at the hospital. He was at the station. Somehow, Hekla ended up there after the hospital. It could have just been the drugs and shock, but she recalled sensing a shift in mood when she returned to headquarters. It was like she had walked up to a group of carelessly gabbing teenagers who abruptly became quiet when she arrived. Kjartan asked a lot of questions about her decision to go to the house early. To her, the necessity of her actions was self-evident. Clearly, she needed to move *even sooner* if she were to keep Elísa safe. It seemed like Kjartan, or whomever was in his ear, was suggesting that she had led the assailants to the house. Maybe a "detective disobeys orders, causes chaos, and endangers the public" narrative was more palatable to those in power than the truth. To be fair, she only had bits and pieces of the truth herself.

She knew the only people who had known where Elísa had been hiding were the Americans and top-level law enforcement. The four goons at the house were clearly trained and had access to advanced weapons. Other than the police, the only people who would have any motive to seek out Elísa were those who were afraid of what she knew—or what information she might have. The only people who would have such fear were those associated with the mining deal. Most of this was obvious, but the answer to the question, "Why was Elísa at Keeper's house to begin with?" was more complicated, and not something Hekla could articulate right now.

It was easy to cast Hekla as a renegade. The police could make vague comments suggesting that the people who raided the house and shot Elísa were the same ones who killed Jack and Steingrímur. The implication was that the intruders were trying to eliminate a witness or co-conspirator—without, of course, explicitly calling the dead teenager a co-conspirator.

Hekla needed time to figure things out. She needed time to figure out if she even *wanted* to figure things out.

She took another healthy swig.

She had a vague recollection of driving to the outdoor shopping center near her flat after Einar dropped her off, of filling her prescription, and of walking diagonally across the large parking lot to the state-run liquor store. She had a notion that alcohol might be a better remedy for what ailed her, but the drink didn't ease her thoughts any more than it eased her physical pain. And now she had a few new images to add to the catalog of dead and devastated faces that danced in her mind.

What bothered her most was the knowledge that it really was her fault. She *was* to blame. Whether she had led those men to Keeper's home or not, whether her theories were actual truths, none of that mattered. In her heart, she knew that everything that had gone wrong, everything that led to the death of that girl, was her fault. She wanted desperately to be active, to go after each of the men who broke into Keeper's home and then to go after everyone who was responsible for the thugs being there in the first place. But even if she were well, she knew that this wasn't possible right now. Things had shifted, and she would need to be patient.

Hekla finished the vodka in her glass. Her attention shifted back to the TV. The country's mood, or RUV's coverage and interpretation of the mood, seemed to have changed as well. Where there was shock and outrage before, there was now a more somber and mournful tone. This wasn't just big news, this was tragic news. For Hekla, it was personal news. And she couldn't bear to watch it, to hear stories about the life that Elísa barely got to live.

Hekla turned off the volume but kept the TV on. She was still hoping that the media might help her out. She wondered if Aldís would make a statement.

Aldís. Hekla knew more about Aldís than most, but there was a stretch of Aldís's life she knew relatively little of. This stretch included the time that August was with her. When Hekla looked at the file the NBI had on Aldís, her focus was not on Aldís's romantic partners. But now she was curious. Whatever it was that sent August into his hole in Copenhagen happened after he left Iceland. Maybe his issues with Lisa didn't stem from his time at the legat. Maybe it was from after he left. And maybe Aldís's work during this period could provide some insight into what had happened.

Hekla crawled across the sofa to retrieve her laptop. Next to her laptop, buried within a heap of personal items on the cushion, was her cell phone. She eyed it warily before picking it up. She winced at the sight of Logi's name among the missed calls and messages.

She unlocked her phone and checked his text message. Her reticence was justified.

"I really need to see you. Please."

CHAPTER FORTY-FIVE

August awoke to the sensation of sunlight on
his face. It was the first time since arriving in Iceland that he
could remember beginning a day that way. He stared out the window, trying to determine if he had neglected to draw the curtains
closed the night before, or if he had previously been impervious to
the late-morning rays. It was a pleasantly frivolous thought, no
doubt induced by the time he spent in Patreksfjörður with Aldís
the day before. Even the negative thoughts that greeted him in
the morning were no match for the joyous mood he unexpectedly
found himself in.

His time with Aldís hadn't provided answers to most of the
questions he had about her current situation, but just talking to
her, having a real conversation instead of a reunion interrupted
by a team of overzealous cops provided a sense of relief he hadn't
felt in years. The effect even carried over to his thoughts regarding Lisa and what happened with Client. He was still angry, but
this was a type of anger with defined contours. Somehow, what
had long been a blinding rage and a sense of impotent fury had
become a simple, clear desire for revenge. This was something he
could work with.

He took a deep, free breath. Aldís's defiance and her optimism
in the face of overwhelming odds and relentless enemies made it
hard for him to linger on the past or lament the present. If she
could enjoy his company after everything they had been through,
it was hard for him to spend another day in the darkness. Besides,
things were different now. He might not know whom he could

trust besides Aldís, but he knew for sure whom never to extend the courtesy to again.

He surveyed his room. It was probably time to upgrade his accommodation. Aldís didn't like the idea, but he had decided he was going to stay longer, if for no other reason than Lisa's clearly articulated desire for him to *not* stay any longer. He was unsure what her role was in all of this, but he was intent on finding out. He even dared to hope that he might have an opportunity to assist those who opposed his former employer's machinations.

Two dead billionaires in a winter wonderland, he mused. Fucking Christ.

August never got around to asking Aldís why she had decided to visit the Azure spa the day Jack was killed. He knew she hated that place. He remembered her scathing critiques of the hotel's owners, the influence they had on tourism, and their awful labor record. So, it was odd, to say the least, for her to patronize this establishment on a random Monday in December, when an American she had pointedly criticized just happened to be staying there.

August got out of bed and turned on the TV, hoping to catch a weather forecast either before or after his shower. He froze when he saw a reporter standing outside the police station.

"This is the third homicide in Iceland in five weeks and second Icelandic citizen who has been killed," Margrét declared. "Police have not yet commented on whether this death is connected to the other two killings, but we do know that the victim was an employee of the Azure Hotel, where billionaire American businessman Jack Drumman was killed last month."

August sat on the edge of his bed.

"This death raises serious questions about law enforcement's response to the unprecedented wave of violence," Margrét continued. "We have learned that two police officers were actually at the scene when the four assailants entered the private residence."

August's stomach dropped. *Where were they?* His chest tightened at the mention of a death, but his stomach quaked with dread as he waited for the revelation of circumstance.

"The commissioner told RÚV that officers were conducting a search, but he declined to provide information about why it was necessary to search the home at that hour, or if the police presence played a role in the victim's death. Both officers, whose names were not released, were injured, with one suffering serious, but non-life-threatening injuries from a flash grenade."

What home? What residence? *Where were they?* August's brain practically screamed the questions. He panicked, searching for a way out as his eyes remained glued to the TV. The network cut from Margrét to an anchor at the television station. There was a picture of a young girl on the corner of the screen. She looked like she was in high school or whatever the equivalent was in this country. The image knocked the wind out of August. He helplessly watched the screen, waiting impatiently for the final blow that he was already convinced was coming.

"Thank you Margrét," the anchor said. "To recap, tragic news. Nineteen-year-old Grindavik resident Elísa Pálsdóttir fatally injured by a shotgun blast early this morning in a chaotic scene that included two police officers and several unknown intruders. The incident took place at a private residence in the Suðurnesjabær municipality. The home was originally owned by the keeper of an adjacent lighthouse—"

And then August couldn't hear a thing. He slid off the bed and onto his knees, continuing forward until his bowed head touched the carpet. His eyes thought to cry, but an unexpected force within him deemed his eyes' response inadequate. He screamed. It was a primal, desperate howl that wavered between anguished and angry. It was directed at anyone and everyone, and finally, at August himself—with twice as much fury.

The girl. The runaway teenager. The Keeper's home in Keflavík—Aldís's safe house. August could have done something. He could have saved her. All he had to do was speak up and she would still be alive. She *should* still be alive. But no. He did nothing. And now she was dead.

⁙⁙⁙⁙⁙⁙⁙⁙⁙⁙⁙⁙

August continued to work with Client even after the young man's arrest. He did everything humanly possible to help in the ensuing days, weeks, and months. He called, he wrote, he even flew to the States several times. He spent multiple nights at far-flung motels that were still hours away from the remote locations where Client was being held, all for the opportunity to spend a mere hour or two with him. He wasn't going to give up, but it wasn't a fair fight. The rules of the game applied only to Client. And when August first heard the words "secure housing," he feared the game might already be over.

Special Housing Unit, Administrative Segregation, Restrictive Housing, Security Management Unit—these are all euphemisms for torture. Actually, they are euphemisms for solitary confinement, which is a euphemism for torture. There is no doubt about the effect, if not the purpose, of confining a person to a bathroom-sized cage for 23 hours a day. The only reprieve coming when the guards would shackle the prisoner and lead him or her to another cage—this one outside—that was too small for any activity besides pacing.

August—and many others—believed America's *entire* prison

system, excluding perhaps the places they reserved for the wealthiest criminals, was a highly structured torture system. That put solitary confinement in a special class of evil, the kind of fucked-up, calculated sadism that could only be truly appreciated by "enhanced interrogation" monsters and their predecessors in scientifically calculated atrocity.

So, when August was informed that Client was in solitary confinement, he began to panic. Client was brave and tough, but also rigid and uncompromising. When Client saw a wrong, he tried to fix it. There wasn't really room in his brain for other options. But this approach also removed sentimentality as a moderating force, even as it might apply to one's own life. August was afraid that Client might do the math and simply conclude that his best move was to fold his cards and quit the game.

August knew how difficult it was for inmates to voluntarily end their life in solitary confinement. Only the government was supposed to have the power to release prisoners from that hell. Suicide watch is therefore more like suicide control. The withholding of personal items, the unadorned mattress pad on a concrete slab, being left naked in a too-cold cell illuminated by a yellow light that remains on for days and weeks that might as well be months or years—Client's captors didn't take these measures because they were *concerned* he might end his own life. They were measures taken to make damn sure he *couldn't*.

When Client was temporarily returned to a "normal" cell, he must have seen it as awash with opportunity, as close to freedom as a prison offers. But he also must have been afraid, terrified even, knowing the nightmare that was waiting for him whenever those with power decided he had enough. August imagined it to be like a drowning person who surfaces long enough to get a breath of air, knowing he is about to be dragged back underwater.

It's not just the deprivation of oxygen that waits below, it's the *fear* of being unable to breathe again. In that type of situation, the knowledge that you were once able to survive is not enough. There is no credit for past performance when the brain is trying to protect itself from pain.

What was Client able to see when his head was back above water? August imagined it was overwhelming. The ordinarily dull prison wing must have seemed like a maddening cacophony of sights and sounds after Client had been alone with his thoughts for *97 fucking days*. But after his eyes adjusted and the deafening roar softened to a low buzz, a few things probably would have become clear. First, Client would have at least one night in this cell while officials performed "maintenance" on his solitary confinement unit. Second, the guards followed the same schedule every day, which meant inmates knew where guards were—and when. Finally, of course, was the knowledge that this "break" was temporary. At any time, Client could be sent back to that tiny concrete box with a light that never went off. No matter what, Client would not accept that fate.

August spent the better part of a year searching for answers about Client's death. Eventually, he gave up the quest. He didn't need to find a conspiracy or guard with a conscience. The conclusion would be the same either way. He knew as well as whomever had orchestrated Client's temporary relocation that the move back to solitary was a death sentence—whether Client made the last move or not. Just like the tiny figures he watched on a screen all those years ago, Client was killed by his government. He was tortured and murdered. That's it. That's all August would ever find because that's all there would ever be.

The last interaction August had with Client was when he watched the young man's dead body lowered into the ground. As he stood alone, watching the heavy machinery complete the process of disappearing Client, August vowed that he would never allow something like this to happen again. He would do everything in his power to avoid being responsible for ending another good person's life, even if that meant effectively ending his own.

CHAPTER FORTY-SIX

Eʟísᴀ's ꜰᴜɴᴇʀᴀʟ ᴡᴀs ʜᴇʟᴅ ᴀᴛ ᴀ Lᴜᴛʜᴇʀᴀɴ Cʜᴜʀᴄʜ in the heart of Grindavik. Hekla didn't think the girl shared the religious beliefs of those in charge of the arrangements, nor did she believe these people—ones who had assumed the role of grieving relatives in a spectacularized death with great enthusiasm—ever had been close to her. But the church did have plenty of seating. That was probably the most important part of this whole thing anyway.

Watching the buildup to the event, Hekla knew there was likely to be a large turnout, but as she approached the town, driving south on Grindavíkurvegur, she realized that this had turned into something else entirely. There seemed to be more cars on the road leading to the church than there were people in all Grindavik. Five hundred meters out, people of all ages were walking toward the church, hands full of flowers, cards, and handcrafted items meant to memorialize the deceased.

Hekla considered turning around. Instead, she nearly clipped a mourner as she made a last-second right on Nesvegur. She took Nesvegur around the circumference of the town until she came to a gravel-covered clearing in the residential district a few blocks east of the church. She got out of her car and trekked through about a half a meter of snow in some family's back yard as a child watched with wonder from a window in the house.

⁙⁙⁙⁙⁙⁙⁙⁙⁙⁙

Hekla was slightly unsteady as she stood on the mosaic sidewalk outside the Church. She mostly ignored the dirty looks of people heading toward the building. Every now and then though, she took a defiant drag of her cigarette as she locked eyes with a proper woman or concerned father. This was a funeral for a teenager, Hekla thought. Surely these people could find greater offenses to propriety than her nicotine-infused tribute to impermanence. She tried not to blow smoke directly into their children's lungs, but otherwise had more important things to focus on—namely, who would be walking into or out of the church.

When she arrived, the congregation was singing. The last funeral she attended had no singing. In fact, it had no body. She supposed it wasn't really a funeral. Rather it was a semi-official conclusion to years of misery. At least that was the idea. Some families got closure from the discovery of a body. Hekla was supposed to be satisfied with a check and a letter. She returned the check.

She'd also been to a few masses as a child, part of her parents' periodic attempts to expose her and her brother to other people's faiths. Even at a young age, the behavior of the believers left her feeling frustrated. The focus seemed off, the underpinnings bizarre. She could understand adopting some beliefs as a way of coping with a fear of death, especially when it was almost certainly followed by an eternity of nothingness. Death was some scary shit. What bothered her was how so many invoked "God" instead of taking action. She had always felt that "because God" was an unsatisfactory answer for good, and a downright disturbing justification for bad. It was man, not God, who had an actual and immediate ability to make a more equitable world. Surely humans had the capacity to come up with better organizing principles for living a decent life, and *much* better ways to prevent so many from being so incredibly fucked.

Hekla heard more singing. This was the third round since she had staked out her ground near the Church. She looked at her hand, which held what must have been her third or fourth cigarette of the young day. Several of her digits looked alarmingly white. Everyone going into the church was well bundled-up. She probably should feel colder, she thought.

For a variety of reasons, Hekla had not paid particularly close attention to her outfit this morning. She considered her three-point, wet-wipe-shower, along with her discovery of a pair of knitted, wool sweatpants that she could pull over her legs without disrupting her bandages to be significant enough victories. Any more attention to her appearance would be inappropriately vain given the circumstances, she decided after the fact.

It wasn't until she was well on her way to Grindavik that she realized she was almost certainly still drunk. The pull of vodka she took from a repurposed water bottle before she got out of her car was therefore a precautionary measure.

Her phone vibrated. The state-of-the-art touchscreen didn't recognize her index or middle fingers as belonging to the living, so she dragged her pinkie across the face of her phone to accept the call.

"Yes—here."

"Uh, hello?" Val sounded startled, as though they hadn't expected an answer. "I, um—I'm sorry to bother you. Are you okay? Are you at the funeral?"

"Yes. I'm—I am."

"How are you feeling? I left a few messages."

"Okay. Fine. I'm fine. What is it—what can I help—you?"

"Um . . . well I'm not really sure—"

"Vals. What's it? Just tell me, now." Hekla leaned to the side, almost falling over in the process, as she attempted to get a better look at some people leaving the Church. She couldn't make out anyone's identity, but it appeared someone in the group commanded respect.

"There was an interview. With the bartender at the hotel—the Envoy. The transcript was part of the universal file but then it was pulled. It must have only been there an hour or so."

"Uh-huh." Hekla was only half-listening at this point, her attention focused on the mourners leaving the Church.

"It was taken out of the file right after a meeting between Bjarni and Kjartan, so I imagine it was discussed with Kjartan too. And, um, well . . . "

Hekla noticed the RUV news van a block or two behind the church. "Just—just tells me."

"They know about you and Logi," Val blurted out.

Hekla's attention was immediately brought back to the phone. Her very first thought was, "What does *Val know* about me and Logi?"

Her next thought was, "Not now."

"Okay then," Hekla said.

"Okay?" Val responded with surprise.

"That's good—you telling me for. I'm glad you did. That. Thank you."

After a confused pause, Val's befuddled voice came back. "That's it?"

"Yes. I think so now." Hekla was pretty sure she saw who she was looking for.

"Should we—is there something I can do to help?"

"No. No, not this—no. You did great. Thanks. I have to go."

"Are you sure? Is everything—"

Hekla hung up. The crowd outside of the church was forming a semi-circle, indicating that the dead girl's body was about to be paraded out. She flicked her cigarette and took a few steps toward the crowd when a large hand fell on her shoulder. She looked around, and then up, to see Gunnar. Her eyes widened and her heart sank.

Gunnar wore a formal police uniform, but it looked like he was wearing a mask, as well. His eyes weren't merely black and blue, they were black and blue and gray and red and a few other colors that had no business on a healthy human being. His nose was purple and swollen, and a series of surgical stitches held parts of his face together. Hekla thought about the brutal blows that the rest of his body had absorbed and the injuries she couldn't see.

"Oh—God," she said. "I'm—I'm so—sorry."

Gunnar shook his head. "What are you doing here?" he asked. "You should be resting."

"No. It's fine—I'm good."

"You don't look good."

Hekla guffawed. "You're not—in great—looking great your-self. Big guy."

Gunnar didn't laugh. "That's not what I mean." He looked around. "How'd you get here?"

Hekla noticed that the crowd near the entrance to the church was moving in unison, pulling apart and then back together, like an amoeba or whatever organism it was that did that sort of thing.

"Gunnar. I'm—I . . . " It was hard for her to look at him like this. He also deserved better than what she had put him through. But she didn't have time to devote to him right now. "I have to—have to go now. I'm sorry."

"Hekla!" he shouted. But she was already off, scuttling as fast as she could with the limp that she had adopted to avoid stretch-ing her calf muscle.

Some part of Hekla knew what she was doing was a mistake as

she moved quickly toward a couple standing solemnly near the back of the crowd. A conscious part of Hekla also noticed Kjartan, dressed in formal police attire, a few meters away. But this part of her was present only as an observer. It had no power to influence the actions of its host. It was there to capture just enough of a memory that she would have to accept the truth later. Because later, she would want nothing more than to dismiss all the scattered recollections from a mostly blacked-out period as a sloppy work of fiction assembled by an exhausted brain. If only.

Later, she remembered taking her last few steps toward the couple, forcefully grabbing Aldís by the shoulder and spinning her around. She remembered that Aldís looked shocked and unnerved by Hekla's appearance. Aldís seemed deeply upset, as well. There were no tears in Aldís's eyes, only a look of deep sadness, a look unmistakable to anyone who has experienced deep loss.

For a moment, Hekla was uncertain. But the deep sadness that *she* felt had been taking performance enhancers. And even drunk, Hekla knew exactly what to say. She knew because she had been practicing the words in her mind since Elísa was shot.

"Did you know?" Hekla practically screamed. "Did you know she was there?" Her hand bore into Aldís's shoulder as she shook her. "Answer me! She was there—did you know?"

Aldís shook her head. Her sadness seemed deeper now, as though Hekla's words brought even greater pain.

"A kid!" Hekla continued. "She was a kid!" Her voice cracked on the last word.

Logi appeared, his arm jutting into Hekla's memory as Aldís took a few steps back.

"Get off," Hekla said with venom as she shoved Logi hard. She continued after Aldís. "She was just a fucking—a fucking kid! Why was she there?"

Aldís's face offered no answer.

Hekla reached toward Aldís. It was unclear what she intended to do, since any number of possibilities existed. It was likely a mystery to Hekla as well, and will forever remain that way, because at that precise moment, a power greater than Hekla intervened. It might even have been *powers*, as Hekla doubted that Kjartan alone could produce the force on her body.

Hekla was dragged away. She watched Aldís finally break into tears as Logi embraced her. And with that fond recollection to hold on to, Hekla's brain decided to rest—or retreat—into temporary oblivion.

PART THREE

CHAPTER FORTY-SEVEN

THE FIRST PILL WAS MAGICAL. IT DIDN'T JUST alleviate her physical discomfort, it eliminated all pain. With one dose, the screaming inside her head was muted. In its stead was a radiating joy—a sense of peace, a warmth, a transcendent serenity that exists when there is true harmony between self and the world. She was lifted. Her body subjected to the pull of gravity only long enough to secure a foot, then it was free to twist and turn, merrily in the air above, before just enough weight would return for her to push off with her next step. It was as if a liquid form of light had entered through the top of her head and worked its way down and around her body until she was embraced by a comforting love. It was perfect. And it lasted for hours.

The next pill was okay.

Maybe it was good. Who knows? It was difficult to properly gauge efficacy when the only point of comparison was transmutational orgasm. Whatever the case, it was clear that Hekla needed to be careful with those things.

Hekla had passed the first few weeks of her recovery, and her suspension from the police force, without taking a single pill. She managed with alcohol, abstaining during the 12 hours before a doctor visit. She told her doctor about her enduring pain, refilled her prescription, and left the pill bottles untouched.

Once she was sure her leg was better, she started taking her medication. Her drug use was not medically approved, but neither was it the devised scheme of an addict. She just needed help getting through the days.

After the disappointment of the second pill, she implemented a strict dosage regimen, supplementing with vodka as necessary. She was wary of the cycle of addiction but, more than anything, she was annoyed that she couldn't replicate that initial bliss, and she didn't feel like swallowing a fistful of pills only to *not* get there again. Naturally, the addition of alcohol produced uneven results. At best.

So it was that Hekla found herself passed out on her bathroom floor one spring afternoon, her phone rattling incessantly on the ceramic tiles a meter from her head. The first thing she saw when she opened her eyes was red. Dark red. It covered the back of her fingers and the side of her right hand, which rested beneath her brow. Revulsion rumbled through her, and her stomach clenched. Her skull was like a cymbal, still vibrating after being smashed with an oversized drumstick. She felt alive, alert, and terribly displeased with the gift of consciousness.

She slid her legs up until she was able to rest on her knees and forearms. The floor was cold and hard. It felt particularly drafty on her legs. She tilted her head and realized she was only wearing underwear—barely. She reached back to adjust her waistband so that her panties could at least provide some coverage.

It took her a few tries before she could sit up. As soon as she lifted her head, the pain rushed upward. Eventually, she managed to get to her feet by bracing herself against the toilet. She gingerly shuffled to the sink and stared into the mirror, too shocked to be properly scared.

"Fucking hell," she thought to herself.

It looked like someone had sliced her face open. A trail of blood, at least a centimeter wide in some places ran from the side of her forehead, down and across her nose before stopping just above her lips.

She leaned closer. The line was crooked. It appeared that at least some of what she was seeing was dried blood. She turned the water on and washed the blood away, hoping she wouldn't find a sizable gash. She was lucky in that regard. The laceration on her forehead was not insignificant, but it wasn't terrible. Wouldn't even require stitches. Hekla looked back at the floor. There sure was a lot of blood, she thought, with more than a little concern for her overall supply.

She returned her focus to the mirror. Her face wasn't cut in half, but she didn't look good. *Terrifying* was one of the first words that came to her mind, like a hollow-eyed zombie who had died of consumption. It had been a while since she paid much attention to her appearance. Generally, she thought that to be a good thing. She was comfortable with her appearance, her confidence came from attributes other than her looks. But there was nothing positive in the behavior responsible for her current look.

And now her head was bleeding again.

"Ughhck," she groaned.

She had been standing for far too long. She carefully lowered herself to her knees. The cold tiles bit at her bare legs. She sat back on her ankles, wrapped her arms around her stomach, and bent forward at her waist until her torso was almost parallel with the floor. Then she gently rocked herself, doing the best she could to distract herself from the acute pain that she felt everywhere, all over, again.

*

Hekla chugged two glasses of water from the kitchen sink before refilling her glass and moving to the living room.

The room was hard to recognize at first. At least the room she thought she remembered. There were concentric circles of debris originating from a spot on her couch, where she apparently had set up a nest. On the ground next to the couch, in reaching range of the nest, was a nearly empty 750 ml bottle of vodka. Next to the vodka were her pills.

Hekla picked up the vodka and placed it on the coffee table. She grabbed the pill bottle and inspected its contents. A few loose tablets rattled against the plastic. She tossed the bottle on the couch, took a swig of vodka, and collapsed face-first into the cushions. It seemed like she had deviated from her strict dosage regimen, she concluded with resignation.

She quickly realized that she didn't know how long she had been going on like this. Time and her memory had become fuzzy. Memories from years ago were clear, but she couldn't remember details from yesterday. The soiled clothing, empty bottles, and food cartons strewn around her flat told her she had been in this haze for at least a week.

The sound of her phone vibrating on the tiles echoed from the bathroom.

When Hekla was first informed of her suspension, she dealt with it, in her mind, as well as possible. She did not dispute the authenticity of the texts between Logi and herself. Nor did she contest the conclusions that had been drawn from them. She made sure to note that she never personally interviewed Logi— not because she was trying to avoid the consequences of an undisclosed affair, but because it was important for her to preserve the integrity of the investigation.

She was somewhat surprised that Kjartan didn't mention anything about Elísa's funeral. She had a disturbingly vivid recollection of showing up drunk and yelling at Aldís before being dragged off by Gunnar and Kjartan. She figured Kjartan had done her a favor by omitting it from her departmental record.

Even off-duty, a documented incident with drugs or alcohol could keep her from active duty for a year or more.

As it stood, there was no real timetable for her return. There was an official two-month suspension with pay, followed by an unofficial, but essentially mandatory, month-long leave of absence. She spent the suspension in a stupor and was now almost halfway through a second month of leave. Truthfully, she was in no rush to return to work. There was nothing for her to do there—nothing she *could* do. She had tried her best, and all she did was get a teenager killed. Meanwhile, her efforts at uncovering and exposing the real villains had amounted to nothing. Maybe even worse than that.

Just a few weeks after Elísa's death, the details of the government's new energy partnership—*promising to usher in a new era of prosperity while respecting the traditions, values, and relationship with nature that make Iceland so special*—were announced to the country. Those leading the charge acted as if the revelations made by Aldís were not disqualifying indictments, but an incomplete teaser clip. Dragged from the shadows into the light, the businesspeople acted as if they'd been in the sun all along.

The *new* mining deal group was shameless. Truth was no impediment to business, and neither was death. The people who stood to make a fortune from the deal loudly proclaimed that they were trying to finalize a business transaction to honor a dead man. The phrase "Steingrímur's dream" was repeated ad nauseam during their initial press conference. Sticking a drill into the seabed to grab some mysterious super-rock was being done in *his* name now. It was grotesque. Hekla wondered how Steingrímur would have felt about a life spent acquiring money and power just to be reduced to a marketing ploy designed to make some *other* assholes richer.

Susan and the American partners were conspicuously absent from the rollout. Susan fled to the States shortly after Steingrímur's murder, but Hekla paid enough attention to know that Susan—and the interests she represented—were still intimately involved.

The other current event Hekla kept tabs on was Aldís's bid to be elected to Iceland's parliament. The campaign got more coverage than any Icelandic campaign ever—including races for prime minister. The media couldn't seem to get enough. It was, of course, because of Aldís. Even before her arrest, Aldís running for office would garner significant attention. The events surrounding her entry into the race made the story even more alluring. But seeing the type of articles that were emerging, it was clear that the election was also profoundly important to Aldís's opponent, Ragna María Sigurðardóttir—and the powerful interests that backed Ragna.

It was all about the mining deal. If Aldís won, she could scuttle the whole thing. So Ragna's re-election campaign was an extension of the mining deal consortium's marketing effort. And just as with the media blitz that defined the deal, Ragna's campaign was full of disingenuous claims. Ragna and the consortium promoted the lie that if Aldís were to win and block the deal, the people of Iceland would be deprived of better jobs and more money. Nothing supported this claim. In fact, evidence from the consortium's *own contracts* contradicted this position. But that didn't matter. Ragna and her surrogates repeated the lie over and over, and that appeared to be enough to fix it as a fact in many voters' minds.

Hekla's phone rattled once more. It wasn't going to give up. She feared what she might learn she had done over the past few days. Or weeks. She pried herself off the couch, grabbed the bottle of vodka, and finished what was left in one giant gulp. She knew she'd have to deal with the phone eventually. Might as well get it over with now, she figured.

CHAPTER FORTY-EIGHT

Hekla tried to make sense of all the calls. There was no *good* reason for anyone to try and contact her so many times in such a short period of time. She navigated to the outgoing calls section. "Uhhgh," she groaned. There was no *good* reason for her to have made so many calls while blacked out.

The phone shook in her hand. It was Val, the cause of almost all her phone's recent activity. Reluctantly, she answered.

"Are you okay?" Val asked with alarm before Hekla could get a word out.

"Huh?" Hekla's voice was rasp, barely above a whisper.

"Are you home?"

"Yuh—Yes. I'm here. Why?"

"I'm outside. Let me in. Now."

Val's order did not invite debate. Hekla still hesitated, giving her brain extra time to conjure up an excuse. Her brain did not deliver. "Give me—give me a minute," Hekla mumbled.

In the seven minutes between hanging up the phone and letting Val into her building, Hekla managed to put on pants, wash her face, clean up a blood trail, and shovel almost everything that was on her living room floor into her bedroom. A quick sniff inside her shirt before opening the door revealed that she might not be entirely fresh, but Hekla thought the look of horror on Val's face was a bit much.

Val, by contrast, looked as composed and capable as ever. Hekla realized that she had never seen them out of office attire, or even outside the station. There was a vibrancy that got lost there, she realized now. Their hair was still finely tuned, cropped close on the sides and back, a bit longer on top with the front pushed back. Their outfit loosely resembled what they would wear to work, but with tiny variations that gave an entirely different impression: pants a touch wider at the ankle, shirt untucked, hitting just beneath their hips under a mid-weight jacket. It was a modest look that also managed to be definitively anti-conservative. And their captivating face, enticing with symmetry but alluring in a way that geometry could not account for, shone a bit brighter.

Right now, however, Val's face scared Hekla. "What is it?" she asked.

Val said nothing as they took a few steps inside Hekla's flat. They looked around and then returned their gaze to Hekla, who felt exceedingly uncomfortable. "What?" she asked again. "Why are you looking at me like that?"

Val appeared as if they wanted to respond a certain way but had to stop themself. When they finally did speak, their tone was measured. "How are you feeling?"

"I—" Hekla also had to stop herself, not from speaking an unvarnished truth like Val, but from spinning an instinctual lie. "I've been better."

Val nodded. "You called me. Last night. And then you didn't pick up. I was worried."

Hekla's stomach managed to make a new knot. "I'm sorry. I was—I was drinking."

"Do you remember what you said?"

That seemed like an unfair question to Hekla. Val must have thought the same since they quickly assisted. "It was about Bjarni."

Hekla let out a small sigh of relief. All things considered, that wasn't the worst topic not to remember. She had a good guess about what she had said. "Bjarni and Elísa?" she asked.

"Yes," Val said. "I think you're right. I think I can prove it too."

<hr>

Hekla stared at the mug of coffee in her hands. There wasn't a chance she could take another sip without vomiting.

Val sat diagonally across from her on the couch. They took a few sips from their own mug before resting it on a magazine that had melded with the coffee table to form a permanent coaster. Hekla appreciated the way Val instinctually adapted to the surroundings. Their countenance was softer now, there was no look of condemnation when Hekla had to clear mystery sediment from the couch. They even retrieved a tissue to wipe off blood that seeped from Hekla's forehead.

Hekla was touched by Val's kindness, and she stopped pretending. She admitted she didn't remember much of what she had done over the past weeks, and acknowledged she had spent much of the time since the funeral drunk or on the path to drunkenness. Val did not seem shocked. Their only comment, delivered with a matter-of-fact voice that managed to convey heartfelt urgency but not judgment, was, "Be careful with any medication you might be taking."

Val told Hekla that while they were generally concerned by her prolonged seclusion, they only became truly worried today. Hekla had left several barely comprehensible messages in the early morning hours. After Val woke, while they were listening to the messages, Hekla called again. They answered, but all they heard was a loud thud followed by silence. Val considered calling for an ambulance, but decided, for the sake of discretion, to drive over. They kept calling, and the longer Hekla went without answering, the more anxious they became. What if she was hurt, Val wondered, what if they could have saved her by calling for help right away?

Hekla could see the echoes of fear in Val's eyes as they recounted the story. "I'm so sorry," Hekla said, "Really, I'm—I shouldn't have put you in that position. I'm sorry."

"It's okay. There are other things to focus on. I'm just glad you're alright."

Hekla didn't feel like it was okay, but she was fine with moving on. Val was helpful that way. "Bjarni left the hotel in Vik," they quickly revealed. "Almost as soon as he got there."

Hekla narrowed her eyes.

"You think that Bjarni told someone where Elísa was, right?" Val continued. "The Americans or whoever sent those people in?"

Hekla hesitated a second before responding, "I do." She was almost certain that's what happened, but wasn't thrilled that she had shared those thoughts without remembering.

"It makes sense," Val said. "The Americans didn't know which address was right. Bjarni must have told someone. I think he checked the Vik address by himself as soon as he arrived. He saw that Elísa wasn't there and made a call. He beat you and Gunnar to it."

"But how do you know? You didn't—"

"Talk to him?" Val gave a wry smile. "No. Of course not. I wouldn't—unless you wanted me to."

Hekla smiled appreciatively.

"But I did talk to a clerk at the hotel," Val explained. "Where they were staying in Vik. And the clerk remembered seeing one of them leave. Alone."

"That could have been anyone though. It was months ago. How would they even remember?"

"It was a memorable night. A lot of people remember what they were doing the night Elísa was killed. And they were unusual guests—off-season, late at night, two adults checking into separate rooms."

Hekla nodded.

"I checked though," Val continued. "To make sure."

"Checked what?"

"Security cameras. They put them in after Jack's murder. Fortunately for us, they haven't gotten the hang of them yet. When I went to visit, they still had the footage saved on a drive."

"You have him on tape?" Hekla's face perked up.

Val reached into the pocket of their jacket and took out a flash drive. They handed it to Hekla.

"Wow." Hekla held a dumbstruck expression as she stared at the flash drive. "This is amazing." But another thought quickly intruded, muting her initial optimism.

Val seemed to anticipate her doubt. "It doesn't prove he went the address. Or that he told someone. I know. But the timing tracks perfectly. The footage shows Bjarni leaving the hotel alone just after they checked in. Then it shows him return about thirty minutes later. If we were able to get the car's GPS or his phone records . . . "

"Yeah," Hekla said without much conviction. She did her best to muster up more enthusiasm for Val. "This is great. Really. It's fantastic."

"You don't think it's enough?"

Hekla pursed her lips. *Enough for what,* she thought to herself. She didn't know what justice looked like anymore, she just wanted to make sure no one else got hurt. Her mistake was inspiring people like Val to the point where they thought they could do something positive in the first place. All that did was put them in jeopardy. Now she had Val risking her life and career on the same foolish notions that got Hekla to where she was now. And no one should ever be where she was now.

"I don't know," she finally answered. "It's probably not a great idea to keep poking around." She felt her heart squeeze as she spoke the last sentence.

Val's face fell. A moment passed before they spoke again, "You're not coming back."

"What?"

"To work. You're not coming back, are you?"

"No. What are you talking about—I'm coming back." As Hekla said the words though, she realized that maybe she wasn't ever going to return.

Val nodded politely, as though they shared her doubts in real time. "There's something else," they said. "Gunnar thinks they're trying to pin Steingrímur's murder on Logi."

Hekla's brow furrowed. "How? They know he was with me."

Val shook their head. "I'm not sure. Gunnar wants to talk to you."

Hekla gave a frustrated sigh as she looked away.

"We need your help," Val added, their voice taking on a different tone. "There's no one else we can trust. We need you back."

Hekla returned her focus to Val. She felt another tug in her stomach. It pained her not to be able to give Val the affirmation they sought—not to be there for good people who were trying to do the right thing. She thought it over a few more seconds. "Tell Gunnar he should contact Aldís' old boyfriend."

"The American?" Val asked in disbelief.

"Yeah." Hekla nodded. "August. I think we can trust him."

CHAPTER FORTY-NINE

As soon Val left, Hekla locked the door and retreated to the sofa. She huddled, hunched over on her hands and knees, wincing in pain as waves of heat and nausea rolled through her body. Her gut felt like it was eating itself. She considered swigging her coffee just so she could have something to throw up. "Errrahhh," she moaned with frustration. She couldn't deal with any of this now—she didn't *want* to deal with any of this now.

She slid off the couch and staggered to her bedroom. She plunged her hand into a pile of clothing and emerged with the bottle of pills. No point trying to moderate now, she thought. She made her way to the kitchen and opened the refrigerator. Pathetic. A few condiments, a paper bag full of old leftovers, a nearly empty bottle of sports drink, and a handle of vodka. She opened the freezer. Another bottle of vodka.

Without warning, a tear formed in the corner of her eye. She hastily tossed a pill in her mouth and washed it down with chilled vodka.

~~~~~~~~~~~~~~

Hekla wasn't sure what time it was when she woke. It was light out, but the sun was low. At least she was in bed, she thought. She tried to remain as still as possible, unsure how bad her body would feel if she moved, and in no rush to find out.

Hekla thought about Val's visit. She wasn't sure what August could do for them, but he seemed like a safe ally—if he hadn't already thrown himself off a cliff or rigged a more effective noose than what she suspected he was experimenting with in Copenhagen. She was now certain that August was the unnamed attorney at the center of Aldís's exposé on American drone killings. In that story, the attorney's client was a whistleblower who was imprisoned after his government reneged on a deal. She didn't know how Lisa was involved, but if this was the source of August's ire toward his government, she was confident his interests would align with hers as far as these investigations were concerned.

There wasn't much more Hekla could do herself, even if she were in good standing with the NBI. There was essentially open-air collusion taking place between her government, private corporations, and foreign entities, and no one seemed to care. What good was the truth now? The best she could do was get as much information to the public as possible and let them decide.

That wasn't entirely true. There *was* more that could be done, but she wanted to keep Val and Gunnar as far away as possible in case things didn't turn out well—again. She didn't know what the consortium and its allies were planning with Logi, but she wasn't going to let them hurt him. And she also wasn't going to let them use Logi to defeat Aldís, regardless of any differences she had with the journalist-turned-suspect-turned-candidate. There already had been far too much pain—too much blood, too much death—to allow them to win like that now.

She lifted her head off the pillow. A current of pain shot up through her spine into her skull. She immediately collapsed back to the bed. "Aahhck," she groaned. This wasn't going to be easy.

CHAPTER FIFTY

THE NOISE FROM THE BEACH STARTED EARLY. IT WAS pleasant at first—when it was still dark—the water gently lapping against the rocks, a few chirps and whistles from the birds. But the first human voice signaled trouble. As the sun rose, it was like someone slowly turned the volume up on a slightly out of tune radio station. And they kept increasing that volume until everyone's auditory system was jeopardized. It continued like this until late at night—with only a brief respite late in the afternoon so everyone could rest their voices for an evening of screaming.

Unless it was Monday. On Mondays, August might be able to get some fucking sleep. Even better, on weekdays he could go to the shore himself without fear of a German toddler slamming a bucket full of sand against his shin. Really though, it wasn't that bad. He just adopted a reverse type of schedule. Saturday and Sunday were for work: exploring nearby towns, shopping, and taking care of the odd errand or two that managed to force its way to his attention. And Mondays through Fridays were strictly reserved for relaxation. Or *attempting* relaxation.

August was in Mallorca, staying at a mostly vacant bed and breakfast in a small town on the northeastern end of the island. It was the perfect location, far from major towns. From his room he could see the rocks and the water. To the east there was nothing but rolling hills. A fair number of Germans packed the place on weekends but, occasional miscreant child aside, they were fine.

On weekdays, he would rise some time after the mid-morning sun shone through his window. He would eat breakfast downstairs and then fill his tote bag with provisions for the day—carbonated water, snacks, a towel, and a thick Calvin and Hobbes comic strip anthology that he discovered on one of his excursions to the neighboring towns. He put on a cheap, neon green swimsuit, an oversized, khaki-colored cotton sweater, and overpriced sunglasses. Then he slid into a pair of well-tread boat shoes and walked to the pebbly shore. He'd drag a beach chair as far east and forward as possible and stay until his sweater no longer kept him warm.

After the beach, he'd return to his room and luxuriate in a long shower or bath. He might have a soda or coffee to stay awake. Because it was chilly at night, he tended to wear a linen shirt underneath a cardigan, loose-fitting pants, and colorful socks with his boat shoes when he went back out. He ate at one of the same three places, each establishment providing him with a quasi-off-menu dish to fit his diet. Often there was a football match on TV, so he might watch a bit with the locals, maybe enjoy an espresso or two. He'd return to his room exhausted, and before long he would be asleep.

And that's how August spent his days and nights. Content—or something close to it.

⁓⁓⁓⁓⁓⁓⁓⁓⁓

It was odd leaving Iceland again. After learning of the teenager's death, August was certain that he was done. He had failed to prevent another death, and he was not prepared to live with this one on his conscience as well. He even wrote something for Aldís. But what began as a sort of suicide note ended up reading more like a thank you letter. He told her what their time together meant to him, so inevitably he ended up writing about joy and hope. Before long, he felt he should continue the search for these things again, for joy and hope, despite knowing how elusive they were.

He sent the letter to Aldís anyway, with a few annotations in the margin. He wasn't going to make the same mistake as last time. He was going to say goodbye and share kind thoughts. He'd come to view the practice of keeping positive thoughts secret as some warped shit that too many people considered normal. It was like they were only comfortable in extreme, empty, or repressed emotional states. Maybe that was just him, but he was going to try to change at least.

Before coming to Mallorca, he settled his affairs in Copenhagen. He gave up his flat, sold or donated most of his possessions, and put the rest in storage. There wasn't much he needed, but he refused to ever purchase winter attire again, and there were a few other items that meant something to him, so a locker seemed prudent. He destroyed his laptop and phone and traveled several stops on the train before discarding them. He also broke off whatever it was that he had with Petar. This was a much more difficult task than he expected, even with the casual nature of their relationship and the time already spent apart. It would be nice if Petar were here, he occasionally thought, but after a few nights, he knew he'd want to be alone again.

What exactly he was going to do next was a different matter. He was financially secure, and would be for some time. He had done some rough math and figured that if he kept to unadorned rooms in offbeat locations in the offseason, he could live this way for as long as a decade.

His real problem wasn't money. Writing that note to Aldís did more than extend his desire to live. Against his better instincts, he actually felt like doing something *meaningful* again. The urge was even stronger than the one that led him to Iceland a few months earlier. Back then, he was tired of his life and worried about Aldís. But now, with his comic book and the sun, pleasant evenings watching football and sharing a few laughs with the locals, he had something that damn near approximated a cordial relationship with existence.

And yet, something was missing. As fucked-up as his recent stint in Iceland was, it reminded him of the sense of community he once had there. When he originally moved to Iceland to live with Aldís, he felt, for the first time in his life, like he was truly part of something. He was no longer just one person trying to navigate life on his own. And, as strange and stressful as his more recent visit was, he got a taste of that "belonging" again. It was a feeling that couldn't be replicated by a few nights with someone, or any of the other relationships that he couldn't—or wouldn't—allow to be anything but superficial. Fortunately, he had anticipated this feeling. That's why there was one more vestige of his pseudo-past life that he held on to. Part of it was in his Copenhagen locker. He wasn't quite sure where the rest of it was, but its existence was always floating around on the periphery of his mind.

When August activated his phones five months ago, he was given the option of creating an online account, which would let him remotely access his texts, call log, and voicemail. This type of registration conflicts with the desire for anonymity that motivates most people to buy phones at convenience stores, but August, for better and worse, wasn't most people. He didn't care if someone stole his personal information, he cared only about the robots in the sky. So he had set up the online account. And he didn't destroy *all* his electronics—he kept the working phone intact and left it in the locker.

August was aware that a data center somewhere now had a digital record of his cellular activity, accessible to anyone with the right paperwork. And he knew that record could reveal more significant details of his life than any social media application ever could.

He supposed it was a mistake to set up the account. Stupid, dangerous—an obvious flaw waiting to be exploited by the many entities whose purpose is to exploit. But he didn't blame himself for keeping it active. It was his tie to something. He had brought himself to tears with his letter to Aldís, describing the significance that true community had on him when he first spent time with her. He wasn't going to kill himself after writing that letter and he *also* wasn't going to cut his last line back to that connection.

The thing about lines is, every now and then, you want to pull on them.

CHAPTER FIFTY-ONE

On the day August decided to check his missed calls and messages, he spent the morning planning various routes to travel in search of a publicly accessible computer. He was about to leave when he thought to ask the owner of his bed-and-breakfast for directions. The owner—a friendly guy who knew how to prepare August's coffee—chuckled at August's request for a "café internet."

Instead of giving August an address, he handed him a laptop and wifi code.

"Whenever you need it," the owner said in Spanish.

August gave a sheepish smile and nod. He realized that while he had renounced most technology, the world kept moving. He didn't need an internet cafe or a public library—just a friend.

He took the laptop to a small table near the entrance in the tiny lobby and sat down. He pulled out his notebook, flipping past the pages whose edges had merged, to a sheet with more recent notations. On the page with the information for his cloud-based account, he had also written down several new contacts. They all were either Icelandic cops or U.S. Embassy employees. A bad sign. His search for deeper connection was dependent on a profound message from one of the handful of phone operators in the world with his number, and most of his contacts were cops or cop-adjacent assholes who would, at best, be thrilled to never see him again.

He ran his tongue against the inside of his lower lip. Who was he kidding, he thought, there was nothing for him here. There never really could be. What he wanted was impossible. It had to be Aldís, and, if he were really being honest, he couldn't even think of a message from her that would be satisfying. Did he think now, after all they had been through, she would suddenly decide he was irreplaceable? She hadn't even needed him when he was with her. He didn't know what exactly she was up to, but he knew it was more important to her than his latest epiphany. And if he really cared, it would be more important to him too.

Nonetheless, he entered his account number and password, hammering at the keys to the point where he feared drawing an angry look from the laptop's owner.

His account page opened. Nothing from Aldís. He wasn't surprised, but he was disappointed. Nothing from the cops, either. Even the embassy had decided to leave him alone, though he was sure it was because they already knew what he was up to. In all the time he had been gone, there were only three missed calls and a voicemail, all made within the past week from a number he didn't recognize.

He gave a quick glance around the room before playing the message.

"Hi August, this is Gunnar—Gunnar Ottóson from the Grindavik—actually I'm with the national police now, in Reykjavík, but this is my cell phone. I was hoping to talk to you. We met once, I drove you home—back to your hotel. Hekla suggested I contact you. If you could please call me back, not at the station, just my cell phone. Please. It's this number. I'd really appreciate it. Thank you."

August grimaced. He disappears and the only person who cares to contact him is a cop. A giant cop. How sad, he thought. It was like he was a schoolchild, abandoned at recess and left to play with the teacher—if the teacher were a fucking cop. Truthfully, in that analogy he wasn't sure he'd be the innocent kid.

He spent the rest of the day and next morning thinking about Gunnar's message. At the beach, he found himself having to re-read the panels of the comic strips, sometimes only making it to the second or third box in the marvelous "Sunday edition" spreads before starting over. After a while, he went back to the bed-and-breakfast and asked to borrow the owner's laptop again.

He searched online for stories about the teenager's death. When he was last in Iceland, he was too busy feeling bad about himself to give much thought about the other implications of the shooting. He still didn't want to think about it, but now, with Gunnar reaching out to him, he had questions he needed answers to. Mainly, what the fuck was that girl doing at Aldís's safe house? And how did that cop know she might be there?

The safe house was one of Aldís's most closely guarded secrets. August didn't think even Logi knew its location. Sívar, the ice-blooded man who watched over the place, sure as hell wasn't giving it up. Which brought August back to an uncomfortable conclusion that he was probably subconsciously avoiding all along: Aldís was elbows-deep in some of the grislier aspects of this whole affair.

There was a flip side to this. If Aldís did know Elísa, if Elísa was someone she cared about enough to shelter in her most secret place, then that cop, Hekla, had told him the truth. Elísa's life *was* in danger. He found this to be oddly encouraging despite affirming the grim fact that he could have done more to help. Whatever her true motivation, this cop appeared to have accidentally aligned herself on the right side of something for once. And if she trusted Gunnar, maybe Gunnar's intentions were okay, too.

One other good sign: Gunnar sure as hell didn't want him to accidentally call the station.

nnnnnnnnnn

"**G**unnar speaking."

"Hi. This is . . . this is August. Sorenson."

"Oh, hey." Gunnar didn't sound like he was expecting a call back. "Um, could you just—can you give me a minute?"

"Sure."

August was using the bed-and-breakfast owner's delightfully sleek phone. The owner had told him he could take it to his room, but staying in plain sight seemed more polite.

Finally, Gunnar spoke again, "Hey. Sorry about that.

"You away . . . from the office now?"

Gunnar emitted a hearty chuckle that August recognized from their brief time together. "Yes," he said. "I'm in my car now."

"Good. So . . . how can I help you?"

"I—well I'm not sure, really."

August's lips twisted into a frown.

"You know what happened with Hekla?" Gunnar asked. "The NBI detective you met?"

"Yeah . . . she was hurt. Right? Is she . . . okay?"

"She's fine. Well—she's okay. She was hurt, yes. They also suspended her."

"Suspended?" That surprised August. "Why?"

"Er—well there were some things. It's not really important now though."

"I don't know that. She told you to call . . . right? You're gonna have to tell me . . . something."

August could hear Gunnar exhale.

"She was having a tough time," Gunnar said. "After the girl was killed. And there was also—well . . . " There was another heavy breath before Gunnar continued with a quickly delivered sentence. "There were rumors of an inappropriate relationship with a suspect."

"Suspect? What . . . suspect?"

"Logi Stefánsson."

"Heh," August murmured. The affair didn't surprise him, but the other part did. "He's . . . how is *Logi* a suspect?"

Instead of responding to the question, Gunnar floated a statement. "She trusts you."

"Who?"

"Hekla."

"Okay . . . so?"

"Are you trustworthy?"

"To who?"

Gunnar let out a little laugh, but was serious when he spoke again. "Hekla thought there were—that other people weren't being properly investigated. So we, well, we were investigating the murders but also looking at things that maybe some people wanted us to ignore."

August remained silent, letting Gunnar elaborate.

"I think she was right. I don't—I'm not sure about the focus of the police efforts and there are—there are just things that need to be looked at more."

"Good. . . . You should look at them."

"I am—we are. But we need help. There's not—there are people here who are very powerful. Where I work, where others work. We don't know who we can trust. Just like Hekla, I want to make sure that the right people are held accountable."

"That's great. . . . Really. I don't know . . . why are you calling me though? I'm not a cop."

"Good. I can't trust them."

August's turn to laugh. "It's not . . . it's not just that. I'm not—I'm not anything anymore. I don't know . . . why you think I can help." Gunnar started to speak but August continued over him, "And . . . honestly . . . I have no fucking clue why you'd think I'd want to."

There was another moment of silence before Gunnar spoke. "You knew Logi, right?"

"Yeah. . . . I'm not helping you arrest him."

"I'm not asking you to. I don't think he did anything. Other people want to, though. I think there's a reason they are trying to blame him. Just like Aldís before. Something they both know maybe—I'm not sure yet. But I think you can help. Even if it's just another person we know who isn't connected to the mining deal or Americans."

"You know . . . *I'm* American. Right?"

"Yes." Gunnar paused a second. "How is your relationship with your country—the people in your government? Lisa Harris?"

August closed his eyes as his face grew tight.

"They killed that girl." Gunnar's voice was slightly strained now. "And no one wants to go after the people responsible. You know these people. Better than most and certainly better than me. We could really use your help. Without Hekla, I don't know who else I can turn to."

August let out a slightly defeated grumble.

CHAPTER FIFTY-TWO

YOU DON'T FLY FROM PALMA TO REYKJAVÍK IN MAY.
Iceland is lovely in the spring, but what kind of person would
leave Palma for it? In August's mind, the only thing drearier than
abandoning beaches in paradise for a slowly thawing rock was the
increasingly pathetic circumstance motivating his travel. It had
gone from a noble pursuit of love to a highly questionable quest to
remedy past mistakes. And now, he was heading to Iceland to try
and protect his ex-girlfriend's current lover from police overreach.

Great idea.

In fairness, he wasn't only interested in helping Logi. He would
be tremendously satisfied if he were able to prove a connection
between Lisa and the death of that girl. It seemed as if Gunnar
thought there was at least some American involvement. The publicly available details didn't discount the possibility—the timeline
was odd, and early-morning tactical assassinations were kind of
an American military and law enforcement specialty. Either way,
he was sure Lisa and her friends were involved in some sketchy
shit, and he couldn't help but remain curious, even if he knew the
possibility of them ever being held accountable was basically nil.

As for Logi, August knew he was a good man, and felt that he
should help if he could.

Logi grew up in Akureyri and met Aldís in college. August
figured that Logi selected his activities to endear himself to Aldís,
or at least to occupy the same space as her, but maybe that was
projection. Either way, Logi became a true believer. So much so,
that whatever feelings he had for Aldís took a back seat to their

work. They may have briefly dated, but they couldn't maintain their professional and personal relationships at the same time. Professional came out the winner and they both seemed satisfied. At least that was the story Aldís told.

It would have been easy for August to attribute the friction between Logi and himself to Logi's love for Aldís, but he knew that wasn't really the case. Sure, Logi had been a dick to him, but he thought Logi had a point. Logi had made personal sacrifices for other people his entire life. He did hard things and made no excuses and never compromised integrity to increase his comfort. August, at least up until his mid 30s, was the opposite. He was all compromise and excuse, very little integrity.

∽∽∽∽∽∽∽∽

This trip to Iceland went much smoother than the last. August was significantly less terrified at the airport and on his flight than he was when he traveled in the winter. His sun-infused, socialization exposure therapy seemed to have paid dividends. He was so lost in the pleasant feeling of not feeling miserable that it took him longer than it should to realize that he had been standing in front of a customs officer for quite a significant period. Not that there was anything he could do now. This was a scenario he probably should have prepared for *before* getting on the plane.

The agent looked once more between August and his Danish passport before sneaking a glance at her screen from the corners of her eyes. "Can you just hold on one moment, sir?" she asked with a half-smile.

August didn't respond, but his expression had turned sour. He watched passively as the officer walked toward a supervisor standing several meters behind and whispered a few words in his ear. The supervisor, with practiced perfection, kept a positive disposition, smiling and nodding several times before sending the officer back. It would all appear to be a simple misunderstanding to someone in August's position, no need to freak out or cause a disruption. But he knew better. Looking closely, he could see the supervisor subtly move his hand to his radio as they spoke, before obscuring himself from August's view.

"Sorry for the delay, sir. What was the purpose of your visit to Iceland again?"

August tilted his head at least 30 degrees to the side.

The officer forced an insincere smile.

August let out a dramatic sigh as his rolled eyes led the way for the rest of his head. Then he closed his eyes and waited. It did not take long.

A hand wrapped around his bicep. He flinched, but the tight grip kept him from moving much. "Do you mind coming with us?" a cop of some sort asked.

There were two of them, August noticed. Large, bulky men on both sides of him. It did not matter if he minded. He gave a neutral grunt, and the officers led him away.

⁂

The temporary detention center looked more like a cafeteria or large office break room than the minimum security prison it functioned as. There were padded chairs, coffee, even a television. August knew that it wasn't good fortune that brought him to this space so quickly though. Usually, when someone runs afoul of customs, they are made to pass through an additional security checkpoint, mostly used to steal people's drugs and harangue unloved travelers. Then, quite often, they are taken to an interview room where some prick tries to threaten or blackmail them into divulging incriminating, visa-denying information about the origins of their drugs or anti-democratic downloads. August had skipped the queue, and that made him wonder how exactly his passport had been marked.

He was far too familiar with the ability of the U.S. government to forever fuck with someone's ability to move about the world. There were different passport markings, nominally associated with the "risk level" that a person presented. It was a joke, of course. Half the people required to go through extra screening were journalists. The truly dangerous people didn't fly commercial, and the most effective way to devastate a country these days wasn't by getting onto a plane, it was through trade agreements, and loans from the International Monetary Fund and World Bank that were conditioned on "austerity measures."

August leaned forward in one of the padded folding chairs as his face contorted into a grimace. His thumb and the knuckle of his forefinger pressed hard into the bridge of his nose. It had been a while since he noticed the semi-voluntary clenching of his facial muscles.

He tried to stay calm and think things through. He was sure that it was Lisa who caused his passport to be flagged. There hadn't been any issues when he had flown from Iceland to Copenhagen, or Copenhagen to Mallorca. So it was clear that she was okay with letting him live in relative peace if he didn't bother her. And for some reason, his presence in Iceland again *bothered her*. It *bothered her* enough that she found it necessary to *bother him*. That was notable. She was the one who kicked his bed while he was sleeping in the first place, what did she think he was still capable of, he wondered. What *hadn't* she been able to do already?

The opaque process for being added to the fuck-your-flight-up list made removal from that list very difficult. He believed he had successfully removed, or at least lowered the designation of, a few people while he was at the legat. That took time though. He doubted an appeal to the Danes would go anywhere. Whatever had occurred was done with their blessing. Ultimately, his freedom of mobility would be dependent on a return to their good graces, but that was long-term. His chief concern now was what this all meant for him and the people he cared about.

If Lisa knew he was coming, he needed to be careful. It was probably best if he didn't shine too bright a light on anyone who was so afraid of being caught communicating with him that they kept him on hold for five minutes while they snuck off into their car. That crossed the big man off his list of potential helpers. It removed Hekla, too. That didn't leave him with many options. He had one idea though. If it worked, it should get him in while giving everyone the option of disassociating themselves from him as necessary. *If* it worked.

CHAPTER FIFTY-THREE

"Hey . . . it's August."

"What do you want?"

"How . . . how are you?"

"What do you want?"

"Uh . . . well . . . I could use your help—"

"No."

"Haha," August laughed nervously, he was struggling to walk the line between cheerful and serious. "I know. . . . It's funny, but . . . seriously. See . . . I'm at the airport—"

The line cut off.

August looked at the phone as though something must be wrong with its wiring. He smiled at the unamused immigration officer sitting across from him in the room. "Bad . . . connection. Let me just . . . "

He redialed. Logi answered before a full ring. "I'm *detained . . .* " August emphasized before Logi could yell or hang up, "at the airport. I explained that I needed to see *my client . . .* that it's urgent. As his *attorney . . .* I need to be let in . . . to protect his rights." Logi didn't respond but he didn't hang up, which August took as a good sign. It crossed his mind that his license to practice law had lapsed several years ago, and he cursed himself for not bothering to pay the small fee that would give his claim of attorney-client relationship some added legitimacy. "So . . . it has to be *you* who gets me. You understand? I know . . . it's crazy." He let out another stilted laugh as he snuck a glance at the immigration officer. "But you're familiar . . . with things . . . how crazy they can be . . . and how you have to trust the people trying to do the right thing." Still silence on the other line. "Well . . . think you can give your lawyer a ride?"

Finally, Logi spoke. "I think the world would be a better place if more lawyers spent time in detention." And then he hung up.

✶✶✶✶✶✶✶✶✶✶✶✶

He looked tired, August thought. Angry and annoyed too, but mostly just tired. It wasn't until much later that August realized what he was really seeing on Logi's face was worry.

August didn't feel particularly great himself. After seven hours spent slouched on the chairs in the detention center, nothing to eat or drink but vending machine snacks, small cups of water and stale coffee, he was more than ready for a hot shower and long sleep. But he wasn't going to complain. Logi had worked wonders for him. Shortly after he had hung up, Logi must have made a convincing call or two, because within an hour, another agent informed August that he would be permitted to enter the country on condition of him applying for an emergency temporary work visa with either the American or Danish Embassy. August still predicted this would end either with deportation or unlawful residence, but he would worry about that later.

It seemed like Lisa had only been able to inconvenience him. Maybe he'd lose the extra few privileges that stuck with him from his days working for the U.S., ones that people like him didn't really need in the first place. Whatever. She probably wanted to label him a terrorist, but that would have required a degree of open communication with other agencies and governments that she wasn't willing to engage in.

It wasn't until after Logi had successfully extracted August from the detention center that his demeanor took on its present form. Logi didn't say another word, didn't even look at August, during their entire walk through, and out of, the airport. August periodically glanced up at him, hoping for an indication of levity, or at least acknowledgement, but he got nothing. Once they were both inside his Jeep, Logi finally spoke again—still without looking at August. "You need to stay out of this," he said in a quiet and raspy voice while staring blankly at his steering wheel.

August's eyebrows tilted.

"You don't know what you're doing," Logi continued somberly. "You don't understand what's going on."

"Do *you*? I'm . . . I'm trying to help you."

Logi turned to August, looking studiously at him for a moment. Then he shook his head and returned his attention to his car. "This isn't for you," he said as he started the engine.

August grumbled. "Why . . . why'd you come then?"

Logi backed out of the parking spot and navigated across the airport's parking lot. "I figured you'd do more harm if I left you here. Besides, you'd probably just call Aldís." He shot August a quick look. "Why *didn't* you just call her?"

August shook his head. "I'm not . . . here for her. She's busy . . . enough. I don't want—I'm trying not . . . to interfere with that."

Logi scoffed. "No problem bothering me though, huh?"

"They—they're trying to pin a murder on you," August's voice rose slightly with indignation. "It's . . . it's fucking serious."

"I know it's serious," Logi remained calm. "That's why I'm telling you to let it go. Not just for us. But for you. Nothing good will come out of you getting involved."

"Pfff . . . " August rolled his eyes and looked out the window.

After a few seconds, Logi spoke again. "What murder?"

Now August inspected Logi's face. "Steingrímur. I think."

"Who told you that?"

"Another cop. . . . Big guy. Gunnar . . . Ottóson. You know him?"

Logi shook his head.

"It was . . . Hekla Rafney . . . told him to call me. You *do* know her. Don't you?"

"Yeah." Logi's eyes darted over. "I know who she is. She questioned me."

"Right. Well . . . he asked me to come. He says you're innocent. . . . Wants my help."

"Hah," Logi laughed derisively. "Trusting cops again? That didn't take long."

"No. . . . Not really. But . . . if I listened earlier . . . that . . . that girl might still be alive."

"What do you mean?"

August face pinched tight. "She . . . came to me. Hekla. Your cop . . . *friend*. She wanted to know where Aldís might hide out. Thought . . . the girl might be there."

"You knew?"

"Yeah. . . . I had an idea . . . but I didn't say anything."

"Mmh." Logi looked thoughtful. "That's not your fault."

"Why . . . why *was* she there?"

"Who?"

"The girl."

Logi just shook his head.

"Of course." August sighed. "So . . . should I trust them or not?"

Logi slowed the car to a stop near the exit of the parking lot. "What you should do is leave. Stay out of this." He took a deep breath. "I know you won't listen though, so—yeah. You can trust Hekla. Or whoever she trusts. They're cops, but I think they're after the right people."

August nodded. He wasn't going to press Logi on how he came

to believe that a particular cop that had supposedly questioned him on suspicion of murder had come to gain his trust.

The car remained still.

Logi looked expectantly at August.

"What?"

"Where am I taking you?"

"Oh. Right. . . . Yeah. You can just take me to the hotel. It's—fuck." August's shoulders sank. "Oh Fuck!" He closed his eyes tight. "Fuck fuck fuck fuck."

"What is it?"

"Argh!" August wrapped his hand around his eyes. "I need . . . ahh . . . I need to check something. I'm sorry. Is there a bank . . . or . . . I guess a computer . . . I can use?"

Logi narrowed his eyes. He held out his phone. "How about this?"

٭٭٭٭٭٭٭٭٭٭٭٭٭٭٭

August smoked a cigarette with his back pressed against the side of the Jeep. He looked slightly defeated. Logi stared at him a few meters away. He looked slightly bewildered.

"So, they can just take your money?" Logi asked.

August gave a half shrug. "Not . . . take. Really. Not yet. . . . But they can keep me from accessing it."

Logi's face still showed confusion.

August took a long drag. "They froze them. . . . My accounts. And my cards . . . so . . . " He held his palms up, "Kinda fucked."

"When?"

"I dunno." He shook his head. "It was fine the other day. I bet . . . I dunno—probably an emergency application after I arrived . . . or when I bought the ticket. That's good. I guess. It means it's temporary . . . they'd need a real proceeding to keep it. Still . . . for now . . . not great."

"What's wrong with you?"

"Huh?"

"What's wrong with you?" Logi repeated.

"I don't . . . understand . . . what—"

"No one wants you here. They block your entrance, take your money. It's not your fault, but every time you're here—and I think you'd have to agree—things don't exactly go well for you. Would that be a fair statement?"

August pressed his tongue against his lip. "That's not . . . an unfair . . . assessment."

"So—why the hell do you keep coming back?"

A bittersweet smile emerged on August's face. He took one last drag of his cigarette before rolling the butt between his fingers until the cherry fell off. "Do you know . . . *why* they don't want me here?"

"No. Why?"

"No clue." August gave an exaggerated shrug. "But . . . I want to find out. Fuck them. All this stuff . . . that just means I'm on the right path."

Logi let out an exasperated sigh as he shook his head. "You're a child."

"Am I wrong? It's the same . . . what Aldís is fighting . . . that mining deal . . . whoever killed that girl. Something there . . . that's why they don't want me here. Don't you want me to find out what they're doing next?"

August locked eyes with Logi. Logi held his stare several seconds before finally relenting with another, more measured, sigh. "So what? You want to stay with us now?"

"No. . . . I have another idea."

"Great," Logi muttered.

A few minutes later, both men were back inside the Jeep, and August was yelling into the new disposable phone he had purchased for the trip. "Fuck you! . . . Okay? Keep the fucking money! I'm not going . . . anywhere." He hung up. His demeanor didn't match his language or volume. He smiled at Logi and held out his phone. "So just . . . keep it with you. Leave it at the house . . . just a day or two. . . . Then destroy it. Okay?"

Logi took the phone and put it in the center console. "And you just want me to leave you here? You don't want me to call anyone—someone to pick you up?"

"No. I'll be . . . fine." August flashed another smile as he opened the door. "I hope. Thanks for your help. Thanks for . . . everything."

CHAPTER FIFTY-FOUR

Aᴜɢᴜꜱᴛ ᴍᴀʀᴠᴇʟᴇᴅ ᴀᴛ ᴛʜᴇ ᴘɪᴄᴛᴜʀᴇꜱQᴜᴇ ʟɪᴛᴛʟᴇ house in Grindavik. It was late when Gunnar picked him up near the airport. Gunnar came quickly after he called, but August still spent too much time outside, shivering in his breathable sweater. His stomach was queasy, he was lightheaded and exhausted, and all he wanted was to take a long, hot shower and go to sleep. But there was something he needed to ask first.

The two had spent most of the drive from the airport discussing police activity, and *inactivity*, in response to the murders. Driving through town, August noticed several makeshift memorials, and signs in the windows of homes and cars, commemorating the life of Elísa. It was still so easy for him to forget how different this country was from the one he grew up in, even from the one he spent most of adulthood in. Tragedy wasn't expected, accepted, and forgotten here quite so quickly. And it was small. About 2,500 people lived in Grindavik. American high schools had more people.

"Did you . . . know her?" he asked after Gunnar parked in front of the house.

Gunnar gave him a searching look, as though he had an idea who August was speaking about but wanted to be sure. August's solemn expression seemed to resolve any doubt. "No. Not really. I'd see her, but mostly because I was at the hotel a lot for work. I don't think I ever saw her in town." Gunnar's voice hardened. "I know her parents though. They're shit."

August nodded. He looked back at the house. "Are you . . . sure this is a good idea?"

"No."

August furrowed his brow.

"Best option we have." Gunnar shrugged. "I'd have to meet you if you stayed somewhere else anyway."

"Right. And . . . if someone does find out?"

"I'll say we became friends."

"With a . . . suspect?"

"Not in the murders. And charges were never filed for that . . . " Gunnar gave a half-smile, "other thing."

"It was . . . a small push." August smiled along with Gunnar.

"It's hard not to hit those Viking Squad guys sometimes. I understand."

They both laughed before August grew serious again, "If you're . . . using me . . . to get to Logi or Aldís . . . "

"It's only risky for *me* keeping you here," Gunnar jumped in. "Even speaking with you." August was grateful Gunnar didn't force him to finish a threat they both knew he'd have trouble seeing through.

"So why . . . why are you doing this? What's so . . . important to you?"

"It's what I told you. I want to know who's involved in this." Gunnar paused. "And if any of them is responsible for killing Elísa."

"Mmh," August grunted, he could accept that motivation. "Okay." He reached for the door but stopped when he noticed Gunnar hadn't moved.

"What did you do to them anyway?"

"To . . . who?"

"The Americans. The people at the embassy. Seems like you really pissed them off. What happened?"

"Erh." The left side of August's face twitched, it looked like his was trying, and failing, to smile.

"Sorry. It's okay if you don't—"

"After . . . after I moved here," August spoke with his eyes closed, "to be with Aldís. "There was an analyst with the U.S. military . . . he came to us—well Aldís really. I just . . . happened to be there. He had all this data with him. It was evidence . . . of war crimes." August opened his eyes and faced Gunnar. "Drones. . . . Other stuff too—videos, records, anything you could imagine. I thought I could help. I thought I could protect him." August's face contracted again. "It didn't . . . work out. Lisa Harris—from the embassy—she was one of the people involved."

"She gave us the address where Elísa was located."

August nodded. "Yeah. Well . . . we had a deal, but they . . . they had it thrown out. They arrested him. . . . The analyst."

"Oh. I'm sorry—"

"He died. In prison . . . not long after." August's words hung in the air for several heavy seconds.

"Do you think they killed him or . . . ?"

"I dunno. He was . . . he was in solitary confinement . . . a long time." August gave a look as if to suggest this was explanation enough, Gunnar acknowledged as much with a small nod. "I think they're responsible though . . . for his death. And the others."

"But what does that have to do with you?" Gunnar looked puzzled. "Why would Lisa, or any of them still care what you do—do you have something on them?"

August let out a rueful chuckle. "No. . . . Nothing not public already. Maybe they still think I'm a loose end. . . . I dunno." There was another long pause before he continued. "I . . . I wasn't on the right side of things . . . for a long time. You know? People . . . in my position . . . who did what I did, know what I know . . . we don't usually wake up and declare our life's work immoral. Too much . . . to lose."

"What—you mean like what they did to your money?"

"I mean . . . there's that." August smirked. "They try and keep us . . . fat and happy. But no . . . it's more. It's not easy . . . living alone . . . with the truth of what you've done. It's easier . . . telling yourself the little lies. Taking the paychecks."

"Hmm. So, you think that's why they don't want you here? Not anything to do with the murders?"

"Oh . . . No. I do think it's related. Somehow . . . there's something here. Something . . . worth the risk of giving me nothing to lose. I'm not fat . . . and I'm not happy."

Gunnar chuckled. "Alright. Then let's see what we can find out."

August nodded. He opened the door.

"Hey," Gunnar called out before August could get out of the car. "Just so you know—I don't think you're ever alone if you're trying to do the right thing. No matter what happened in the past."

⁓⁓⁓⁓⁓⁓⁓

A cold, blunt object pressed against August's temple. His body responded to the sensation in his dreams before the part of his brain responsible for recognizing danger woke him up. It felt like the middle of the night, but the first thing he saw as he opened his eyes was light sneaking in through the windows across the room. He remembered he had fallen asleep on Gunnar's couch. Then he saw the source of his initial discomfort. Standing just a meter away was a small child with a wooden block in her hand and a mischievous grin on her face.

He stared at the young girl for a long moment. Then he threw open his mouth in mock surprise, leaning off the couch as his face took on an exaggerated and playful look. The girl burst into laughter and ran away.

A short while later, August sat cross-legged on the ground next to Anna, helping her build a wooden block fortress to protect her puffin and lamb plush toys. In between supervising construction and maintaining supplies, he sipped coffee and practiced Icelandic with the girl. To his dismay, she didn't offer much help clarifying the significance of phrases like, "the middle of the night," in a land with such a unique relationship to darkness. After being roused, he also had the pleasure of meeting Gunnar's sister. Ingibjörg patiently taught him the ins and outs of the coffee-making operation before she prepared for the day. Occasionally, she stopped in the living room, or called out from another room, to correct August, Anna, or both, on their pronunciation and grammar.

Gunnar seemed surprised by all the activity when he finally got around to joining the group.

"Good morning," August said with a wide smile.

"Morning," Gunnar yawned. "How'd you sleep?"

August made a silly face at Anna. She giggled wildly. Gunnar looked to his sister for an explanation. Ingibjörg just smiled and shrugged her shoulders.

⁖⁖⁖⁖⁖⁖⁖⁖⁖⁖

After breakfast, Ingibjörg dropped off Anna at school and then drove to work. Gunnar was due at the station, but before he left, he spent a half-hour introducing August to the materials that they had gathered as part of their shadow investigation.

August trusted Gunnar. There were few, if any people he had opened up to like he had with Gunnar the previous night. He was still a little wary though. He'd been burned at both ends, first giving too much credence and then, being so fearful of manipulation that he walled off opportunities to help. Eventually, he knew he'd have to take a leap of faith if he was going to be of any use. Working with Hekla and Gunnar, particularly after receiving tacit approval from Logi, seemed like a safe enough place to start. He didn't need to commit himself and, if nothing else, this association might give him access to otherwise confidential police information.

Almost any concerns August did have vanished as soon as he saw the wildly comprehensive case files the team had created. The setup alone suggested they were serious about keeping their investigation independent. All information was shared on a secure network, and what they did have was impressive: thousands of hours of CCTV footage, transcripts and videos of interviews, photographs, timelines, charts, notes. Every piece of evidence that could be reduced to electronic form, and it was all categorized in folders, with a hyperlinked table of contents and short summary document at the top.

The file regarding Elísa's murder was significantly smaller, but no less intriguing. The real highlight though were the files relating to Aldís, which Gunnar explained were no longer available to the police. Apparently, after the police seized her records, private contractors seized them from the police. This seemed suspicious to August, as it would to anyone.

August was impressed. There was no way it was acceptable to have all this information outside of police control. Unless one of the two cops he knew, or the special assistant he had yet to meet, were operating the most inefficient sting operation he had ever seen, they were risking a lot just by having this material, let alone sharing it with him. He wasn't going to let his guard down, or miss an opportunity to protect Aldís or Logi, but it seemed safe to assume that these rogue officers had more noble priorities than any other cops he'd encountered.

⁕⁕⁕⁕⁕⁕⁕⁕⁕⁕⁕⁕⁕

August spent the next week at Gunnar and Ingibjörg's house, doing almost nothing but reviewing evidence, playing with Anna, and sharing meals with the family. It was pleasant, being surrounded by kind people in a warm household, but that made it easy to lose track of his purpose. Every now and then he felt lost, like he was out of orbit or making his way around the wrong planet. It didn't help that his objectives were ill-defined to begin with.

Gunnar had given August almost no new information on what the police had on Logi. There was a fair amount of circumstantial evidence suggesting insider involvement in the murder of Elísa, but nothing that could definitively connect the Americans or members of Icelandic law enforcement. August couldn't figure out why anyone in the consortium would kill a random witness in the investigation into the murder of one of their partners' spouses. What he did know, however, was that Elísa's presence at the safe house meant she was not a *random* witness. And that's where things got complicated for him.

August had already accepted the idea that Aldís was somewhat involved in some aspect of this, but the closer he got to defining her involvement, the more his mind tried to maneuver around the obvious. And then there was the matter of the election. It was fast approaching, and he still couldn't really understand what was going on. When he watched Aldís's announcement months ago, an uneasy feeling settled in his stomach. He had that same feeling now, watching her on the security camera footage from the Azure the morning Jack was killed. There was something off about her appearance, like she was playing the part of herself on TV. She had always been aggressive and unafraid. She wasn't one to shy away from the spotlight if she thought it would help. Here though, she was calling attention to herself in a different way.

August knew he had to compartmentalize these thoughts. He needed to be able to find out all he could to protect Aldís and Logi without accidentally implicating them in something much bigger. That meant keeping strict control over what information he was supposed to share, and with whom—and what information he even wanted to know himself. This was no small task. As he watched video showing Aldís appear on the cameras, blithely moving about a natural wonder-turned investment opportunity, the already blurred lines began to lose all distinction.

CHAPTER FIFTY-FIVE

They were missing documents.

On the private network shared by Gunnar, Hekla and Val, there were basic records relating to Logi's alibi, easily obtainable and routine as part of any criminal investigation, that should have been part of the file. August asked Gunnar if there were any police records that they couldn't get, but Gunnar assured him that they had everything the police did. Outside of stunning incompetence, the likes of which didn't match the thoroughness displayed by the police in every *other* aspect of the investigation, it was hard to view this as an innocent omission.

Either Gunnar was lying, and there was a cache of records that hadn't been made available to August for one reason or another, or someone within Iceland's police force was purposely concealing relevant information. The likely exculpatory nature of the records suggested that someone with the police was hiding the information. But the fact that group made no effort to supplement their secret file made August suspicious of Gunnar and Hekla.

It made no sense that none of the text messages between Logi and Hekla were here. There were enough phone records to establish Logi's location and the fact that he did communicate, but the nature of these conversations remained a mystery. The police obviously had Logi's texts. That's how they found out about his affair with Hekla. August wondered if the police planned to pretend the texts no longer existed, to "misplace" evidence that would establish an alibi for Logi after using it to sideline Hekla. Regardless of their intention, August couldn't believe that Hekla was letting this continue. Why wasn't she putting up a fight, he asked himself. Why wasn't she doing *anything*?

August didn't like it. The police had digitally or forensically reconstructed everything Logi had done in the hours before and after Steingrímur's murder. But Logi said he'd been making extended trips to the capital for almost a year. Where were all the records for those visits? August would have expected at least some detail about those visits to the capital, but there wasn't even an invoice. To August, this seemed intentional, like it was designed to cast suspicion on Logi's innocent travel. Maybe Logi's excuse was nonsense. August certainly didn't believe Logi's explanation for spending extra time in Reykjavík. In fact, he scoffed when he read the transcript. But the police should have at least checked into it.

A strategy of willful ignorance, or even deliberate obfuscation, didn't make sense in the long term. There was just too much that was too public for these types of records to disappear entirely. If everything pointed to an affair, the truth would come out sooner or later.

What the hell are they trying to do? Are they really going to play another game of Arrest First, Learn Facts Later? Even when they already know the most critical fact—that the only reason Logi was ever at the hotel was to visit Hekla? Do they just not care?

All the unanswered questions made August incredibly uneasy. He knew that whoever was pulling the strings of law enforcement had shown a willingness to move without regard for consequence: They arrested Aldís before checking her alibi and they threw a concussion grenade into the safe house while their own detectives were inside. They were jittery, trigger-happy. There was something they cared about much more than appearances. Jittery, trigger-happy forces were next to impossible to predict. And that scared the hell out of him.

⁕⁕⁕⁕⁕⁕⁕⁕⁕⁕⁕

"There's no one . . . no one here killed him."

Gunnar looked up from the kitchen table.

August was sitting at the narrow table against the wall, next to the kitchen. He was going through video files on the family's desktop computer, which had been repurposed and complemented with an extra monitor. Next to him was a pad of paper with a few numbers and a list of names. He crossed out the last name, just as he had crossed out the ten or so above it. He had reviewed the actions of every single person in the vicinity of Jack's suite when the American was killed. August followed their movements across multiple cameras, comparing approximations the team had compiled regarding the time needed for certain activities with the video evidence and Jack's time of death estimate. No one came close to being able to commit the murder.

"From outside . . . " August continued, "they had to have come from the outside."

"It's impossible," Gunnar replied. "And there were cameras there too. Someone would have seen them."

"It's not . . . it's not impossible. Look." August opened a satellite image photo of the hotel. Val had highlighted Jack's suite and labeled all entrances and exits, camera locations, and other key information.

Gunnar stayed seated.

"Just . . . look." August implored Gunnar to come over with a pull of his head.

Gunnar let out a low growl, but complied and looked over August at the monitor.

"There," August said, pointing to an access road at the edge of the frame. "They could have come . . . from there. Then . . . " he drew an imaginary line with his finger from the access road through a mass of white space to a spot just outside of Jack's suite, "straight to the spa . . . like that."

He turned to look at Gunnar, who grunted as he shook his head.

"Why . . . why not?" August asked.

"This." Gunnar reached over August and ran his thick finger back and forth over the white mass that August had just delicately swiped through. "You can't just hop through it. It'd take at least an hour. And that's moving fast. Winter, in the dark?" Gunnar answered his own question with another shake of his head.

"It's not . . . impossible though. Right?" After staring at the same images for days, August wasn't going to give up on his new theory that easily. "It's a blind spot . . . see." He pointed at the shaded area used to indicate regions not covered by surveillance cameras. "No one would have seen . . . them. They could have gotten in and out . . . undetected."

"Maybe in, but then what?"

"Huh?"

"Outside the spa, it's four—five meters of rock, and then water."

"So?"

"So, what would they do? If they made it there, somehow, across that icy ground in the dark. And then also made it down the rocks, without anyone seeing or hearing them—what would they do then? Where would they go?"

"They could have . . . stayed in the water. It was dark . . . right? When Jack went out."

"There was a light on next to his door. I think he would have seen them. At least when they moved toward him. But there wasn't even a struggle. They were able to kill him with basically one movement."

"Mmh."

"But that's not the biggest problem."

August raised his brow.

"How would they know?" Gunnar asked.

"Know . . . what?"

"That it *was* a blind spot, for one. But also, like I said, this is two or three hours, early in the morning. It's freezing. There's no margin for error. Even if they got lucky with the cameras, you can't just make a run like that on chance. You'd have to be prepared. You'd have to know for certain."

August pondered this for a moment. He knew Gunnar was right—to an extent. His new theory had simply led them back to a different version of the same conclusion they had already reached. "Someone else . . . there was . . . someone else involved. Someone who knew the place . . . and his schedule."

"I think more than just one," Gunnar said.

"Yeah. . . . " August rested his head in his hand as he stared at the screen. After a moment he gave Gunnar another look. "What—what are you working on?"

"Bjarni."

August didn't need to ask any follow up questions. Gunnar was convinced Bjarni was responsible for Elísa's death. There was a noticeable change in his demeanor whenever Bjarni's name came up. It was like glimpsing the angry, vengeful aspects of Gunnar's personality that the man must have learned to control. But August also knew that Bjarni was now the lead detective on the case. He couldn't imagine how difficult it must be for Gunnar to stay calm while taking orders from Bjarni.

August adjusted the image of the hotel on his screen, focusing on the area where he had predicted Jack's killer had traveled from. He traced along the access road until he found a spot that had a camera. He moved his pen to the time he had written down for Jack's death, added 45 minutes, wrote down the new time, and then added another three hours so that he had a range of three hours and 45 minutes. He opened the folder with footage from cameras located near the hotel and found the subfolder for the camera he had identified. He scanned the list of movie files until he spotted one within his range and double clicked the file. CCTV footage popped up on the screen.

He gave a quick glance at Gunnar before pressing play. He fast-forwarded through the video. It wasn't long before he had to stop.

Objectively, there wasn't much to look at. The angle wasn't great. The camera was from a power station, so its focus was primarily the entrance to the building rather than the road in the background. There was also one major exit before the hotel, so even if a car was driving along the road at this specific time, there was no way to know for certain if it even made it to the space that August had stowed away in his mind.

Still, someone must have viewed this footage, August thought. They must have at least given it a cursory glance. He wondered which one of the three cops he was working with saw it—the streak across the top of the screen. Who stopped the video and zoomed in on the car? They wouldn't have been able to identify any individual, and wouldn't have been able to see the license plate. It was black and white footage, so the furthest they could have gotten would be the make and model of car. August didn't know much about cars, but this one was easy to recognize. All he could do was hope it wasn't rust-orange.

llllllllllllllllll

The next morning, after breakfast, August asked Ingibjörg if he could borrow her car. She had offered it to him "whenever you want," but he felt bad further inconveniencing the family. He was a fugitive deadbeat crashing on their couch, and now he was going behind one of their backs. He didn't feel like he had any other choice. There were questions he needed answers to, and he wasn't going to find them here.

CHAPTER FIFTY-SIX

August wasn't sure what he would find in Akureyri. He figured he would learn more about Hekla's background and Logi's relationship with her. The real reason for the trip though—a trip he was certain would piss off the people he was most dependent on—was the memory of a single look.

Back when August was living with Aldís, Logi was often at the house. After the two men had developed enough of a rapport that August no longer feared a fist to the nose, he would occasionally tease Logi about his hometown, sharing a knowingly ignorant opinion or dramatically reading copy from the tourism bureau's website. Logi was a good sport, sometimes offering an anecdote about his upbringing to counter August's barbs, or just threatening to read headlines from a U.S. news publication. It was on one such occasion that August saw it—a look that Logi gave to Aldís.

On the surface it was innocuous. The group had just finished chuckling at some undoubtedly juvenile joke August told, when he asked Logi a question. "Are you still close with anyone you grew up with?"

Logi answered with a story that focused more on his and Aldís's shared biography. Mostly things August already knew—how the two met, friends they had in common, relationships that faded or strengthened over time. There was something different this time though, a new character, along with a terse explanation about why this person and Logi were no longer in contact. And that's when Logi gave Aldís the look. August could still picture it clearly: Logi's eyes, vulnerable and melancholic, focused on the floor a fraction of a second before finding Aldís; and Aldís's response too, the way she understood and empathized, as though she were embracing him with her expression alone.

The look meant little to August at the time, but now it was all he could think of. He was convinced that it meant something, or explained something, or answered some question that he couldn't articulate just yet. If he could figure out its significance, he believed most of the other pieces to this puzzle would fall into place. He didn't know exactly what he was looking for, but he was pretty sure that the answer was in Akureyri.

⸻⸻⸻

While August had come to terms with his real motivations for *leaving* the U.S., there was more to his decision to *stay* abroad. The events of the past few years had shifted his focus to politics and ideology. But psychological factors played more than a small role. Recently, as he found new places to *not* call home, and certainly now, as he knocked on strangers' doors in Akureyri, it was obvious how much easier it was for him to be a foreigner.

When away, he felt protected. Even when there was no language barrier, there were other invisible layers that shielded his most vulnerable parts and kept him from feeling too exposed. He'd lost that in Copenhagen over the past few years. Whenever he left his flat there, his senses were all overwhelmed. He became fearful of any interaction because his nerves couldn't take any more stimulation. In contrast, when he was seen as an obvious outsider, he felt like he had more leeway. He could process things at his own speed, be himself while also hiding himself.

This was a tremendous value to his investigative work. Besides the obvious benefit of being able to comfortably approach strangers, he found that they tended to let their guard down. It was most notable when they spoke in a language other than English. Someone would switch from English to another language to keep August in the dark, but they would then give away every detail with their tone and body language. Plus, August often understood at least a few words the stranger was saying in the other language. He thought those trying to deceive would have better luck telling him the truth in English—at least then he might question what he was being told.

August didn't need to rely on his sensitivity to subtle signs when he asked questions about Hekla. Almost no one wanted to talk to him, but when he posed the right question to the right person, the look on their faces told a story even when their words would not. There was something here—something in Hekla's past triggered discomfort in everyone August approached.

When he was about halfway back to Gunnar's house, August pulled Ingibjörg's car to the side of the road and called Jenson. He left his standard message with his latest number, got out of the car, lit a cigarette, and waited for a return call. He had another favor to ask, but he felt better about this imposition because Jenson had missed something. August was confident that for a man as diligent as Jenson, professional pride alone would have him fix the error. Of course, he had more than one request. For this new ask, his debt to Jenson would be significant. August also promised himself he'd put more effort into a friendship that he really did value beyond the access to confidential materials that it provided.

CHAPTER FIFTY-SEVEN

"How was your trip?" Ingibjörg asked.

August froze. It had been two days since he returned from Akureyri, and he hadn't discussed his trip with anyone. Gunnar, purposefully he presumed, hadn't inquired, but this was his first real, unimpeded time with Ingibjörg since he got back. Anna was asleep and the adults were unwinding a bit before they either went to bed or put in a shift of unpaid work. Gunnar was in the kitchen making coffee, and August had just sat down on the couch next to Ingibjörg after helping with the dishes.

"Good," he answered, his voice much higher-pitched than he intended.

"Are you sure?" Ingibjörg smiled, her warmth still unmistakable even when she teased.

August caught a subtle glance from Gunnar. "Yes. It . . . it was." He did his best to manufacture a convincing smile. "Feels like . . . a long time ago. Different country up there."

"You were visiting a friend?"

"Yeah." He could feel Gunnar's eyes on him. "From . . . when I lived here."

"How are they?"

"Um . . . good." August didn't want to alienate Gunnar before he knew where everyone stood, but he also knew that he needed to act soon. Right now, getting more information was more important than keeping his secret. "Actually . . . " he continued, "it's not really . . . a great time for him."

Ingibjörg raised her eyebrows. "Oh no, what's wrong?"

Gunnar took a step into the living room.

"Well, it . . . it kind of has to do . . . with what we're working on." He nodded in Gunnar's direction.

"The case."

"Yeah. My friend . . . he's a suspect. But I don't . . . *we* don't . . . think he did anything wrong." He looked to Gunnar. "Right?"

"You visited Logi?" Gunnar's flat affect and indecipherable expression sent a chill through August's spine. If he had any inclination to tell an outright lie, Gunnar's tone sent that notion running.

"People . . . people who knew him," August clarified.

Gunnar nodded. "They want to arrest him," he explained to his sister. "He's the person of interest they keep talking about in the news. I think they've mentioned him by name more than once."

"Yes." She looked to August. "I didn't know you were friends with him too."

August smiled and lifted a shoulder. "If it's . . . someone your brother's bosses are after . . . fifty-fifty chance we were friends."

Ingibjörg chuckled. She gave a smile in solidarity and placed her hand on top of August's. Then she got up, took her glass from the coffee table, and kissed Gunnar on the cheek. "Well, I'm glad you're here helping my brother balance things out by working for the good guys." She put her glass in the sink and said goodnight before retreating to her room.

After the door shut, August and Gunnar stared at each other for several seconds. August's mouth parted, and he started to turn his palms up as part of a conciliatory shrug, but Gunnar shook him off.

"It's okay," Gunnar said. "I'm not sure what's going on."

 "What . . . what do you mean?"

"They've given his name out and stopped any real investigation, but we still aren't doing anything."

"Mmh. Do you think . . . they're waiting until the election?"

"What good would that do? When they released his name, I thought we would be arresting him. When that didn't happen, I thought they were just trying to influence the vote."

August nodded. He had read stories that were clearly intended to hurt Aldís's credibility by tying her to a murder suspect. It struck August as a bit clumsy or naive for them to think that a candidate whose campaign originated from a false arrest would be hurt by another rumor. There were many things that could be said about people like Lisa, but clumsy and naive were not among them. "You don't think . . . that's what they're doing anymore?"

"I don't know. It doesn't make sense to wait this long. He's still considered our lead suspect—we're just not doing anything. There must be something else. I just can't figure it out."

August nodded again. He wondered when Gunnar would figure out that he was looking into Hekla, rather than Logi when he drove to Akureyri. He hoped to have more than just instinct and theory by the time Gunnar realized that August was investigating the insiders along with the outsiders, the good guys as well as the bad.

⁓⁓⁓⁓⁓⁓

The rest of the week was tense.

Every day, after the siblings left for work, August would make the short walk to the Pósturinn to see if a package waited for him. The clerk would answer 'no' and then tell him how he could be notified remotely. He would politely decline and then smoke a cigarette on the walk back, mixing up his route so neighbors didn't start noticing him.

Every night, after Anna was in bed, August, Gunnar, and Ingibjörg would watch coverage of the upcoming election. August would ask questions about the process and receive unsatisfying responses. He was concerned that so much could hinge on a single election and disheartened that this country, like his own, could be vulnerable to the money disease that plagued much of the world. After the others went to bed, he'd have another smoke, then spend another hour or two trying to figure out why Aldís was so much more confident, bold, and hopeful in *her* actions than he could ever imagine for himself.

It went on like this, with more cigarettes and less sleep until the day before the election. On this day, as August walked into the Pósturinn, he noticed that the clerk was smiling. His heart skipped a beat. He eagerly signed for the package and ran back to Gunnar's house. He was so excited, he didn't even think about the lost opportunity for a smoke until he had reached the door.

Once inside, he opened Jenson's package with a pair of scissors from the kitchen and removed three packets of paper, one much thicker than the other two. Just as with the first package, he found a note from Jenson affixed to the top of the pile:

> *August — let me know when you are back in Copenhagen.*
> *Be careful.*

August stared at the note for several seconds. He was hoping for a lighthearted rebuke. Even a "never again" would have been preferable to "Be careful." A wisp of worry rose in his chest as he turned his attention to the documents Jenson had sent.

The first group of contained billing statements from all Logi's visits to the Envoy over the past year. August wrote down the dates and times that Logi checked in and out of the hotel. Then he reviewed the charges Logi made during those various stays. August's eyes narrowed as he saw a pattern emerge. A copy of Logi and Hekla's text messages would have been nice, but he felt like he could read these numbers like a script just the same.

August put down the hotel records and moved to the next packet of papers. These were Aldís's election registration documents. He quickly scanned each page looking for a date. When he found what he was looking for—what he had generally anticipated—he kept staring at it as if could change the numbers with his mind.

Aldís had decided to run for office *well before* she was arrested.

August's gaze became empty, and his mouth twisted into a frown. He had a hunch this was the case. It was why he wanted the records in the first place, but it still stung. On the surface, it was a neutral piece of information. These records were public, and the date alone didn't prove guilt or innocence in any crime or conspiracy. But in August's mind, combined with the other documents and as part of his elaborate theory, the date of her decision was damning. It might as well have been a signed confession, it hurt him so much.

August gathered himself and turned his attention to the last packet. His eyes widened. In any other circumstance, this would be an investigative coup. Even as low as he was feeling, he had to smile and marvel at what was in front of him.

Spreadsheets don't typically inspire awe, but this one sure did. There were columns for name, city and country, U.S. dollar and converted currencies, recipient name and address, and several different dates. It was voluminous, over 50 tightly laid out pages, with small, barely legible font.

This was clearly the source of Jenson's concern, he figured.

Unlike the other two sets of records, Jenson hadn't had to figure out a way to covertly retrieve the spreadsheet. August knew it existed, he knew where it was kept, who to ask, and what name to use to get it. He learned all of this from Client. He still didn't really believe he would ever see it, and he certainly didn't believe he would receive a copy that wasn't redacted to the point of illegibility. But here it was. Client's source clearly wanted to share what they had been sitting on for who knows how many years.

The spreadsheet was a record of payments that the U.S. government had made to the families of individuals it had inadvertently killed in some of its missile strikes. It was a record of death and a statement of values. More than anything, it was an indictment of the society that had come to dominate the modern world. Something got fucked up somewhere if human existence could now be reduced to a half of a profit and loss statement, August mused.

He ran his finger along the pages, hastily scanning the column that listed who had received money. After about 20 pages, he stopped. He gave a cursory glance at the rest of the pages, but he had found what—or who—he was looking for. A pseudonym was associated with the address, but August knew the real identity. It was one of only a handful of entries with a notation that indicated the payment had been declined. This was it. This was the proof he was looking for.

He glanced at a clock. It wasn't even noon. He knew whom he had to speak with, but his visions of a grand confrontation that would result in some sort of righteous order being restored seemed silly now. The election was a day away, and neither Gunnar nor anyone else he knew of had any inkling that the police were going to arrest Logi any time soon. It might not be the best time to hire a car just so he could hurl accusations at someone—especially since he probably would only have one chance to do so. Still, this was a lot for him to sit on.

He tapped the ring, middle and forefinger of his right hand against the table in rapid succession. Then he stood up. He couldn't just sit around. He had to do *something*.

CHAPTER FIFTY-EIGHT

AUGUST WAS SILENT AT DINNER. HE WAS MORE fidgety than usual, and his eyes had trouble focusing on anything other than Anna, playing nearby on the ground after playing with her food, for more than a second.

After reviewing the records, the only action he had taken were several walks to smoke cigarettes and a thorough cleaning of the house's common areas. He looked up information for cab services a few times and counted the cash that had been loaned to him, but that was as far as he got before he abandoned his plan to visit Hekla. He was decisive only in his imagination. He fantasized the conversation he would have. But each flight of fancy was inevitably grounded by the harsh reality that he had nothing of substance to offer. Even if he was right, he thought, what good would his knowledge do for anyone now? All he could do was sit back with the rest of the country and wait to see what would happen next.

"Are you okay?" Ingibjörg asked.

"Huh?" August turned to her. Gunnar looked up, pausing with his fork on his plate. "Oh . . . yeah. I'm just . . . nervous . . . about the election."

"I think she'll win."

August forced a smile. That was possible. Probable even. But then what?

⁓⁓⁓⁓⁓⁓⁓

After all the buildup, the actual election didn't have any drama. Aldís won handily. The objectively good news, however, did nothing to alleviate August's angst. If anything, he was more worried. He promised himself he would act if there was even the slightest hint of danger—if Gunnar added so much as a half-second of hesitation while delivering his customary update. But nothing happened. There was no hesitation, no bad news, nothing at all that might put him or anyone else from the team on alert.

A full day and night passed. Aldís was the decisive victor. One day turned into two, then three and four. Soon the reality of the situation intruded upon August's nightmarish visions. He thought it would be weird if he *didn't* call Aldís. Ostensibly, the call was to congratulate her, but he was still searching for even a trace of fear or doubt in her voice—anything that might be capable of breathing life back into his worst suspicions. But there was nothing there. Just Aldís on the other end of the line. Logi was at her home too, and they both seemed fine—better than fine, really.

More days and nights passed. Aldís gave a rousing speech that drew a bigger audience than most Icelandic club football matches.

Things quickly became so routine and uneventful that August was forced to consider his future once off the island. He was entirely unprepared for such thought. He had become convinced that events here would dictate the course of his life one way or another. He placed all his chips on the table, he didn't think there was a scenario where, after a spin or roll of the dice, someone would hand him back the same number of chips and ask him what he planned to do next with his life.

"You're going to hire a lawyer?" Ingibjörg asked one night, about a week after the election. "Can't you just do it yourself?"

August chuckled. They had just finished a late dinner. Gunnar was still at work. With August around to help, Gunnar had taken the opportunity to work different shifts, ensuring that either he or

Val knew what was going on at the station. Now Ingibjörg was sitting at the kitchen table sipping coffee. August was at the computer, reviewing an email he had composed to an attorney who once offered to help Client. August needed a lawyer who could help him with all the immigration issues that were waiting for him upon his reintroduction to polite society.

"No," he responded. "I'm not even licensed now. It's worth it . . . whatever they charge . . . to not deal with any of these people again."

"You can stay longer you know. We really do like having you here."

August furrowed his brow skeptically. He was sure they liked him, confident he offered some value when he watched Anna, but there was no way that they weren't looking forward to a living area that wasn't permanently occupied by another adult.

"I mean it!" Ingibjörg declared with a smile that was both playful and defensive. "And you know Anna loves having you around."

August tilted his head in acknowledgment. He did thoroughly enjoy spending time with Anna as well. A few hours playing with the child were a few hours he didn't have to spend with his own thoughts. "I'll visit," he said. "It might . . . take a bit of time anyway. I'm not sure—"

The front door swung open. Gunnar clambered inside. "They're going to arrest him," he said, breathless, as though he had run here from the station. "Logi. Tomorrow morning."

August immediately closed the email. He crossed the room and picked up his backpack.

"What're you doing?" Gunnar asked.

August gave him a piercing look, as if he either knew, or should be able to easily figure out, the answer to his own question.

Instead of responding to Gunnar, he took a few steps toward Ingibjörg. "Can I . . . borrow your car?"

Suddenly, August's body jerked backward. He stumbled as his body turned. He managed to find his footing and immediately placed his hand on his shoulder—it felt like someone had hit him with a hammer. He looked up at Gunnar.

Gunnar appeared remorseful for the physicality, but his voice was stern. "You can't go there. Not now. I'll be with them tomorrow morning. I'll make sure nothing bad happens."

August narrowed his eyes. "Where . . . do you think I'm going . . . exactly?"

"Patreksfjörður. Aren't you?"

"No."

Gunnar's large brow twitched slightly.

"Hekla," August whispered.

Gunnar emitted an exasperated growl as his shoulders dropped.

August turned back to Ingibjörg, who offered him the keys. "Be careful," she urged.

Gunnar stared daggers at his sister. August looked between the two.

"She's on your side, isn't she?" Ingibjörg chided her brother. "Our police haven't exactly distinguished themselves in any of this. Let him do what he needs to do."

August was speechless. "Th-thank you," he eventually mumbled as he took the keys.

Gunnar's large body remained between August and the door. They locked eyes again.

"Can I . . . go?" August asked gently but with conviction, as though he were affording Gunnar the opportunity to claim as much or as little ownership over an inevitable outcome as he wished.

Gunnar held August's stare for several seconds. Finally, with another low growl, he stepped to the side.

CHAPTER FIFTY-NINE

Aᴜɢᴜsᴛ ᴅʀᴏᴠᴇ ᴀs ꜰᴀsᴛ ᴀs ʜᴇ ᴄᴏᴜʟᴅ ᴛᴏ Hᴇᴋʟᴀ's place—needing to frequently glance at the navigation panel on the car's dashboard to stay on course. The whole time, he practiced what he would say to Hekla when he arrived. These imaginary conversations were volatile. Sometimes he seethed with rage, other times it was as if the two were mutually supportive participants in group therapy. Right now, as he neared her building, he was mostly angry.

Gunnar and Val had given Hekla a great deal of deference. Too much, in August's opinion. They seemed to revere her. Consciously or not, this blinded them to her shortcomings, or otherwise prevented them from confronting her. She got to get drunk while everyone else fought the battle she had started. August did have some empathy for her. She was distraught over the death of Elísa, and she blamed herself for what happened. At the same time, the steadying influence of her career had not only vanished, but was in many ways responsible for the loss and heartache she experienced in the first place. He knew what that felt like. In many ways, her story was his story.

But Hekla was not August. He knew something about her that neither Gunnar nor Val did. This information, in his mind, negated any excuse that she might have for remaining on the sidelines. She had the power to protect people she obviously cared deeply about. So, whatever her excuse for remaining disengaged, and whatever reason Gunnar and Val had for leaving her alone, enough was enough. They needed her help, and they needed it now.

It was past 11 p.m. when August arrived at her flat, but Hekla was fully dressed when she answered the door.

She greeted him with four words: "What do you want?"

He didn't respond. Instead, he gently pushed open the door and stepped inside. She shut the door behind him as he looked around. The living room was tidy. The only thing that stood out was the coffee table, which Hekla had turned into a makeshift workspace, with her phone, an open laptop, a few cables, and what looked like an external hard drive lying on top.

"How long . . . " he turned to face her, "how far . . . are you going to let this go?"

"I don't know what you're talking about."

"You're going to let them arrest him?"

Hekla hesitated a moment, narrowing her eyes. "What exactly do you want me to do about it?"

"Say something."

"Like what?"

"Tell them . . . where he was. With you. . . . Right?"

"They have all the information. Clearly it doesn't matter."

"So tell someone else—the news . . . RUV . . . fucking someone. They can't keep him in jail . . . if people see proof that he's innocent."

Hekla exhaled dismissively and shook her head. "I'm surprised how naive you still are. After everything you've been through . . . "

She turned her back on him and started walking toward the kitchen.

"I know about your brother," August called out.

Hekla winced. Her body jerked a half-centimeter and then

froze, as if a fine arrow had pierced her spine and lodged itself in her heart. She rolled her bottom lip in and out of her mouth, grating it against her top teeth. With the muscles in her neck and face still tight, she tried to compose herself, forcing a breath through her nostrils, widening her eyes, and doing all she could to present herself in a way that didn't betray her true emotions. Then she turned around.

August could see he was right. It *was* her brother who was killed by his government. Her family *was* the recipient of the check identified on the spreadsheet. And she had refused to accept the blood money.

August nodded slowly. "I'm . . . sorry."

"No," she replied in a voice that would barely qualify as a whisper. She swallowed hard and tried to clear her throat. "Why—why are you here?"

"I can't . . . I can't let Logi take the fall for you. I'm sorry but . . . I just can't."

She remained silent.

"I know it was you. I know . . . you killed them both."

Still nothing from Hekla. August continued, "I don't care. Really . . . I don't. I'm not . . . here to judge. If things were different . . . I don't know. But . . . he can't go to jail for something he didn't do. I'm not . . . I'm not going to let that happen."

"You don't know what you're talking about."

"I know there was no affair."

Her mouth parted ahead of her words. "Is that right?"

"You weren't sleeping with him. I saw the records . . . from the hotel visits."

"And?"

"It was the same thing . . . every time. Where you'd meet—when—place, time, room. Even what you ordered. Room service . . . fifteen or twenty minutes after you arrived. Only the date changed."

"That doesn't mean anything."

"People don't have affairs for the thrill of routine."

She scoffed. "Okay. Let me get this straight—now you want me to admit to an affair that you think *didn't* happen? An affair that pretty much destroyed my career? Have you thought this through?"

August gave a half-shrug. "You . . . you have to do something. He risked everything . . . to give *you* an alibi. You're going to abandon him now?"

Hekla sighed, frustrated, closing her eyelids as she pressed her fingers against her forehead. "Go home August. Or back to Gunnar's. I don't have time for this." She turned back around and continued into the kitchen.

"Really?" He bounded over to her side. "You're not gonna do . . . *anything*? After all they sacrificed for you?"

Hekla clenched her jaw. She crouched down to open a cabinet and retrieved a large water bottle. August hovered over her.

"Am I wrong?" he asked.

She looked up at him. "You're wrong. Could you please move now?"

He didn't budge.

She stood straight up, her face just a centimeter or two from his. Then she stepped to the side and walked over to the sink. "I have stuff to do," she said as she turned on the faucet. "I'm asking you nicely. Please. Leave."

"No," he spoke louder now. "I'm not going to . . . just let you go . . . let you keep living your life . . . while everyone else suffers for you."

Hekla slammed the water bottle on the far edge of the sink.

August flinched. The bottle bounced out of her hand, flew back over the sink, and fell to the floor where it rattled around for a few seconds.

"What do you think I'm doing!?" she roared as she took a step toward him. "Huh? Why do you think I'm still here?"

He backpedaled, too stunned by the reproach to answer.

"You know nothing," she continued ferociously. "Do you understand? Nothing! You think because you learned a thing or two about my past, you have any idea about my present? You think I'm *living*?"

Her eyes burned with rage, but August could hear the pain in her voice too. She hesitated a moment, as if deciding which way to take the conversation. Finally, she said it:

"Logi wasn't at the hotel for me. I was there for him."

August's brow furrowed in confusion.

"He wasn't my alibi," she explained, "I was *his*."

"What?" August finally managed to mumble.

"I don't know how someone so aware can be so fucking blind."

"I don't . . . I don't get it."

"I know you don't."

Hekla growled as she scooped up the water bottle. August looked lost as he tried to process this new information. Hekla filled the bottle and tightened the lid. She opened a cabinet above the sink and grabbed a few protein bars.

"What . . . are you doing?" he asked quietly, clearly chastened.

"I'm going to protect them."

"Them?"

She gave him an incredulous look. "Why do you think they're going there now—do you really think they care about arresting him?"

He had no response. He was still lost in his head trying to sort out the implications of her admission.

"Think," she ordered.

There was a high-pitched rumble, followed closely by an even higher-pitched ring. They both looked over at Hekla's phone, vibrating on the coffee table in the living room. She disdainfully rolled her eyes at him before marching to the other room to answer.

"Yes?" she said. Almost immediately, her face turned to a grimace. "How do you know? You're there now?" She sighed. "You shouldn't be there. No—it's okay, I understand. It's good. Yeah. Does Gunnar know?"

Hekla looked over at August. "Yeah," she continued into the phone. "He's here. I don't know, but I'm leaving now. I'll call you from the road. Okay. Good job—thanks."

"What . . . what is it?" August asked as she hung up.

"Bjarni's gone. He's not at the station and Val just checked his home. I think he's going to Patreksfjörður early. To Logi. I need to leave. Now."

Hekla swiftly moved past August to grab the water bottle and protein bars from the kitchen. She returned to the living room and shut down several applications before closing her laptop. Then she stood up and looked expectantly at August, who hadn't moved more than a centimeter. "Are you coming?" August remained silent. Hekla shook her head. "I'll meet you there."

CHAPTER SIXTY

AUGUST WASN'T PREPARED FOR ANOTHER LONG drive north. That would have been the case no matter what the circumstance that night, but it was particularly true given what Hekla had just told him. There was too much time to think. About Aldís and Logi of course, about the gulf between what he thought he knew about them and the reality of their existence, about *everything.*

August had told Aldís only part of the story that winter in Copenhagen, when he revealed his reason for seeking employment with the U.S. government. He wanted a better life. That was true. But his initial motivation was much more straightforward: It was spite. Spite led him to Denmark.

Growing up, August loved listening to his mother tell stories of her activist youth. It was enthralling stuff for a kid to hear, the defiant stands and risks she took to improve the lives of those without a voice in society. Inevitably, he would ask her something along the lines of "what happened?" or "why did you stop fighting?" These were childish questions, but he was a child. At the time, his mother was one of the most active members of one of the most active unions in all of California—a union that, largely because of her efforts, threw around its sizable weight on behalf of worthy causes. His mother patiently explained the importance of the work she was engaged in, how sticking together was one of the few tools those with less money and power had against those who wanted it all for themselves.

Every now and then, she hinted at an additional reason for the more cautious approach she had adopted over the years: The birth of her children. Young August was unsatisfied by these explanations. He was a stupid kid, as ignorant as the next American pre-teen was back then. The value of solidarity, like other less flashy forms of activism, was lost on him.

But there was more to the story than his mother was willing to share. It wasn't until she was dead that he learned the full version. The person who filled him in on the details was the last person he would ever want to hear speak a word about his mother—his father, Erling Sorenson.

Erling—or Earl as he took to calling himself—was born in Denmark. He graduated the Copenhagen School of Business and worked in logistics for a giant shipping firm. Earl hated Denmark, thought it was small and stifling, no place for a future titan of business like himself. He wanted out, and when he met August's mother, he found his ticket. August's mother was a recent college graduate nearing the end of a summer spent backpacking around Europe. When she met his father, she extended her stay. Earl was quite handsome, and, if he could keep his goddamn mouth shut about his theories on free enterprise, August imagined he was charming, too. But August also wondered if his mother might have been harboring a secret desire to abandon her native land as well. There was some reason for hope with America back then, but perhaps she saw the writing on the wall.

Whatever their intentions going into the relationship, August's parents' decision on the future took on some urgency when his mother became pregnant. She made it clear that she wanted to stay in Denmark. There was no doubt in her mind that it would be a better place to raise a family. Earl, however, was similarly adamant that they make a life for themselves back in the States. In the end, his father prevailed, and they ended up moving to Southern California.

August had always known the broad strokes of the story but was not privy to the details until the night after his mother's funeral. That night, in a tear-and-alcohol-soaked confession, Earl told him the lengths he went to ensure he got what he wanted. Earl wanted desperately to be a great businessman and knew his future would always be limited in Denmark. When August's mother became pregnant, he took advantage of every moment of weakness or doubt she had. He led her to believe that his concern was for her and the child, when really it was always about his personal ambition. Earl pressured her, he exaggerated, he told outright lies about his homeland. And he succeeded. Once they had moved to America, and after August's mother was pregnant with a second child, Earl left her for another woman. His American dream was complete.

August could still picture Earl sitting in the armchair in the darkened living room of his mother's house, playing the part of a pitiful, heartbroken old man as he revealed the despicable truth about how he manipulated August's just-deceased mother. When Earl finished, he calmly stood up, wiped away tears that probably never were there, shook August's hand, gave him his drink, and walked to a waiting car so he could be driven back to his real family.

What an asshole, August thought now, just as he thought then. At the time, he was still in law school. He had recently quit drinking, a fact Earl was keenly aware of. His father equated temperance with weakness. Real men, he said, could handle their liquor. Real men. What bullshit. Earl had shared similarly asinine views on masculinity when he learned August liked men *and* women. If there were ever an example of someone failing to live up to the ideals of manhood, it would be Earl Sorenson. Erling. Prick.

August remembered holding Earl's half-full drink in his hand. He had competing desires to down the drink in one gulp and throw the glass against the wall.

He did neither.

Instead, he began researching opportunities to work abroad. He was particularly interested in any benefit he might be able to gain from his citizenship in a country that his father wanted nothing to do with. Only then, August realized the significance of the extended vacation his mother had forced upon him when he was an obstinate teenager who preferred a summer doing nothing to a holiday abroad. Through uncontrolled tears, it dawned on him that his mother had preserved his Danish citizenship in those weeks. He wondered why she never told him. His sobs were painful when he thought of the grief he had given her for that magical summer—a summer that provided him with options that almost no one else in his peer group would ever have.

⁓⁓⁓⁓⁓⁓⁓

August was driving far too fast on roads he barely knew. After two hours and a few close calls, he eased up somewhat. He wasn't going to catch Hekla, and the last thing he needed was a return trip to the hospital. He already had placed several calls to Logi and to Aldís. As instructed by Hekla, he left messages for both, telling them to be on alert, to come outside if they heard or saw anything, to make the scene as public as possible, and, no matter what, to ensure that Logi was never alone with Bjarni.

What an insane message. August wondered how he repeatedly managed to be so wrong about so much. Aldís, Logi, Hekla, it was like he was unable to see people clearly until it was too late.

Or maybe part of him always knew, but like always, retreated to a comfortable lie instead of accepting a difficult truth. He knew Aldís was involved in all of this, yet until several hours ago, he pretended there was some explanation—maybe she knew but didn't *really* know—that might keep his image of her pristine. It was pathetic. The truth was, if Logi killed Steingrímur, Aldís must have been aware. And given everything else that had transpired, it was much more likely that she was an active participant.

Truthfully, he was probably just scared. Murder scared him. Even the murder of bad men by good people.

But why shouldn't Jack and Steingrímur, two men who were steadfastly devoted to enterprises of devastation, be treated as inhumanely as the poor saps on the wrong end of their business endeavors? Particularly if their deaths led to other lives being saved. Was he just a coward, August asked himself, letting others stand on the front line while he critiqued their form? Or maybe killing these assholes was still wrong, no matter the reason or the benefits. He didn't really know.

His mind turned to the others. If he had misjudged Aldís and Logi and the lengths they were willing to go for the causes they believed in, it was likely he had misjudged the people running the show in Iceland. He had pegged them as corrupt bullies, dangerous, but mostly in the way all amoral forces tend to be. They don't care. It's not their goal to kill, but if they want something and you're in the way, too bad for you. But it *was* different here. If the good was its own kind of good, he thought, why wouldn't the bad also be its own kind of bad?

Whether it was Lisa and the Americans, or the most powerful people in Iceland's law enforcement, they all apparently knew Aldís better than he did. And they were right about her. She *was* a real threat to them, and they *did* try to stop her at every turn. This meant she and Logi were in real danger.

He sped up. Aldís and Logi usually put their phones away in the evening, so he wasn't surprised when they didn't answer. Unless they had changed their routines, there was little chance they would get his messages until morning. August had to get to the house before Bjarni. Luckily, he already had an opportunity to familiarize himself with the car because he was going to test its full capabilities tonight. He leaned forward in his seat, gripped the steering wheel tight, and pressed his foot on the gas pedal.

CHAPTER SIXTY-ONE

Aᴜɢᴜsᴛ ᴡᴀs ᴀʙᴏᴜᴛ 15 ᴍɪɴᴜᴛᴇs ᴀᴡᴀʏ ғʀᴏᴍ Patreksfjörður when his phone rang. His heart felt like it escaped his rib cage as he scrambled to answer. He had been driving in near-total silence for an hour now. Maybe two. He was certain he was about to receive bad news.

"Yes?"

"They arrested him." Hekla's voice was clear and calm on the other end.

"What?"

"He's okay. Logi. He's at the station now."

"What . . . what happened?" August asked, still not believing such a simple resolution was possible. "I don't . . . understand."

"I'm not sure exactly. Gunnar talked to someone in Patreksfjörður. They told him that Bjarni brought Logi in just a little while ago. Apparently, Logi was outside when Bjarni showed up. He must have gotten your message."

There was a light, freeing sensation in August's chest, as though interlocking muscles and nerves had unwound themselves. "I . . . " he began, but he didn't want to leave this feeling.

As if sensing the same, Hekla allowed the unspoken relief to hang in the air a few more seconds. "I'm right near the Patreksfjörður station," she eventually shared. "I'm going to stop in. Do you want me to meet you outside?"

It was remarkable that Hekla managed to stay in front of him the entire drive, he thought, she must have been going *fast.*

"Um . . . no. That's okay. I think . . . I'm gonna go check on Aldís. I'll call you after."

"Okay. Sounds good."

⁓⁓⁓⁓⁓⁓⁓⁓⁓

A manic giddiness, the type that only comes after certain near-death experiences, stayed with August for the whole drive to Aldís's house. They were *that* close. At least that's what it felt like. He wondered if Aldís was thinking the same.

He pulled his car over directly in front of her house and hopped out. Only as he was taking the final few steps to her door did he start to question the appropriateness of his exuberance. It was somewhere around 3 a.m., Aldís's best friend and partner had just been arrested, and August had not been invited. Why would he think it would be a good idea to show up now?

His hand had already begun to turn the doorknob when his doubts reached their zenith. But as the latch clicked and the door opened, his concerns were quickly replaced with a frantic quest to remember—*was the door usually left open?* Answers begged even more urgent questions as his mind raced. The door used to be open, he was pretty sure, but that was years ago. Surely, Aldís was more cautious these days. Hekla had said that Logi was outside when he was arrested, so the door was open at some point, but either Logi or Aldís would have locked it after, wouldn't they? On the other hand, he reasoned, if someone else had come into the home afterward, intending to do harm, they almost certainly would lock the door behind them.

This somewhat comforting thought, that bad guys lock doors, was as far as his mind got, because by the time he had two feet inside the house, he knew something was wrong. Aldís wasn't here. She should be here. There was no way that she would have gone back to bed so soon after Logi's arrest. She would have heard the car. She would have met him at the door. Even if she were in the bathroom, he could at least expect a muffled call. But there was nothing. Just silence. *Where was she?*

August's heart raced. It felt like it was beating twice as fast as when he had answered Hekla's call earlier. He kept still and listened. The quiet seemed unnatural in Aldís' house, like it was forced. He tried to recall if he had heard something when he first entered.

"Police!" a voice from the kitchen shouted.

His body stiffened.

"Stay right where you are," the voice commanded.

August moved without thought, striding through the living room, where he saw no sign of a struggle. He rounded the corner to the room adjacent to the kitchen and froze. Standing tall, just outside the entryway to the kitchen, was Bjarni.

August locked eyes with the cop, trying to read his expression. It seemed like Bjarni was surprised, like he wasn't expecting anyone. There was also a glint of recognition—Bjarni remembered him, and seemed to be trying to figure out how much August knew.

August glanced at Bjarni's hands. They were empty. He marched forward.

"Stop!" Bjarni yelled.

As August approached, Bjarni moved decisively to restrain him. He twisted August's right arm and pressed his own forearm against the back of August's neck. Even in top form, August would have trouble escaping such a hold. But then Bjarni tried to justify himself.

"This is a *crime scene.*"

A surge of adrenaline rushed through August. He spun out of Bjarni's grasp and shoved him away. Bjarni stumbled backward and August raced into the kitchen.

And then his body stopped working. First, his legs gave out, and he stumbled to the floor. Next, his hearing went. Bjarni's furious shouts transformed to mere outlines in the air. Finally, August's lungs stopped working. His lips parted but no air came in or out. The only organs that still functioned properly were his eyes, and he would have given anything for them to be as broken as the rest of him.

On the floor, pitched forward awkwardly, arms at the side, knees bent, and weight resting on the side of her face and shoulder, was Aldís. A fresh pool of blood slowly expanded around her head. The dark red throw pillow was near her hip. A hole pierced its center and pieces of fill scattered about. And there was a revolver.

Aldís looked uncomfortable. Tremendously uncomfortable. Bodies shouldn't look like that. No one would choose to be in that position. August had seen dead bodies before, and they were all horrifying—grizzly reminders of the cruel indifference that marked the end. But he never had trouble accepting them for what they were. But this was Aldís. She was not supposed to look like this. Not ever.

August closed his eyes and expelled the air that his lungs had been holding. He *felt* the emptiness now. It was painful. Then a hand touched his shoulder.

Adrenaline shot through his body. He threw himself across the floor, grabbed the gun, and scrambled to his feet. Before his brain had any idea what he was doing, he had pointed the gun at Bjarni's chest. It was heavy and felt awkward in his grip. It must be Logi's, he figured. Aldís refused to allow so much as a hunting rifle in her presence, and he knew this wasn't Bjarni's weapon, at least not the one issued to the police. August had never fired this type of gun before, but he had a good guess as to how it worked and was more than willing to take a chance.

Bjarni lifted his hands and took a cautious step toward him. "She was like that when——"

"Don't!" August screamed as he moved his finger to the trigger. "Don't fucking move." Bjarni stopped and remained still, several paces from him in the kitchen.

It felt to August as if his head were pounding in sync with his heart. He was just aware enough to know that he was out of control, but he didn't care. He didn't need to see the slight indentation around Aldís wrist, nor recognize the logical inconsistency of Logi trying to silence a gunshot before turning himself in, to know what happened. Bjarni did this. Bjarni ended the life of a person he loved. Bjarni turned a spectacular creature, someone capable of appreciating, enjoying, and sharing the nearly limitless array of wonders in the world into a lifeless lump of flesh and bone. Bjarni stole that from the world. He stole that potential from Aldís, and he stole that person from August.

So now August was going to end Bjarni's life. It was all he could do. And he had to do something. Anything to alter the reality of what was in front of him. Fury and anguish consumed him. As a result, he missed things. Like Bjarni subtly moving his arm down to his side.

CHAPTER SIXTY-TWO

In all the Westfjords there were only about 20 active police officers. The station in Patreksfjörður, therefore, was a notable outpost in the region. Still, Hekla flew right by it as she drove along the Strandgata, shortly after entering the village. She kept going a bit, looking in vain for a place to turn off before angrily skidding her car into a three-point turn and traveling back the way she came.

She eyed the cars in and around the station as she stepped out of her vehicle and walked to the entrance. It occurred to her that she hadn't been inside *any* police station in months. She also had no badge and no good reason for being here—at least none she was willing to articulate. On the other hand, it was unlikely that anyone here knew all this information. So she pulled open the doors and took a confident step inside.

"Bjarni," she called out.

There were two officers in the station—an older, tired-looking man, sitting behind a desk on the far side, and a chipper young man, already on his feet and moving toward her.

"Excuse me," the young officer said, "how can I help you?"

Hekla recognized the officer's voice. She scoured the room, trying to make sure she wasn't missing anything. "My name is Hekla Rafney, I'm with the NBI. I'm looking for one of our detectives. Bjarni Pálsson. Is he here?"

The young officer looked to his senior colleague. Hekla wondered if perhaps they *had* heard about what happened with her. The older officer held the look of the young officer for a second before giving an indistinct shrug. She had no idea what that was supposed to mean, but the young officer nodded before speaking, "He was here a few minutes ago, but he said he had to go back out—"

Hekla threw the doors open and sprinted back to her car. The officer followed her outside. "Hey," he shouted. "What'd you say your name was again?"

She was in her car with the door shut by the time he finished the question. She peeled backward out of the lot, angled her car on the road, and threw it into drive. Her tires screeched on the pavement as she sped off.

⁕⁕⁕⁕⁕⁕⁕⁕⁕⁕⁕⁕

Hekla drove far too fast for Patreksfjörður's small, sometimes precariously paved roads. In less than two minutes she was on Aldís's block. She pulled her car between two homes around 100 meters from Aldís' place and jumped out.

She wasted too much time, she thought, as she raced along the back of the houses leading to Aldís's home. She should have come straight here. *Why hadn't she?* The thought of being too late, of everything she had put herself through—of everything that she had *done*—in the past year-and-a-half, being for naught terrified her.

Hekla stumbled. She placed her hand on the ground to keep from falling. This *was* enough, wasn't it, she asked herself. She didn't need to see the result of her failure. She had done her best. The few meters left in her journey suddenly seemed as far a distance to travel as the many marathons behind her. Still, she fought forward, against the strong current of both her mind and body. But it was a struggle. Her legs burned. Her lungs ached.

She crawled on hands and knees toward the back corner of Aldís's home, then sat with her back against the exterior wall. At least this would be it for her, she thought. Even if she was too late, this would be the end. Nothing she could see on the other side of this wall would haunt her any more than what she already saw whenever her mind had a second of time to itself. She didn't even need to close her eyes anymore to experience the nightmare. Once she finished here, she would finally be done. With everything. Forever.

This thought freed her slightly. It opened a reserve of energy and willpower she didn't think she had. Before she knew it, she was crawling along the side of the home. She could breathe again. Breathing allowed her to think. And thinking allowed her to look, to listen, to let her senses work for her.

She saw August's car in front of the house and noted that the driver's side door was shut. That meant that Bjarni would have heard him coming. The front door was open. Hekla heard a shout. It sounded like August. Maybe she wasn't too late, she thought. She sprung toward the door and slipped inside.

⁕⁕⁕⁕⁕⁕⁕⁕⁕⁕⁕⁕⁕⁕⁕⁕

Bjarni had his police-issued gun tucked into the back of his waistband. He was standing motionless, with his gaze fixed on something or someone in the kitchen. It must be August, Hekla thought, but why did Bjarni even have his gun with him? The answer came to her immediately. She knew what, besides August, was inside the kitchen. Bjarni had done what he came to do. He had killed Aldís.

Hekla stood up from her crouching position and walked toward the kitchen. There was no point in hiding anymore, no point in discretion. Nothing mattered. She kept going until she was flush with the entrance to the kitchen. On her last step, Bjarni could see her, and several things occurred in rapid succession. In her mind, however, they all occurred at once: she recognized Logi's gun in August's hands, Bjarni turned his head, August's eyes glimpsed hers only to focus back on Bjarni with furious resolve, and Bjarni reached behind his back to grab his gun.

Somewhere, among the rapidly firing synapses, Hekla concluded that Logi's gun must be loaded. Bjarni would have drawn already if he had emptied the ammunition in the other weapon. So Logi's gun would fire, and from that distance, even with August's terrible stance and shaky grip, it would hit its mark. If August's finger moved just a millimeter, maybe less, there was almost no chance Bjarni would get a shot off before a bullet tore through his chest.

It was less than a second of real time, but everything had slowed down enough for Hekla to weigh all the variables and be certain of what would happen if she did nothing. Bjarni, already distracted by her appearance, and never particularly graceful with a firearm to begin with, would likely only get his arm back to his side before August shot. Bjarni might get a round off, probably in the ground or in the wall, but no one else would be hurt. Bjarni would almost certainly die though, and August would be the one who killed him. Hekla saw this outcome and, calmly and deliberately in the same fraction of a second, made a decision. She wasn't going to let August take someone's life in revenge. She knew what that was like. He deserved better. She decided to change the ending.

She whipped out her gun and fired.

Her shot pierced Bjarni's skull just behind his left ear. She held her weapon on Bjarni as she moved forward. She kept the gun on him as he crumpled to the floor. She stayed there, hovering over his lifeless body, looking down on him but not really *looking* at him. She certainly wasn't thinking of him when a tear crept into her eye.

CHAPTER SIXTY-THREE

AUGUST WATCHED IN SILENCE AS HEKLA TOOK Logi's gun from his hands and wiped off his fingerprints. She asked him where he had found it and he pointed to a spot on the floor. He didn't say a word when she called the police and told them she shot Bjarni. And he stood quietly by her side in front of Aldís's house as they waited for the police to arrive.

It must have come as a surprise to her then, when as soon as the two officers from Patreksfjörður got out of their car, August shouted, "Kill me . . . he was . . . he was going to kill me!" There was an unrestrained emotion in his voice, as though the dam holding back his pain had burst. "I came . . . I came in and he was leaning over. I saw . . . he was wiping off the gun. I didn't know . . . I didn't know what he was doing—"

"What *who* was doing?" the young officer who had just spoken with Hekla a half-hour earlier asked. The older officer signaled for his partner to stay with August as he went to check on Hekla and look inside the house.

"That cop . . . the one inside." Tears streamed from August's eyes now. "He left the gun . . . on the ground. I didn't know what he was doing . . . I kept going and . . . and . . . that's when I saw . . . " He sobbed. "Aldís. . . . She was dead."

"Okay," the officer swallowed hard. "What happened next?"

August shook his head back and forth in tiny quick movements. "He . . . he had another gun. I didn't see . . . he pointed it at me . . . he . . . he was going to shoot me." He took a heavy breath. "But . . . she saved me." He gestured toward Hekla, who was watching them with a dumbstruck expression a few meters away. "She saved me . . . she was there . . . just in time."

August was barely able to focus, but he could tell that Hekla was not expecting him to hem her in as far as any confession was concerned. That was good. The emotion he displayed was organic, but his words were carefully selected. His intention was to give her as little room for her own narrative as possible. She had done something for him and, whether she liked it or not, he was going to return the favor.

He was now convinced that Hekla was driving Logi's car early that winter morning— that *she* had killed Jack. He recognized the look on her face as she reset the scene in Aldís's kitchen. It was *his* look, a countenance he had adopted for years, so he knew better than anyone that it was bullshit. Regardless of what she had done, and regardless of what she thought about any of it now, she deserved a future. And he was going to do his best to ensure she had one.

August spent the next several hours telling and retelling the story of how he and Hekla wound up in the same room as the deceased Aldís and Bjarni. His version came close enough to the truth that he had no problem with consistency. The entire time though, whenever he had a moment of reprieve from his agonizing heartache, his thoughts would turn to Hekla. Over the course of several hours, she had gone from someone he barely trusted to a person he could barely comprehend.

The scope of what Hekla had been through was beyond him. All of this really, what she and Logi and Aldís had done, how they managed to do it, it boggled his mind. And now what? What was left? Aldís was dead, Logi was in jail, and Hekla had been denied an opportunity to be punished for her actions. August didn't know if Logi intended to confess, but he was sure if he did, it would be to not one, but two murders. August was equally certain that Hekla would feel as though her lot was the worst of them all.

His attempts to make sense of everything and his empathy for the survivors were the only things preventing his despair from reaching new depths. He felt at odds with the planet again. This time it was as if the earth had made several quick orbits around the sun while he was asleep. He wasn't sure what occurred, but felt the pains of existence just the same. "Now what?" he asked himself again, this time wondering what kind of future *he* could have after all that transpired.

CHAPTER SIXTY-FOUR

Aᴜɢᴜsᴛ ғᴏᴜɴᴅ ɪᴛ ᴅɪғғɪᴄᴜʟᴛ ᴛᴏ ʙᴇ sᴀᴅ ᴀʀᴏᴜɴᴅ other people. He didn't mind others knowing, but there was a special sort of pain he liked to reserve for himself when he was alone. He wasn't content with just feeling bad, he also needed to feel bad about feeling bad, to blame himself for the state and revel in all the noxious mental and physical habits that accompany the otherwise normal emotion. Being around other people made that difficult. Living primarily on a couch in someone else's house, subjected daily to the intuitive compassion of a toddler and the gentle warmth of two Icelandic giants, made it damn near impossible.

But Gunnar didn't really give him much choice in the matter. After August was done speaking with the police, Gunnar practically dragged him back to the house. He could mourn as long as he'd like, the siblings told him, but he wouldn't be doing it alone.

The first few days, he did little but cry and sleep. He wound up keeping reverse hours, staring through the TV all night, pretending to wake as Gunnar and his sister got ready for work, and sleeping until they returned. The crying was harder to predict, but it usually came on when he found himself enjoying a moment or situation, like when he was chatting with the neighbor's children while having a smoke, only for the parents to pull the kids away. Or the time he was enjoying dinner with the family, laughing at something Anna had said, and it crossed his mind that he might be happy one day.

He and Gunnar didn't talk much about what happened. He got the distinct impression that there was only so much that Gunnar wanted to know. They had spent enough time investigating together for him to know that Gunnar was aware of discrepancies, if not outright impossibilities, in the case against Logi for the murder of Jack. But if Gunnar doubted anything, he kept it to himself. Gunnar graciously continued to provide August with police updates, and maybe every now and then, Gunnar's eyes would linger a little longer on his face, almost involuntarily searching for any reaction he might have to a piece of news.

It was easy for August to keep a straight face. Nothing Gunnar told him came as a surprise: Bjarni was labeled a rogue officer who had it out for Aldís. The murder of Aldís and the attempt to frame Logi were unrelated to any other incident, individual, entity or group, the police decided. Case closed.

Similarly, there was no further movement in the investigation into Elísa's death. It was being treated as a botched robbery, and none of the ensuing events provided a sufficient basis to reconsider this theory. Hekla had resigned. Attempts to reach her by phone went straight to voicemail, and there was no response when Val visited her flat. The investigations into the most infamous murders in modern Icelandic history, two of which would also likely make the top ten list of most other countries, were closed.

August took the news in stride. In truth, he didn't really care. Part of him felt like he should continue the work of pulling at threads, following leads, figuring out exactly what Lisa, the U.S. ambassador, and their business partners knew and when they knew it. But he didn't have the heart for it anymore. Some people were capable of that kind of work, but he wasn't one of them. He was done with this shit. It was too much. He *felt* too much, and he really, really, didn't want to feel any of it anymore. He was grateful that Gunnar and Val planned to keep investigating. It just wasn't for him.

August was done involving himself in affairs that led to death—whether he was safe behind a desk at the Embassy or holding a gun on a cop in Patreksfjörður. But he still was curious about how Aldís, Logi, and Hekla had managed to pull off the murders. He couldn't help himself. It was incredible. He figured they must have had help, but when he thought of what help they would need, every possibility seemed too remote or far-fetched to be true. There wasn't a single conspirator who could tie things together. In his experience, it was nearly impossible to get more than two people to maintain the confidence, diligence, and discipline necessary to successfully execute such a high-level conspiracy. Hell, if three people plotted to steal a candy bar, one of them would almost inevitably give up the game in a text or stray CCTV appearance.

Here, in addition to the three main players and Elísa, the group would have needed at least two other people. Probably a whole lot more. There was no way so many people could keep quiet. Someone would make a mistake, or crack at the first question from a detective. It didn't make sense, but here they were. And they probably would have gotten away with it if those in power had followed their own rules.

August couldn't think about it for too long. For months he had managed to maintain some sort of cognitive dissonance regarding Aldís's role in the murders. Now, he was finally willing to admit she was involved, but he still couldn't really face the truth. The hardest part of all this was that he knew that Aldís would be the first to take issue with his refusal to look directly at the messy, complicated, reality of who she was. It was one of those thoughts that made him smile and then immediately cry.

<hr>

After a month or so of mourning, August decided to return to the States. A few days after Aldís's murder, the embassy informed him that his money and passport issues had miraculously resolved. He could stay longer, but there definitely wasn't anything here for him anymore. He'd go to the U.S. after a visit to Copenhagen, where he'd spend some time with Jenson. Good friends were hard to find, and the durability of August's few meaningful relationships seemed precarious. Best not to let this one rust, he thought.

After Copenhagen, he would fly back to California. He didn't really know what he would do there. He hadn't told any of his remaining relatives he'd be there. He wasn't even sure where he would stay. But he wanted to go. It was an odd sensation. It felt like a mixture of a long-delayed return home and a final visit to say goodbye. Maybe it was both.

August was set to leave in a few days when there was a knock at the front door. He opened it to see a woman holding a letter-sized manila envelope.

"Is there a David August Sorenson here?" she asked.

He eyed the woman warily. "Who gave you this address?"

"Are you Mr. Sorenson?"

He held her stare another two seconds before relenting with an affirmative grunt and a nod. He signed for the envelope and shut the door as the woman walked away.

He sat down at the kitchen table and inspected the envelope. A label on the center of the envelope displayed his name—his full, legal name. Only a handful of people in the world even knew it.

The return address indicated it was from Patreksfjörður. He recognized a word that was printed above the return address. Something relating to law.

He closed his eyes and let out a sigh. This can't be good, he thought. Might as well get it over with. He tore the damn thing open.

Inside was a single-page letter written in English and typed on sturdy paper, along with a smaller, sealed envelope. August's Icelandic comprehension had been correct: The package was from a lawyer who purported to represent Aldís's estate, and the letter detailed the instructions Aldís had left. After a specified period following her death, provided August was still alive, the lawyer was to cause the enclosed envelope to be delivered to him.

The lawyer included some information about the disposition of Aldís's assets. An unnamed individual would be given a life estate in her house and a new charitable trust would have the remaining interest. That was information August didn't need. He wondered whether the lawyer charged a flat fee or billed for time.

August picked up the smaller envelope. "August" was written on the front. He instantly recognized Aldís's handwriting.

He braced himself. This was going to hurt. He could feel it in his chest already. He stared at his name for several more seconds before carefully opening the envelope. Inside was a letter, several pages long, handwritten on lined stationery:

Dear August,

    Hopefully you never have to read this. I'm afraid though. I think we might win, and I'm not sure they will allow that. I feel the need to write you just in case. There was something you said in your letter to me. Something that I've been thinking about since we last saw each other. I think, maybe, some part of it has been on my mind since you left Iceland years ago. It's been bothering me. I don't know what will happen, and in case I don't get another opportunity, I need to tell you this now. I know you think I always need to get the last word, but I hope you'll forgive me in this instance. Trust that I would much prefer to hear your rebuttal.

I hope you are okay. I really do. I know it's been hard and if you are reading this, I know it must seem like it's only gotten harder. I'm so sorry you had to become involved in all of this. It's not fair. It really isn't. You've been through so much. I know it is probably too much to ask for you to be okay now, but please have faith. I love you so much, August. I truly believe that this can be the beginning. For all of us, and for you too.

In your letter, you wrote that I was always "better than you," and that there are other people more "deserving" of what I have to offer. I know that you had similar thoughts after what happened when you were first here. In both instances, and in any variation you can come up with, I need you to know that you are wrong. I wish you were here right now, so you could see my face and hear my voice and understand just how wrong I believe you to be. This is nonsense and it must end now.

I am not better than you. No one is better than you and you are better than no one. It doesn't work that way. There isn't one person who is more or less deserving than another. It is fine that we have our favorite creatures. We get to choose our loves and who we spend time with. And we are unique. It's amazing and special and should be cherished. But I am not what made our time together so special. I am not what made us great, and I am not what will make things great for others. I'm just one person. I'm not a reason or an excuse. It's like everything else. If it was good together, then it was together that made it good. It was us. It wasn't me and it wasn't you.

I think you have always put too much value in the individual instead of the group, and I think this is the cause of much of your pain. Maybe it is hard to see what the group is sometimes. I understand that. The world doesn't make it easy. But every one of us has always been part of something bigger. As individuals, we will falter and fail. We can't help it. Even the best of us will compromise our values. At some point we will have to make a sacrifice or a choice. It could be a preference as to who we love, or maybe an act to further our own ideas about greater good. Look at me. Could I have possibly provided you with a better example? Together though, we can be more. It does not have to hurt so much. We don't have to be dependent on one person or even a group of many. I know deep in my heart that there is a way where we can all triumph without sacrifice, and no one will ever have to make choices like I did.

I know you've heard me speak like this before. Hopefully you didn't start skimming after you saw the words "individual" and "group" in such close proximity. Let me try another way, just in case. We can make it personal if we must. Do you want to know how I know that I am not better than you? It's because I know that you would have talked them out of it. You would not have allowed what happened to take place. You would have done everything you could to convince them of another course of action. I didn't do that. I barely even tried. I was fine with it, really. I probably still am. So there. Maybe it's just that simple.

I don't want to make you more upset. I'd much rather use this opportunity to share nice thoughts like you did, but even if I had the strength, I don't have the luxury. I need you to know these things. You are going to have to decide how to spend the rest of your life. There are many things that I am willing to accept, but I cannot stand the thought of you placing any more significance in my life or death than is warranted. You need to know that it was never me alone who made something good before, and I am not necessary for good things to happen in the future.

It's tough writing this now. I can't believe these could be the last words I ever get to share with you. I'm sorry for that. I'm sorry for everything that's led up to this and everything that is happening now that I am not there for. It breaks my heart. I wish I could change my mind like you did and alter the nature of the correspondence. But it is too late for that. What happens next will be out of my hands.

I love you August. I love you so so much. I admire you deeply. But dead or alive, I will not tolerate any more of your bullshit. Your capacity to feel bad is one of your greatest strengths. Stop wasting this gift on yourself. Please. There is so much to love in this world and so little time.

Love forever and always,

Aldís Eva

CHAPTER SIXTY-FIVE

THE BLOODSTAIN WAS STILL VISIBLE ON THE FLOOR. The cabinets were open, and stacks of dishes and silverware were scattered about the counter. The police had gone through Aldís's house twice while investigating Hekla's shooting of Bjarni and pretending to investigate Bjarni's murder of Aldís.

"Why would she think I'd want anything to do with this crypt," Hekla wondered as she sat at the kitchen table.

Her mind drifted. She thought back to the interview Aldís had given all those years ago. She thought about purpose and consequence.

It was over now. Hekla and Aldís and Logi and how many others had made sure that powerful people had been held to account. Jack Drumman, a man she believed to be as culpable for her brother's murder as those who authorized the missile strike, had faced repercussions in a world he thought he was above. Steingrímur, too. And what good had it done? When she first returned to Logi and Aldís after almost a decade apart, all she wanted was revenge. Aldís did her best to give purpose to her bloodlust, but even if Jack's death saved a thousand people, nothing could ever undue the harm that taking a life had done *to her.*

She spun Aldís's chef knife back and forth on the table with her middle finger. There needed to be an end.

Aldís believed that the lack of consequences for immoral action was one of the fundamental problems in modern society. There were no exceptions. The way Aldís saw it, anyone who unjustifiably killed someone else had to face punishment. Even the powerful.

And even the weak.

When August lied to the police after Hekla shot Bjarni, he denied her a chance to be punished for what she had done. A life without consequence is as bad for the individual as it is for society. Now, Hekla was left alone with the weight of all she had done pressing down on her. It felt even worse than being alone with her anger, as she had been for so long after her brother was killed.

August didn't know any of that, though. How could he? Hekla imagined she stole *his* opportunity—his chance to finally act.

The noise coming from the bathroom upstairs had changed. The tub was filling.

She stood up, grabbed the knife, and walked to the staircase at the front of the house, unbuttoning her flannel as she made her way. She crossed the hallway, walked through Aldís's bedroom and into the bathroom.

She stared at the tub and thought about Kjartan. He had been kind to her all those years ago. He tried to warn her about the pain she felt after her brother was killed on the humanitarian mission. He told her that she had to accept the grief and decide what kind of person she wanted to be moving forward.

What kind of person *had* she become? She couldn't imagine he would have had any idea that she could end up like this. Or maybe he was trying to protect her from this exact fate. In her quest to restore balance to the world, she had lost track of what her world even was. Now she was alone again, but without the life-preserving fuel of anger.

Not for long, she thought.

Hekla turned off the water. She had only been in this bathroom once before. She took a moment to appreciate how much sunlight filled the room. It was peaceful.

She carefully laid the knife across the corner of the tub, the handle on one edge and tip of the blade on the other. She removed her flannel, folded it once over her arm, and placed it on a wooden stool. She took off her T-shirt and placed it on top of the flannel. She pulled off her pants, folded them and put them underneath her shirts. Finally, she removed her socks, unclasped her bra, slid off her panties, and placed each item neatly on top of the pile.

Hekla had avoided looking at her reflection in the tall mirror over the sink as she undressed. Now, naked, she looked at the figure in the mirror. She placed her hand gently against her cheek, like a new lover exploring a partner for the first time. She felt pressure behind her eyes and looked away. It was too late to start caring for someone new.

All this time, she had managed to avoid asking herself the ultimate question. For all her nightmares and remorse, despite the clear recognition that she had done wrong, she never allowed herself to truly consider regret. *Did she* regret what she had done? She still wasn't sure the extent to which she wished to pull back the past, but when she saw her reflection in the mirror, she felt something new. She felt sorry for the person she saw, for what she had done to herself, for the other life—full of possibility and promise—that she had extinguished that cold, dark morning.

A thin layer of steam danced across the top of the water. She lifted her leg and placed it in the tub.

"Yah!" she yelped as she pulled her leg back out. It was *hot*.

She took a deep breath and quickly put both feet in the water, giving herself no choice but to adjust to the temperature. Her shoulders shot up and face pulled tight, but she stayed in the tub. The thought of lowering the rest of her body into the water frightened her. It struck her as slightly ridiculous. After all she had been through, was hot water really going to stop her now? She allowed herself a melancholy smile, grabbed the sides of the tub, took another deep breath, and lowered her backside into the water.

"Ahh," she gasped. Her eyes shut tight, but she continued moving until the water was at a level just below her breasts. Before she was able to fully acclimate, she let go of the sides and slid into the tub until she was submerged up to her chin. She gasped again. It was incredibly painful, but the lower half of her body immediately felt some relief, and before long it all just melted together.

She grabbed the sides of the tub again and pulled herself back into a seated position. Nothing was easy, she thought, as she reached back over her shoulder and grabbed the knife.

She held the knife in her right hand with both arms extended, palm-side up, forearms and wrists barely breaching the water. Her plan was to cut her right wrist first, then use her dominant hand to cut the left. Her thinking was that the right hand would have more strength to complete the task even if weakened. She realized now that she wasn't sure this would work. And when a teardrop made a tiny splash in the water, she realized she was crying.

She kept the knife in her right hand. She didn't think she would be able to do this twice. She placed the blade against her wrist. One good cut should do the trick, she figured. She adjusted the knife slightly, tightened her grip, and closed her eyes.

She was afraid. The feeling came on suddenly, but she recognized it clearly—she was afraid, terribly afraid. It felt like she was under water, except her eyes were now her mouth and her lungs—closed she couldn't breathe, but open there was air and life.

She allowed herself one last breath. She opened her eyes and inhaled at the same time. It was beautiful. Even the mundane bathroom seemed extraordinary. The light, the colors, the shapes, the sounds, the way she could feel *everything* without even trying. There was so much here. Far too much to say goodbye to.

So, she shouldn't try.

She pressed the blade into her flesh and closed her eyes again.

A new sound.

It's nothing, she thought, just a selfish part of her brain playing tricks on her. She kept her eyes closed, clenching her jaw as she steeled herself against the possibility of any more intrusions.

But there it was again. Knocking. She opened her eyes. Someone was at the front door. It was a persistent rap, light but repetitive, five strikes, a tiny break, and then five more. They would go away soon, she figured. She let out a small sigh, disappointed that she would have to go through this process again, but willing to accept a slight delay. Then she remembered: She left the door unlocked. They might *not* leave. They might not let *her* leave.

"Hell," she murmured as she stood up.

She chastised herself. For all she was willing to endure, this was where she drew the line, she just had to leave the door unlocked. Her goal was to prevent someone from having to break down the door but, in truth, she was probably more unnerved by the thought of her dead body remaining indefinitely in the unoccupied house, and she believed an unlocked entrance might hasten discovery. Why she found it necessary to comfort herself with thoughts of a less-frightening corpse as she prepared to die wasn't something she cared to consider, so instead, she focused on the sanctity of door frames.

⁓⁓⁓⁓⁓⁓⁓

Hekla's T-shirt was practically soaked through. Her pants clung to her legs and a small puddle of water had formed near her feet as she stood near the door. She tried to conjure a phrase in her mind that would send her neighbor off in the quickest amount of time without risking further inquiry. She noticed a bit of blood trickling from a mark on her left wrist, so she tucked that arm behind her back as she reached for the door with her right.

She pulled the door open. Her eyes widened. All the words she had considered fell from her mind.

August's eyes were puffy and red, as though he had been crying for hours. There was desperation in his look but also hope, like he thought she might be able to provide an answer that no one else had been able to.

"Huh—hey," his voice was gravely and unsteady, even more stilted than usual. "I'm . . . I . . . I . . ." His mouth remained open, but no further sound came out. Eventually his lips merged back together into a frown. The tears that could not have been absent long, reappeared in his eyes.

"August," she said, lightly and with wonder, "what are you doing here?"

His face pulled into a grimace. "Um . . . is it . . . is it okay if . . . if I . . . can I . . . " He blinked hard, his entire face scrunching together momentarily. "Can I come in . . . for a bit?"

Now her mouth parted involuntarily. She felt pressure behind her eyes again. Her body answered before her words could as she nodded enthusiastically.

"Yes," she said while waving him inside. "Of course."

August exhaled hard. A smile emerged on his face.

Hekla couldn't help but chuckle to herself. She held a tight smile—a joyful, desperate, loving, grateful smile—as August passed her on his way to the living room. Then she took a deep breath and let her eyes close.